FORWARD
THE
MAGE

ERIC FLINT &
RICHARD ROACH

Forward The Mage

This is a work of fiction. All the characters and events portrayed in this book are fictional, and any resemblance to real people or incidents is purely coincidental.

A Baen Books Original

Baen Publishing Enterprises
P.O. Box 1403
Riverdale, NY 10471
www.baen.com

ISBN: 0-7434-7146-6

Cover art by Larry Elmore

First paperback printing, August 2003

Library of Congress Catalog Number 2001056468

Distributed by Simon & Schuster
1230 Avenue of the Americas
New York, NY 10020

Production by Windhaven Press, Auburn, NH
Printed in the United States of America

WATCH IT! HE'S GOT AN EASEL!

It was only then that I noticed the odd sheen of their knives. Poisoned blades!

It was that outrage which finally snapped my trance. I dropped my baggage and charged forward carrying my easel like a three-pronged lance. An easel! You laugh! But no ordinary easel, this. For, combining the teachings of my various uncles, I had long ago designed this easel with a condottiere's sense of art. Each of the legs came to a sharp point, edged like a razor. Furthermore—but that in a moment.

For now, let me say with all due modesty that I slew three of the scoundrels with a perfectly executed *coup d'arrière tripodiste*. Then, before their bodies had even hit the ground, I drew my sword from its cunningly disguised sheath in the upright of the easel. A moment later it was plunged through the back of the nearest poisoner, piercing his heart. A quick twist of the wrist to free the blade, and a moment later another poisoner was run through the back. Another quick twist of the wrist—

"Through the back?" you say. Certainly! Though I am an artist, I am also a most proficient swordsman. I was trained by my uncle Rodrigo from the time I was six.

"As pretty-faced and brash a boy as you are, Benvenuti," he'd said to me (not without a sneer), "you'll be bound to land in a duel by the time you're sixteen. Some outraged husband, no doubt. So you'd best learn to use a blade at least as well as you learn to use a paintbrush."

I was a good student, and even my uncle eventually admitted that I had the knack of swordplay. But his instruction was stern and severe. Many was the time I was soundly cuffed—even thrashed—for committing what my uncle Rodrigo considered the greatest of all swordsman's sins.

Chivalry.

This book is dedicated to our wives
and mothers, who always believed;

and to those great pioneers who
first aroused our enthusiasm for
fantasy: Francois Rabelais,
Miguel Cervantes, Voltaire, and
Jonathan Swift;

and, of course, to the world's
Sancho Panzas.

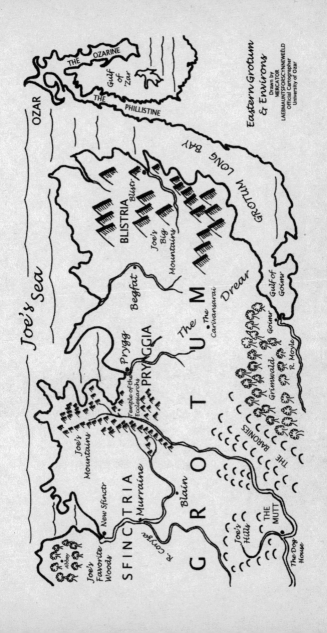

OZAR

THE OZARINE

Gulf of Zur

THE PHILLISTINE

Joe's Sea

GROTUM LONG BAY

BLISTRIA

Blistr

Joe's Big Mountains

Begfat

The Drear

Gulf of Goinu

Goinu

R. Moyle

Joe's Mountains

Prygg

Temple of the Ecclesiarchs

PRYGGIA

The Carawanserai

GROTUM

THE BARONIES

Grimwald

SFINCTRIA

New Sfinctr

Murraine

R. Conga

Blain

Joe's Favorite Woods

abbey

Joe's Hills

THE MUTT

The Dog House

Eastern Grotum & Environs

Drawn by
MERCATOR

Drawn by
LAEBMAUNTSFOISCYNNEWEÉLD
Official Cartographer
University of Ozar

Wisely hath it been written that those great upheavals which so enflame the passions of society that they excite the masses to rebellion and enmity against all lawful custom and sovereignty, wherefore the common herd is led to commit many profane mischiefs against the peace, including both mad foreign adventures and rude civil revolts, may not be comprehended as mere brutish conflicts between vast opposed powers, each bent on conquering for itself the Helm of State. Rather, we say that they are compounded of many societal atoms, indeed, of a multitude of small dramas, mere chance encounters, perhaps, 'twixt private persons of divers degrees and sorts.

Vulgar history will, of course, take no heed of these events, for they will appear to those witless sycophants of Clio's muse to be so contemptible, prosaic and inglorious, compared to the deeds of kings, ministers, generals, revolutionists and agitators, to the discordant flux of the classes and the masses, that they will be blinded to their import and, forsooth, will roundly and churlishly despise them. Yet these small episodes, we say, are the true stuff of History. For, though men go their way quietly in tranquil times, yet, in such epochs when storm clouds gather o'er the State and insurrectionary thoughts steal into the minds of the pauper classes, then may the separate lives of men be severally fused as if by a lightning bolt of social hatred, wherein all of society is transformed, and, like the wounded Leviathan, vents its unleashed fury at mute and fear-filled Nature.

Of course, we find in the literature other theories,

1

chiefly opposed to our own. These, however, we may
dismiss, for they are all of them perniciously false and
utterly repugnant to the human intellect in every
respect.

The College of Historians
University of Ozarae (in Exile)

PRELUDE. *In Which We Introduce the Gentle Reader to Our Tale Through a Most Cunning Usage of the Ancient Narrative Device of The Plunge Direct Into the Turbulence of the Times. Taken From the Autobiography of the Notorious Scapegrace, Benvenuti Sfondrati-Piccolomini.*

Autobiography of Benvenuti Sfondrati-Piccolomini, Episode 1: Police, Potters, Pedants and Plunderers

I arrived in the city of Goimr upon the most wretched ship imaginable. The CSS *Lucre*, it was called, a name which was as inappropriate as possible. The CSS *Pigsty* would have served better; the *Shipwreck-in-the-Making*, ideal.

Yet, upon my first glimpse of Goimr, I was almost sorry to disembark. The sight which greeted my eyes was even more disheartening than the ship. I had expected, without really giving it much thought, to find Goimr's harbor a smaller version of my native Ozar's great port, the Horn of Surfeit. At the very least, I should have thought Goimr—which is, after all, the chief port of southeastern Grotum—to be a match for any of the smaller harbors of the Philistine at which my ship had stopped on the voyage from Ozar.

Not so. I was encountering my first taste of that reality which has given rise, throughout Grotum, to the expression "grubby as Goimr." Upon the oily, sluggish waters of the harbor bobbed a variety of vessels, which seemed to compete with each other in their disrepair and desuetude, not to mention their antiquity and obsolescence. Numerous dilapidated warehouses dotted the quays, most of them boarded up, if not burnt and gutted. Everything was covered with a deep layer of grime. Roofs sagged, doors were unhinged, steps were cracked and broken. The very stones of the quays seemed corroded by some foul reagent.

The sole exception to the general miasma of decay was the building in front of which my ship was docked. The building was gigantic, stretching a full two hundred yards along the center of Goimr's waterfront. Above it, facing the waterfront, rested a huge sign announcing to the world:

GREAT GROTUM NORTHERN, EASTERN,
SOUTHERN, WESTERN,
CENTRAL AND ENVIRONS EXPRESS
AND TRAVEL COMPANY
(a subsidiary of THE CONSORTIUM)

"At least there's a trace of Ozarine energy in this miserable place," I muttered to myself, descending the gangway. And indeed, the Consortium building—though it shared the general aura of squalor—was bustling with activity. Numerous barges, skiffs, scows and hoys plied the waters adjacent, bringing cargoes to and from the several ships moored nearby. A constant bustle of men and wagons carrying goods, supplies or passengers swarmed about the quayside in front of the building.

The moment I stepped ashore, I was delivered into this seething frenzy of commercial and maritime activity. Wending my slow way past oxen teams drawing huge loads, dodging gangs of stevedores, I left the docks and entered the relative calm of the building. After some inquiries, I eventually made my way out of the labyrinthine edifice and into the passenger area on the far side, from which transportation into the city proper was available. There I rented a large locker, into which I placed my traveling sack and my easel. It wouldn't do, of course, to visit the King of Goimr with luggage under my arm.

As I was heading out the main archway to the plaza beyond, I stepped aside to let a man hurry by. Strange-looking fellow! Strange, not so much in his features—for he was normal enough in that regard, aside from the excessively severe look on his bearded face. But his clothing! A long, shabby, flowing robe, covered with obscure and cabalistic symbols. A wide-brimmed, floppy pointed hat. In his hand he bore a long staff, carved with runes. I realized that I was actually face to face with one of that legendary breed of sorcerers which are peculiar to Grotum.

As I stepped aside, I heard the mage say: "Make haste, wretched gnome, make haste! For even as I speak, time wanes!"

I looked to see the person to whom he was speaking. My jaw dropped with astonishment. Wizard indeed! For behind him—as if transported by levitation— loomed an immense sack, bulging at every seam, from which protruded the snouts and extremities of weird instruments too bizarre to describe.

From beneath the sack I heard a whining voice: "But master, it's heavy, and I can't see." I now saw a pair of spindly legs under the sack, twinkling in their efforts to keep pace with the wizard's long stride.

"Watch out!" I cried. "There's—"

But my effort to warn the servant of the portmanteau just ahead of him did not come in time. In an instant, the little legs tripped and the gigantic sack went flying.

At the sound, the sorcerer spun about. A look of great fury came upon his face.

"Unspeakable wretch!" he cried. "Did I not entrust to your care the safekeeping of my possessions?" And so saying, the wizard began smiting the prostrate servant with his staff.

"Hold there, sirrah!" I exclaimed. "It was but an accident! Your man could not possibly have seen the obstacle before him—did he not tell you himself that he couldn't see? If there is any fault here, it is yours alone. You should have warned him."

The wizard's look of wrath was transferred onto me.

"You are impudent, youth!" he bellowed.

Ignoring him, I stepped over and took the arm of the servant, who was now on his knees, shaking his head. I lifted the tiny fellow to his feet.

"Th-thank you, s-sir," he stammered. His voice was very clear and sweet.

I did not reply, so great was my astonishment. I had thought the wizard a strange looking fellow! His servant, I now perceived, was a dwarf. And while I myself did not share the general prejudice against dwarves, I was struck speechless by his appearance. For, truly, this was the hairiest and ugliest dwarf I had ever encountered. It was only the freshness of his voice which enabled me to determine that the servant was a young man—not much more than a boy, really. From his appearance alone, I would have thought him an ancient and horrid sub-human, a miniature demi-troll, escaped from some cavern of the earth.

But the boy seemed harmless enough. He immediately dove under the sack, positioning himself to lift it. I reached down and seized a fold of the sack, attempting to aid him.

The thing was unbelievably heavy! I am a large man, well muscled and strong, but I do not think I could have possibly lifted it by myself. Yet here was this dwarf—smaller than a stripling—even now hoisting the monstrous sack onto his back. In but two seconds, he was back on his feet.

"Thank you very much for your help, sir," came his little voice from beneath the sack.

"Not at all," I replied.

"Cease and desist this unconscionable chitchat, wretched dwarf!" exclaimed the wizard. "By your clumsiness, you have already delayed me!"

I had had quite enough of this fellow, thank you. I stepped up to him and said: "You, sirrah, are the only wretch about!"

The wizard's face began to redden with anger. But after a moment he turned away.

"Bah!" he exclaimed. "I have no time to bandy words with a layabout. The coach to Prygg departs momentarily, and I cannot afford to miss it. Good day to you, sirrah, and may we never meet again!"

"My sentiments exactly," I growled to his retreating back.

Little did I know then . . . Not only was I destined to meet again with the wizard and his servant, but in the years to come my life and fate was to become inextricably intertwined with theirs.

Indeed, the first coil of that intertwining was even now upon me. For no sooner did I emerge from the archway onto the plaza, looking about for a means of transport to the Royal Palace, than a black coach came careening up. A half-dozen black-garbed men were precariously perched on top. GOIMR SECRET POLICE was painted on its side in bold red letters. In slightly smaller letters beneath:

Classified information!
Tell no one on pain of death!

As soon as the coach stopped, the men on top leapt to the ground. The doors to the coach opened and another half-dozen men spilled out from the interior. I was so struck by the improbable sight that I stood motionless. My artist's sense of perception was attempting to determine by what magic means so many men— beefy types, to boot—had managed to fit inside the not very commodious coach. I would have done better to have noticed the fact that every other person in the crowded plaza had disappeared.

One of the policemen pointed to me and cried: "Seize him!" A moment later I was brought down by the horde, chained and manacled, protesting my innocence all the while.

"He must be guilty as sin, Sergeant," I heard a policeman chortle. "The only one who didn't run! And listen to him pleading his innocence!"

"A foreigner, too!" cackled another. "Listen to that outlandish accent!"

"I'm from Ozar," I protested. A momentary pause in the bustle of binding, manacling and chaining. Then: "The blackguard! Impersonating an Ozarine!"

"Gag him," came a tone of command. "No need for honest secret policemen to listen to the honeyed words of treason."

Before I knew it—now gagged, to boot—I was

hustled into the coach. As I was forced into its dark interior, I heard the sergeant say: "You two stay here and search the area for the other one." A moment later, the coach careened into motion.

By now I was in a dark and gloomy mood, full of self-reproach. In my mind's eye, I could already hear my uncle Ludovigo's sneering voice.

"Forgot everything I taught you, you fool—and at the very first opportunity!" Here he would glower in his inimitable style. "Idiot. Cretin. Moron." This would go on for no little time, accompanied by much clapping of despairing hands to aggrieved forehead. Then the lecturing voice of my uncle:

"What is the first law of secret police?"

The innocent flee where no man pursueth.

"The second law?"

Protestations of innocence stand in direct proportion to guilt.

"The third law?"

Who wants to hear it, anyway?

I was not looking forward to my next meeting with my uncle, let me tell you. No point lying to him, either—he'd see right through it. After the heaping of foul names upon my head, the ritual clapping of despairing hands onto his own head, there would come the great sigh—a genius casting pearls before a swine— and then, horror, the inevitable lecture.

"I will try again, my witless nephew. As I have told you before, time and again"—here would follow the history of the universe, beginning with the coalescence of the galaxies—"and so—will you try to remember?— if you wish to be a great artist you must expect many encounters with the secret police, many an interrogation by the forces of Church and State, many a long stay in the donjons and bastilles, many a beating and torture. Especially in Grotum! For these ineluctable modalities of the risible, you must be as well trained and prepared as your uncles Giotto, Algardi, Donatello and Salviati have made you for the actual exercise of your art itself."

Here would follow the ceremonial chewing of mustachios. Then:

"And why do you want to be an artist, anyway? It's a foolish ambition, no matter what those other uncles tell you! Much better for you to become a condottiere like myself or your uncles Rodrigo and Filoberto and the others. You have a talent for arms, and it's a much safer occupation than being an artist!"

The rest of his future lecture I was able to rehearse in advance, as the coach banged and clattered its way along the cobblestoned streets. And there was this benefit from the gloomy experience, that by the time the secret police of Goimr reached their destination, I was well-prepared for the immediate prospect of torture, having reviewed in my mind all of my uncle's instructions.

I was hustled into a great, gray, windowless building, which shared the general shabbiness which I was coming to realize was inseparable from Goimr. SECRET POLICE HEADQUARTERS read the sign above the door. (With, needless to say, the same bloodcurdling threat concerning classified information below.) Down a long corridor, a turn to the left, and there it was—the interrogation room, replete with all the requisite engines and tools of torture.

And then—

My rigorous rehearsal for the ordeal proved greatly excessive. For—would you believe it?—the incompetent fools began with a bastinado! My greatest problem was not to burst into laughter. The soles of my feet were covered with iron-hard calluses a half-inch thick—this the product of my uncle's rigorous training, which included walking on coals and soaking in brine. The blows of the cudgels were like a tickle.

But, of course, I never once lost my now-firm grasp on the fourth law of secret police:

Shrieks of agony soothe the savage beast.

Nor the fifth:

Stoic silence inflames the policeman's heart.

Nor—most important—the sixth:

Admissions of guilt stand in direct proportion to innocence. This, you will of course recognize, is but the obverse of the second law.

And so I interspersed my screams of agony with the most lurid confessions:

"Yes! Yes! I did it! I admit everything!" (Here I emitted a horrid shriek.) "I murdered the Popes—all twelve of them at once! The blood flowed like a river! O hideous impiety! And then!" (Here I dissolved into broken blubbering.) "I dismembered them! And ate them! O foul ecclesiophagy!" (Here I threw in the cackle of the criminally insane.) "And then! And then! After letting nature take its course, I defecated on holy ground! Like a wolf staking its territorial claim! Oh! Oh! I am a monster of depravity!"

"Not that, you idiot!" roared the sergeant. "Not the Popes! What about the King? What did you do to the King?"

"Which king?" Then, thinking I was bordering dangerously on proclaiming innocence, I immediately howled with glee and pain. "There have been so many! Butchered kings by the score, I have! The Kaysor of Kushrau I poisoned! And then—I fed the poisoned meat to his hounds! They died in agony! And then I cut the canines from the canines"—(here followed demonic shrieks of ecstasy at the pun)—"and with these newfound weapons I slew the Great Mogul of Juahaca! Plunged the teeth into his throat while he slept! Gave him a dog's collar of his own!" (Lunatic laughter.) "And then! Oh! I murdered the Doges of the Philistine! All of them at one swoop! Crept up on them while—"

"Not that, you idiot!" roared the sergeant. "The King of Goimr! Here—in Goimr! What did you do to the King of Goimr!"

"Oh! Him!" Here I fell into a minute or two of insensate ululation, for at the mention of the King of Goimr, the two policemen applying the bastinadoes had fallen into a truly vigorous beating of my feet. Then: "I forgot him! There've been so many kings! But him! Yes! Yes! I remember now! I disemboweled him with a scythe! Danced a fandango with his guts!"

"The King's still alive, you idiot! And not a mark on him! But he's insane! How did you drive him mad?"

I gasped with shock. "Still alive! You mean I missed? With a scythe? Missed! I'm going mad myself! But that's it! That's it! It must have been the horrible sight of my demented leer—the ghastly scythe in my hands!—drove the King of Goimr mad! O wondrous! O wondrous! I am such a criminal! Such an archdevil! A paragon of purest evil! Drove the King mad! Yes! Yes! I remember now!"

"It's looking bad, sir," I heard one of the policemen say, his voice filled with discouragement. The bastinado slacked off.

But the sergeant was made of sterner stuff. "I'll have none of it!" he roared. "You there! Apply the cudgels smartly! D'you hear me, you laggards?"

The bastinado renewed itself with a frenzy. Not to be thwarted, I immediately launched into a semi-coherent confessionary babble, recalling to mind all of the various crimes which my uncle Ludovigo had made me memorize. Fortunate I was in my training! On my own, I couldn't have thought up a tenth of those deeds of villainy.

At length, the bastinado fell off again.

"It's hopeless, sir," came the same policeman's voice, now sullen in its failure.

"Yes, I know," came the sergeant's morose reply. "Truth to tell, I lost heart earlier, when he confessed to seducing the Elf Queen's unicorn and abandoning the beast in her pregnancy. But this latest! Kidnapped the magnetic monopoles. Prevented the decay of the proton. And then—did you hear him? Murdered every one of the world's astronomers and cosmologists to protect the dark secret."

"Perhaps," came the obsequious voice of another policeman, "we could try the rack?"

"To what purpose, you fool?" demanded the sergeant. "What crime has he not confessed already?"

"Well," hemmed the obsequious voice, "he hasn't confessed to buggering and murdering the Maharaj of Naham."

"Oh, but I did!" I screeched. "It was my greatest crime! Through the use of cunning potions I brought all his mahouts under my sway! Taught them to sodomize the great war elephants! And then! The elephants now corrupted! The immense creatures filled with unnatural passion! I had but to wave the King's bed-clothes under their snouts! The hideous sight! The herd of aroused pachyderms! Their tusks and trunks raised to the heavens! Their great bellows of lust! The palace trampled flat! The King fleeing for his life! But in vain! My greatest coup! There! The King! Racing across the Royal Grounds! There! The pachyderms in hot pursuit! And then! Oh! Oh! The—"

"Shut up!" roared the sergeant. "*Just shut up!*" I fell silent, grimacing in an effort to hide my smirk.

"Untie him," grumbled the sergeant. "We'll take him to Gerard." Then, very gloomily: "There's going to be hell to pay when the Chief Counselor hears about this."

A minute later I was carried out of the building, a burly policeman hoisting me by each arm. I could have walked quite easily, though I wouldn't have cared to dance a gavotte. But I saw no reason to enlighten the brutes as to the true condition of my hardened feet.

Another rough ride followed—the cobblestones of Goimr's streets shared the general state of disrepair—and we debouched onto a large plaza bordering a sluggish river. This, I realized, must be the river Moyle, at whose mouth the city of Goimr is located. And there, on an island in the middle of the river, lay the Royal Palace—just as described in the travel brochures.

Ha! The actual palace bore the same relation to the one pictured on the travel brochures as the corpulent and toad-faced Madame Hexe bore to my grandfather Goya's portrait of her, *The Naked Madame*.

"Isn't there one building in this city that isn't half-crumbling?" I asked.

"Silence!" roared the sergeant. Then, sourly: "It's a poor country, we are. Not like your precious Ozarae."

His own gloom was no deeper than my own. To Goimr had I come, my brain flushed with visions of making my fame and fortune—invited by the King himself. A Royal Artist already—and me not yet twenty-four years of age! But now, gazing at the Royal Hovel, I reflected that I would be lucky if the King of Goimr could afford the paints, much less any decent fee. And I was not pleased by the suggestion, during my interrogation, that the King was not quite in possession of his senses.

But I had little time for reflection. Soon enough, a barge was found to transport the policemen and myself over to the Isle Royale, and from there it was but a few minutes before I was ushered into a large chamber.

The furnishings in the chamber were of the sort I

was coming to expect. The tapestries were particularly wretched, although they did serve to cover most of the grime and water stains on the walls. Behind a desk sat a man of easy grace.

"What's this, Sergeant?" he demanded, as soon as we entered the room. "Have you captured the wizard?"

The sergeant coughed apologetically. "Well, Chief Counselor Gerard, the truth is—we believe this man's innocent."

Chief Counselor Gerard's face was a study in confusion.

"What man?" he demanded.

"Why, this man here, sir," explained the sergeant, pointing to me. "The one we caught red-handed at the travel station. But after we put him to the question, it became clear that—"

"Imbecile!" The Chief Counselor's face was flushed with anger. "What has this man to do with anything? I told you to capture the wizard! Does this man look like a wizard to you? Look at his clothes—he's obviously from the Ozarine. Why would you seize *him*?"

The sergeant looked embarrassed. "Well, sir, when we arrived at the travel station—following your instructions, sir, I must point out—everyone fled but this man here. Stood there as guilty as sin, he did. Well, sir, as you know, it's the first law of secret police work. Only a guilty man would attempt to act innocent. And then, after we caught him, he pleaded his innocence! Well, sir, as you know, only a guilty man—"

"Oh, be quiet," snapped the Chief Counselor. A look of weariness crossed his face. "The end result of all this is that if the wizard did make his escape from the city through the travel station, then he's long gone by now."

"Well, yes, sir. They move along right quick, sir, the Consortium's transports do. Not at all like it was in the good old days. The bad old days, I mean to say."

The sergeant drew himself up, attempting a gesture of subtle reproof aimed at a superior. "And in any event, if you don't mind my saying so, sir, we really have no reason to think the wizard would have tried such an obvious escape route as the official travel station of the city. More likely, sir, he'd have tried to leave through one of the lesser-used gates."

"Yes, yes, I know. I've got police squads covering all the gates. We should know something soon. Fortunately, the wizard's a noticeable man. That ridiculous gown! The hat and the staff! The perfect image of the sorcerer of popular superstition. And that horrid servant. God, Sergeant, did you ever see such a frightful dwarf? And that incredible sack he carries!"

Well, I am neither stupid nor unobservant, and it was immediately obvious to me that the wizard of the police search was the very same unpleasant fellow I had encountered on my way out of the station. Had the police not been distracted by my stupidity they would have apprehended their culprit but moments later.

Warring impulses—I should say, warring advice— raged within my mind.

On the one hand, I was mindful of the unanimous advice of my artist uncles:

Always curry favor with the rich and powerful. As long as you curry favor with the swine, you can do anything else—cheat 'em, take their money, seduce their wives, whatever. But always curry their favor.

On the other, there was the unanimous advice of my condottiere uncles:

Don't tell the high and mighty anything. There's nothing more suspicious than a man who volunteers information. The torture chambers are full of blabbermouths. It's the seventh law of secret police:

"If he spills his guts freely, just think what he'll do under The Question."

In the end, oddly enough, the question was resolved for me by the memory of the pitiful dwarf. A nice enough boy he'd seemed, ugly though he was. And I had no illusions as to a dwarf's fate in the hands of the secret police. So I kept my mouth shut. And in so doing, I sealed not only my own fate but that of the world.

"You may go, Sergeant," said Chief Counselor Gerard. Then, as the sergeant took my arm and made to drag me away, Gerard added: "Leave him here."

The sergeant began to say something, thought better of it, and left.

When the door closed, Gerard turned to me. "Who are you, sir? Am I not correct, that you are from the Ozarine? What are you doing here in Goimr?"

"Quite so, Chief Counselor. My name is Benvenuti Sfondrati-Piccolomini, of the famous clan of scholars and artists. I just arrived from Ozar on board the CSS *Lucre*. Indeed, I do not believe I had spent more than ten minutes on Goimric soil before I was seized by your secret police."

The look of embarrassment on Gerard's face encouraged me to press home the advantage.

"As to the reason for my being here, I was invited by the King of Goimr to set up as the Royal Artist." With a flourish, I drew the King's letter from my pocket—which the secret police of Goimr, in that inefficient manner which I was coming to associate with everything Goimric, had not even searched.

"And here," I added dramatically, as soon as Gerard finished reading the King's letter, "is a letter of recommendation from the Consortium's Director of Companies."

I handed him the second letter. Gerard's face grew

gloomy. The King's letter had not seemed to produce much effect on him. But the letter from the Director of Companies was a different story altogether.

"'Upstanding young man,'" he read from the Director's letter, "'scion of a great family' . . . 'one of Ozar's most promising new artists.'" Etc., etc., etc.

Actually, I'd never met the Director of Companies. My uncle Giotto, however, is one of his favorite artists, and he'd persuaded the Director to sign the letter, which, needless to say, Giotto had written himself.

"This letter wouldn't do you much good in Ozar, of course," my uncle had said to me as he handed it over. "Everybody here knows that wretched plutocrat hasn't the faintest sense of art. But in Grotum it'll stand you in good stead. Fawn all over Ozarine wealth, they do, the nobility of Grotum. A miserable, medieval place. But there's no denying it's the greatest source of the world's art as well as most of its mischief."

The truth of his words was attested to by Gerard's very evident discomfort.

"Recommended by the Director of Companies himself! Um. A fine man. No—a great man! Been a mighty blessing to us here in poor and backward Goimr, he has. Um. No need to mention this recent unpleasantness to him, I should think?"

I nodded my head graciously, mentally rubbing my hands with glee. *Get something over the bastards as soon as you can*, my uncles had told me—artists and condottiere alike.

Gerard smiled feebly. Then he heaved a sigh.

"Unfortunately, sir, I'm afraid you've arrived at a bad time. Our blessed King has become unhinged—driven to insanity by the machinations of the villainous sorcerer Zulkeh. The realm is in an uproar. The King mad. The Heir Apparent a hopeless incompetent. All the heirs, indeed—well! No need to go into that here. But the point is, my good young man, that there's simply no place at the moment in Goimr for a Royal Artist. Not likely to be for—for some time, I should think."

I pleaded and remonstrated, but all to no avail. Truth to tell, now that Goimr was a reality rather than an illusion, I was none too sure myself that a promising young artist's career would be much advanced by lingering in such a place.

I did, however, in the course of my ensuing discussion with the Chief Counselor, manage to achieve a modest victory in what my uncles call The Artist's Quest.

I squeezed some money out of him.

Not much, I admit. But then, I found myself not disbelieving his claim that the treasury of Goimr was practically empty. But I got enough to enable me to survive, while I decided on my next course of action. I also obtained a brief letter with his signature which would, so he assured me, avoid any further complications with the police.

When I left the palace, it was sundown. My first task, clear enough, was to find lodgings for the night. I hired a small boat to transport me back across the river and began searching for a hotel.

Imagine, if you will, the tedium of looking for lodgings in Goimr. Even in the vicinity of the palace, the choices seem to vary from shabby to grim to hazardous. In the end, I settled on a run-down boardinghouse, whose proprietor seemed not quite as avaricious and slovenly as most I had encountered. Not saying much, that. Exhausted as I was by the day's travails, I was up half the night confronting the most sullen and difficult batch of rodents it has ever been my displeasure to encounter.

The next morning—not much rested, I can tell

you—I returned to the travel station and obtained my belongings from the locker. I then set out in search of other lodgings in a poorer part of town. My experiences of Goimr had so quickly lowered my threshold of fastidiousness that I was determined, at the least, to find lodgings which were not exorbitant in their price.

By early afternoon, I had wended my way into a truly disreputable part of the city. Truth to tell, I had long since forgotten about finding new lodgings. I had become absolutely fascinated by the baroque squalor which surrounded me. Ozar, of course, has its miserable tenements and ghettoes, like any great city. But nothing to compare to these slums!

The determination to capture this *nonpareil* wretchedness on canvas seized me. In part, this determination was prompted by my artist's instinct. But, in the other part, it was prompted by my artist's reason. For, as my uncle Giotto had told me many times, there are two subjects which—captured with paints—the rich will always pay through the nose to hang on the walls of their mansions: their own glorified features, and the misery of the poor. The misery of the poor, because it comforts them to ponder the tragedy of the human condition. Their own idealized portraits, because it comforts them to ponder their own worth in escaping that condition.

Rounding a corner, I found myself on a particularly odious street. Not only were the cobblestones in severe disrepair, not only were the gutters strewn with garbage and less mentionable items, not only were the ramshackle buildings which loomed over the street the very epitome of tenements, but—

There—not twenty feet before me—a woman was being attacked by a mob of cutthroats!

I was taken completely off guard. Until I rounded the corner, I had heard not a hint of clamor. The struggle under way was being waged in complete silence, save the occasional hiss and grunt.

For a moment, I was paralyzed, like a statue, rooted to the spot. From horror, you would think. But no, it wasn't that. I am an artist, with an artist's eye, and it was the impossible drama of the scene which transfixed me—like a tableau from ancient legend.

The struggle bore little if any resemblance to the image which might normally come to mind when one hears of "a woman assaulted by a mob of cutthroats." Think rather of "a lioness assaulted by a pack of hyenas."

The woman was a striking figure. This, in three ways. First, she was—not beautiful; not, at least, in the normal sense of the term—but so fierce in her countenance as to burn every feature into my mind. More so, indeed, even in the first instant I saw her than any woman I had ever seen before, or have seen since. The regal poise, the nose with the pure curve of a hawk's, the gleaming black eyes, the firm jaw and chin, the full lips, the great mass of kinky hair like midnight, the swarthy complexion now even more flushed with passion and fury. No, not exactly beautiful, but what has a goddess to do with earthly concepts of beauty?

Then, she was *big*. Not obese, you understand. To the contrary. Her every movement—and these were fierce and energetic even as I took in the scene— bespoke a body that was muscular and sinewy. Even shrouded as her body was in a plain and baggy set of tunic and trousers, there was no denying its quite evidently female nature. The woman seemed almost a giantess. She matched my six feet of height, if not exceeded it. And though I am considered a large and well-built man, I had no doubt that she weighed perhaps as much.

She certainly outsized her opponents! For these

men, as I saw when I finally tore my gaze from this
fantastic vision of a demi-goddess out of a desert
nomad's legend, were rather small and rattish in their
every aspect. Yet they pressed their assault with great
vigor, lunging at the woman from every side. They
seemed actually in a frenzy, leaping at her with drawn
knifes, attempting to stab and slash any portion of her
body they could reach.

I said that the woman was striking in three ways.
And the third of these ways was the unbelievable
ferocity of her defense. With her right hand she would
pluck an assailant out of the air—in mid-leap—and with
her left hand, which clasped an immense butcher knife,
she would remove her opponent's head with one blow
of the blade. For all the world like a farmer's wife
beheading chickens! Even as I watched, two heads
joined the half dozen which—I now noticed—were
lying about in the street like an urchin's rag balls.

Despite her ferocity, she was vastly outnumbered.
There were still a good dozen assailants remaining.
And even with her back to the wall of a building,
they could come at her from three sides. The end
of such an uneven contest was inevitable, given a
willingness on the part of her opposition to press the
fight to its conclusion, disregarding their own casualties. And small though they might be, and rattish
in their countenance, there was no denying that her
assailants were possessed of a ferocity the equal of
her own. As I watched, a knife blade slashed the
woman's hip. It was not a particularly deep cut,
hardly more than a scratch, but she immediately
hissed. A look of great pain came into her face. Her
opponents squealed with triumph.

It was only then that I noticed the odd sheen of
their knives. Poisoned blades!

It was that outrage which finally snapped my trance.

I dropped my baggage and charged forward carrying my easel like a three-pronged lance. An easel! You laugh! But no ordinary easel, this. For, combining the teachings of my various uncles, I had long ago designed this easel with a condottiere's sense of art. Each of the legs came to a sharp point, edged like a razor. Furthermore—but that in a moment.

For now, let me say with all due modesty that I slew three of the scoundrels with a perfectly executed *coup d'arrière tripodiste*. Then, before their bodies had even hit the ground, I drew my sword from its cunningly disguised sheath in the upright of the easel. A moment later it was plunged through the back of the nearest poisoner, piercing his heart. A quick twist of the wrist to free the blade, and a moment later another poisoner was run through the back. Another quick twist of the wrist—

"Through the back?" you say. Certainly! Though I am an artist, I am also a most proficient swordsman. I was trained by my uncle Rodrigo from the time I was six.

"As pretty-faced and brash a boy as you are, Benvenuti," he'd said to me (not without a sneer), "you'll be bound to land in a duel by the time you're sixteen. Some outraged husband, no doubt. So you'd best learn to use a blade at least as well as you learn to use a paintbrush."

I was a good student, and even my uncle eventually admitted that I had the knack of swordplay. But his instruction was stern and severe. Many was the time I was soundly cuffed—even thrashed—for committing what my uncle Rodrigo considered the greatest of all swordsman's sins.

Chivalry.

"Who d'you think you are, you little snot?" he would roar, applying the whip. "Some great lord of the land

parading around with airs? You're a wretch of an artist, you dolt! None of this bowing and posturing for
the likes of you!"

Whimper and plead though I would, each transgres-
sion of my uncle's code would earn me the full ten
lashes. A stern regimen, but by the time I was seven
I could recite the code in my sleep:

Whenever you can, stab 'em in the back.

Better yet, stab 'em in the back in the dead of night.

*Best of all, stab 'em in the back in the dead of night
while they're asleep.*

If you've got to stab 'em in the front, try a low blow.

*If none of that works, then use all your skills as best
you can, you stupid dummy.*

My uncle would, I believe, have been pleased. The
masterpiece with the easel. The next two, felled with
a backstab. From then on, of course, my foes were
alerted and I was forced to face them from the front.
But the next two went down before my low blow—
not without bestowing a look of great indignation upon
me as they expired. A strange morality—set upon a
woman with poisoned knives, but take offense at a
sword through the groin.

Alas, after that it became sticky. Two more of the
villains were dispatched by the woman before the poison
began to take effect upon her. She half-collapsed against
the wall, dropping her knife. Hissing with triumph, one
of the men hurled himself upon her, blade high. Foolish
move! Even as the impetuous hyena moves in too
quickly for the kill of a wounded lioness. For the woman
seized his throat in both hands and wrung his neck. A
most horrible sound, really. She then flung the body at
the others, bowling two of them over like tenpins. But
that was her last gasp. She slumped to the ground, dead
or unconscious.

In a frenzy, I forced my way to her side, in order

to protect her now-helpless form from certain death. Six assailants were still left alive.

No, five. For as they came in upon me, I suddenly changed tactics and thrust high, piercing one right through the throat.

Unfortunately, my blade was momentarily caught in his neck bones as he fell, and I was unable to withdraw it in time to parry a blow from another. His knife sank into my side.

Not deeply, not deeply, for I twisted aside even as the thrust came in. But the pain! It was as if I had been injected with acid! I recall my astonishment that the woman had simply hissed when so struck. I myself screamed like a banshee.

But there was this much to be said for the agony, that for a brief few seconds it galvanized me to a pure fury. A moment later, two more of my opponents were overborne by my rage, their blades beaten down, their faces slashed, their guts spilled onto the street.

Alas, the galvanizing pain was soon replaced by a great weakness. I staggered back, lost my footing. Then I fell against the wall of the building, right next to a door. It is strange how, at such moments, one notices the most insignificant thing. For my eyes fixed themselves upon a small, much-worn placard dangling by one screw from the door. DEATH HOUSE OF GOIMR, it read.

The irony of it caused me to laugh. I think it was that wild laugh which momentarily stayed my remaining opponents. The three paused, stooping over me. It was that pause, perhaps, which saved my life.

For at that moment, the door to the death house opened and a giant emerged. A true giant—even in my dazed state, I now realized that the woman whom I had taken for a giantess was but a very large woman. But this man! He had to stoop in order to get out of the door—and it was a large door. Eight feet tall, at least, he must have been.

My three opponents were transfixed by the sight. Not the size of the newcomer alone, but the way his eyes rolled about, the way he giggled like a madman, the drool issuing from his loose lips. And the words he spoke: "Isn't this just the craziest thing? Who would have thought it would come to this! And in Goimr— of all places!"

He beamed down at the three knifemen.

"Don't you just love it?" he asked. Then he raised the huge club which I now noticed for the first time— and so, judging from their expressions, did my opponents—and crushed one of them like an insect.

The other two—no cowards, I will say it—instantly launched themselves at the giant. In vain. Another swipe of that immense cudgel and both of them went flying. One of them was clearly dead—I could see the rib cage shattered like the side of a barrel. For a moment, I thought the other dead as well. But he struggled to his feet, shaking his head to clear the daze. He stared up at the giant, who was shambling toward him, club raised high.

"Madness and confusion, madness and confusion, oh it's so lovely," babbled the giant. He cackled with glee. I think it was that insane cackle which finally broke the villain's nerve. He turned and raced down the street.

Or, I should say, tried to race down the street. It took the giant but four huge strides to catch up with his prey and smash him to the ground. I could hear the skull splatter.

Then darkness claimed me and I knew no more.

My consciousness returned slowly, my hearing leading the way.

"And how is my dear aunt?" Such was the first sound I recalled. It was spoken in a high-pitched man's voice.

"The same as usual," came the reply, this in a female voice pitched so low that I don't know what to call it. Contralto profundo? The voice continued: "Head in the clouds."

"Oh, Gwendolyn—always so stern! When did you join the Sisterhood, by the way?"

"Me? A Sister?" A snort. "Not likely!"

"But I understood you to say you were carrying a message for Zulkeh from the Abbess Hildegard. I assumed—but then! Perhaps I misunderstood. Probably did. Probably imagined the whole thing. I'm crazy, you know." Mad cackling. "Hear voices all the time."

"Stop drooling! It's disgusting."

"Sorry. Can't be helped. Goes with my dementia. The head psychiatrist at the asylum's told me many times that—"

"Wolfgang, shut up!"

Even in my semiconscious state, the momentary silence which followed seemed filled with reproach. Then, a sigh, and the contralto profundo spoke again. Quite a beautiful voice, really, once you got used to the rumble.

"I didn't mean to hurt your feelings. I just don't want to hear it. And to answer your question, the reason I was carrying Hildegard's message is because she asked me to. She said the Sisters were being watched too closely."

"This is a long way to come just as a favor."

Another sigh. "Tell me about it. Halfway across Grotum, a good part of it on foot, with a knife fight at the end of the trip. And I never did get to deliver the message."

"Can't be helped. Zulkeh left yesterday. Just as

well, all things considered. The Fangs would have taken him before he finished his first sentence, replete with arcane allusions to the classics."

"Is he really that bad?"

The male voice snorted. "The world's greatest pedant, my dear Gwendolyn. I take it you've never made his acquaintance?"

"Don't meet too many pedants in my circles."

"I should think not!"

"Must you roll your eyes like that?"

Mad cackling. "Such intolerance! Quite odd, really, given your extreme ideological views."

The female voice snorted. "Eight-foot-tall lunatics who can afford to buy their own private insane asylums don't qualify as members of the downtrodden masses."

"I should hope not! But tell me, what exactly was this message you were to deliver?"

Silence.

"Oh, come, come, Gwendolyn. If you can't trust a madman, who can you trust? After all, who'd believe me anyway? Can you picture the scene? It's marvelous! Myself, strapped to the rack—wouldn't fit actually, they'd have to build one special—the dungeon filled with Inquisitors and Cruds and Fangs! The great ones! Cardinal Ignomini! The Angel Jimmy Jesus! God's Own Tooth! They speak! Their voices filled with hate! 'Tell us, Wolfgang, what were you doing down there in the secret passageways leading off from the abandoned death house?' Myself, screaming with pain! 'Oh! That feels good! Excruciating agony! Just what the head psychiatrist at the asylum recommends—'"

"Wolfgang!"

"What? Oh, sorry. But the man's a genius, you know? A giant in the field of psychology. Anyway, where was I? Oh, yes, strapped to the rack, screaming with ecstasy. 'I was talking with the notorious agitator Gwendolyn—

the demoness herself! The Queen of the Railroad. And she was telling me how the Abbess Hildegard asked her to hike all the way across Grotum—just as a personal favor, you know?—in order to tell Zulkeh, the world's egghead supreme, that he was mixed up in Joe business.' And then—"

"How did you know?" demanded the woman's voice. A voice now frighteningly harsh.

"But it's obvious! Why else would Hildegard get involved? And why else would you agree to come?"

"I didn't do it because of Joe! Can't stand all this Joe nonsense. It's one of the reasons I'd never join the Sisterhood. It's idiotic. We're all supposed to stand around contemplating our navels. And meantime Ozar gobbles up Grotum along with the rest of the world. Let the poor starve! Let the dwarves be butchered!" Her voice assumed a clipped high-pitched tone. "'When Joe comes back, dear, these things will all get straightened out. In the meantime, we must do our best to salvage what we can.'"

"I must say, that's quite a good imitation of Hildegard. My favorite aunt—I'm really very fond of her. She's quite mad, you know? A classic obsessive-compulsive—especially when it comes to her correspondence with God! The head psychiatrist at—"

"Wolfgang!"

"Oh. Sorry. Where was I? Other than in a state of lunacy? Oh, yes. You were about to tell me the message you were to deliver to the wizard."

"I was not. Besides, you seem to know all about it already. And while we're on the subject, just exactly what were you doing in the death house?"

"When?"

"When you came out and clubbed the rest of the Fangs, you idiot! What were you doing here?"

"I was watching you, actually. There's a peephole

in the door. You were marvelous. Just marvelous! Hacking and hewing Fangs right and left! Reminded me of this ax murderer we have in the asylum. Wonderful man, really. Of course, the head psychiatrist took away his ax. Can't blame him, I suppose. Therapy's difficult with an ax in your skull, even if you're the world's greatest psychiatrist. But it was horrible the way the poor madman wailed and—"

"Wolfgang—shut up! Just shut up about your damned asylum! You mean to tell me you stood there and watched the whole thing? And didn't do anything? You lousy bastard!"

The male voice sounded aggrieved. "Didn't do anything? That's crazy! If you'll pardon the expression. Didn't I come out and finish the job?"

"Not until I was already cut and for all you knew dead from those damned poisoned blades!"

"Nonsense. It was obvious the Fangs were trying to capture you alive. To put you to The Question, don't you know? Better to be dead, of course. But if they'd been an assassination team they'd have been wearing green cockades. Green for gangrene, you know? They're really quite maniacal, the Fangs, in a horribly sane sort of way."

"You mean they weren't trying to kill me? It sure seemed that way! No sooner did I knock on the door than they came piling out of the death house. Didn't say a word, just started stabbing at me right away."

"Yes, yes, I know. As I said, a lot of maniacs. They've gotten it into their heads that Zulkeh's meddling with the King's dream would stir up awful things. You should have heard them carrying on in here. They came in not six hours ago. Absolutely furious that they'd missed the wizard. Ransacked the whole place. A frightful scene! There's nothing here except a lot of old bones, of course. The wizard took all his stuff with him when

he left. I watched the whole thing from my hideout."
Mad cackling. "Amazing! Such disrespect for the dead
from such paragons of piety! Crypts dumped, bones
scattered, urns shattered! I'm afraid that by the time
you knocked on the door they'd worked themselves up
into quite the devout frenzy. You should have heard
them pouring out of the catacombs and racing up to
the main level."

"What if I'd been an innocent bystander?" demanded
the woman.

Absolutely insane and hysterical laughter followed
this question.

"What's so damned funny?"

"My dear Gwendolyn! Are you such a naïf?
What a question—and coming from you! Gwendolyn
Greyboar! The Terror of Theocracy! The Lady of the
Lowlife! The Nabobs' Nemesis! Dumb as a schoolgirl!"
Suddenly the mad voice was tinged with anger. "When
has anyone been an innocent bystander in the eyes of
the Godferrets?"

"All right, all right," grumbled the woman. "But I'd
still like to know why you didn't come out sooner."

"Well, actually, I was about to take the plunge
when this marvelous young man came along. Such a
hero! And so young and handsome! The coup with
the tripod! Brilliant! And what an exquisite backstab
he's got. You were probably too busy to notice, dear.
A pity, really. Best backstab I've seen in years.
Skewered two of them in a trice. And then! When
the Fangs turned to face him! The low blows! Oh,
marvelous! Marvelous! That kind of treacherous
swordwork's a lost art, nowadays. Haven't seen such
cunning bladesmanship since Rodrigo Sfondrati-
Piccolomini. It was—"

"My uncle," I mumbled. I tried to open my eyes,
but I couldn't.

"He's waking up!" exclaimed the woman.

"What a silly goose you are. He's been awake for some time. Now he's regaining consciousness." Clucking sounds. "Really should require you sane people to take courses in psychology. Won't find a lunatic who can't tell the difference between being awake and being conscious. It's the key to the whole thing, you know? Insanity, I mean. The head psychiatrist at the asylum wrote a wonderful—"

"Wolfgang! You mean he's been listening to us talk?"

"Well, not exactly. More accurate to say he's been hearing us talk. 'Listening' implies consciousness, you see. And I was just explaining that in his article the—"

"Shut up! You idiot! He's heard too much!"

The sound of motion, somehow ominous. Then the man's voice: "Gwendolyn!"

I opened my eyes. The woman—yes, it was she, the lioness—stood crouched above me, her great knife upraised for a death blow, her eyes blazing.

"Perfect!" I cried. "Right there! Don't move! My brushes! My paints!" I tried to move, couldn't.

The woman frowned. Her frown had to be seen to be believed. I began weeping with frustration. A masterpiece it would have been! *Goddess In Judgement.*

"What did he say?" she said, turning her head. My eyes followed her gaze. There, sitting on a stone slab, was the shambling giant who had emerged from the doorway and administered the final blows to the knifemen. A lunatic, it was now obvious. He began a wild and insane cackling.

"He wants to paint your portrait!" he howled. "A true Sfondrati-Piccolomini! Of the artistic branch! Can't bear to die without painting his doom first—oh, marvelous. Marvelous!"

He wiped tears from his eyes, then babbled further.

"Really a much finer lot than my own clan, I'll be the first to say it. Not such good scholars, the Sfondrati-Piccolominis, but you'll never find such great mad artists among the Laebmauntsforscynneweëlds."

"He wants to *what*?"

"Portrait," I whispered. "Your portrait. You're perfect. Just like you were before—in the fight."

She gazed down at me. Slowly lowered her cleaver. Shook her head.

"You're as crazy as he is," she growled.

"Perhaps some introductions are in order," said the giant in his oddly high-pitched voice. "I am Wolfgang Laebmauntsforscynneweëld, of the noted scholarly clan of that name. This magnificent lady with the great cleaver in her hand is Gwendolyn Greyboar, famous throughout Grotum for—"

"Shut up, Wolfgang! He's an Ozarine, by the looks of him."

"Well, of course he's an Ozarine. As I was just about to say, Benvenuti Sfondrati-Piccolomini, of the noted scholarly clan of that name—and not just scholars! Oh no! Artists and condottiere galore! Come to Goimr to seek his fame and fortune." Here he broke into a horrid cackling. "And they say I'm crazy!"

My feebleness was rapidly fading. I muscled myself up into a sitting position. In the process, I noticed that my wound had been expertly bandaged. Looking around, I saw that I was in a chamber hewn directly out of bare rock. Along one side was a stone bench, where Wolfgang was sitting. Behind him, bored into the rock wall, were some odd-looking holes. The chamber was otherwise bare, except for the entrance to a dim tunnel which loomed in the far wall. The woman leaned against the wall next to the tunnel.

"How do you know so much about me?" I demanded.

The giant stopped cackling and shrugged. "Well, I

read the letters in your pocket, while Gwendolyn was bandaging you up. Quite impressive. An invitation from the King. A recommendation from the Consortium's Director of Companies. A letter of—*Gwendolyn!*"

I turned, flinched. The woman was looming above me again, cleaver upraised.

"An Ozarine agent!" she raged. "A Consortium spy!"

"Nonsense!" boomed Wolfgang. "He's an artist."

"What kind of artist would have letters in his pocket from the Director of Companies?" hissed Gwendolyn.

"A Sfondrati-Piccolomini, of course. They didn't get to be one of the two great learned clans in the world by being wallflowers, you know? Great self-promoters, the Sfondrati-Piccolominis—take it from a Laebmauntsforscynneweëld! Besides, the letter wasn't even written by the Director. I recognized Giotto's handwriting. Been corresponding with him for years. Oh, I've no doubt the Director's signature was genuine enough. Never catch a Sfondrati-Piccolomini in outright forgery! And so what? The man must sign twenty letters like that a day. He's not much better than a parvenu, the Director, and he knows full well that if he's to take his place at the summit of Ozarine society he's got to develop a reputation as a Patron of the Arts. It's part of the plutocrat ritual."

Gwendolyn was still frowning, that amazing frown. And it's odd, looking back after all these years, how my life went off course so early. Can't say as I regret it, mind you. But still, it's odd. A young man's heart is supposed to be caught by a young girl's eye, or the smile on her lips, or the curve of her neck, or the toss of her hair.

At that very moment a faint sound was heard. Wolfgang held up his hand, motioning us silent. He pressed his ear to one of the holes in the wall behind him. A moment later Gwendolyn had joined him on the bench, her ear pressed to another hole. And it was but another moment before my ear was pressed to a third.

"Make your report," I heard a voice say. A hard, cold, cruel voice.

"The dead men are all Fangs, Mr. Inkman."

Again, the cold sneering voice: "Tell me something I don't know."

"It's hard to tell exactly what happened, sir. The wounds are strangely varied. Some were decapitated, as by an ax. Others skewered. An expert swordsman's work, that—a cunning one, to boot. Perfect backstabs and low blows, the most of those killed by the sword. And then there are the three who look like they were clubbed by an ogre. Crushed flat, those were."

"Three killers," mused Inkman. Silence. Then, he spoke again: "What did you do with the bodies?"

A harsh laugh. "We put them in the lower catacombs. Rolled them right back up in the shrouds and bones they'd pitched. Nobody'll look for them there. Certainly not the Goimr police! Couldn't find their dicks in the dark, those clowns. And I don't think there are any Fangs left alive in Goimria. Leastways, all the ones I knew are lying right now on cold stone slabs below. By the time God's Own Tooth finds out what happened and sends another ferret pack, these'll all be moldy bones."

"Excellent! We're the only ones who know what happened, then?"

A cough. "Well, not exactly, Mr. Inkman. The killers know what happened. Know more than we do, actually."

"Them! Who cares? Hasn't the Angel said it a thousand times? 'It's your friends who are the problem. Enemies take care of themselves.'"

"Yes, sir. That's what he says, sir."

"So! What could be more perfect? For once, the miserable Fangs will be in the dark, instead of us. The Angel will be very pleased. He's been trying to convince the Committee and the Nabobs for months that it was time to send a Rap Sheet to Grotum. They've been stalling, listening to the damned Fangs whispering in their ear. 'Don't rouse the Groutch beast from its sleep.' 'Let Grotum lie.' That's all the Fangs ever say! Bah! Is the swelling grandeur of Ozar to be denied by these ancient legends of Grotum? Nonsense! It's long past time we took firm and direct measures. The Senators will whine and whimper, of course, like a typical lot of politicians. But the Nabobs are made of sterner stuff. Especially the Director of Companies! Now there's a man of action, after my own heart."

"The Fangs won't like it much, sir," responded the second voice.

"There's the beauty of it," replied Inkman. "This little massacre here will throw them into a panic. And well it should! When was the last time a whole pack was wiped out to the last ferret?"

Silence. Then, Inkman again: "Never, that's when. I can't stand the holier-than-thou bastards, but there's no denying they're a murderous crew. Can you imagine the reaction of God's Own Tooth when he hears? He'll be baying for Groutch blood!"

"He'll want to know who did it, too. Don't you think we should—"

"Nonsense. What? Are we to waste our time trying to sort out which lot of Groutch malcontents butchered the Fangs? No, no, it won't do. Remember the Angel's motto: 'Do in your friends first, and your enemies are bound to follow.'"

"As you say, sir."

"So, let's be off. You are sure you cleaned up all the evidence?"

"All except the bloodstains on the street. But who'll notice that, in Grotum?"

"Well said! It won't be long now before this entire miserable sub-continent bends its knee to Ozar. Not with a Rap Sheet here on the scene to help us."

"Goimr will fall into our laps for sure, with a Rap Sheet."

"Bah! Who wants Goimr? No, I'll be proposing to the Angel that we start with the Rap Sheet in Prygg. I know he'll agree. He's often said Prygg was the key to Grotum."

The last sentence I only heard faintly, for the voices were dwindling into the distance. When I looked up, I was struck by the differing ways in which my two companions in the cell were reacting to the conversation we had just overheard.

Wolfgang was grinning from ear to ear.

Gwendolyn's face was flushed with fury.

"The Ozarine dogs!" she cried. "The filthy Cruds!"

"The vainglorious fools!" cackled Wolfgang. "The incredible idiots!" He began laughing insanely.

Gwendolyn glared at him. "They're going to bring a Rap Sheet to Grotum to complete their conquest of our homeland. And you think that's funny?"

Wolfgang wiped tears from his eyes. "But, my dear Gwendolyn, don't you see the irony of the whole thing? The fools propose to bring one of Joe's great relics to subdue Joe's own homeland. Doesn't it strike you that there's a hint of folly in the logic? Typical Cruds!" Here the giant imitated Inkman's cold voice: "'As the Angel says, first do in your friends. Then your enemies will fall.'" He fell again into his horrible mad laughter.

"I love it!" he cried. "The Ozarine paranoids will hide the massacre of the ferret pack from the Fangs, so the Fangs—who know the lurking danger in Grotum better than anyone!—won't be able to get in the way of the Ozarines when they come trampling all over the place and rouse the lurking danger to full fury."

Gwendolyn was still glaring at him.

Wolfgang shook his head. "Gwendolyn, the whole problem here is that you don't really understand the Joe question."

"I don't want to hear about it!" she snapped. "All I know is that the Ozarine Empire—which has already half swallowed Grotum!—now intends to gulp us down complete. What do you propose to do? Sit around drooling and giggling while we wait for some myth to rescue us?"

"Well, not exactly. I do believe Joe will need a little help along the way. But don't let me stop you. I quite admire your efforts! Sally forth—by all means! Smite the Ozarine with your cleaver!"

I thought that last was an unfortunate turn of phrase—the more so when Gwendolyn turned her hot glare onto me.

I spread my hands in a calming gesture. "Madame, let me assure you that—"

"Don't call me 'Madame'!" she barked.

I took a deep breath, tried again. "Gwendolyn, then. It's true I'm an Ozarine. What of it? I'm an artist, before all else. I care not a fig for the pomposities of the rulers of Ozar. Certainly not the Angel Jimmy Jesus and that whole lot of Cruds! Nasty creatures. Besides, like every genuine artist I know, my heart lies with Grotum. It's the center of the world's art! Its music!"

"Its mischief!" giggled Wolfgang.

I nodded at him. "Perhaps, perhaps. It's certainly a livelier place than Ozar. At first, I thought Goimr an unutterably dull place—"

"It is," spoke Wolfgang and Gwendolyn in unison.

"—but here I am—not a day since I landed—and

already I've been arrested, tortured, been in a bloody swordfight, hidden in a secret hidey-hole, spied on Cruds—what next? What next?"

"Next you'll have to make your escape," said Wolfgang. "The both of you."

He turned to Gwendolyn, who was—and I was glad to see it—calmer in her aspect.

"I assume you'll be trying to follow Zulkeh—when you discover where he went—to deliver Hildegard's message."

"A pox on Zulkeh!" came the response. "A pox on Hildegard and her damned schemes! I've got better things to do than be chasing all over Grotum looking for some obscure sorcerer. I've got to warn my comrades. If the movement isn't prepared for it, the Rap Sheet will cut through us like a scythe. Even with an advance warning, it's going to be bad enough. Besides, I don't even know where the wizard went."

The key moments of decision come unexpected in life. If I have learned nothing else, this I have. And when they come, it amazes me how instantly they are made. Later, musing over the events, I was struck by how light were the feathers that wafted my fortune. A dwarf's voice, a woman's frown—these the things that sent me off on a road unforeseen.

I had told the police nothing, but now I spoke.

"The wizard—Zulkeh, that is his name? Accompanied by a dwarf servant?"

"His apprentice," corrected Wolfgang. "Shelyid, his name is."

"Yes—an ugly creature. But he seemed a sweet boy. Anyway, they've gone to Prygg." I told them of my encounter with Zulkeh and Shelyid at the travel station, and the words I overheard spoken by the wizard.

"But why would he go to Prygg?" asked Gwendolyn. She peered closely at Wolfgang.

"It's time for some answers, you lunatic. You've been keeping things from me."

Wolfgang looked aggrieved. "My dear Gwendolyn!" He began rolling his eyes wildly.

"Cut out the act, Wolfgang!" she snarled. "Who is this wizard, anyway? And why is everyone so interested in him? Including you!"

"Me?"

Gwendolyn waved at the chamber. "This hidey-hole. This wasn't put here by the wizard. Look at the scale of the chamber—and that tunnel. This was built by you. Why?"

Wolfgang coughed, then smiled. "Can't put a thing past you, can I? Well, yes, actually I built this chamber so I could keep an eye on the wizard. Built it years ago. Zulkeh's never known about it. The room beyond—the one which these holes enable you to listen to—that's the wizard's study."

"Why?" demanded Gwendolyn fiercely. "What's so damned important about this sorcerer? You said yourself he was just a pedant."

Wolfgang looked hurt. "I said nothing of the sort. I said he was the world's greatest pedant, that's true. But I never said he was *just* a pedant. Dear me, no! Ridiculous!"

Gwendolyn threw up her hands. "Enough. Enough! I'll never get any sense out of you. And I don't care, anyway. I'll let lunatics like you worry about the legendary Joe. I've got real things to worry about—real enemies, and real comrades, and real struggles. And I've wasted enough of my time already. The wizard's gone to Prygg—let him go! I'm not chasing after him. I've got to get back to the Mutt. The Ozarines with a Rap Sheet here in Grotum will wreak havoc. I've got to get the warning out—and quick."

She rose, like a tiger, and turned to the tunnel. Then stopped abruptly.

"Where does this tunnel lead to, anyway?"

"Where else?" giggled Wolfgang. "To my secret door. But, Gwendolyn, will you please stop long enough to think?"

He raised his hands, as if to fend off the blow of her glare.

"Please, my dear, please! I'm not trying to talk you out of your plans. Forget the wizard—by all means! It's no problem, anyway. I've had a hankering to visit Prygg again. It's Magrit, you know." He smirked, for all the world like a schoolboy. "She and I are quite the item! Such a passionate witch!"

He coughed. "Well, enough of that. The point is, I'll follow the wizard. But if you want to warn your people, you first have to get out of Goimr. The police will be everywhere. You heard Benvenuti—they'll be watching every gate. You're rather a noticeable woman, you know? How do you think you'll get out?"

Gwendolyn frowned. "Well, I hadn't really thought about it. I just walked in, I thought I'd just walk out."

"If I might make a suggestion, and"—here he cackled—"if you can manage to overcome your anti-Ozarine prejudices for a moment, I believe that Benvenuti might be the solution to your problem."

He turned to me. "Tell me, my boy, have you given any thought to your future?"

It took me a moment to grasp his meaning.

"No, I hadn't. Not really. My original plans seem to have fallen through."

"I should say! Idiotic plans, to begin with. Imagine. Wanting to be the Royal Artist of Goimr!"

He and Gwendolyn both burst into a fit of laughter. Now that I'd experienced Goimr, I admit I found it impossible not to laugh myself.

"You see, Gwendolyn?" demanded Wolfgang. "Just as I said! A marvelous young man! The perfect traveling companion for you."

"What are you talking about?" she demanded.

"Don't you see? It's perfect! For both of you. Benvenuti has a letter vouching for him, signed by Chief Counselor Gerard. That'll get him through the gates with no questions asked. As for himself, the sooner he shakes the mud of this wretched city off his boots, the better."

He smiled at me. A wonderful smile he had, actually, if you left aside its demented aura.

"The place for an aspiring young artist, my boy, is New Sfinctr! There's the ticket! Oh, it's a horribly wicked city, I admit. 'The pesthole of the planet,' they call it. But exciting! Alive! Vigorous! Just the place for you. But your problem, of course, is how to get there. It's all the way across Grotum. You'll have to traverse forests, mountains—the Groutch wilderness. On your own, you'd lose your way. Lose your life, no doubt. But with Gwendolyn as your guide, it'll be a Sunday stroll, near enough."

"I'm not going to New Sfinctr," growled Gwendolyn.

Wolfgang dismissed her protest with a wave. "Quibbles, quibbles—and you know it! You're going as far as the Mutt, aren't you?"

She nodded.

"And isn't New Sfinctr but a hop, skip and a stumble from there? Of course it is! A well-traveled route, too. Even a simpleton could find his way from the Mutt to New Sfinctr. And Benvenuti's no simpleton. Not even today—and he certainly won't be one by then. No, not at all! He'll be what the Ozarine call 'an old Groutch hand.' "

I wished he'd left off that last bit. Needless to say,

the mention of the Ozarine brought a scowl from Gwendolyn.

"And that's another thing! There are people I've got to meet." She glared at me. "People I don't want this damned Ozarine to see, so he can run and tell his people who they are."

"Damn you, madame!" I overrode her bellow with one of my own. "And don't tell me not to call you 'madame'! Aren't you acting the perfect high and mighty lady? I assure you, no Ozarine heiress could do it better. I told you once—I will say it again—I am an artist, not a politician. And I'm certainly not a policeman! Make any detour you wish. See anyone you desire. If you want me to remain off to one side while you undertake your mysterious missions—why, so I will. If you choose to have me accompany you—why, I will say nothing to anyone."

I spat on the floor. "And finally—*madame*—you may rest assured that not all Ozarines are pig-bellied plutocrats. My own branch of the Sfondrati-Piccolominis has known its share of poverty and hard times. But we've always been artists, or scholars, or soldiers of fortune. Or—if those words don't suit you!—call us potters and pedants and plunderers. But there've been precious few respectable bourgeois in the lot. And never a police informer!"

We were glaring at each other fiercely, practically nose to nose. It was she who stepped back, with a new look in her eyes. Respect, I thought, and I was stunned by how much I cared.

"Got quite the bite, this boy does," she chuckled.

"No boy, Gwendolyn!" exclaimed Wolfgang. "No boy could have carved up so many Godferrets. Skill and training be damned—that takes an adult passion. He did save your life, you know. Well, actually, I would have saved it if he hadn't—but he didn't know that at the time. Quite the hero lurking somewhere inside this young fellow, if my twin powers of madness and amnesia are to be trusted—and they are! They are!"

The round of insane laughter which followed from the giant's mouth enabled both Gwendolyn and me to catch our breath and take new stock.

And then she smiled, for the first time since I had met her. Not a sunny smile, Gwendolyn's, never—too many scars had forged that smile. But there was a great cool gleam in it, like moonlight, and friendship, and a sense of unyielding courage.

"All right," she said. "I'm willing, if you are. I warn you, the trip will be long, hard, and dangerous."

I didn't need to answer with words. I was grinning from ear to ear, and laughing, and happier than I'd been—ever, I think. An adventurous life, I'd wanted, since I was a lad. And here it was!

But after Wolfgang explained the details of his plan, I wasn't happy at all. And the look on Gwendolyn's face was positively terrifying.

"But—but—" I was stammering like a schoolboy. "I'd thought—perhaps—Gwendolyn could pose as my wife—well, local girlfriend, in any event—the police might know I'd just arrived unaccompanied—but—" I was actually blushing.

"Nonsense!" boomed Wolfgang. "The whole idea's preposterous! Look at her. Oh, don't mistake me—she's an immensely handsome woman, Gwendolyn is. But—let's face it. Would the dullest-witted policeman in the world believe, for one moment, that this Amazon would be some Ozarine playboy's skirt of the evening?"

Gwendolyn's face was like an iron mask.

"He's right, damn him. His plan will work, I've no doubt of it. That's why I hate it."

Even Wolfgang's air of perpetual good cheer seemed clouded, for a moment.

"I know, my dear. But that's partly why it'll work. The police may have learned by now that you're here in Goimr. If they have, they'll be looking for you, as sure as the sunrise. But not as a draywoman! Not ever! Not Gwendolyn Greyboar!"

His gaiety returned. "No, the real problem here is with Benvenuti. It's his part in the play I'm concerned about. You'll need nerves of steel, my boy! And I hope you've as good a hand with a whip as you have with a sword. The whole thing will have to look real, you know?"

I took a breath. "I'm actually better with a whip."

"Oh, good!" cried Wolfgang. "Oh, that's very good!" He coughed, chuckled. "Actually, I'd say your life may depend on it."

Looking at Gwendolyn, I had no doubt of it. Even before—as if by an involuntary reflex—the cleaver appeared in her huge hand.

"If that whip so much as scratches me!" It was amazing, really, how deep her voice was.

"If it does," she continued, "when we reach the forest, I'll gut you like a pig."

The times were most rank. For the Old Geister brooded alone and disconsolate far away in the bowels of his cloud-shrouded citadel, taking scant heed of the affairs of men. Meanwhile eons passed, millennium upon millennium, and the world fell into corruption. Skepticism and unreason swept across the land, even as the wench's oestrus inflames the pubert's loins. Yet the Old Geister acted not, for his rancor was overcome by melancholia.

Worse than the damage to human morals was the damage to human minds. Men began to doubt, then question, then snigger at, then openly scorn, the once revered mysteries of old. Soon it was apparent that humanity preferred natural acts to unnatural lore. Thus, as generation followed upon generation, the candle of the old knowledge flickered out, and expired in the common memory of mankind.

Yet, as we approach the time of our tale, there remained abroad in the world a few score scholars devoted to the retrieval of lost arts and philosophies. They could be found scratching among the rubble of ruined libraries and ancient temples, hoping thereby to unearth fragments of old writ. Each believed that there was to be discovered by the perusal of old scrolls and tablets, and the cunning exegesis thereof, the deepest secrets of the powers of the universe.

Their lot was hard. As a result, their numbers, never great, declined steadily as the time of our tale draws near. Many factors contributed to this end. Some were martyrs to their own experiments, falling victim to spells ill-cast, demons misconjured, potions botched, talismans malwrought. Others were undone by the perils of the itinerant life attendant upon their pursuit of wisdom: the cholers of nature, the intemperance of wild beasts, the deprivations of disease, and the like. Still others, and these the most numerous of all, fell prey to the brutish acts of their fellow humans—for these latter are, as is well known, an unruly lot, given to sudden tempers and disputes. Hence the popular aphorism: "He who lives by reason, dies by the sword."

The survivor of these happenstances would yearn at length for a sanctum, some refuge wherein to contemplate the mysteries of Truth, unhampered by the pogroms of man and nature. Perforce they would forego, for a time, the peripatetic life and repair to some town or city, therein to peruse at leisure whatever ancient pearl of wisdom might have been acquired in their travels.

To support a domicile for these scholarly pursuits, the sorcerer would typically apply his or her learning as a scrivener, teacher, lecturer, tutor, or healer of incurable maladies. Of these, of the mere handful of wizards populating the earth now at the time when our tale is ripe for the telling, we note that the least notable was a certain Zulkeh of Goimr, physician.

The ancient city of Goimr is located on the underbelly of the great sub-continent of Grotum, at the place where the river Moyle joins the sea. Here, in a vast old abandoned death house, replete with many strange vaulted chambers connected by dark and crumbling passageways winding convolutedly like so many intestines deep into the bowels of the earth, down ever downward, into small niche-pocked vaults filled with damp worm-eaten caskets, many askew and half-opened crypts of the long dead, urns of dust, and the scattered bones of dogs and man, here, chose Zulkeh to rest and ponder his wealth of artifacts and relics, his scrolls and tablets, his talismans and tomes, the fruit gathered of his many journeys.

An individual of such marked cerebral bent as the thaumaturge of Goimr could not, of course, afford to be troubled by the vulgar exigencies of attending his own person. Accordingly, Zulkeh had taken for the purpose an apprentice. This individual, one Shelyid, was evidently an orphan, for he had been discovered one evening by the wizard in a crude basket placed before the door to the death house. Zulkeh had at once taken in the wretch, not, it must be admitted, as an act of kindness, but rather in the pursuit of science. For the unfortunate Shelyid had been cursed with a most disgusting physiognomy. The victim of dwarfdom, the wretched Shelyid's runtish body was ill served and thus doubly cursed by bad nerves, the slightest agitation of which would produce the most indecorous results: pox, palsy, jitters, quivers, tremors, convulsions, paroxysms, fevers, the staggers, the jerks, shortness of breath, frequent and uncontrolled excretion, irregularities of the pulse, lock-jaw, ague, fidgets, timorousness, and a general feeling of social inferiority. These, of course, the classic symptoms of that most dread of nervous conditions, *hysteria follicularia*, the uncontrolled growth and spread of hair upon the body.

The sorcerer had taken in the much-afflicted Shelyid in the belief that the dwarf was unnaturally wrought, the creature of some puissant though unknown power in the universe. For many years did the wizard peruse his scrolls and tomes, searching for some clue to the dwarf's provenance. Finding nothing, he turned to a consideration of events in the world at large which might be relevant to Shelyid's origin. But in truth the year of the gnome's discovery was a remarkably quiescent year, at least by the standards of the modern turmoil. Only two events of general historic interest had occurred: the publication—much to the outrage of the Ecclesiarchs—of Father Cosmo Sfondrati-Piccolomini's infamous letter from the Sssuj, and the mysterious disappearance of the Colossus of Ozarae. As both these events occurred in lands far distant from Goimr, and as no connection with Shelyid's arrival was discernible, the wizard dismissed these coincidences from his mind.

The time came when Zulkeh drew his conclusions and summoned the dwarf to his chambers.

"Shelyid," spoke the mage, "I have determined the source of your squalidness."

"Oh, master!" cried Shelyid, fairly fainting from joy and expectation. "You are the wisest and most powerful of wizards!"

"Indeed," concurred Zulkeh. "The truth was most trickily hidden from my powers, most cunningly disguised from my perceptions."

"Yes, yes!" quivered the dwarf.

"I perceive now that my error lay in my too great wisdom, for it was natural that I should assume that your affliction lay in some supernatural source, whereas it is in fact purely commonplace. Thus I tell you that you are in truth not an occult but a genetic specimen. And though the world in its ignorance perceives in you nothing but an odious eyesore—scrofulous, repulsive and loathsome—that behind this veneer my genius has penetrated to the truth. To wit, that you are in fact nothing but an odious eyesore—scrofulous, repulsive and loathsome."

The wizard continued in this vein, opening up to Shelyid's understanding the wondrous and tortured path of logic whereby Zulkeh had arrived at the essence beneath the appearance. But it must be admitted that his labor was in vain, for the dwarf had long since fainted dead away, whether in awe of such deep and profound thoughts or in horror at the now-revealed permanence of his fate, it is difficult to say. Fortunately for the dwarf, his years of service to the wizard had reconciled this latter to Shelyid's limitations, and Zulkeh concluded that he would retain the runt as his apprentice, despite Shelyid's now-demonstrated lack of worth.

Thus, at this the beginning of our tale, do we find our principal *dramatis personae* ensconced at Goimr, the sorcerer earning an irregular income by his knowledge of physic, or, on those all too frequent occasions when none sought his services, by dispatching Shelyid into the tombs to scratch over the possessions of the long dead, extract the occasional gold tooth, and whatnot.

And now it is time to introduce myself, for I am your narrator; and, though I subscribe to the ancient wisdom that a tale's narrator should be as unobtrusive

as possible, yet it is mete that the gentle reader should
know somewhat of the provenance of this tale, lest he
become afflicted with false doubts concerning its
veracity and authenticity.

"Your narrator," I named myself, yet this term must
at once be qualified. In truth, it would be more proper
to call myself the compiler of this narration, rather than
the narrator himself. The principal source of our tale,
the central thread around which I have been forced
to weave other annals and accounts, is the *Chronicle
of the Great Calamity* scribed by my illustrious forefathers, the Alfredae. I say, "around which I have been
forced to weave other annals and accounts," for among
the hazards and adventures of my ancestors' flight from
the Great Calamity many portions of their manuscript
were, alas, lost forever. Nor, in the nature of things,
was it always possible for my ancestors to directly
observe various events and incidents of great moment
to our history.

Thus did it fall to my unworthy self, Alfred
CCLXXIX, despite my frailties and paltry skills in
comparison to my incomparable forebears, to attempt
to fill the *lacunae* in their chronicle with other sources.
As for these latter, I will vouch for their authenticity
but not their veracity, as they are all of them the
product of human hands and thus inherently suspect,
due to the well-known mendacious proclivities of that
malign race.

No better example to illustrate this last point could
be found than the very same *Autobiography* of
Benvenuti Sfondrati-Piccolomini which I chose as the
prelude to our tale. A strange choice for an introduction to scrupulous history! For the autobiography of
this artist is, of course, notorious for its unreliability,
inexactitude, and preposterous self-aggrandizement. Yet,
it seemed to me that any chronicle seeking to clarify

the events and inner forces leading to the Great Calamity must, of necessity, include within its compass the tale told by Benvenuti Sfondrati-Piccolomini. This, for two reasons.

Imprimis, Benvenuti himself played no small part in the ruination of civilization which we know by the name of the Great Calamity. At each and every critical juncture of that tangled skein of events and episodes which led to the Great Calamity, does his presence and influence make itself felt. And not his alone, nay, but those of the maleficent characters which he attracted about him like flies to honey, as well. Name all the individuals prominent in the destruction of our lost heritage, beginning with the Rebel himself, and you will find, in four instances out of five, this lowest common denominator—an association with the scoundrel Benvenuti Sfondrati-Piccolomini.

Secundus, the wizard Zulkeh himself, blamed by all gentility for the Great Calamity, insisted to his dying day that a proper analysis of Benvenuti's *Autobiography* made clear the truth of the matter. Of this thesis, I myself remain dubious. Yet, in fairness to the historical personage of the sorcerer, I felt it both judicious and proper to incorporate into this chronicle the *Autobiography* of the infamous artist.

With those portions of our tale directly transcribed from my ancestors' account, the matter is naturally otherwise. These may be regarded as unblemished truth, and this for two reasons. *Imprimis*, my peerless forefathers accompanied Zulkeh and Shelyid throughout their famous odyssey, in the course of which the hidden meaning of the Great Calamity was revealed. They were present at every juncture, there to observe and record both the event and its inner purport. *Secundus*, my ancestors' chronicle was not compiled by witless humans but by members of that infinitely superior race to which my ancestors and I belong. I speak, of course, of *pediculus humanus*.

"A *louse!*" you exclaim.

Yes, I say proudly, a louse. And typical 'tis that even you, gentle reader, will automatically respond with the genocidal impulse of your bestial race, so evident even in ancient times and now, since the Great Calamity, grown systematic and ruthless in its horror. I am a louse, and my ancestors were lice before me. And not just any lice!—but lice whose devotion to science was of such all-consuming passion that they readily resided upon the none-too-well-fed Shelyid, taking advantage of the latter's hirsute plenitude to record a history of our modern times which is *nonpareil*. Would humans have done as much? To ask the question is to answer it.

I urge you thus, gentle reader, to suppress your barbarous instincts and heed attentively the tale which follows. For though you despise us, consider this patent truth—that while you squat here in wretched exile, dreaming with bitter regret of your lost wealth and luxuries, we squat here upon you and regret much less, for by your squalid existence you assure our sustenance.

Cease then your fruitless scratching! say I, and attend rather to my tale. For though the Great Calamity has cast us into ruination, yet it is said that History moves in its cycles. The time may come again when we—or rather, our descendants—regain that high estate to which our breeds are entitled. Such latter Restoration, however, depends in no small part upon the diligence with which you and your ilk absorb the lessons of the past. Thus I say again: attend to my tale, putting aside all useless antipathies. For we are companions in misfortune.

PART I

The Which
Consists of Alfred CCLVI's
Account of Zulkeh's Last Days
in Goimr, the Events and Thoughts
of Those Final Days, and His Decision
and Departure. Taken From the First
Chapters of the Great
Chronicle of the
Alfredae.

———∞∞∞———

CHAPTER I. *A Sublime Discourse on the*
Nature of Gravity. A Knock on the Door.
The Wizard Is Summoned by the King!

It was Zulkeh's habit of the evening to instruct Shelyid
in the art of wizardry and the lore of science. With the
dwarf ensconced upon a stool in a corner of the
study, the wizard would pace to and fro, expounding

at length upon whatever subject struck his fancy. On this particular evening, Zulkeh had chosen to enlighten the dwarf upon the nature of gravity.

"So you see then, Shelyid," spoke the mage, "this question of *gravity* has gripped the mind of man since time immemorial. The great ancient philosopher Disquo was the first to provide a general answer to the question: *Why do all objects rest where they do?* His answer was of the piercing simplicity of all true genius.

"'Because they belong there,' said Disquo, and no one has been able to refute this proposition since. This is because it is irrefutable, for 'tis clear to even the dullest intellect that all things exist in their place because they belong there. Indeed, it must be so, for if they did not belong there, they would be somewhere else. Is this clear?"

"Oh yes, master!" cried Shelyid.

"Good. We may continue. Following the destruction of ancient civilization for those reasons which I have on earlier occasions opened up to your understanding, Disquo's great truth disappeared in the chaos of barbarism. Only centuries later, after a passing semblance of culture had been resurrected under the aegis of the Ecclesiarchy, was the insight of Disquo revived, albeit in a form more suited to the needs of Religion. For it was then that the famed theologian St. Quinine brought forth Disquo's dictum anew, but now with the caveat that all things belong where they are because God wills it. This thesis was to dominate human thought for a millennium. It is, of course, utterly specious.

"'How so?' you ask, groping in the dimness of your runtish intellect. It is self-evident. The true scientist understands by the nature of inquiry that such is designed to answer such questions as are posed through the examination of the question which is posed, and no other. Thus, the answer to the question: 'Why do objects rest where they do?' can only be scientifically answered by explaining why objects rest where they do. This Disquo had already done: 'Because they belong there.' To add to this truth the quibble that this is so because God wills it, adds nothing whatever to the investigation. If God exists, then 'tis rampant tautology to say that he causes all objects to belong where they are, for He is naturally the source of all objects, being and belonging. If God does not exist, then He has nothing to do with any of these. The revered saint's thesis thus merely posits the existence of God under the guise of explaining the nature of gravity. But it advances us no further than Disquo's formula. Indeed, it throws confusion over the problem. Is this clear, dwarf?"

"Oh yes, master!" cried Shelyid.

"Good. We may continue." A sudden frown enveloped the wizard's brow. Zulkeh peered fiercely at his apprentice, who shrank before his gaze.

"Misinterpret not my words," spoke the mage. "My intent is not to cast aspersions upon Religion, for such is necessary to discipline the passions of the common herd. In this task, the servants of Religion perform a most exemplary service. For this work they deserve all just credit and due, despite their superstitious habit of cloaking the Old Geister's immanence in all manner of frivolous and ridiculous trappings. Is this understood?"

"Oh yes, master!" cried Shelyid.

"Nevertheless," continued Zulkeh, "it is apparent, from the standpoint of the higher reason, that St. Quinine's contribution to the study of gravity is nought but a diversion. Even so, infinitely more sublime was Quinine's thinking to that of his historical successor, whose advent was but another symptom of the sad decline of science in the modern world.

"For know, Shelyid, that the most significant figure following Quinine to treat of this question—significant not, as I shall in a moment expose, for his contribution, but for the vulgar popularity which it has received among the plebeians—was Oldgram. Sir Oldgram, for such was he titled in the barbarous land whence he originated, invented what he pompously called the Law of Gravity, thereby arrogating to himself, before his time and without reason, an honor which is properly mine. This law, or rather, 'law' so-called (for it is nothing of the sort), states the following impudent proposition: to wit, that objects attract each other in direct proportion to their mass and in inverse proportion to their distance.

"This imbecility has long since swept the modern world, and it grieves me to relate that the Law of Gravity is today considered synonymous with the name of Oldgram. Yet so far from representing an advance of science, much less the formulation of an actual Law (most sublime of Theses), this outrage to all reason has rather dragged the level of scientific thought far below the stage earlier attained by Disquo, even in ancient times.

"For look you, gnome, what is the purpose of science?" demanded the wizard.

"I d-don't know, master," stammered Shelyid.

"An excellent response," spoke the wizard, patting the dwarf's head. "For it is only mete that a lowly apprentice should first learn science, then the higher truth of which it is the expression, and only at the last its purpose. But I will open up a small portion of this secret to your understanding."

Here Zulkeh struck a solemn pose. "The purpose of science, Shelyid, is to answer the question *Why?* Is this clear?"

"Oh yes, master!" cried Shelyid, pleased to be asked the normal question.

"With this understood, it is immediately apparent that Oldgram's proposition is sheer effrontery. Does Oldgram explain *why* objects rest where they do? By no means! He merely correlates the relationship of all objects to each other according to some crude ratio evident to the base senses.

"We may thus dismiss Oldgram as an importunate impostor, a parasitic empiricist, a flea upon the body of science. To the question 'why do objects rest where they do?' Disquo had already answered correctly— 'because they belong there.' Neither the necessities of Religion nor the jackanapes of Oldgram have advanced the study a single inch beyond. It was left to me, and to me alone, to unravel the riddle. And this I have done according to that mode of subtle reasoning which is my wont and habitude. Is this clear, dwarf?"

"Oh yes, master!" cried Shelyid instantly, for this was a question whose answer he had long since mastered.

"Excellent. To the question 'why do all objects rest where they belong?' or, to phrase it differently: 'why do all objects obey the Law of Gravity?' (properly so named only by myself) I have provided the following astonishing insight—because all objects contain *graveness*. Yes, Shelyid, *graveness*, the illusive essence of gravity which has hitherto escaped the ken of all mankind save myself.

"And thus we have it, Shelyid. The Law of Gravity, the *true* Law of Gravity discovered first—and so far only, I might add—by myself. The Law may be stated as follows: *Objects come to rest where they do because all objects contain greater or lesser amounts of graveness and hence gravitate downward to the precise degree determined by the quantity of graveness present within them.*

"Immediately we see that this keen postulate not only brings the problem of gravity into full accord with all rational cosmography, but sheds as well a broad beam of light upon the most diverse questions hitherto unanswered. To give just one example, from the field of ethnology: why, Shelyid, is it the custom to bury the dead?"

"I d-don't know, master," stammered the dwarf.

"Of course you don't!" exclaimed the mage. "How could you, without understanding the Law of Gravity? The reason is simple, my stupid but loyal apprentice. The dead are buried because it is only proper that the final end of life, which is a grave undertaking, should be death, which is graver still. And what more fitting place for the dead, therefore, than the grave?

"But with all these mysteries resolved," went on the wizard, "surely your mind has begun to grope at a related but contradictory problem. To wit, the gravitation of objects having been explained, why do certain objects *rise*?

"The answer to this question, Shelyid—whose discovery is also a monopoly of my genius—is to be found in the explication of the Law of Levity. What is the Law of Levity? The Law of Levity postulates that objects rise in accordance with the—"

At that moment the sorcerer's discourse was suddenly interrupted by a loud knocking on the door of the study.

"Shelyid!" spoke Zulkeh. "Someone is at the door."

"I know, master," muttered Shelyid, his anxious visage peering from behind the cabinet where he had instantly retreated at the sound of knocking.

"Then answer it, dolt!"

"But, master," whined the dwarf, "what if it's a stranger?"

"Bah!" oathed Zulkeh. "Who else would it be, cretin? I command you, open the door!"

"Yes, master," grumbled the runt. Shelyid inched from behind the cabinet and, apprehension writ plain upon his face, slowly approached and opened the door.

Now, the gentle reader is perhaps puzzled by the peculiar attitude evidenced by the misshapen apprentice toward this mundane task of opening a door in response to a knock. But the matter is, in truth, simple of explanation. We have already alluded most delicately to the dwarf's unfortunate nervous condition. By his nature, Shelyid greeted all events not strictly routine as incipient calamities. The attitude, common to the general run of mankind, that the grass is always greener on the other side of the fence, was incomprehensible to Shelyid. In the dwarf's mind, grass was not green to begin with. It was brown and coarse and grew only in rare clumps. Fences were not challenges to an audacious spirit, they were excellent constructs which served the salutary purpose of keeping at bay the monsters with which Shelyid's mind peopled the universe, according to them as well the fixed and unilateral purpose of doing him harm. So, far from finding his own clump of crabgrass inadequate and longing for other pastures, the dwarf found in fences the sole complaint that they were invariably too short, too flimsy, too low and too few.

Yet the gentle reader should not conclude that this *outré* world view was solely the product of Shelyid's fevered fantasies. Alas, no, the dwarf's *weltschmerz* was all too well grounded in brute fact. For Shelyid, as we have explained, was cursed not simply with a grotesque nervous condition but with an equally grotesque appearance. All too often had he been mistaken, at first sight, for some strange and loathsome beast— if not a vicious carnivore then at the least some disease-ridden creature escaped from the bowels of the earth, perhaps unnatural, certainly abnormal, a suitable object for curses and blows. More than once, opening the door of their abode to a stranger, had the pitiful gnome been greeted with a gasp and a boot.

Upon this occasion, however, his luck was better. The door open, Shelyid and his master perceived in the dim entryway a small and wiry man, well dressed and bearing an air of self-importance. This worthy stared at the apprentice for some long moments and then, wrinkling his nose, looked to the wizard.

"Is the sorcerer Zulkeh present?" he inquired.

"I am he," spoke the mage.

"In that case, I have a message to deliver." He reached into his cloak and brought forth a letter, sealed with wax.

"Bring me the letter, Shelyid," spoke Zulkeh. The dwarf took the proffered missive and scurried to his master's side. Zulkeh broke the seal and examined the contents of the letter.

"This is a summons from King Roy, King of Goimr!" he exclaimed.

"Quite so," agreed the stranger. "You are to present yourself at the palace tomorrow morning following the eighth bell. See to it that you are prompt." He turned to go.

"Hold there!" spoke Zulkeh. "What is the King's purpose in summoning me to his side?"

The man inspected the wizard, his apprentice, and their lodgings. "That," he sneered, "is a good question," and strode off.

"Impudent rogue!" oathed the wizard. "King Roy would be well advised to dispense with his services!"

"But what could the King want with us, master?" queried Shelyid.

"As to the specifics of your question," responded

Zulkeh, "I know not. But 'tis hardly strange that the King should call for me. Rather the contrary—'tis most apt that the mighty of the earth should flock to my side for counsel and sagacity. That they have never done so is but further proof of the decrepitude of these our modern times. In truth, it is King Roy who should come to me, not I to King Roy. But as I have always been a respecter of temporal authority, we shall answer his summons. And now, Shelyid, to bed."

CHAPTER II. *Journey Through Goimr. A Discourse on the Geography and History of the City. The Palace Doors Swing Wide!*

The following morning, Zulkeh and Shelyid set forth to the palace. As the distance to be traveled was great, the wizard determined to engage a hansom, though his meager funds normally precluded such extravagance.

We take here the occasion to educate the gentle reader in the geography and history of Goimr. The realm of Goimr is a small kingdom located on the southeastern coast of the sub-continent of Grotum. The city of Goimr itself is located at the extremity of the Gulf of Goimr, the which extends westward from Grotum Long Bay. To the north and west, the kingdom is surrounded by mountains, with only the Dreary Gap on its northwest frontier offering access to the Grimwald and the other lands of Grotum which lie beyond that noisome forest. To the south, the farmlands of Goimr steadily give way to the Great Southern Steppes, which are more or less considered to begin at a line bounded on the west by Joe's Lakes and on the east by Joe's Dunes. Further still to the south lies the Great Wall of Grotum, an ancient stone palisade erected in the dim mists of the Groutch past by the legendary Emperor of the Grinding Hegemony, as a bulwark protecting Grotum from the incursions of the various nomadic tribes which infest the Great Southern Steppes.

The Great Wall itself, sad to say, is but a pitiable remnant of its ancient glory. Over the eons, the forces of man and nature have taken their grim toll upon the once mighty rampart. In many places along its length large breaches occur, and even at its best the Wall is crumbly and dilapidated. Not for many centuries has it served as an effective barrier to the outrages of the nomadic hordes, the which plunder and pillage the southern portions of Goimria at will. So regular and frequent are these barbarous incursions that the much-ravaged peasantry of the realm commonly refers to the ancient bastion as the Great Hall of Grotum. This practice is, of course, forbidden by royal decree, but as the police of Goimr are hardly more efficient than its army, it continues unchecked nonetheless.

As the hansom made its slow way to the Royal Palace, which was located on an island in the middle of the river which bisected Goimr, Zulkeh took the occasion to educate his apprentice on the historiography involved.

"The existence of this ancient ruler, my stupid but loyal apprentice, is a matter of much controversy among historians. Indeed, the subject has become one of the major arenas of contention between the two great scholarly clans, the Laebmauntsforscynneweëlds and the Sfondrati-Piccolominis."

Here Zulkeh stroked his beard vigorously, as he was wont to do when deep in scholarly exposition. "For millennia, the account of this monarch presented in the classic annals of the ancient Herodotus Laebmaunts-forscynneweëld were considered to be, in the main, accurate. Herodotus depicted the Emperor of the Grinding Hegemony as a mighty despot whose power held sway over all of Grotum and other lands bordering on Joe's Sea. So august was this ancient ruler, so near divine in his aspect, that it was considered sacrilege for either himself, his entourage, or even his means of transport, to touch anything but human flesh in his travels about the realm."

Shelyid's eyes widened. Seeing the expression of shock and surprise in his ward's face, the wizard nodded sagely. "Indeed so, dwarf. A most superstitious and barbarous lot, our ancestors. 'Twas even the custom for the Emperor's chariot to be drawn over the prostrate bodies of his subjects, the which laid themselves upon every inch of every road whence his frequent journeys took him."

Zulkeh's brows lowered as he weighed the various aspects of the question in his mind. "From a mathematic viewpoint, of course, the policy was ill-advised. As the Emperor's chariot was an immense vehicle carved from a single block of jade, resting upon two great iron wheels inlaid with gold and gems, and drawn by four buffalo, the practice weighed heavily upon the populace. Hence, according to Herodotus, the derivation of the Emperor's cognomen. Hence also, according to Herodotus, the rapid decline of his empire."

Here, glowering fiercely, Zulkeh's eyes ranged across the dilapidated slums through whose narrow and crooked streets the hansom was passing. "Since that time—as even you can no doubt deduce from our miserable surroundings—the history of Goimr can most politely be described as undistinguished."

"Everybody says it's a dump, master," agreed the

apprentice cheerfully. "Most wretched place in Grotum, they say."

"Nonsense!" exclaimed the mage. "Squalid though it be, Goimr is a veritable paradise compared to Kankr." His brow furrowed. "Nor do I recall giving you leave to insult what is, when all is said and done, my chosen place of study and cogitation."

The dwarf's head lowered, acknowledging the deserved reproof. Zulkeh continued:

"The official historical account, perpetuated by the royal family at great expense, has it that Goimr was once the seat of a great empire ruling all of Grotum, which was brought to an end by the unfortunate pile-up of silt at the mouth of the Moyle. This interpretation leans heavily on the aforementioned legend of the Emperor of the Grinding Hegemony, and is considered utterly preposterous by the entire population. But we must leave off this fascinating but perhaps not pressing matter. For I see we have arrived at the ferry which will convey us to King Roy's island."

Eventually, Zulkeh and Shelyid arrived at the palace door, upon which the wizard rapped imperiously with his staff.

"Who's there?" queried a voice within.

"It is the wizard Zulkeh, come in response to King Roy's summons."

Moments later the door creaked open. A slovenly individual in the livery of the Royal Guard peered forth, then stood aside.

"You may enter. Go that way," he muttered, pointing down a long corridor to their right with one hand as he scratched his stomach with the other. Zulkeh attempted to solicit more precise directions, but the guard ignored him and slouched into a rickety chair.

Grumbling at the discourtesy, Zulkeh strode forth

down the hallway. Ere long, however, his humor improved as he regarded the multitude of portraits which hung along both sides of the hall, the which depicted the long line of the royalty of Goimr.

"Respect for one's ancestors, Shelyid, is a sure sign of good breeding," spoke the wizard as he inspected the portraits. "Pity 'tis in this regard that you have no known ancestry to respect." The dwarf hung his head in shame. "On the other hand, given your malformities, 'tis perhaps as well that your provenance remains unknown."

At the end of the hall stood two guards before another door. These wights were as unprepossessing as the first. Informing them of his name and the nature of his visit, Zulkeh and Shelyid obtained admittance to the room beyond. In this antechamber, bare of all furnishings, they were joined shortly by a man of easy grace, yclept Gerard, who pronounced himself Chief Counselor to the Throne.

"Ah, Zulkeh," said this latter. He regarded the wizard and his apprentice for some long moments, not, or so it seemed, with any great pleasure. "You are here at the behest of King Roy, who bade me search the city for a sorcerer to aid him in his current melancholia. You were the only one I could find. I will tell you straight out, sirrah, that I view the King's hope in your assistance with considerable skepticism."

"Such is the folly of men," spoke the wizard, stiffly erect.

"Indeed," sniffed Gerard. "Well, be that as it may. The King has made his wishes clear. The matter stands thus. King Roy has had a dream, a most terrible dream, or so it seems, and certain of my colleagues"—here he gestured vaguely toward a small body of men who appeared in the entry beyond—"took it upon themselves to alarm His Majesty and to intimate that this

dream bodes ill for the realm. I, of course, have no
truck with these fantasies, for it is plain to the man
of reason that dreams are nothing but dreams, and
thus—I am frank with you, sirrah—it seems misguided
to raise such commotion about a paltry matter. You are
here thus against my advice, but we must make the
best of it. In this respect, I am certain that you, as a
man of science, will see the matter in the same light
as do I, and thus aid me to assuage King Roy's fears
and dispel the fog of misgiving which currently clouds
his brain."

"Indeed, sirrah," spoke the wizard, "being, as you
so rightly put it, a man of science, I am forced to
hold precisely the opposite opinion, if so pallid a term
as 'opinion' can be used to describe the crystalline
certainty of my views."

"What?" demanded the courtier. "Do I understand
you to believe in dreams?"

"Certainly not. You mistake my meaning. I do not
believe in dreams, but in Reason, which resides in
dreams, however obfuscated and difficult to interpret.
You grasp, of course, the distinction?"

Zulkeh squinted at the courtier and awaited acknowl-
edgment. He, in turn, squinted back. Once again
Gerard examined the eccentric raiment of the sorcerer
and the oddities of his apprentice.

"I am not at all sure that I do," he said at length.
"But the King has called for you and I will therefore
introduce you to the August Presence. Whatever else,
do nothing to alarm him."

With that, Gerard passed through the far entry,
Zulkeh and Shelyid following behind. Beyond, they
perceived a drawn and haggard visage, who rose from
a rather shabby throne, eyes streaming with tears.

"Oh Gerard!" moaned this figure. "Who have you
brought to torment me now?" His face contorted,

became vicious with remembered treasons. "I have kenned your plot—you seek to drive me mad!"

King Roy tottered forth, gesticulating with some energy. "And what are my loyal subjects about today? Setting mantraps for my police? Cutting down my forests? Poaching my game? Eating my herds? Scoffing my heralds? Stoning my tax collectors?"

He scuttled forward, in an obliquely crablike manner, and thrust his face into Zulkeh's. "And who're you?" he demanded.

"I am Zulkeh," spoke the mage, "the sorcerer whom you summoned."

"I summoned?" King Roy frowned. "Why, yes, so I did." He peered at Zulkeh suspiciously. "You don't look like a sorcerer."

Before Zulkeh could respond, the King waved his hand in a gesture of infinite weariness.

"Well, I'm the King of Goimr. And believe me, it's no picnic. When my grandfather was King nobody fooled with him, let me tell you. If they did, he took their property, sold their family into slavery, and cut them up to feed his racing dogs. But today the plebes are so wanton nobody knows who their families are, and all their belongings are already mortgaged to the Consortium. The last peon I cut up for feed gave my kennel the runs and I missed the sweepstakes." King Roy paused, disconsolate. "I needed the money, too."

Zulkeh made to speak. "Your Majesty's Chief Counselor, Gerard—"

"That traitor!" shrieked the King. He leveled a quavering finger at Gerard and the other courtiers, who were gathered on the opposite side of the room. "They're all miscreants, the lot of 'em. I pay them a fortune to sit on my Council of Ministers, but their avarice knows no bounds. Gerard, here, is in the pay of the Ecclesiarchs, and that one—there!—he's the

Minister of War, runs a pool on the exact time of my assassination. Were it not for my sense of duty I'd abdicate and let that ingrate who claims to be my son try his hand at this miserable business, assuming he could learn to count his fingers."

Gerard detached himself from the knot of councilors and came to Zulkeh's side.

"Your Majesty is ill-served by lending credence to such rumors," he soothed. "I dally with the Ecclesiarchs to obtain information, not to give it out. Naturally I must accept their bribes, lest they suspect my motives. As for the War Minister's pool, its purpose is solely to draw forth would-be assassins that they might be the more promptly dispatched by your efficient executioners.

"But let us now to the business at hand," he continued, spreading his arms in a calming gesture. "The wizard Zulkeh is here at your express request, to dispel the fears roused by—"

"Dispel the fears!" shrilled King Roy. "What good can a wizard do? I was mad to even think of it!" Here he glared most ferociously at Zulkeh.

"Ha! You—wizard! Can you conjure up a battalion of troops who won't flee from their own shadows? Can you cast a stupefying spell over the entire populace, so that these ministers of mine could deal with them as equals? Can you? Can you? Ha! Wizard—ha! Fraud! Impostor!"

Then, even as the thundercloud enfolds its roiling fury round the granite crown of the awesome peak, so did the mage's brow o'erboil with rage.

"Silence!" he spoke. "I perceive that civilization has decayed even further than I feared, since respect for Knowledge has fled not only the brute masses upon whom its hold was always faint, but the puissant as well."

The King of Goimr gibbered in outrage, but the wizard paid no heed. Indeed, he spoke further.

"Yet in these paltrous times do I live, and living so must need support the temporal power, no matter its feeble merit, lest chaos reign supreme. This truth, however, renders it imperative for the secular representatives of Order to grasp at least the rudiments of science. For know, Your Majesty, that truth reveals not itself as itself. Nay, fie upon such witless notions! Rather does Reason insinuate itself through the obscure—to most, the opaque. It moves through the angularities of logic, the vectors of analysis, the immanence of the unfolding speculation. Surely you grasp my point?"

Zulkeh paused to observe the King's response. As the latter was still gabbling in mindless fury, the wizard cut impatiently to the core.

"What, then," he demanded, "was the nature and content of this dream?"

And at that, at the very mention of the word, King Roy's distemper fled like a ghost. His eyes rolled wildly. "My dream!" he shrieked, and collapsed to the floor.

CHAPTER III. *A Portentous Dream—Its Contents Revealed. The Mage Is Troubled in His Mind. King Roy's Wrath. The Mage Elucidates. King Roy's Anxiety. The Wizard Is Commanded!*

"The hair—the hair!—everywhere I turned—pulling me down, binding my limbs—then! My tongue—caught! Caught, I say, caught!—grasped by a great beard sprung suddenly up before me, coiling about like a thousand serpents, writhing and twisting—but worse— it spoke! Yes, it spoke, I say! The beard spoke! Oh God, did it speak—on and on and on and on, babbling in some heathen tongue.

"But I couldn't speak—it was horrible! I couldn't give orders—not a one!—and me, a King! And who ever heard of a beard speaking, anyway? Certainly not to a King! I mean, what's happened here to the basic rules?

"Then it was worse still—for suddenly it wasn't just the one great beard, oh no! Thousands of beards, millions of them, millions I tell you! Little ones mostly—but so many! Everywhere—growing over the whole palace, sprouting up everywhere—right on my dinner plate, I tell you!

"I couldn't move, couldn't lift a finger—every finger was held down by beards! And worst of all—I couldn't give orders, not a one—and me, a King! The great beard still had me by the tongue!

"But it got worse! For then—all the beards started to speak! Oh God and what a fearful racket they made—millions and millions of little beards, all of them gabbling away in hundreds of barbarous tongues, not one of which made any proper sense.

"Then—suddenly—the beards let me go! I jumped up—ran away—they all hissed at me but they let me go—I thought—but I was wrong! For just when I thought I was getting away I saw this figure before me. Not much—something small. But it was hideous! Hairy and frightful!—and then! It started to grow! It wasn't small at all! No! It tricked me! And me—a King! It was huge! It was gigantic! And it kept growing and growing, higher and higher—o horrible! Horrible! Horrible!

"No more," wept King Roy. "No more—the rest is lost, I remember no more. It is all like a black stain, all other memory is lost." He fell silent, hunched on his throne, scepter clenched in bony fist, ashen-faced, eyes haggard and unseeing.

"So," spoke Zulkeh, musing in deep thought. At length he emerged from his contemplation. "I must ponder upon this matter, Your Majesty. A most profound maloneirophrenia! Now had it been snakes which grasped you so, 'twould be a simple problem. Snakes are a trifle. Ropes are also quickly fathomed. Tentacles, likewise. But beards? That is quite a different matter."

The mage fell silent, lost for some moments in his thoughts, then spoke again. "Your Majesty, this problem will require my full study, the application of my most cunning dialectic. But rest assured—the solution will emerge in due time."

"Time?" demanded King Roy. "How much time?"

"'Tis difficult to say, Your Majesty. Certainly weeks, probably months, possibly years."

"Months!" screeched King Roy. "Years!" His eyes bulged. "I don't have years! I must know now! I must know the danger, that I may take steps to avert it!"

"Bah!" oathed Zulkeh. "Think you a question of such gravity—a portent of such overwhelming peril—can be discerned in its unveiled essence in the twinkling of an eye? Years, I said, and years it may well be. I shall almost certainly be forced to travel to divers and odd locations, heathen lands and the like, where beard lore is most fully developed."

Then did apoplexy seize upon the royal visage. "You are hereby commanded by royal edict to report to me at this palace one week from today!"

"Utterly impossible!" spoke the mage. "One week could barely allow me to scratch the surface of the problem."

"Two weeks, then—and not a minute more!" And with these words King Roy lowered his head, grasping it in both hands. "Go now!" he groaned.

"What does it all mean, master?" asked the dwarf later, as they rode through the crooked alleys back to their domicile.

"It means ill, Shelyid, great ill," spoke the wizard in a dark voice. "Of what ill, and whence, I know nothing as yet. But the truth is there, and I shall unearth it—never fear!—wherever the search may take us."

"Us?" queried Shelyid. "Us, master?" His beady eyes began to glaze. "But what have I to do with searching out great ills, master?" He whined in his throat. "That sounds dangerous, searching for great ills and perils and such. I am no mighty mage such as yourself, to wander about the world like that. I'm just a dwarf, a wretched dwarf."

"True, quite true," agreed Zulkeh, patting the gnome's head. "But you will be needed to carry my things."

And then did the wizard launch into a most learned discourse, opening up to Shelyid's understanding the necessary place of the burden carrier in history, recounting tales of faithful servitors of yore and their role in sundry legendary exploits of ancient sorcerers and warlocks, in which these humble drudges found not only their proper place but a share as well (paltry though it was) of the glory and—alas, usually—the gory end of these selfsame puissant probers of the unknown. But, in truth, his exposition was in vain, for his apprentice had long since fainted dead away, whether in awe at such deep and profound thoughts or in horror at the now-revealed impermanence of his fate, it is difficult to say.

CHAPTER IV. *A Wizard's Travail. Failure—But the Truth Revealed Therein. The Dwarf Reproved. The Wizard's Decision. The Dwarf Reproved. The Wizard's Command. The Dwarf Reproved.*

In the days which followed, Shelyid's fears slowly abated. For it seemed, after all, that the wizard had no intention of departing his domicile. To the contrary, Zulkeh did now forego even the morning promenades which he had in the past enjoyed upon occasion. Not once did he leave the death house.

Yet this sedentary life bespoke not sloth on the mage's part. Quite the contrary—never had Shelyid seen the wizard so engrossed in his work. At all times Zulkeh could be found in his study or laboratory, delving into the sorcerous arts, taking neither rest nor sustenance. Soon the multitude of tomes, tablets and scrolls which filled their domicile became disarranged even further, as the mage investigated their arcanities. Odd experiments did he conduct, in the course of which many revolutionary advances in the field of alchemy were achieved, only to be impatiently discarded as irrelevant to the task at hand. Bizarre talismans did he bring forth, applying to them the most peculiar incantations. Conjurations, summonings—more than once did Shelyid flee in terror as the misty form of some fell creature from the netherworld took shape, called up by the wizard's lore.

But all was in vain. The truth lay hidden, the secret of the King's dream obscure. At length, after a week of frenzied study, Zulkeh ceased his travails. Then for four days did he remain ensconced in his chair in the study, pondering silently. Around him Shelyid tiptoed, careful not to disturb his master's musings—although on one occasion the loyal apprentice made so bold as to brush off the dust which had accumulated upon the wizard's immobile person.

The wizard remained undisturbed during this period, despite the incessant arrival of messengers from King Roy demanding to know what progress could be reported. For the loyal Shelyid rebuffed these assaults with unwonted determination. Indeed, he became rather adept at opening the communication port in the door and shouting out: "Go away! The master is busy, can't be disturbed, go away!"

Alas, the day came when a whole squad of Royal Constabulary arrived.

"Open up in the name of King Roy of Goimr, open up in the name of the law!" bellowed the lieutenant in charge, all the while pounding on the great oaken door with his truncheon of office. Shelyid, to his credit, attempted to stand fast. But, when six burly troopers began to apply their shoulders to the door, the dwarf undid the bolts and lifted the bar, swinging the door wide just as the staunch six hurtled at it. They came crashing through into the entry hall where they piled up like so many falling duckpins, dislodging as they fell a neat pyramid of mummified heads. These

unpleasant items, not much more than skulls, really—
strands of beard still attached to their mandibles—had
been stacked there by Shelyid pursuant to his master's
command to retrieve the heads of all bearded men from
the crypts as part of the wizard's investigation.

Shelyid shrank back into an alcove as the policemen made frantic efforts to arise from the carpet of
heads, the sight of which objects did little for their
morale, judging, at least, from their wails. At length
the officer entered and commanded his troopers to
silence and order. As they moodily regrouped, casting fearful glances down the various dark and dank
passages which emanated from the foyer, the officer
addressed himself to Shelyid.

"You—there in the alcove—present yourself! Where
is the wizard Zulkeh?"

Shelyid stood mute, his teeth chattering.

"Speak, grotesque dwarf! Or I'll set the squad on
you!"

The constables brightened visibly and began to finger
their various belts, clubs, coshes, sticks, straps, gloves,
knucks and other instruments of lawful persuasion. One
of the beefy policemen reached out a hand and dragged
Shelyid forward by the scruff of the neck.

"You want I should give him the third degree,
Lieutenant?" he demanded with a leer.

"Wait! Wait!" cried Shelyid. "I'll take you to the
master!"

"Do so, then!" barked the lieutenant. Released by the
constable, Shelyid started toward a flight of steps at
the opposite end of the hall. As he headed down the
steps, followed by the Royal Constabulary, the dwarf
said timidly: "Things'll look a little weird, but you don't
have to be afraid. It's just that the master's trying the
cantrips of Escher Laebmauntsforscynneweëld and I
always hate it when he does because—"

The gnome's words were cut off by great cries of fear and shock from the Constabulary. Of a sudden, the staircase they were descending was inverted and tipped to a ninety degree horizontal angle. The policemen dropped to their knees in startlement, despite the dwarf's warning cries.

"No! No! Don't do that! The staircase isn't really—"

Alas, the warning came too late. In a trice, the policemen had inadvertently rolled themselves down the staircase, even though it appeared they were rolling up and sideways. Their progress down—up? along?— it was difficult to say—the staircase was precipitous in the extreme, and most painful to boot, judging by their cries of hurt and distress. Shelyid sprang aside as the squad made their way forward like so many fleshy tumbleweeds, the lieutenant rolling up the rear.

The dwarf hurriedly followed the law enforcement bowling balls, calling out:

"When you get to the bottom—I mean, the top— I mean, the end—don't move! Don't move!"

Alas, his words went unheeded. No sooner did the Constabulary pile up at the terminus of the staircase than they staggered to their feet, bellowing with outrage like bulls. A moment later they were flattened by the arrival of a giant tarot card onto their heads. The Knave of Batons, fittingly enough.

Shelyid raced up and pried the card off the backs and buttocks of the minions of order, now squealing with outrage like so many boars. The policemen staggered to their feet again, and looked around. They were standing on top of an enormous desk, next to a huge bowl containing a pipe the size of a buffalo and two used matches the size of logs. Nearby loomed a gigantic humidor. A bit farther off, huge books leaned against buildings, the which marched in stately progression, side by side, down a normal looking street. The street was filled with people going about their business.

Average men would have been paralyzed with astonishment. But these were stalwart officers of the law, trained and disciplined, ready to handle the unexpected. At once they drew their billy clubs and advanced upon Shelyid. Things would no doubt have gone badly for the dwarf, save for the intervention of the wizard.

Or rather, the wizard's voice, which instrument of wrath descended on the Constabulary like the proverbial Word of God.

"Cease this intolerable impertinence!"

Stunned into frozen statues by the great voice, the Constabulary stared up in shock. There, at a great distance, loomed the gigantic visage of the wizard Zulkeh. The mage was holding a pack of cards in his left hand, a single card in his right. Judging by the expression on his face, he was wroth with wrath—and it was impossible not to judge correctly, for his face was the size of a great monument.

"By what right do you interrupt my studies?"

The lieutenant, his expression no longer arrogant, cleared his voice. "Sirrah wizard, a thousand apologies! But I have been sent by King Roy to oversee your studies and report on your progress."

"Bah! Impudent knave! You are in no wise competent to oversee my studies! Nor, I misdoubt me not, are you capable of accurately reporting so much as a sliver of my science."

The wizard glowered in the distance like a volcano. Suddenly, he flicked his wrist. The knot of policemen were flattened by the arrival of another giant card onto their heads.

"I shall tell your fortune. Ah—the Knight of Swords! You are headstrong, careless, heedless of warnings."

"Oh yes, master!" cried Shelyid. "I tried to warn them!"

Another card landed atop the thrashing Constabulary.

"The Fool, reversed. Foretells of major problems arising from reckless, impulsive action."

Another card. The policemen were now buried from sight.

"The Tower, reversed. Predicts the calling down of a disaster which might have been avoided. Unnecessary suffering. Self-undoing."

Great squeals of fear and pain emanated from beneath the growing pile of cards. The wizard drew another card.

"I shall now predict my own future. Ah—excellent! The Six of Swords! Indicates that some obstacle has been overcome and progress can now be resumed."

The wizard stretched out his hand and scooped up the knot of squirming constables onto the card. With a quick flick of the wrist, he flung them into a corner of the room. As they left the tabletop, the policemen resumed their normal size. Not to their great satisfaction, however, judging from the bellows of displeasure with which they greeted their landing on the floor.

The lieutenant scrambled to his feet and began to speak. He was immediately interrupted by the wizard.

"Silence, dolt!" oathed the mage. "You desire to oversee my studies, do you? Well, then, be silent and observe!"

And so saying, the mage reached out and drew forth one of the books leaning against the buildings on the desk. He slammed the book down flat on the table. The clapping sound caused the desk top to shimmer. A moment later, the previous objects were seen to have vanished, replaced by several others. In the brief glimpse they were allowed, the constables saw an oddly shaped, multisided object, a bowl containing a cactus, a corked bottle and a glass, and—suddenly, a horde of hideous reptiles began to emerge from a drawing pad lying beneath the book. Lizards, newts—it was difficult to say. In the blink of an eye, the reptiles were racing about in a circle, appearing and reappearing, squirming about in a most nauseating manner. The lieutenant and his men became dizzy.

Their discomfort soon passed, however, driven away by a greater unease. For the circling reptiles were picking up their pace. In but three seconds, their individual figures had vanished in a swirling scaly maelstrom.

A moment later a new form—indistinct in shape, but strange and fearful in its aspect—materialized above the desk, wavering like a flame in the wind. The officer moaned. The squad of constables herded together in a corner, lowing in fear.

"Officer, let me introduce you to the devil KKR," said the wizard. "I have summoned it to assist me in my investigation of the King's dream." The devil glowed a bit brighter. A cackling sound came from its—mouth?

"Devil!" spoke the mage. "Do you have anything to report regarding King Roy's dream?"

"Not a thing."

"Explain yourself!" demanded the mage. "I have given you ample time to investigate the matter."

The devil—sneered? It was difficult to say—but certainly unpleasant.

"Kiss off, Zulkeh. I'm not one of those puny devilkins you've been summoning with the hexes of Hieronymus

Sfrondrati-Piccolomini. So don't try that tone with me! Besides, we've got orders from the top—from the CEO himself. King Roy's dream is off limits."

There came the impression of a satanic leer.

"Then again, I might be open to a little insider trading. Against all the rules, of course—but what's the point of being a devil if you can't make a little on the side?"

Zulkeh frowned. "And what would you demand in exchange? An eternal soul, I assume?"

KKR howled with laughter. The constabulary huddled yet closer in the corner. The officer's face was white as a sheet.

"Oh, Zulkeh, you are such an incorrigible romantic," cackled the devil. "An absolute throwback! A pure medievalist! No, no, my dear mage—souls aren't worth a thing in these modern times. Progress, progress! Nowadays, I only deal in commodities. Bulk commodities."

"Bah!" oathed the wizard. "I do not possess bulk commodities, evil dullard! Look about you—do you see any such mundane trivia?"

"Well, as a matter of fact—" The devil flared an ominous purple, like the sky before a hurricane. A great bloodshot eye emerged from its vague form, waving about on a stalk. The eye fixed its gaze on the policemen in the corner, who, for their part, bayed in fear and distress.

"There's always a good market in pork bellies."

The constables stampeded from the room, trampling their superior underfoot. They blundered up the staircase and into the entry hall above, stumbling over mummy heads, and jammed themselves—all six at once—out of the front doorway. A moment later the king's officer leapt to his feet and raced out. In a few seconds all trace of the Royal Constabulary had vanished.

✦✦   ✦✦   ✦✦

Neither on the next day nor on any day that followed did a messenger come from King Roy to inquire of the wizard Zulkeh. Then, two days before he was to return to the Royal Palace, the mage arose from his chair and summoned Shelyid to his presence.

"Shelyid," he spoke, "I have determined the true state of things."

"Oh master! You have discovered the secret of the King's dream!"

"Nay, dwarf, I have not. And therein lies the mystery—for, of itself, the secret of King Roy's dream should long since have yielded itself up to my science, the which is superb in all fields and without equal—here I eschew false modesty—in the art of divination. Yet I have failed, failed utterly, to unveil it."

"Oh." After a moment, the apprentice assumed a mien of cheerful consolation. "Don't feel bad, master. After all, even a mighty sorcerer such as yourself can't always succeed."

"Bah!" oathed Zulkeh. "You are impertinent, gnome!" The wizard glowered fiercely. "Dolt of an apprentice! Product of idiot loins!"

Shelyid cringed before his master's fury, groveling at his feet. "Please, master," he whimpered, "I won't do it again."

"See to it that you do not!" A deep sigh issued from the wizard's lips. "But then, perhaps you are not to blame. Oft do I forget me that error is the result of intelligence misapplied. Thus, where intelligence is absent, we are confronted not with error but with the natural, if repugnant, behavior of the common brute."

"Thank you, master," bubbled Shelyid, pleased to have escaped a thrashing.

"But now, Shelyid, attend me closely, and ponder upon my words, each and every one of them. For the

concepts which I am about to unfold are wondrous in
their construction, impeccable in the geometry of their
logic."

"Yes, master!" The dwarf knitted his brows in prepa-
ration for thought.

"We begin with the major premise, to wit, that I am
peerless in the art of divination. It is thus in the nature
of things that there exists no dream which—*all other
things equal*—I cannot decipher through the application of my powers. Is this clear?"

"Oh yes, master!"

"Good. Let us now move to the minor premise, to
wit, the fact that I have, nevertheless, failed in the task
of unveiling the meaning of King Roy's dream. Is this
clear?"

"Oh yes, master!"

"The conclusion follows as night from day. All else
is *not* equal. Why have I been unable to discern the
secret? Clearly, *because I have been prevented from
doing so.*"

"But by whom, master?"

"Yes! Precisely! Well done, Shelyid! You have instantly
penetrated to the heart of the matter. By whom, indeed?
The answer is clear—*by my enemies.*"

"Enemies, master?" queried the dwarf, confusion and
alarm writ plain upon his face. "I didn't know you had
any enemies."

"Neither did I, dwarf. But enemies I clearly have.
And most puissant enemies, to boot, for not only have
these fiends succeeded in preventing me from discovering the import of the King's dream, they have, as
well—the villainous rogues!—kept their identity, nay,
even their existence, hidden from my sight, the which
resembles clairvoyance in its precision. But—ha! I have
foiled their plot! Yea, verily, I have uncovered the foul
schemers!"

The wizard paced to and fro, gesticulating with great vehemence. "Yet here confront we now a difficulty, Shelyid, for though my grasp of thaumaturgy is, as you know, equaled by none, yet there exist certain minor and esoteric branches of science which remain, if I may indulge in metaphor, outlying provinces not yet fully incorporated into the empire of my intellect. Of these, of these few—mere handful, in fact—does foety include itself."

"Foety, master? What is foety?"

"It is the study and lore of foes, Shelyid, including within its compass such fields as antagonology, enmitics, opponent psychology, developmental feudery, vindictrism, oppugnatic calculus, and, of course, the applied arts—revenge-work, table-turning, and so forth."

For some moments did the mage stand silent, motionless, poised in deep thought.

At length he spoke. "Well! There is nothing else for it, Shelyid. The true man of wisdom recognizes as well his limitations, few and meager though these be. My skills in foety have remained dormant, lo these many years, having as I do no foes, due to my invariant courtesy of manner and demeanor. Yet foes it now appears I have, and powerful ones. I shall need assistance. So. Let us be off!"

"Off, master?" queried Shelyid, a hint of anxiety creeping forth upon his simian brow. "Off where?"

"To Prygg, of course. Where else? There does the witch Magrit dwell, and there is none on earth who has her mastery of foety. And well 'tis for her sake, the vile harridan, for rudeness and intemperance have made her a host of enemies. Indeed, were it not for my well-known forbearance, I should number myself among them. As it is, the encounter will not be pleasant, indeed, may even be fraught with danger."

"Danger, master?" cried Shelyid, the hint of anxiety now grown to full stature.

"Of course, danger! What did you think? And not just from Magrit! Nay, much more, for the road to Prygg is long and oft perilous, replete as it is with savage beasts and diverse odd-fellows, ruffians and the like."

Then did the dwarf cry out in anguish, blubbering most pathetically, calling upon his master to leave him behind, extolling the cleanliness and order of the domicile which would await the sorcerer upon his triumphant return from great deeds of renown, if left to the loving care of his loyal apprentice during the mage's absence. But it was to no avail. Indeed, for his pains the dwarf was most soundly chastised by his master.

"And thus I command you, unworthy wretch, prepare the necessities of our journey," concluded the wizard's reproof. Grumbling, but now obedient, the dwarf set about his newfound task. As the mage and his apprentice possessed but little in the way of clothing, toiletries, and other such paraphernalia of human existence, the gathering together and packing of these items took but a moment.

"We can go now, master," piped Shelyid, depositing two small haversacks on the floor. "We're all packed."

Zulkeh frowned. "Do you trifle with me, gnome?"

"No, master," protested Shelyid. "Of course not."

"See to it that you do not. Hasten then and attend to the packing of the necessities of our journey. This I have already bade you do, and I am not pleased by your sloth in carrying out my command."

"But, master" whined Shelyid, "we *are* packed. See— here are our bags. I put everything in them: your spare robe, your other pair of socks, and all my stuff. That's all we have."

"Bah!" oathed Zulkeh. "I am in no mood for bumptious jests! What do I care for these trifles? Again, I command you—pack the necessities of our journey!"

"But what are they, master?" queried the puzzled dwarf.

"My instruments, dolt! What else? My scrolls! My tomes! My talismans! My artifacts!"

"H-how many of th-them do you w-want, master?" stammered the dwarf, his rapidly glazing eyes roving about their quarters, noting the many thousand scrolls heaped untidily upon workbenches and shelves, the stone figurines and clay tablets scattered about the floor, the thick leather-bound tomes of great weight stacked precariously hither and yon, the vials, beakers, jars, jugs, amulets, talismans, vessels, bowls, ladles, retorts, pincers, tweezers, pins, the bound bundles of sandalwood, ebony and dwarf pine, the bags and sacks of incense, herbs, mushrooms, dried grue of animal parts, the bottles of every shape and description filled with liquids of multitudinous variety of color, content and viscosity, the charms, the curios, the relics, the urns of meteor dust, the cartons of saints' bones and the coffers of criminals' skulls, and all the other artifacts of stupendous thaumaturgic potency crammed into every nook and cranny of every niche, room, closet and hallway in the death house, not excluding the heavy iron engines in the lower vaults.

"All of them, of course!" spoke the wizard. "Everything. Not a single item necessary to my science can be left behind—and they are all of them necessary, for I am not in the habit of collecting useless trivia."

Most piteous were Shelyid's moans.

CHAPTER V. *A Dwarf's Travails, and the Wizard's Comments Thereon. The Dwarf Succeeds. An Imminent Departure, Forestalled by a Gnome's Subterfuge. A Pathetic Scene!*

Long were the labors of the dwarf Shelyid which ensued, following his master's clarification of the task at hand. For, 'twas not simply the immensity of the actual collection and storage of the mage's possessions which faced the apprentice. Early on, as the small mountain of said possessions began to pile up in the wizard's study, it occurred to the dwarf that he had no vehicle, no vessel, within which to stow these objects for transport.

This realization come, Shelyid pointed out to the wizard the vast disparity between the hillock of objects to be conveyed and the small size of their haversacks. The dwarf then proposed, as a solution to the quandary, the ruthless elimination of all possessions not absolutely necessary to the wizard's work. Indeed, the diminutive apprentice waxed eloquent. He extolled the sorcerer's great powers of mind, the titanic scope of his intellect, the oceanic breadth and depth of his spirit, all of which, argued the gnome, led to the inexorable conclusion that so puissant a thaumaturge as Zulkeh required, in actual point of fact, no more in the way of possessions than his staff—which he would, naturally, wish to carry himself—and his spare robe and extra pair of socks.

The mage was not convinced. Indeed, he now waxed most eloquently himself. He excoriated the apprentice's feeble powers of mind, his stupefying lack of wits, the oceanic formlessness and viscous sludge of his spirit, all of which, contended Zulkeh, led to the inexorable conclusion that so sullen an apprentice as Shelyid required, in actual point of fact, the application of the wizard's staff to his backside. Theory here led at once to practice.

The dwarf now properly chastened, Zulkeh ordered him to manufacture some suitable sack in which to stow the possessions in question. And so did the apprentice set about this newfound task.

Here, as well, his labors were long and arduous. For the wizard himself possessed no cloth of a size sufficient to make such a sack. Thus was Shelyid perforce required to descend into the catacombs, gravely disturbing, your narrator is pained to relate, the slumbers of the dead. For the apprentice did tumble out of their eternal resting place many a skeleton and many a mummy, seeking, by the collection of their burial shrouds, to amass together a quantity of cloths out of which he could manufacture the great sack.

Alas, these labors seemed in vain. The dwarf was no more nimble-fingered than he was nimble-witted. His attempts at cutting and sewing, not to mention the more subtle of the tailoring arts, were inept in the extreme. Of course, this proved to be something of a boon. For the dwarf was, by virtue of his clumsiness, blessed with a most educational lecture on the part of his master. Zulkeh sat in his chair in the study, observing the gnome at his work, and lightened Shelyid's labors with a lengthy monologue on the subject of bungling and botchery, opening up to the dwarf's understanding various theoretical and historical subtleties of the question which had heretofore escaped Shelyid's attention, this, though the subject itself was actually one of the more frequent of the mage's topics of discourse.

Then, the sack at last stitched and knotted together, in a most crude and unsightly fashion, the apprentice discovered that his labors not only seemed to be, but were in actual fact, in vain. For no sooner had but the fourth part of the mage's belongings been stuffed into the sack than this would-be conveyance ripped at a dozen places, disgorging its would-be contents back onto the floor of the study.

In fairness to the dwarf, it should be said that the fault lay not with his seam-manship. Indeed, his rough-hewn seams were the *only* places where the sack did not rip. The fault lay rather in the fact, now obvious to the slow-witted Shelyid—especially with the wizard's accompanying and most lucid exposition on the related subjects of idiocy and cretinism to assist him in his reasoning—that the moldy and worm-eaten shrouds of the long dead are not, all things considered, the most suitable material out of which to forge a sturdy traveling sack designed to carry objects not only of vast multitude and great collective weight, but sporting many sharp points and edges as well.

"But master, I don't have anything else to make a sack from," whined the dwarf.

"Bah!" oathed the mage. Zulkeh rose from his chair and stalked over to a shelf, from which he drew forth a book and a box.

"Thoughtless lout!" The mage extended the box to Shelyid. "Have you forgotten this?"

Shelyid gingerly took the box.

"But, master, you told me never to open this box. So I don't know what's in it."

"Do not attempt to excuse your ignorance with ignorance, wretched gnome! Of course I forbade you to open the box, for it contains nothing less valuable than the hide of a guthfish."

Shelyid's brow furrowed.

"What's a guthfish?"

"Lazy dwarf! The nature of said magical piscoid is recounted in this penetrating volume by the Potentates Laebmauntsforscynneweëld, *The Guthfish of Grotum, its history and natural philosophy.*"

The wizard now extended the book.

"Had you but read this tome—instead of lolling about in idleness—it would have opened up to your understanding the divers uses of the creature's hide as well as the strange and wonderful characteristics thereof."

"But, master, you told me never to read that book, lest I should be felled in my mind—actually you said the cluttered pit which passes for my mind—by the subtle and cunning things which are contained therein."

"Bah!" oathed the mage. "Do you seek to excuse your disobedience with obedience?"

Zulkeh thrust the book into Shelyid's hands.

"Read this, unworthy wretch!—and proceed to fashion the sack according to its instructions."

"Yes, master," sighed the dwarf, seating himself on his stool.

Shelyid quickly read through the first chapters, in which was recounted the history and habits of the rare guthfish of Grotum. Therein he learned that the fabled fish had once—or so, at least, was the legend—

swallowed the entire universe when it was tiny and disgorged it back out when it was huge. He was then introduced to the lore of the guthfish hide itself, its many attributes and curious characteristics, which included the fact that it was not only the strongest and most elastic material known to exist, that it could not only conform to whatever object or objects it encompassed, but that, in addition, it possessed the strange power of infinite expansion—this last property being apparently magical, since it could be analyzed by the use of any mathematical formula known to man, including several which were mutually contradictory.

The last chapter contained instructions for fashioning the guthfish hide into a useful sack. This Shelyid read carefully, noting that the hide could only be cut with a singularity (left drawer, upper cabinet), could only be sewn with a needle made from the square root of -1 (middle shelf, small box under the curious amulet from Obpont), and could only be stitched with superstring thread made from the Theory of Everything, of which, needless to say, the wizard had a vast amount stored on spools scattered all over the abandoned death house.

After reading the last chapter twice, Shelyid took up the box and examined it. The following was written on the front of the box:

GENUINE GUTHFISH HIDE

100% Pure and Undiluted!
Large Economy Size!!
Use It For Everything!!!
Fits Anything!!!!

WARNING: Studies by pettifogging government agencies and alarm-
ist environmental fanatics have indicated that guthfish hide is toxic
to the health of some people. Further study, however, by sober and
reputable industrial scientists has shown that such people are not worth
a damn and would be better off dead anyway. Symptoms may include
the onset of bad nerves, pox, palsy, jitters, quivers, tremors, convulsions, paroxysms, fevers, the staggers, the jerks, shortness of breath,
frequent and uncontrolled excretion, irregularities of the pulse,
lockjaw, ague, fidgets, timorousness and a general feeling of social
inferiority, these, of course, the classic symptoms of that most dread of
nervous conditions, *hysteria follicularia.* Use at your own risk.

Shelyid also read this label carefully, especially the
warning. Having done so, he spoke to his master.

"But, master," whined the dwarf, "it says here that
this stuff can cause—"

"Diminutive cretin!" oathed Zulkeh. "The warning
applies solely to individuals who aren't worth a damn
anyway." The mage glowered. "And while there is
mounting evidence that you fit this description perfectly,
you already suffer from the classic symptoms of *hysteria
follicularia*—so where is the harm that can befall you?"

Unable to counter this impeccable line of reasoning,
the reluctant gnome opened the box and drew out the
contents. Several things became apparent. First, the
guthfish hide seemed infinitely large, for there seemed
no end to the number of folds Shelyid could open.
Then, once the dwarf had unfolded the thing to a
sufficient size for the sack required, he saw that the
shape of the hide itself seemed to suggest the very sack
into which it would be made. Finally, it was either
utterly colorless or colored in every shade of the
rainbow—it was impossible to tell.

Quickly assembling the required tools and supplies,
Shelyid launched himself into the making of the sack.
All afternoon he labored, stretching and trimming,
shaping and fitting, adjusting and improving. Under
his fingers (the which seemed less clumsy and more
adept than before) a huge sack soon emerged, the
interior divided and subdivided into numerous com-

partments and regions, the exterior liberally bestowed with divers pockets and pouches. At last, all was ready.

Shelyid proudly announced to the wizard: "Master, I've finished the sack."

"Bah!" oathed Zulkeh, not looking up from the tome he was examining. "Do you seek to excuse your indolence with diligence? See to the packing of my possessions—for even as you dawdle, time wanes!"

It was the work of many hours for Shelyid to collect, categorize, store, restore, arrange, rearrange and pack and repack the sack, fitting each tome, artifact, talisman, scroll and all else carefully therein. When everything was complete, just before sunrise, he fell into an exhausted slumber. Only to be awakened, just after sunrise, by his master.

"Come, wretched gnome, arise and hoist the sack! You have wasted an entire day in your inefficiency. We must be off at once—for even as you rub the sleep from your eyes, time wanes!"

Shelyid bent to hoist the burden over his shoulder. More accurately, Shelyid got down on his knees preparatory to burrowing under the enormous sack and hoisting the several-times-larger-than-himself object onto his entire diminutive person. But, at that moment, a thought seized him—or so, at least, one can surmise from his pale and distraught expression.

"Wait! Wait!" he cried. "I forgot something!" And so saying, Shelyid charged from the room, ignoring his master's expressions of impatience and displeasure.

Back into the catacombs plunged the dwarf, his little legs scurrying frantically. Down and down he went, into the lowest depths, arriving at last in a small and dark crypt. He went into a corner of the chamber and squatted, clucking softly.

A moment later, a large and horrid-looking brown spider emerged from a hole. Shelyid extended his hand,

onto which the hideous creature clambered. He raised
the thing before his eyes. The arachnid stretched out
a gruesome limb and touched the dwarf's nose.

"Hullo," whispered Shelyid. Then he began to weep.
The spider touched his nose several times with a
motion which, were the idea not absurd, one would
have called a caress.

"I have to leave," choked Shelyid. Then, a few sobs
later: "I'll miss you so much. You're the only friend I've
ever had. What will I do without you?"

He looked about the dank little grotto, not much
more than a cave, actually.

"My happiest times've been the times here with
you." He sniffed. "Actually, been my only happy
times."

He stroked the monster. "I know I should enjoy the
master's lectures, 'cause they're good for my brain and
stuff." Wretched sniffles and snuffles. "It's hard to
understand what th'master says, 'cause I'm so stupid.
And then he gets impatient with me and he—well, he's
sort of mean to me." More wretched sniffles and
snuffles. "Real mean, actually."

A great sob burst from the dwarf's chest. "Oh, what'll
become of me? I'm just a dwarf. I'm just a stupid, ugly
dwarf. I don't want to go off and have adventures! I'm
no good for it. I'll get killed—eaten by ogres or something! Or maimed, or—" He stopped, overcome. Then:
"Oh, and what's the difference? I guess I'm no good for
anything, anyway. Might as well get eaten."

He gazed down at the spider, great tears leaking
down his hairy cheeks. He stroked the horrible creature again.

"But I'll sure miss you," he whispered. "I sure will.
If I come back, I mean, if I don't get eaten or whatever, I'll come see you right away. I promise." The
spider touched his nose.

A faint sound echoed in the room. It bore about it the aura of the voice of a most outraged sorcerer.

"That's th'master. I gotta go, or I'll be beaten." He sniffled. "Probably be beaten, anyway. But I just had to see you one last time."

He placed the monster back on the ground. "G'bye," he whispered, and fled from the chamber.

CHAPTER VI. *A Journey Begun. A Coach Ride. The Royal Palace. King Roy's Dream Redux. Calamities. A Tumultuous Departure. The Central Travel House of Goimr. The Wizard Inquires. A Commercial Philosophy Explained. A Purchase. "We're Off!"*

Thus it came to pass that wizard and servant abandoned the abandoned death house and set forth on their journey of renown.

Their initial progress was slow. Shelyid, his diminutive figure buried under the enormous bundle on his back, from which protruded here and there the snouts, corners and extensions of sundry wizardrous objects too bizarre to describe, staggered to and fro, lurching with every step, careening wildly from house wall to house wall, from lamppost to trash bin, from corner to midstreet to gutter.

"Shelyid!" spoke Zulkeh. "Cease this inefficient mode of travel! And take care lest you damage the items I have entrusted to your care."

"But, master," whined the dwarf's voice from somewhere beneath the sack, "it's *heavy*. And I can't *see*."

"Bah!" oathed Zulkeh. "Is the odyssey of science to be impeded by the physical frailties of such as you? Too long now, wretch, have you lolled about in the comfort of luxurious surroundings. The rigors of travel will do you good. It will improve your muscular tone, enhance your respiratory capacity, strengthen your stamina, harden your will, hone the edge of the blunt instrument that is your mind, and expose you to new knowledge and lore. Enough of this childish petulance! Make haste! For, even as I speak, time wanes."

And with that the wizard resumed his progress, Shelyid caroming behind.

But before our heroes had rounded the first corner, a great clattering of hooves and jingling of harness was heard to approach. Zulkeh stood to one side as a coach-and-four thundered down the narrow street accompanied by a mounted squad of the Goimr Royal Coachmen. Shelyid, unfortunately, bent double in concentration, failed to apprehend the approach of these worthies. He lurched into the center of the street just as they passed. Two of the riders were bowled over— horses and riders going asses over teacups—while the others frantically avoided the staggering dwarf and his pack. The coach skidded dangerously but came to a halt without upsetting.

The coach door flew open and a courtier leapt out. He hurried up to the wizard.

"Are you not the wizard Zulkeh?" he demanded. Then, not bothering to wait for a reply, he continued:

"Excellent, excellent! I've just come from the palace—Chief Counselor Gerard sent me to bring you to the King. Please, please—get into the coach! We must hurry! The King is at his wits' end!"

Even as the courtier spoke, the coach and four was brought up next to Zulkeh and Shelyid. A footman jumped down and opened the door. Alas, it soon became evident that Shelyid and his sack could not be crammed into the coach, the which was more of a dainty and elegant carriage than a sturdy means of transport. The courtier instantly called up the detachment of Royal Coachmen who helped Shelyid load the sack onto the rear of the coach. The vehicle settled deeply, with an ominous creaking and groaning.

That done, Zulkeh and the courtier climbed into the coach. Shelyid made to follow them but was arrested by his master's fierce glare.

"Wretched gnome! Have you forgotten your duty?"

"No, master, the sack is loaded and tied," explained the dwarf, his legs fairly vibrating in relief from their burden.

"Yes, but who will watch it?"

So saying, Zulkeh slammed the door. Shelyid, with a shrug of resignation, found a perch on the top of the sack where he grabbed onto one of the straps as the coach rushed off down the street toward the palace.

With a squad of Royal Coachmen to clear the streets, the coach careened unimpeded through various lanes and byways before it debouched onto a main thoroughfare, where it continued pell-mell toward the landing. It was but the work of a minute for the passengers to alight and, with the assistance of many hands, to transfer the sack onto a water taxi. The boat—now deep in the water—instantly departed for the royal isle. Once upon land, the courtier conducted them to Chief Counselor Gerard's chamber, hissing his anxiety and haste all the while.

Gerard was equally agitated. "Egbert, what took you so long? King Roy has been screaming for the wizard. And you—Zulkeh! I warn you once again—say nothing to disturb King Roy! He is in a most unstable state."

Zulkeh nodded curtly. He and Shelyid followed

Gerard into the royal audience chamber. The King's cries of distress could be heard from a considerable distance. They grew positively clamorous upon the entrance of the mage.

Indeed, King Roy was a shocking sight. In the two weeks which had elapsed since the last interview, he had aged twenty years. His hair was straggling and gray, tufts of it plucked out. His clothes were disheveled, his eyes were wild. He gave off the odor of a hunted roebuck.

"Wizard! Tell me, what does it all mean? I must know, I must know!"

"Your Highness, as I have previously explained, this matter is too deep for facile explication. In fact, I have but recently discovered that the import of your dream is considerably more complex, with many more hidden and obscure attributes than I had at first appreciated. Much additional study is required. Even at this moment I am undertaking a journey for—"

"No! No! No! I must know, know, know! Now! Now! Now!" So shrieked King Roy, in a most unregal manner.

"Your Majesty—please! There is no need for this unseemly distress. You may rest easy in your mind. For the magnitude of the danger which is so clearly indicated by your dream is such as to preclude the thought that a mere monarch might forestall its occurrence."

"What?" cried the King. "But I must do something! What of my kingdom? My dynasty? My palace? My— why, even my royal person!"

A look of surprise came upon Zulkeh's face. "It is, then, the meaning of this dream for your *personal* fortunes that concerns you?"

"Of course! What does this dream mean for me? I must have an answer—and now! Do you hear? Now! Now! Now!"

The wizard made a soothing gesture. "Calm yourself, Sire. If 'tis only the personal import of the dream that you seek, the matter is simple, even commonplace. The mystery lies entirely in its deeper and more obscure elements."

King Roy goggled. "You know, then, the meaning of this dream for myself?"

"Certes!" spoke Zulkeh, his voice full of good cheer. "The problem in this regard is transparent. The grasping of the tongue is alone a sure sign, the forcible restraint of speech being, of course, the third of the seven great oneiric portents. I refer you, in this regard, to the classic exposition by Sigmund Laebmauntsforscynneweëld, *The Interpretation of Auguries*, as well as to his more specific examination of the fear of mutism, *Tongue and Taboo*, wherein the great scholar—"

"A pox on your blithering pedantry!" shrieked King Roy. "What does the dream mean? For me! You hear? For me! Me! Answer, you wretched scholiast!"

Stiffly, the wizard drew himself up. "Well, then! Your dream foretells the utter and complete destruction of your kingdom, your palace, your dynasty and your royal person. The destruction will naturally encompass the entire male line of your family down to three generations, including all collateral branches. Whether ruination will as well sweep into its train the female line of your family is a matter open to some doubt—for here there is much dispute among the savants. Sigmund would have it so, as would his famed relative Adler Laebmauntsforscynneweëld. But, as is well know, Piaget Sfondrati-Piccolomini advances the proposition that ruination portents apply only irregularly to the distaff line, this due to their childbearing functions, the which, as he is known for saying, provide certain immunities from calamitous events due to the providence-favored innocence of babes. As to this latter, I myself have formed as yet no firm opinion, for it seems that there is some question—"

But the mage expounded no further. For at that very moment, King Roy—whose complexion had undergone in recent moments a marvelous display of the colors of the spectrum—sprang up and cried, "No!" (in a most undignified manner) and hurled himself to the floor.

"But 'tis plain as day, Your Majesty," spoke Zulkeh to the writhing monarch, "the signs are unmistakable. For as I was saying, 'twas none other than Sigmund Laebmauntsforscynneweëld himself who enunciated that most basic principle of oneiromancy which holds that the seizure and immobilization of the tongue—"

"Stop! Cease! Desist!" bellowed Gerard, advancing to the fore. "Did I not instruct you to quell King Roy's fears? What have you done? Your mad babble has driven the King to this state! Fiend! Miscreant!"

With this latest affront the mage's reserve broke, even as the stately dike shatters 'neath the blow of the mighty tidal bore. Smoke and lightning issued from his ears; his eyes blazed hotly forth.

"Silence, ye witless sycophant! Abuse me not, lest I chastise you in my affront! Science is what it is, had you the sense to see it. And what boots it, the downfall of a King? This, a trifle, when far greater matters hang in the balance!"

Then, even as the tide ebbs, so the wizard's wrath subsided. "But I forget me. To ask perception of such as you would be to drown in folly. I can tarry no longer. For I must tend to the greater matters of which I am now apprised."

With that, the sorcerer turned and strode down the long audience chamber, Shelyid twinkling behind.

Gerard cried out: "Stop these fiends, stop these criminals! Alarum! Alarum! Guards! Constables! Arrest these villains!"

In an instant, the trample of many jackbooted feet was to be heard coming from the left. Moments later another thunder of boots was heard on the right. Two squads of Royal Guards and Royal Constabulary appeared in doorways on either side. The lieutenant of the Constabulary drew his sword and advanced into the audience chamber, but, before he took three steps, he was hailed by the captain of the Guard.

"Lieutenant—halt! I must remind you that the Royal Guard—and the Royal Guard alone!—has jurisdiction within the walls of the palace."

So saying, the captain of the Guard drew his own sword and charged after Zulkeh and Shelyid, who—the first preoccupied with thought, the latter with sack—continued their progress toward the far door. But the captain had not taken three steps of his own before the lieutenant of the Constabulary planted himself in the way. A lively discussion concerning legal jurisdiction ensued. The debate escalated in lockstep with the paces of our heroes, until, by the time the wizard and his apprentice were halfway down the long chamber, the entire Guard and Constabulary were hacking and hewing each other with a vigorous display of swordsmanship.

Drawn by the sound of clashing steel, a platoon of the Praetorian Guard burst into the chamber through the very door toward which our heroes made their way.

"Stop them!" cried Gerard. In an instant, the fierce Praetorians charged the struggling mob of guards and constables, pouring around Zulkeh and Shelyid like water around rocks in midstream. The brawl in the center of the chamber now became three-sided.

Then, as our heroes were but ten paces from the far door, two new bodies of armed men poured into the chamber from doors behind the throne—

Janissaries from the west, Mamelukes from the east. Recognizing his earlier error, Gerard now issued explicit instructions to these newly entered soldiery, detailing with unmistakable exactitude the necessity of immediately arresting the wizard and his apprentice, not forgetting to point directly toward the culprits, all of which precision was pointless since the Janissaries and Mamelukes had immediately started slaughtering each other with the gusto derived from hallowed and historic rivalry.

Zulkeh and Shelyid passed through the far door into the corridor beyond.

Dodging and weaving his way through the slashing mob, Gerard pursued. By the time he entered the corridor, his prey were almost to the lobby at the far end. Not twenty feet beyond, a squad of Secret Police stood in the lobby, fingering their cudgels, frowning with concern, gazing down the corridor, wondering at the sounds of struggle issuing from the royal audience chamber.

The quick-witted Gerard seized the moment. To the Secret Police, he cried: "Arrest the wizard!" To the wizard he cried: "Stop, Zulkeh—stop!"

Shouting with fierce enthusiasm, the Secret Police charged toward the wizard and his apprentice. The wizard turned abruptly at the sound of his name. Attempting to avoid his master, Shelyid tripped over the loose fringe of the faded and worn carpet and lost his footing. Head down, locked in concentration, completely overbalanced by the giant sack, Shelyid—or rather, the sack—plunged directly into the onrushing squad of policemen, with much the same results as a bowling ball striking pins.

Half the squad was down, senseless. The ones who managed to avoid the direct blow of the sack now flung themselves upon the dwarf. Alas, as he recoiled from the collision, Shelyid turned a complete 360 degrees, knocking over another two or three of the policemen as he did so. Still struggling to regain his balance, the dwarf now lurched to the left, crushing one wight against the entry wall; then to the right, crushing another; then he caromed right into the lobby, rolling over the last secret policeman still conscious, and burst through the large entry door leading to the plaza beyond. The door shattered into pieces. In a moment the tumult and chaos were left behind as Zulkeh and Shelyid exited the palace and headed down to the lake, oblivious to the cries and alarm behind them.

The last sight Gerard had of them, as he stood fuming in what was left of the doorway to the palace, was of Zulkeh and Shelyid climbing into the water taxi and making their way back across the Moyle. Throwing up his hands with rage, the Chief Counselor charged back into the palace. His voice could dimly be heard:

"Call out the Royal Janitors! The Royal Cooks! The Royal Gardeners! Arrest the wizard!"

Moments later, the sound of martial clangor resounded from within—mops clashing with pots, pans against shears, clippers versus brooms.

For their part, Zulkeh and Shelyid went their way unmolested. At length they arrived at the central travel station of Goimr. This edifice, huge and many-winged, had once housed a vast assortment of enterprises dedicated to the provision of transport for those citizens of Goimr seeking egress from the dismal city. In times past, the would-be traveler could hire or purchase a coach, a dray, a chariot, a wagon, a cart or, indeed, any other conceivable means of land transport. In recent times, however, all of these enterprises had been acquired by the Consortium, as one of that ubiquitous firm's projects in its conquest of the commerce of Grotum. Their assets had been combined, and the entire travel station had been consolidated under the aegis of a newly founded corporation, the Great Grotum Northern, Eastern, Southern, Western, Central and Environs Express and Transport Company, a subsidiary of Grotum Cultural Endeavor, Ltd. (a non-profit enterprise), itself a subsidiary of Colonial Exploitation, Inc. (a philanthropic foundation), itself, in turn, a subsidiary of the Consortium. This latter was headquartered, as was the case with most commercial enterprises of any note in the civilized world, in the famed and far distant city of splendid Ozar.

Zulkeh paused for a moment before the archway over the entrance to the great building.

"Look you, Shelyid, at this example of the inexorable progress of Reason through Time. In days gone by, chaos reigned here supreme. We should have been forced to waste many an hour in demeaning squabble with divers fellows and odd sorts of avaricious mien, quarreling over fare and form of travel. Today, however, this has gone the way of all unreason confronted by science, and we need but apply for an established and harmonized method of transportation suited to our needs, all of it organized, systematized and regularized by this most eminent and stable of firms."

And with that he passed through the archway into the central court. Shelyid followed, tripping over a portmanteau. The sack went flying. The wizard was greatly displeased, the more so by the unwarranted intervention of a brash and impudent youth.

But at length, this unpleasantness behind them, the wizard and his apprentice made their way to a door over which was suspended the sign: "GGNESWC&EE&T Co.—Tickets."

Once inside, Shelyid unburdened himself of his sack

and sat upon a bench against one wall. He seemed
oppressed by the atmosphere, although the low gloomy
ceiling, the unpainted benches equipped with shackles for the restraint of criminals and children, the dirty
walls covered with graffiti and obscure signs of no
doubt cabalistic origin, should have lent to the establishment a most homelike ambience.

Meanwhile, Zulkeh approached the ticket vendor's
window and examined an enormous sign suspended on
the wall above. The sign read:

TABLE OF TRAVEL RATES
AND COACH CLASSES

Rates	Classes
Family	Deluxe
Convention	Superb
Party	Royal
Merchant	First
Commercial	Second
Clinical	Third
Military	Fourth
Clerical	Fifth
Official	Coach
Secret	Economy
Vacation	Poor
Common	Scum

After pondering this table for a moment, Zulkeh
stepped forward to the vendor's window. In the small
room beyond, he discerned the dim figure of the
vendor and a row of boxes holding tickets of different sizes and colors.

"Sirrah," spoke the mage. "Are there, as would seem
reasonable, twelve classes each with twelve rates, or
twelve classes each with only one rate, or twelve rates,
each with only one class?"

"Sir," replied the ticket vendor in a voice devoid of inflection or discernible tone, "am I to understand that you are calling into question the commercial philosophy and *weltanschauung* of the Great Grotum Northern, Eastern, Southern, Western, Central and Environs Express and Travel Company, a subsidiary of Grotum Cultural Endeavor, Ltd. (a non-profit enterprise), itself a subsidiary of Colonial Exploitation, Inc. (a philanthropic foundation), itself, in turn, a subsidiary of the Consortium? If so, that is to say, if such be the case, you may, if you wish, file a formal complaint, that, be assured, will receive the fullest consideration by those officials of our firm who have been appointed to deal with precisely the aforementioned matters. Should your complaint, after due process and close examination, be adjudged picayune, idle, foolish, bothersome, trivial, malicious, ill-advised, inconvenient, well-taken, or justified, your travel privileges on the GGNESWC&EE&T Co. will be revoked, now and for perpetuity; in addition, you will be fined the full administrative cost of processing your complaint, in addition to a punitive surcharge, such surcharge to be monetary in nature, though not excluding, at the discretion of that office of the Company which has been duly assigned to handle such matters, a thorough investigation of your ancestry, habits, character and associations by the Consortium Constabulary, the results of said investigation to be, at the whim of the Consortium, or any of its subsidiaries involved in the case, or any of its subsidiaries not involved in the case, broadcast to the world at large, with the intention, and the invariable result, of blackening your character, destroying your career, and breaking your spirit."

Zulkeh thought upon these words. At length he spoke.

"Sirrah, I see that your establishment does not take

these matters lightly. An attitude, I might say, with which I find myself in complete accord! I would, however, appreciate your telling me of the difference between the various classes and rates listed in yon table."

"The tickets."

"I beg your pardon?"

"The tickets. Size and color. Size is class, color is rate."

"That is all?"

"That is what I said. Am I to understand that you are calling into question the—"

"No, no, no," spoke the mage hastily. "By no means. I am simply seeking to clarify the matter. As I now understand it, the only difference in the tickets is the tickets themselves. Each ticket, of no matter which class or rate, will purchase the same transport, the same lodgings en route, the same accommodations, etc.?"

"That is correct."

"An excellent policy! In former times, prior to your acquisition of a monopoly over this industry, the desirous voyager was beset by impudent hagglers, each offering a different service for a different fee. You have cut through this mindless hurly-burly at one stroke, reducing the question to its intrinsic essence of prestige and social snobbery."

"That is correct. And now, sir, I am busy and you have taken much of my time. Where are you going? And what is your preference in class and rate?"

"As for destination, my apprentice and I journey to Prygg. As for class and rate, whichever is the cheapest—for my worldly wealth is little, and the subliminity of my intellect requires no social trappings to sustain it."

"Common scum," announced the ticket vendor. "Twelve piasters for two common scum to Prygg."

"I shall take them," spoke Zulkeh, pushing twelve small coins through the slot in the bars. In return, two torn and greasy scraps of paper upon which were scrawled "Prygg" were carelessly tossed back. Picking them up off the floor, Zulkeh gathered up his apprentice and proceeded through the gate leading to the outer court. There the tickets were inspected by an employee, who bestowed upon our heroes a well-practiced sneer. "To the left!" he barked.

They followed these directions and, after walking through a further passageway, came upon their vehicle. It was a huge old coach, easily large enough to accommodate twelve passengers. The coach was rakishly tilted, not by design but simply because it rested on four wheels of varying design and diameter, the which had clearly been salvaged from other vehicles.

Within, the coach gave evidence of a past glory now sadly gone. The seats had originally been dyed a deep green, but were now much faded with age. The padding had a tendency to protrude from the many rips and tears in the covers. The floor was covered by a once-plush carpet now stained and soiled. Ingress and egress to the coach were provided by two large and much-weathered doors, hanging on rusty hinges. Tattered curtains hung in the windows.

Barely had Zulkeh and Shelyid entered the coach when the vehicle lurched into motion. Shelyid sprawled onto the floor.

"Master!" he cried. "We're off!"

"Well spoken, dwarf. Our journey has begun."

PART II

In Which We Follow the
Further Progress of the Terrorist
Trio in Their Unlawful Escape From Goimr,
Revealing Therein Fell Visions and Portents.
Taken, As Before, From the *Autobiography* of the
Renegade Benvenuti Sfondrati-Piccolomini,
the Veracity of Whose Account, We Must
Emphatically Repeat, Is In No Wise
Guaranteed by the Noble Alfredae.

*The Autobiography of Benvenuti Sfondrati-Piccolomini,
Episode 2: Statues, Soldiers, Snarls, and Soothsayers*

So it was on such a wretched cart that I left the city
of Goimr.

Strangely enough, the real difficulty we encountered
in making our escape was none of the things I had
foreseen. It was not the police, not the soldiers, not
even the absurd spectacle of Wolfgang posing as a
gigantic statue being hauled in the back of the cart.

It was the damned draymasters. When we entered
the boulevard leading to the Dreary Gate on the

northwest edge of the city, there was a great mob of
them lounging about in front of the stables. No sooner
did they catch sight of Gwendolyn in her yoke, hauling the cart, than they rushed up and began a fierce
bidding for her.

I was appalled, really. Often enough had I heard my
uncles describe Grotum as backward and medieval, but
the reality of it had never truly penetrated until then.

"And will you look at the size of that mare!" cried
one.

"I'll give you three quid!" exclaimed another.

"I'll make it four!" came from a third.

"Five!"

"Six!"

The indignity was bad enough. Worse yet was that
our escape ploy stood in imminent danger of being
ruined. I did not require Wolfgang's *sotto voce* hissing in my ear to realize that Gwendolyn would not
tolerate the situation much longer. The ensuing mayhem would, of course, be gratifying—fierce joy filled
my heart at the image of draymasters hacked and
chopped into pieces. But it would, as the saying goes,
"blow our cover."

The situation came to a crisis when one of the swine
actually made so bold as to advance upon Gwendolyn,
open her mouth with his hands, and begin inspecting
her teeth, while a second began poking her thighs and
buttocks with his thumb.

Wolfgang's coaching now came into its own.

"Get your filthy paws off my property!" I roared,
cracking the bullwhip. The tooth inspector backed up
a step, but the buttock prodder merely sneered and
continued his examination.

A moment later he was rolling on the ground,
howling in pain. And well he should! I dare say I
removed a good piece of his own buttock with the

whip, whose tip was reinforced with steel wire. Two pieces, actually, one from each haunch—for the sight of his great ass in the air as he flopped on his belly was irresistible.

Perhaps I should have resisted, for the second lash seemed to arouse the mob of draymasters as the first had not. No doubt I had transgressed some quaint local custom.

A moment later they had surrounded the cart, bellowing their fury, shaking their fists, and cursing my person.

"Ozarine whelp!" cried one. (I fear my accent was pronounced.)

"We'll teach you better!"

"Proper Groutch manners you're about to learn!"

Wolfgang was whispering some advice into my ear, but I was not paying the slightest attention. I should listen to a lunatic, when I had been trained by my uncle Larue?

"It's a fearsome arm, the bullwhip," he'd said to me, "but remember—of all weapons, it's the one that relies the most on panache and the psychologic flair. The perfect weapon for you, you sassy, disrespectful little wretch."

"Would you, base curs?" I roared. The first I had lashed from my seat, but now I arose and began laying about with a fine touch—fine, not only in the hand, but in the jocularity of the remarks which I sent along with the strokes. The key, however, was the scalps.

Pain will dissuade a mob, of course, as humor will depress their spirits. But there's nothing like the sight of a few scalps lifted from bully heads by smart cracks of the lash to drain their passions. The more so when the cunning of the stroke causes the scalps to fly directly into the whipmaster's free hand. After I had collected four scalps, stuffing the bloody things into my belt, the draymasters fled in all directions, howling with terror. All but two, who made the mistake of trying to hide behind (I should say, in front of) Gwendolyn. Without breaking stride, she shouldered them down, trampled them under, and hauled the iron-rimmed wheels of the cart directly over their bodies. A cart, mind you, bearing not only my weight but that of the giant Wolfgang as well!

I was adapting to Grotum, I could tell. The sound of crunching bones was a pure musical delight.

"Oh, well done! Well done!" hissed Wolfgang.

"Thank you," muttered Gwendolyn.

"I wasn't talking to you, dear," chuckled Wolfgang. "I was referring to the masterful whipwork. Are you by any chance related to Larue Sfrondrati-Piccolomini?"

"My uncle," I whispered. "And will you please shut up? You'll give it away, people see your lips moving—you're supposed to be a damned statue!"

"Not to fear, my boy. I'm a ventriloquist, you know."

Casually I turned my head, looking into the back of the cart. There was Wolfgang, posed cross-legged like a saint—a statue of a saint, more properly. Quite a good likeness, if I say so myself. I had discovered that painting a man up to look like a huge wooden icon was not all that difficult—not, at least, for an artist like myself who had carved and painted more wooden icons by the time I was nine than I could remember.

Wolfgang's stance was perfect. He was absolutely rigid and unmoving, for all the world like—well, actually, like a wooden statue.

"It'll be the easiest thing in the world for me to manage," he'd said after he'd explained the scheme. "The head psychiatrist at the asylum says I've got the finest catatonic trance he's ever examined! Such a compliment!"

And I'll admit his ventriloquism was as good as his

catatonia. I couldn't see a trace of his lips moving, even as he continued to babble on.

"I knew it! I knew it! The wonderful touch with the scalps! The unmistakable style! And the bon mots!" He bubbled with mad laughter—a strange sound and sight, let me tell you, coming from unmoving lips! Grotesque, really.

"I was there, you know," he continued, "at the Criticism of the Critics. I was actually there in person!"

I was stunned. "You were there? You saw it?"

The smug voice: "Every moment. From the preface, to the disclaimer, to the rebuttal, to the conclusion. One of my fondest memories."

It was before my time, of course, but it was a legend in the clan. Over the years, I'll admit to growing a bit skeptical. But as we made our slow way down the boulevard, Gwendolyn stolidly hauling the cart through the fetid crowd, Wolfgang hissed a full description of the great event.

"Amazing arrogance, when I look back on it," he whispered. "But then, what can you expect from a lot of critics? A vile, contumacious breed. And quite unstable mentally. An incredible percentage of megalomaniacs were critics in early life, you know? Still, it's astonishing. Had I been a critic invited to express my criticism of a young Sfondrati-Piccolomini before his assembled condottiere brothers and cousins, I believe I should have declined. And I'm a madman! But damned if they didn't show up—a hundred of the parasites, at the least. Gabbling away as soon as they took their seats. The condottiere listened politely for an hour or so, while the critics dissected every error of the young artist—Alessandro, wasn't it?—"

"Domenico," I corrected.

"Ah, yes! Anyway, on and on they went, explaining how the lad had done everything wrong—the colors, the strokes, the perspective—even the quality of the canvas and the grain of the wood on the frame. But they reserved their fiercest criticism for the actual content of the painting. On this the critics were united—unusual circumstance!—that the depiction of five soldiers of fortune sitting about a table quaffing their wine was a most unsuitable subject for a portrait entitled *Gods At Their Pleasure*."

"The critics never grew up in the Sfondrati-Piccolomini clan," I remarked, "where respect for one's elders is not to be taken lightly. As it happens, my uncles were the models for the portrait."

"You don't say! Odd, really. I myself didn't see any resemblance at all between the divine, serene, and radiant features in the portrait and the—you will take no offense?—scarred, raffish and altogether wicked-looked visages of your uncles. The more so once they began their own criticism of the critics! Such a scene! It was marvelous! I don't imagine half of the critics managed to escape the auditorium alive."

"Not many critics left in Ozar to this day, that's a fact," I commented.

"Just think of it! Such a civilized place, the Ozarine! Rapacious, grasping lot of imperialists, of course. But civilized. Here in Grotum, your critics are a positive plague, a scandal, a threat to public health! Ask any sullen, malcontented little boy or girl who can't tie their shoelaces what they want to be when they grow up and they'll not hesitate for an instant—want to be a critic! Even find a few in the mental asylums. Not many—criticism is in the main a disease of sane people. And they don't last long, of course. It's not conducive to long life, being a critic locked up with a bunch of psychopaths."

Wolfgang continued on in this vein for a minute or so longer, but then he discontinued his discourse. We

were now almost at the Dreary Gate. We were about
to discover if Wolfgang's plan would work.

But just as we drew up before the gate, an interruption occurred. A pack of cavalry horses were drawn
up before a saloon located right next to the gate—if
the noble term "cavalry horses" can be applied to as
sorry and broken-down a lot of nags as I ever laid eyes
on. Just as our dray pulled even with the saloon, a disordered mob of soldiery poured out of its swinging
doors, most still clutching their jugs. In their middle,
hoisted on their shoulders, was a portly captain.

"Make way! Make way!" bellowed this wight. "Clear
the gate for the Royal Goimr Commandos!"

The soldiers manning the Dreary Gate shooed all
civilians to one side and opened the portal. In the
event, their bustling energy was wasted, for it took the
Commandos a full ten minutes to saddle up and ride
off. A good bit of this time was consumed by the actual
difficulty of attaining their seats on the high perches
of the saddles, being, as they were, utterly drunken.
But most of the delay was caused by the captain's
command to "blacken their faces." This act, the blacking
of commandos' faces to ensure stealth in the night,
seemed somewhat inappropriate for horsemen in broad
daylight. But the commandos clearly prized this cherished privilege of their status, and they set about blacking their faces with a vigor. The martial effect, however,
was ruined by their childish levity in smearing each
other with the greasepaint.

"Goimr is not, I am beginning to deduce, one of the
military behemoths of Grotum," was my whispered
comment to Wolfgang.

He even managed a ventriloquist snort.

Eventually, the Commandos assembled into a ragged
file, their horses looking gloomier by the minute. The
captain whipped his plumed hat off his head (the bright

ostrich feather clashed, I thought, with the logic of the blackened face) and waved it about.

"Citizens of Goimr!" he cried, addressing the small crowd which was gazing upon the Commandos. "Your noble Commandos are off to capture the renegade Zulkeh—the sorcerer satanic!—the—" Here he fell off his horse. When he clambered back on, he made to resume his speech, but his now-surly horse would have none of it, and charged through the gate. The rest of the Commandos lunged off in pursuit.

The guards at the gate drew their swords in a ragged salute.

"Hail the noble Royal Commandos!" cried the sergeant.

"Hail the nobleroilcomdos," muttered the guards in response.

"Death to the satanic sorcerer Zulkeh!" cried the sergeant.

"Death to the s'tancsorcerZully," muttered the guards apathetically.

These duties performed, the sergeant and the guards resumed their inspection of the papers of those seeking passage through the gate. My hopes of success in deceiving these vigilant men of war, let me say, were now quite high.

Soon enough, it was our turn. My papers were examined cursorily. The sergeant essayed a squaring of the shoulders in respect of Gerard's signature, failed miserably, resumed his slouch, and waved us through.

Since he seemed harmless enough, I decided to satisfy my curiosity.

"Who is this sorcerer the Commandos are pursuing?" I asked.

I got back in reply a garbled and not very coherent account of the misdeeds of the wizard Zulkeh, in which the kernel of driving the King mad was intermingling with a bouillabaisse of other crimes. I particularly enjoyed the charge of "public urination."

Then, we were delayed by the soldiers gawking at Wolfgang.

"Ay, an' is he the great icon, or what, lads?" demanded one of the guards. His fellows indicated, with none-too-convincing expressions of piety, their agreement with his awed opinion.

"St. Athelbert, idn't he?" asked the devout guard.

I frowned fiercely. "Ignorant dolt! 'Tis the spitting image of St. Abblerede—patron saint of lunatics and criminals!"

The fellow looked properly abashed, and with no further ado I cracked the whip and ordered Gwendolyn to move smartly, d'ye hear? I suspected, from the hunch of her shoulders and the tightening of her jaws, that I would pay for it later.

Once we were beyond earshot of the gate, now on a dirt road leading into the countryside, Wolfgang spoke in a more normal tone of voice.

"There is no patron saint of lunatics," he cackled. "Plenty for criminals, of course, but we raving types have been read out of the state of Holy Grace. Quite absurd, really, when you consider that almost all saints were obviously demented. How they get sanctified, you know? Going off and irritating all sorts of aborigines who boil them in oil or shoot them full of arrows or whatnot. I ask you, who but a madman would do such things?"

I interrupted what, with my growing experience, I could detect as a new round of witless babble.

"I should think the Commandos will capture the wizard soon enough," I remarked.

That set off a new round of cackling from the icon. Gwendolyn's shoulders were quivering—with humor, I realized, considerably relieved.

"And why not? Sure, they're as sorry a lot of soldiery as I've ever seen, but they're still soldiers on horseback pursuing a coach. I grant you, the coach left two days ago, but they should still be able to catch up easily, even allowing for drunken binges along the way."

"No doubt, if they could simply follow the coach. But the coach took the direct route, through the Grimwald, whereas the soldiers will have to take the roundabout road, through the marsh and the mountains."

"Why don't they just follow the coach?"

More cackling.

"My boy, you are such an innocent! Clear enough, you're a stranger to Grotum. The Grimwald, lad, is Grotum's oldest and greatest forest."

"So?"

"So! Are you that ignorant? Snarls, boy, snarls! They abound in the Grimwald—and forest snarls, to boot! Goes without saying, of course—what other kind of snarls would you find in a forest but forest snarls?"

I pondered his words, trying to decide if I was the butt of a joke. It's a crude but common form of humor—to mock a newcomer by telling him tall tales of the local surroundings. I had heard of snarls, of course. What Ozarine was not enthralled, as a child, by the endless tales of those monsters of the Groutch wilds? But as I grew older, I wrote the tales off as fiction for children—in a class with Good Saint Nick and the Tooth Fairy.

I decided Wolfgang was too weird for crude mockery.

"So the snarls actually exist?"

"Of course they exist! You can find them in all the wild parts of Grotum! Forest snarls, mountain snarls, swamp snarls, rock snarls, prairie snarls—the list is well nigh endless. Rather rare creatures, mostly, except in some places. Joe's Favorite Woods swarms with them, of course. And they're very abundant in the Grimwald."

"I still don't understand why the soldiers can't traverse the forest. I mean, if a coach can get through, then I should think a body of armed men would have no difficulty whatsoever."

"My boy, my boy, it's not like that at all. The coach will get through because the snarls will probably leave it alone. Snarls generally don't pester simple travelers. But soldiers! Oh, no, it simply won't do. Take great offense at soldiery, snarls do. Gobble them up with a ferocity. Police too."

"You mean neither soldiers nor police can enter the Grimwald?"

"Not sane ones. Insane ones could, it goes without saying. Snarls are rather fond of lunatics. But what madman would be so crazy as to enlist in the army? Not to mention the police!"

"The Grimwald must be a haven for poachers, then."

This last remark of mine not only set off a new round of cackling but caused Gwendolyn's shoulders to positively heave with humor.

"Such an innocent!" giggled Wolfgang. "Such an ignoramus! Lad, one does not poach in a snarl forest. Believe me, one doesn't. Not, at least, unless one is seeking a quick and messy form of suicide."

I fell silent, disgruntled, if the truth be told, by this unseemly mirth at my expense. The day wore on, our cart making slow but steady progress. Gwendolyn showed no signs of tiring, even hauling our great heavy load. I now realized that she was not only extraordinarily large, but incredibly strong. At first, I would have said, incredibly strong for a woman. By the end of the day, when we finally decided to stop for the night by the roadside, and I observed her lowering the cart without so much as a drop of sweat on her brow, it finally dawned on me that she was easily the strongest human I had ever known. In the years to come, I was only forced to qualify that assessment once, when I met her brother.

That realization only made the ensuing situation the more uncomfortable!

For, after the few minutes required to make our camp for the night—some few yards from the road-side, in a small grove—I realized that Gwendolyn and Wolfgang were gazing at me with a strange intensity. Wolfgang's expression positively radiated amusement. Gwendolyn's was much harder to read. Repressed anger, an odd, cold kind of humor. I was not certain.

"What's this about?" I queried.

Gwendolyn said nothing, her face now like a mask. Wolfgang giggled.

"Well," he said, "it's actually the immemorial and time-honored custom in Grotum, at the end of a day's haul, for the draywoman to provide sexual service for the draymaster."

My face must have flushed red. Partly from embarrassment, partly—I cannot deny it—because the image his words brought to my mind caused a sudden rush of passion to fall over me.

"Barbarous!" I cried. "Barbarous!" I broke into a fit of coughing. Once recovered, I looked at Gwendolyn and said: "I assure you, Gwendolyn, I have no intention of respecting such an infamous custom."

Contrary woman!

Far from bringing praise for my couth gentility, my words brought down on my unoffending head a veritable torrent of abuse! The gist of which was:

And who was I, the slimy Ozarine, to give myself great airs and sneer at the barbarous backwardness of Grotum, when that barbarous state was maintained with Ozarine influence and money?

This was but the prelude to an impassioned speech on the nefarious imperial plots of Ozarae, its vampiric grasp on Grotum, its suborning of all official Groutch institutions (not, to hear her speak, that she was filled with any great admiration for these institutions to begin with!), and so on, and so on, and so on. I was lost after a few minutes—not so much because I disagreed with her logic but because I simply couldn't follow it. Politics, statesmanship, all that, were of no interest to me whatsoever. I was an artist, not a diplomat! Ironic, actually, in light of subsequent events.

Finally, she wound down. Wolfgang cackled.

"I do believe you've left the poor confused lad out at sea without a compass," he giggled.

"But surely," I protested to Gwendolyn, "you have no liking for this hallowed Groutch draymaster's custom?"

"Of course not!" she snarled. "Of course it's barbarous! Women are treated like beasts of burden in Grotum, for the most part. And most of the sexual customs belong in a cesspool. I've met few enough draymasters I wouldn't cheerfully butcher. Will butcher some of them, come the revolution. Reactionary dogs! Not much better than slavers!"

She growled, then burst into a sudden grin.

"I will admit you handle that whip well. The hardest part of the whole day, that was, trying to keep from laughing at the sight of the draymasters howling and scurrying for cover. And I thoroughly enjoyed trampling the two of them."

She eyed me speculatively. "You might want to get rid of those scalps, by the way. They're drawing flies."

I had forgotten them. I yanked them out of my belt and flung them into the woods. When I turned back, alas, the fierce scowl was back on her face.

"I just don't want to hear it from an Ozarine. I think

it's what angers me the most. If the Ozarines were honest about their imperialism, it'd be bad enough. But to have to listen to the vultures chide we crude and uncouth Groutch for our uncivilized ways—while they plunder us like pirates!" She took a deep breath. "Damn all hypocrites!"

I made an unwise attempt to mollify her.

"Actually, Gwendolyn, there's quite a great admiration and fascination for Grotum among many Ozarines. Myself included! Why, as a—"

"Oh, spare me!" She snorted. "Think I don't know every Ozarine bratling isn't brought up on tales of mysterious and romantic Grotum? Hah! I've even read a few of those romantic adventure novels which are so popular in Ozar. One of them even had the hero magically incarnated as a Groutch himself. A knight, naturally, gallivanting about the countryside with noble Groutch companions, rescuing fair maidens. Typical Ozarine horseshit! Why doesn't somebody write a true novel? You know, where the hero's magically incarnated as a Groutch peasant—better yet, the wife of a Groutch peasant! It'd be such a jolly romantic book! Half her children—and she'll drop 'em once a year till she dries up or dies—dead of disease or hunger before they're five years of age. Plowing the fields day after day, toil from the time she's old enough to walk to the time she can't move from her deathbed. A despairing, beaten down husband, drunk half the time—and why not?—except all his rage will fall on her and the children."

She fell silent for a moment, breathing heavily. Wolfgang interjected, saying mildly: "Actually, the boy's not really responsible for all that, Gwendolyn. At least, in the short time we've made his acquaintance, I haven't noticed him charging about spreading mass disease and misery."

Gwendolyn glared at him, then sighed.

"I know, I know. It's unfair of me to throw it on to Benvenuti's head. I shouldn't personalize these things. But still, it infuriates me, the way the Ozarines create a world that perpetuates—makes worse!—every injustice in it, and then cluck their tongues at the barbarity of it all."

It was the first time in my life that I didn't just walk away from a political argument. I think it was the fierce flame in her, that drew me like a moth—and didn't I know, even then, that it usually turns out badly for the moth! Then, too, there was this—which, I admit, cut a little close to Gwendolyn's point, so I always kept it to myself—that she made every Ozarine lass I'd known seem like a pale shadow. Fact is, the damned woman was a romanticist's dream! And what artist isn't a romantic? Not any Sfondrati-Piccomolinis. At least, not from my—admittedly somewhat disreputable—branch of the clan. My branch of the clan, truth to tell, has always produced a lot more adventurers than scholars.

I did not, of course, attempt to argue the politics of her persuasion. For one thing, I would have been completely over my head. Even at that young age, I had enough sense not to dispute doctrine with a hardened Groutch revolutionist! For another, I wasn't at all sure I didn't agree with her, insofar as I'd ever given any thought to political questions. My uncles had certainly never instilled in me any great feeling of pride in "the grandeur of Ozar."

But I did make the attempt to present myself in a different perspective. And so, as our campfire burned a spot of light in the darkness, I spoke quietly of my lifelong fascination with Grotum. Begun, to be sure, from a child's fairy tales. But, as I grew older, I came to understand the centrality of Grotum to all the world's art and literature. This reality was known to all students of the arts, and often commented on by the scholars—some with admiration, most with rueful asperity, some even with despair. But directly or indirectly, Grotum acted like a great dark planet, which drew into its orbit all the brighter but smaller orbs.

She said nothing, but she listened to me. Rather intently, I think. When I was done, she did not break her silence. But I thought—or so I hoped—that there was less tension in the set of her shoulders.

"We'd best get some sleep," she said. Then, as she was rolling up in her blanket, a little chuckle, and she added: "You'll need to be well rested tomorrow, Benvenuti, so your whip hand doesn't waver. But I owe you for the draymasters, so I'll give you one scratch if you cut it too fine. One only, mind! Or it's the gutting blade."

It took us two days to get through the Goimric countryside to the edge of the forest. The trip was uneventful, save for one occasion late in the afternoon of the second day, when we were overtaken by a platoon of cavalry. They came galloping up the road behind us, waving their sabers and hallooing war cries. But it became obvious that they were not interested in us. The platoon charged right by without so much as a glance in our direction. One of the cavalrymen, however, fell off his horse as he tried to ride around the cart. He landed in the road with a great thump.

I hopped off and went over to him. He was sitting up, shaking his head. I leaned over and helped him to his feet.

"Are you all right?" I asked.

"Guess so," he muttered. He looked around for his horse. The nag was off in a field some thirty yards distant. The soldier pursed his lips and whistled. The nag looked at him, defecated, and trotted away.

"Damn the beast!" snarled the soldier. "Now I'll have to finish the charge on foot."

"Is there a battle ahead?" I asked.

The soldier looked at me like I was retarded.

"Would I be charging into a battle?" he demanded. "Haven't you heard? The palace burned down! The heirs to the throne are all dead. The word is we'll have a new government." He swelled his scrawny chest. "A military government!"

He dusted off his clothes. "So, anyway, the captain ordered us to charge the tavern up the road. Free drinks, there'll be." He puffed out his chest again. "After that, we'll maybe burn one or two villages."

He retrieved his sword from the road and waved it above his head.

"For junta and country!" he cried, and began a shambling run up the road.

After I resumed my seat, Gwendolyn started the cart in motion.

"That sounds bad," I commented.

"What do you care about the Royal Palace?" demanded Gwendolyn.

"Not that. Favor to the world, burning down that pile of refuse. No, I meant the part about the military government. You heard him. It's obvious the soldiery'll take it as an excuse to commit atrocities on the population."

Gwendolyn laughed. Behind me, Wolfgang giggled.

"What's so funny?" I asked, in a resigned voice. I was getting tired of being the butt of their humor.

"This is Goimr, my boy," cackled Wolfgang. "Now, if this was Sfinctria, or even Pryggia, your fears would have substance. Quite the proper committers of atrocities, your Sfinctrian army. And the Pryggs are no slouches, either. But Goimric soldiers? Commit atrocities? I fear you overestimate their capabilities."

"The last time the Goimric army tried to plunder a village," commented Gwendolyn, "the inhabitants sent them packing." She looked back at me, grinning like a wolf. "And they were lucky the men were still in the fields. They suffered thirty percent casualties at the hands of the women and children."

"They're really that bad?"

"As you have earlier surmised yourself," remarked Wolfgang, "Grotum does not tremble at the rattling of Goimric sabers."

I shook my head. "They'll get better, I'm afraid. I don't know much about politics, but I spent enough time around my uncles to know that Ozar will be sending in military advisers, soon enough."

"With your uncles along, no doubt," came Gwendolyn's sneering voice, "like proper soldiers of fortune."

I controlled my temper. "Actually," I replied in a calm voice, "they'll not be involved. They refuse to participate in such affairs. It's one of the reasons they always turn down the offers of the Ozarine government to give them regular commissions. They say occupation work corrodes the soul."

Wolfgang cackled. "Such a crazy world! Mercenaries with honor! Of course, they are Sfondrati-Piccolominis."

I remembered the last emissary of the Senate, sent packing from our house with a boot mark on his behind. Ludovigo's boot, that'd been—he was always the most ill-tempered of my condottiere uncles.

"Have you got a war somewhere?" he'd demanded of the emissary. "A real war, I'm talking about?"

The emissary had hemmed and hawed, rambling on about the geostrategic significance of the pacification of some far distant land I'd never heard of. But he didn't get very far along. Ludovigo is not a patient man.

The boot had followed, with my other uncles contrib-
uting verbal mayhem.

When the emissary was gone, scuttling down the
street, Ludovigo had turned to me, scowling and chewing his mustachios.

"Remember this, boy," he'd growled. "Seventeen, you
are now. You'll be a grown man soon, responsible for
your actions." His glare was joined by that of my other
uncles. "The family will forgive a wolf, but we've no
mercy for jackals."

"Certainly not!" I'd exclaimed, not really understanding the ins and outs of the matter. But I understood
my uncle's boot.

"What a world we've produced," sighed Ludovigo.
He'd resumed his seat, planted his boot on the table,
drained his mug. "There was a time when it was a
proud thing, to be an Ozarine. Go back in the family
line, you'll find that plenty of Sfondrati-Piccolominis
served in the army of Ozarae. With pride and distinction. Pride and distinction." He sneered. "Now, I'd as
soon join a pack of hyenas."

"I'd rather join a pack of hyenas," my uncle Rodrigo
had contributed. "Never claim to be more than scav-
engers, your honest hyenas."

"Won't hear a hyena prate on and on about the
grandeur of the pack and the glory of the carrion,"
added Larue.

"Unless it's a scholar hyena," chuckled Filoberto. "I
hear our distant cousin, Rhodes Sfondrati-Piccolomini,
has just come out with a new book—*The Ozarine
Century*, it's called."

"I've read it," said Larue. "Drones on and on about
the Burden of Ozar, as he calls it. That's scholar-speak
for 'let's loot everything, for the lootee's best interest.'
Would you believe, the fool even calls for a new
attempt at conquering the Sssuj?"

Great gales of laughter had greeted that last statement. When their glee subsided, however, my uncles' gloom had returned. The long silence had finally been broken by my uncle Ludovigo, his voice hard as stone.

"That fool belongs to another branch of the clan. In our branch, in our family—we've had eagles and falcons, and owls, and more than a few peacocks and dodos. But there's never been a vulture." He'd fixed me with his glare. "You hear me, boy?"

I was recalled back to the present by Wolfgang's voice.

"There it is. The Grimwald."

I looked up. On the horizon, ahead and to my right, I could see a ragged, dark green line. Even from the distance, it looked somehow foreboding.

I said as much, and Wolfgang giggled. "Nonsense! It's a marvelous place, the Grimwald. Full of wonder and enchantment! Unicorns, even! The world's greatest mystery, you know."

"What's that?" I asked.

"Why, it's obvious! How do unicorns propagate, when they've got this fetish about virginity?" He cackled. "I've spent years trying to figure it out. Even asked the head psychiatrist at the asylum. The man's a genius, you know? But he was no help, at all. Said that unicorns were just a figment of my imagination."

"They are," said Gwendolyn forcefully.

"Well, of course, I know that!" Wolfgang's voice was full of aggrievement. "I'm not stupid, you know, just insane. But that's the whole point! How do unicorns propagate in my imagination, when they've got this fetish about virginity? My imagination certainly doesn't. Have a fetish about virginity, I mean." He howled like a lunatic. "Quite the contrary! A cornucopia of sexual perversion, it is, my imagination. I've scolded it many times, but it keeps coming up with the wildest ideas! For instance—"

"Wolfgang, shut up!" roared Gwendolyn.

"Such a prude! Oh, very well. But, anyway, for some reason my imagination comes up short whenever it tries to picture unicorns propagating. Years, I've spent, trying to figure out why. It's very important, you know, for a lunatic to understand his imagination. Sane people never have to worry about it, of course. You can just pass things off by saying 'it's just my imagination.' But a dement can't do that, because we live in the world of our imagination. So—"

"Wolfgang, shut up!" roared Gwendolyn.

"But, my dear Gwendolyn, you're missing the whole point! Sane people are such cripples! Hamstrung, you are, by the real world. Whereas a madman can just dismiss the problem by saying 'it's just the real world,' and go on about the important business, which is imagining—"

Gwendolyn heaved herself out of the yoke and stalked back to the cart. She glared up at the towering figure of the madman, still sitting in the pose of an icon.

"If you don't shut up," she hissed between her teeth, "the real world will intrude upon your imagination this very minute."

I was afraid a row might break out, with me caught between a giant and an Amazon. But Wolfgang only smirked and said: "I shall become quite the proper icon, then. Full of grace."

And, indeed, he fell silent for the rest of the journey into the Grimwald, except for a whisper meant only for my ears.

"Such a solemn woman, she is. You really must try and brighten up her spirits, young man."

Such was, in fact, my very hope. But I wasn't about to acknowledge the same to a lunatic. Still, my stiff back must have transmitted some of my feelings, for I could hear Wolfgang chuckling behind me.

A short distance further, Gwendolyn turned the cart down a narrow, rutted dirt path. We were now headed directly for the forest, and she began to pick up the pace. A half hour later, the path entered beneath the loom of the Grimwald. Gwendolyn shrugged out of the yoke.

"We can leave the cart here," she said. "No one will find it for days. By then we'll be long gone, deep into the forest."

I hopped off the cart. Wolfgang arose, as limber as if he hadn't spent the last three days posing as a statue. For him, stepping off the cart was not much more than for a boy to step off a stool. It took but a moment for the three of us to push the cart into some bushes, out of sight of any casual passer-by.

Gwendolyn led the way into the forest. The dirt path quickly became a faint trail winding through the immense trees of the forest. Those trees! Never had I seen anything like them, so huge they were, and so densely packed. Every variety of tree, to boot, ever-green and hardwoods mixed together with no rhyme or reason that I could see.

Crazy he might have been, but Wolfgang had an uncanny ability to discern a person's thoughts.

"Don't try to figure out the ecology of the Grimwald, Benvenuti. Can't be done, you know? The scholars gave it up long ago, after my great-grandfather Kirkpatrick went mad in the attempt. Locked him up, poor man, after he started babbling at the annual meeting of the Philosophical Society that the Grimwald was the last surviving remnant of the primeval *Eozoon*. Such a brilliant naturalist! I'm quite partial to his theory of the nummulosphere, myself. You're familiar with it, of course?"

I shook my head.

"What? Never heard of Kirkpatrick's theory?" He grimaced. "Such a horrible state modern education's fallen to! Not surprising, of course, in Ozar. You Ozarines are such incorrigible rationalists. But even here in Grotum the children are not instructed in the theory of the nummulosphere. And such a marvelous theory! Kirkpatrick claims the whole world was built up, bit by bit, by the action of single-celled forams—amoebas, sort of. Claims you can see their fossils everywhere, if you just look closely enough. Unfortunately, he's been the only one able to look closely enough, so they say he's a crackpot. Too bad, really. His theory's so much more imaginative than all this dry stuff about tectonic plates. Can there be anything more boring than igneous rock? Forams, now—there's a lively basis for world-building!" And on he droned, making absolutely no sense at all. But I had gotten accustomed to shutting out his prattle.

By nightfall, we had penetrated a fair distance into the forest. Gwendolyn apparently knew where we were going—I myself was hopelessly lost—for when we entered a small clearing, she said: "This is it. We'll camp here for the night."

The next morning, Wolfgang announced that we would have to part company.

"I'll be going that way," he said, gesturing vaguely to the northeast. "Got to catch up with the wizard, you know, and you two are off to quite different parts."

Gwendolyn looked at him, hesitated, then spoke. "I will ask you again. Why are you—and everyone else in the world, it seems—so interested in this wizard?"

A look of pure innocence came upon Wolfgang's face. "Me? Interested in Zulkeh?"

Gwendolyn exploded. *"Don't lie to me, Wolfgang!*

It must have taken you years to build those secret rooms and tunnels under the death house. And all so you could spy on this Zulkeh! Why? And why is everyone else so concerned with him? Why did Hildegard send me off on this wild goose chase? *Why?*"

"I've been interested in Zulkeh and his doings for years," responded Wolfgang, a rare tone of seriousness in his voice. "Impossible to explain why, in any terms that would make sense to you. But it's my main project in life, actually. It's because of Joe, of course."

Seeing the fierce frown on Gwendolyn's face, Wolfgang sighed.

"You are so unreasonable about this, Gwendolyn! Don't you think you should take the Joe question a bit more seriously, seeing as how everyone else does— friends and foes alike? Or do you really think the Fangs of Piety—not to mention Hildegard—are all as crazy as me?"

"They're crazier," snapped Gwendolyn. "At least you admit you're a lunatic. Hildegard lives in the clouds. Oh, I love her dearly. And she's a friend to the underground, I'd be the last to deny it. That's why I agreed to carry out this mission for her. I owe her plenty of favors—the whole movement does, for that matter. But she's still nuts! She claims to correspond with God!"

"Oh, but she does!" exclaimed Wolfgang. "Has a whole room in the Abbey just to store the Old Geister's stone tablets. Absolutely compulsive, that woman. Won't throw away anything. I'd certainly throw away God's stone tablets, if He sent me the kind of nasty notes He sends her!" He shook his head. "But she keeps right on with her correspondence. Says it's her bounden duty as a pious Abbess to tell God the plain and simple truth about Himself, even if He doesn't want to hear it. Which He certainly doesn't! The Deity doesn't take well to criticism, you know, and my aunt has quite the sharp tongue."

Gwendolyn threw up her hands. "I give up! The Fangs I can understand. Those reactionary maniacs are just as crazy as you are, but at least they deal with the real world."

"Well, of course they do!" exclaimed Wolfgang. "What's the point of being a vicious reactionary, if you're not going to deal with the real world? Might as well be a liberal!" He shuddered. "Such sane people, liberals. Really ought to be locked up, the bunch of them. For their own sake, if nothing else. Not that I'd wish a pack of whining liberals on a lunatic asylum! The rest of the inmates would all commit suicide, just to escape the platitudes."

He paused, beaming down on Gwendolyn.

"I can see you're about to get angry with me, again. Can't be helped, I suppose. Not too many sweet-tempered revolutionaries around. Executions, torture, imprisonment—doesn't make for placid, jolly types. Still, I think you should—"

Gwendolyn silenced him with a sharp gesture. "Never mind what you think I should do." Suddenly she laughed. "After all these years, you'd think I'd know better than to try to get any sense out of you."

She stared off into the forest for a moment, then turned back to the giant.

"All right," she said, "I suppose I can trust you. And it means nothing to me, anyway. The message which I was to deliver to Zulkeh from Hildegard was this. I was to tell him that Hildegard had a vision—"

"I knew it! She's had another vision!" cried Wolfgang, clapping his huge hands like a child filled with glee.

"—and in this vision she saw Zulkeh, with a long

beard—long, all the way down to his feet. And then, out from under his wizard's hat, crawled a monster. The monster made its way down to the ground, using the wizard's beard like a rope. It took the monster a long time to get down, she said, but once—"

"Of course it took the monster a long time!" cried Wolfgang. "That's such a long and perilous journey, climbing down a sorcerer's beard!"

Gwendolyn scowled at the interruption, then continued.

"But once the monster reached the ground, it began to swell, and grow, like a storm cloud. And it was very angry. And then the world ended."

She took a breath. "And that's it. That's the message. Makes no sense to me, at all."

She stopped, gaping with astonishment. For the giant lunatic started capering around the meadow, leaping and doing cartwheels, and howling like a banshee.

"He's finally flipped," I said.

Gwendolyn shook her head. "No—at least, no more than usual. He's just very happy and excited."

Sure enough, after a couple of minutes of these bizarre acrobatics, Wolfgang calmed down and shambled back over to where we were standing. Tears of joy were streaming down his cheeks.

"Best news I've heard in years!" he boomed. "Marvelous! Absolutely marvelous! I'd be ecstatic even if I'd had the vision in one of my hallucinations—but coming from Hildegard!" He grinned, drooling. "Her visions are infallible, you know."

"I don't suppose you'd explain what it means?" asked Gwendolyn.

Wolfgang looked about, like a little boy trying to keep a secret.

"Well, I suppose I could give you a hint. It means

the world's going to end. Way ahead of my schedule, it looks like."

Gwendolyn visibly restrained her temper. "This is good news?"

Wolfgang was shocked. "Well, of course it's good news!" Then he clapped his head with his hand. "Oh, of course! You think—no! no! Dear Gwendolyn! You have such a grim, apocalyptic view of things! Twilight of the gods, all that rot. No, dear, the world's going to end like—like, how shall I put it?—yes! Like all the low things in life end! That's it! Like all the things that crawl, and lie in the mud, and stink, and wriggle."

He stooped, bringing his face down. "Now do you see?"

"No, I don't!" exclaimed Gwendolyn.

Wolfgang straightened, sighed. "We look at things so differently, dear. From different angles, you might say."

He reached out and stroked her cheek.

"But I don't care, Gwendolyn. On the last day of the world—if you don't get yourself killed!—we'll see everything just the same. And in the meantime, go your way with all my love and hope. For I cherish you."

Gwendolyn took his hand and held it to her cheek.

Suddenly, she stepped back. "Be off with you! You damned lunatic. Off to chase after the wizard, I suppose."

Wolfgang beamed. "Yes! Off to Prygg!" And with no further ado he charged into the forest. The trees shook with his passage, the underbrush hissed their protest. But, not more than a minute later, while Gwendolyn and I remained unmoving in the clearing, the sights and sounds of his return became evident. Wolfgang reappeared, moving toward us in that awkward-looking shamble that covered ground amazingly quickly.

Two seconds later he was standing in front of me, waving his arms about.

"I'm so forgetful!" he cried. "I forgot to say good-bye to Benvenuti! Can you forgive me, dear boy?"

I nodded. "Think nothing of it."

"Such a polite lad! Such a credit to his family!"

He extended his hand and shook mine. My—by normal standards—large hand was completely lost in his huge fist.

"Perhaps we will meet again," I said, not really taking the formula seriously.

"Of course we will!" cried the giant. "It's inevitable! You're up to your knees in Joe business, boy, and sinking fast! Of course we'll meet again! But until then, take care."

And again he was off. Within a minute, all sign of him was gone. I turned to Gwendolyn.

"What now?"

For a few seconds longer, she continued to stare into the forest where Wolfgang had disappeared. Then she motioned to the left with her head.

"That way."

PART III

The Which Represents a
Lacuna in my Illustrious Ancestors'
Account, Fortunately Made Good By My
Discovery of a Long Lost Manuscript by
the Undeservedly Obscure *Littérateur*,
Korzeniowski Laebmauntsforscynneweëld,
Companion of the Consortium Director of
Companies in That Superlative
Financier's Most Bitter and
Troubled Exile.

The manuscript which follows herein requires a brief
introduction, if I may take this liberty as your narrator.
For, alas, my ancestors' chronicle suffers from an unfortunate *lacuna* with regard to the account of the wizard
Zulkeh's journey from Goimr to the Caravanserai.

The gentle reader will recall that the precipitous
departure of the coach from the travel station of Goimr
caused the dwarf Shelyid to be hurtled to the floor.
"Master, we're off!" cried the gnome, to which the
wizard responded: "Well spoken, dwarf. Our journey
has begun." Know, gentle reader, that these words were

scribed by the illustrious Alfred CCLVI even as he was himself flying through the air, having lost his perch on Shelyid's eyebrow (this precarious vantage point being the preferred scribal seat of the intrepid chronicler) due to the gnome's clumsiness. In his devotion to duty, Alfred CCLVI did not notice that his airborne trajectory was taking him through the window and out of the coach entirely. This fact was only brought to his attention when the industrious scribe found himself sprawled in six-legged disarray upon the cobblestones, the coach wherein reposed his life's work racing away at great speed. Hastily retrieving his scattered notes, Alfred CCLVI set off in hot pursuit.

Of the odyssey which followed, the epic tale of Alfred CCLVI's endeavor to regain the wizard's coach, I will say nothing. The interested reader is referred to Alfred CCLVI's own account of his adventures, the classic *Across the Grimwald On 80 Hosts*. For our purposes here, it suffices to say that Alfred CCLVI did not rejoin his clan until the arrival of the wizard in the Caravanserai.

At once, Alfred CCLVI inquired if any of his senior apprentices had compiled sufficiently competent notes to enable the great scribe to reconstruct the events of the wizard's journey. Alas, he found their haphazard jottings entirely inadequate. Hence did the irate chronicler order the immediate fumigation of his senior apprentices.

This act was perhaps hasty and ill-considered. For it resulted in the rise to senior apprenticeship of that unfortunate individual later to become the notorious Alfred CCLVII. But that disgraceful episode belongs to a later portion of our chronicle. For the moment, we are left with the embarrassment of a yawning gap in the smooth unfolding of our tale.

It gives me great pleasure to announce, however, that

this gap has now been filled. After years of diligent search, your humble narrator was eventually able to uncover a long lost manuscript written by Korzeniowski Laebmauntsforscynneweëld. The author of this manuscript is one of the least well known illuminati of the famed scholarly clan. Yet, as the gentle reader will soon have occasion to determine for himself, Korzeniowski's obscurity is entirely undeserved. It results solely from the fact that—unlike the vast majority of his clan, who made a pusillanimous accommodation to the forces which triumphed in the Great Calamity—Korzeniowski Laebmauntsforscynneweëld remained true to Reason and chose exile over surrender. Thus did he accompany the Director of Companies in that latter's precipitous flight from the Great Calamity.

Of the odyssey which followed, the epic tale of the voyage of Ozarae's greatest nabob and his companions across the uncharted oceans in a luxury yacht to their final exile in the islands, I will say nothing. The interested reader is referred to Nordhoffandhall Laebmauntsforscynneweëld's classic account, *Financiers Against The Sea*.

The troubled and bitter exile of the Director of Companies in the heathen islands was, as the gentle reader will soon discover, brief. The final end of the leader who, prior to the Great Calamity, was recognized the world over as the supreme embodiment of social discipline, can now be told. For not only does Korzeniowski's tale recount, long after the event, the journey of the wizard Zulkeh from Goimr to the Caravanserai, but it unfolds as well the last moments of the life of the Director of Companies, the greatest man of his epoch.

Thus, it is with great pleasure as a chronicler, combined with deep sadness as a louse of Reason, that I herewith present the tale.

~~~

The Last of the Line
By Korzeniowski Laebmauntsforscynneweëld
(beginning portion)

The native boy came onto the deck bearing a tray; upon it rested four glasses—filled with an amber liquid. He moved silently to the railing; set the tray upon the stool by the Director's side. The Director of Companies turned from his view of the ocean—glanced down at the tray—glared fiercely at the servant.

"Lord!" he exclaimed. "Jim, I told you to bring drinks for everyone!"

The boy gazed impassively at the Director; then, his eyes sweeping the deck in a glance, took in the other four of us.

"But, sahib," he said in his barbarous accent, "tuan tu maik fo."

"I know two and two makes four, you ninny!" roared the Director. "There are five of us!"

No expression crossed Jim's face; his black eyes stared opaquely at the four glasses; leaning over the rail, he peered at his reflection in the waters; unknowable thoughts moved through his mind.

"Mistaik iz mine," he muttered, and left the deck.

"Lord in heaven, rescue me!" snarled the Director. "I don't believe the incompetence of these damned natives. Can't even count the fingers on one hand." He sighed heavily and stared out over the ocean. The rays of the setting sun gleamed in the mirror of the sea; of a sudden, he thrust to his feet and gripped the railing.

"Under Western's eyes," he said sadly, "this sort of thing never happened."

We watched his back affectionately as he stood looking seaward. We knew how sorely he felt the loss of his old and trusted valet; and while this loss was but the least of the calamities which had befallen him, perhaps, for that very reason, it vexed him the most. For me, things were what they were; Barley—well, Barley was Barley; as for the accountant and the lawyer, the worst of it was—that it was. But for the Director it was an affront to his entire spirit. The typhoon of his youth had brought him to the pinnacle of success and power; only then, as he stretched forth the maturity of his grasp, to find his victory swept away by the sudden madness; leaving him as he was now, an outcast of the islands in an alien world.

"It was all Mayer's folly!" he roared suddenly, without looking around. "He should have crushed the rebel when he had the chance! The idiots! All of them!" He glowered out to sea; then spoke again. "Then—then! God, to think of it—the opportunities lost! Bungled from the beginning; Mayer was only the last of the fools. From the beginning, I say! Inkman and the Angel could have done it—at one stroke—they had the chance! I gave them all they asked—then!—at the beginning!—even the Rap Sheet! And for what? For what? To think of it!" He hurled his glass into the sea.

A long silence followed his outburst. All of us shared his gloom. Barring an unexpected smile of fortune, there was no reason to believe the usurpers would not remain the inheritors of the labor and the brilliance of the past. The Director had let slip enough of the tale of his informer—his secret agent just arrived from Ozar—for us to understand the depth of the disaster.

The shadow line of barbarism had engulfed the world, taken civilization in captivity. What had seemed just another outburst in Grotum—cursed Grotum, the nature of a crime itself; age-old nursery of the craft

of treason—had spread like wildfire around the whole
of Joe's Sea—to Ozar itself! Madness; vile, unreason-
ing madness; so complete the victory of lawlessness that
there was no longer any suspense in our hearts. We,
once rulers of east and west, had lost our grip of the
land. The heroic age was over—naught left of it but
tales of hearsay, cobwebs and gossamer.

The weight of the burden lay heaviest on the
Director's heart. He had lost his entire fortune—but
it was not because of the dollars that the Director's
every waking hour was an endless torment of
recrimination; and—yes—self-recrimination. It was the
warrior's soul of the man that shriveled, not the
merchant's brain. He had told us, with a false smile
on his face, and an empty laugh, of his plans for a
peaceful old age. "What matters it in the end?" he had
asked. We said nothing; he went on, "I shall forego the
active life; after all, I'm getting on in years. Let savagery reign! I did my best. Here, in this far-off corner of the world, I shall maintain a little outpost of
progress, a small beacon—no, no, dear friends, let us
not fool ourselves still; not a beacon, a dim lamp, an
ember—let those who come after us, those who will—
someday—turn back the foul tide, let them perhaps
take a little heart, a small sum of fortitude, from our
efforts here—our last essays, you might say. I shall write
some reminiscences—my notes on life and letters; a
personal record, to give what help it may to others."
He lapsed into silence and it burned me to see him
so; he was not a man of letters; could not hope to turn
his mind in that direction.

Remembering that conversation, I looked across the
little lagoon where we anchored; looked to the dim
dusk-shrouded huts of the native village. I thought of
exile—degeneration among the savages.

"I met him once," said Barley suddenly. "The Rebel,

I mean. It was long ago—as I was returning from my first expedition into the Sssuj."

The Director's face turned partly; pain filled it; suddenly I wished Barley had remained silent, much though I found myself filled with curiosity. The Director had enough anguish as it was, without being reminded of the Sssuj.

"Perhaps"—interrupted the accountant—"No," said the Director, "I want to hear the tale. It could hardly bother me now—for years I was tormented by—ah! that brave soul alone amidst the savagery—how much I would have—"

He fell silent, but he hadn't needed to continue; for all his fortune, we knew well he would have given up a considerable portion for the widow's hand in marriage. To him, she was the secret sharer of his fortune—the real partner of his fate beside whom the myriad commercial co-venturers paled into mist. But she felt otherwise—her sense of duty; that sense of duty which had taken her so many years before into the wilds of the Sssuj; to bring godliness into the hearts of the savages—none could dissuade her from her course, fraught though it was with unspeakable peril. No pleas, no entreaties, could stop her; she left that cold morning long ago, never to return—overdue and missing; in all the years since, no word of her had been heard. Thrice had the Director sent Barley into the Sssuj to seek her out; thrice had Barley returned with nought but tales of the endless reaches of the swamp— the swamp, the swamp, the great morass of the world, graveyard of so many brave missions and gallant armies.

"What can it matter now?" demanded the Director. "Can Ozar be any better today than the heart of the Sssuj?" He fell silent for a moment, then turned from the rail and sat himself in our circle.

"Speak on, Barley."

Barley brooded a moment; then, launched into his tale.

"As you may recall, my first essay into the swamp had been from the north; and, following its failure, I returned via the same route—until I reached Torrance. There, rather than return by sea, I chose a more roundabout route—partly for I was loath to bring back my sad news; partly for my rover's feet— you all know my taste for landfalls and departures! So, instead of taking ship straightway from Torrance, I resolved to journey overland through Grotum.

"I had only five companions on the coach ride to Goimr. Two of them were from Malata—a planter, Il Conde de la Manteca, and his young wife—on their way to Prygg. In addition, there was a knight, Sir Carayne, from the Crapaude—like myself, going to New Sfinctr. Finally, there were two bizarre sisters from Torrance, Karian and Ann. They were poor company. Ann giggled the whole way, and her sister contributed nothing to our wayfarers' talk except to exclaim at regular intervals—'Stop laughing, Ann!' Fortunately, they left the coach at Goimr.

"Our stay in Goimr was very brief—only the knight descended from the coach. Sir Carayne returned soon enough; his adventures, I gathered, had not been of the greatest sort, judging from the ardent glances which he bestowed on La Contessa while we waited for the next leg of the trip to begin. On the other hand, that may not be so strange. Sir Carayne was a robust man in the prime of his life, very large, his shoulders and hands of a size suited for his calling; while La Contessa—ah, my friends! you know the smoldering beauty of Grenadine women—short in duration, true enough, but while it blooms—"

"The Rebel!" interrupted the Director, rather rudely; but I thought of the troubles ailing his mighty soul, and smiled at him in the gathering darkness. Barley evidently felt the same, for he nodded his head and continued.

"After the knight returned, the new travelers began arriving. The first was a fat cleric, a local parson on his way to the Temple of the Ecclesiarchs. Following him entered a sallow-faced man of indeterminate years; by his uniform and the briefcase shackled to his wrist, a messenger of the Company. This one sat in a far corner and stared gloomily out the window, ignoring all around him. And thus we sat for some little while, until the driver and the guard appeared and clambered aboard. We seemed to be off, but there was some little delay; suddenly, a final pair of passengers arrived. They had barely entered when the coach jarred into motion. One of them, a little ugly fellow toting an enormous sack, was hurled onto the floor.

" 'Master, we're off!' he squeaked. 'Well spoken, dwarf,' said the other, a strange fellow garbed in an outlandish and scruffy robe, as is the habit of sorcerers in Grotum, 'our journey has begun.' So it was I met the Rebel."

"He was a strange sort, to all appearances the most insignificant—paltry—of persons; how confused reality is!—a veil drawn over a missing jewel in an empty casket. Whatever; they took their seats. The sack itself took up twice the room of the stoutest burgher, but fortunately the coach was not crowded. The other passengers stared at these weird apparitions, their lips beginning to curl with disdain.

"But, before any could express a protest, our attention was drawn elsewhere; for—mind you—Grotum as a whole—certainly Goimr!—was a barbarous place— the populace not yet acclimated to the ways and methods of civilization; thus, when the coach careened through the marketplace at full speed—you all know the efficiency of modern transport—"

"We who made it!" exclaimed the Director; we all smiled fondly.

"—the beggars who infested the place were struck dumb with terror. Two of them, an old man and a young lad with a withered leg, were crushed beneath the wheels. We leaned out the windows, peering back; my first thought, that they had both been killed, was proven false—the boy's screams followed us as he writhed on the cobblestones, his good leg now matched to the other.

" 'Poor lad,' said the cleric sadly, 'to come so close to heaven, only to be thwarted at the pearly gates. But then,' he continued more brightly, resuming his seat, 'no doubt this added disfigurement will enhance his mendicant trade.'

" 'What think you, gentle folk?' he went on, looking at us all with a benign gaze, 'is this not further proof of God's beneficence?'

"Suddenly the wizard spoke. 'The parson has failed to grasp the historic significance of the occasion. The truth of the matter lies elsewhere, not readily apparent to the untutored intellect. For look you, sirrahs and madame, who was that septuagenarian thus timely squashed?' He peered at the coach's passengers most intently.

" 'Yes! It was none other than he!' exclaimed the wizard. 'Even in that brief glimpse I recognized him.' 'Who?' demanded Sir Carayne. ' "Who?" you said,' spoke the wizard. 'And well might you ask, for I see by your thews you are an ignorant man. Well, let me tell you, sirrah, that now deceased deformity was none other than Stromo Sfondrati-Piccolomini.'

" 'Not really?' gasped the cleric. 'Yes, yes,' continued the wizard. 'Not—?' exclaimed the cleric, half rising from his seat in excitement. 'Yes, yes, I say—even he! The author of *The Beggar's Banquet*!'

"'Astonishing!' cried the parson, falling back in his seat; he raised his hands most high. 'O Lord, blessed is Thy spirit, for in this recent crushing, Thy majesty is revealed as was Thy will!'

"'Who is—was—this fellow, this Tromo Svunder—whatever his name?' demanded Sir Carayne.

"'And well should you ask,' approved the cleric, 'for this saint's life is an example for all mankind. Know, Sir Carayne, that Stromo Sfondrati-Piccolomini, of the famed scholarly clan of that name, was a man whose blessed nature in God's eyes is proven by his life. As a youth he entered the field of metallurgy, the which he rapidly revolutionized—or so, at least, I am told, though I know little of these matters myself—yet—'

"'Bah!' oathed the wizard. 'Who does not know Stromo's *Hammer and Tong* is an ignoramus; moreover—'

"'—yes, yes, no doubt!—' expostulated the cleric, 'but the more interesting and uplifting feature of this saint's life is its later portion. For know, sirrahs and madame, that at the prime of his career, Stromo injured himself in a demonstration of the smithing art before a lecture hall full of students.' 'Oh poor man!' cried La Contessa, clutching her bosom.

"''Tis true, I fear,' said the cleric. 'Smashed his knee with a single blow of the hammer. He was, needless to say, disgraced; stripped of his post; cast out; disowned by his clan; but he saw the light, and sought to redeem himself in the eyes of God. Thus did he crawl to Goimr and give himself up to a life of beggary. But he did not satisfy himself with the expiation of his sin merely by this travail, oh no!—as well he seized the opportunity to further the pursuit of knowledge and the Lord's work by publishing his book, *The*

Beggar's Banquet, which plumbs the controversial question of the dietary habits of beggars.'

" 'Bah!' sneered the knight.

" 'But you are wrong, Sir Carayne,' protested the parson. 'For this was no mere monograph, no paltry academic investigation filled with charts and graphs—no! no! a hundred times, no! 'Twas a profoundly religious work, whose entire purpose was the demonstration that the existence of beggars and their noxious diet is one of God's great boons to humanity.'

" ' "How so?" you ask,' he continued," said Barley; then—" 'And well you might, for 'twould appear, on the face of things, a paradox that God's boundless mercy should take the form of a mutilated dotard scrabbling midst garbage-strewn streets for the scant sustenance of his daily life—' '—Bah!' oathed the wizard; 'No paradox, but a conundrum—' '—kicked about by ruffians, tormented by mongrels—is this not passing strange?'

" 'Not at all!' snorted the knight."

"Natural order of things," agreed the Director gruffly.

" 'Yet,' went on the cleric, 'in this seeming mystery the genius and the pure spirit of Stromo, now cleansed by his suffering, perceived the truth. For, as he himself explained, this was not evidence of an ethical paradox but rather the deeper proof of God's justice.'

" 'But therein lay not the source of his genius,' countered the wizard. 'By no means. The demonstration that this is the best of all possible worlds is a commonplace; any student not hopelessly stupid in his mind can prove it by any one of several theorems. No, rather the brilliance of his treatise is found in the specifics of his study of the beggar's diet, for therein he established—with a scrupulous logic which remains an example to all philosophes—that the heretofore presumed connection between social status and diet is subject to the most precise and detailed demonstration, in that through an examination of a man's diet we can determine how he arrives at his social status. This was his contribution to science.'

"'What bullshit!' swore the knight. 'Beggars eat what they deserve.'

"'Precisely, precisely!' exclaimed the wizard. 'But it was Stromo who first *proved* it.'

"At this point the cleric, clearly irritated, resumed his discourse. 'Yes, yes, this is no doubt interesting, and goes to show once again the spiritual essence of Stromo's mind—but the essential feature of the saint's work was the further elaboration of God's justice. This is proven by the very event which we so recently witnessed, the blessed squashing of this holy man. "How so?" you ask—for is it not passing strange that such a virtuous soul should come to such a grisly end? Is this not, on the face of it, an ethical mystery?' 'Preposterous!' interrupted the wizard. 'No mystery, but a paradox, obvious to any half-wit.' The cleric pressed on, his lips pursed with rising ire—'Not so! Rather we see here the greatest example of God's mercy—for look you, sirrahs and madame, the enigma—' 'Clearly we deal here with a third-wit,' commented the wizard.

"'You are impudent, sirrah!' stormed the cleric.

"'In no wise!' contradicted the sorcerer. 'My characterization of your mentality has throughout been guided by the dictates of science, without a trace of spleen or personal malice. Quite the contrary! I find your intellect admirably shaped for your calling—for are you not a shepherd of the Lord, tending his spiritual flock?'

"'Why, quite so,' admitted the cleric, somewhat mollified by these soft words.

"'There you have it, then!' spoke the wizard, smiling

at the parson in a most cordial manner, his hands outspread in a gesture of conciliation. 'What could be more fitting? For as sheep are amongst the stupidest of beasts, it is entirely proper that the shepherd's brain be suited for his work. As lambs stray about the field, it is necessary that the shepherd grasp the difference between right and left; as sheep rise in the morning and sleep at night, so must the tender of the flock be able to distinguish night from day; as they bleat—'

"This was too much. Bellowing with fury, the parson rose from his seat and made to fall upon the wizard. Things might have come to a pretty pass, but for the intervention of the Company messenger. This latter had ignored the entire exchange till then, gazing out the window in the same moody fashion he had maintained since boarding the coach. Without moving his eyes, he snapped, 'It is forbidden to quarrel in a vehicle operated by the Consortium. The fine is ruinously heavy.' The cleric paled slightly and resumed his seat.

"Conversation lagged. Soon Il Conde dozed off, and the knight took advantage of this opportunity to make his approach to La Contessa. Casually extending his leg, he began a surreptitious stroking of the lady's shapely ankle with his mailed and spurred boot. The hot blood of the Grenadine flowed freely; La Contessa uttered several remarks concerning rustic chivalry. Aside from this one-sided romance, the rest of the day passed quietly. Toward the end of the afternoon, the scattered clouds began massing. By evening, the sunny afternoon had become a dreary dusk of pouring rain.

"Fortunately, before long we arrived at the first way station. The coach came to a halt, and the passengers disembarked. Looming in the rain near the coach was a slovenly edifice built of logs and wattle. Above the doorway hung a crude sign which proclaimed this to be the Inn of the Two Whiches. The explanation for this peculiar name was soon forthcoming; for upon the main counter, behind which stood the dumpy form of the innkeeper, rose a rudely lettered placard bearing the inscription: WHICH DO YOU WANT? PALLET OR COT? PORRIDGE OR GRUEL? Opting for porridge and cot, I soon finished the meal—if such it could be called— and went to sleep in a corner of the attic.

"It was still raining the next morning when I arose, though not so heavily as the night before. I descended to the ground floor and made to pay my bill. Ahead of me, the wizard and the innkeeper were quarreling. 'I don't care,' snarled the innkeeper, 'you still owe me money.' 'Nonsense!' spoke the wizard. 'Honest hostels charge only for the services which they provide, and no other. This fine establishment is called the Inn of the Two Whiches for the good and proper reason that it offers a twofold option of two services—porridge or gruel; pallet or cot. As my apprentice and I slept on the floor and eschewed supper, we availed ourselves of none of your services. Hence, we owe you nothing.' And with that the sorcerer strode out the door, followed by the gnome tottering beneath his sack.

"The innkeeper roared with rage, and would no doubt have gone in pursuit, save that I stepped up and blocked his way. 'Innkeeper!' I said loudly, 'I wish to settle my bill.' 'In a minute,' he snarled, 'first I'm gonna get that lousy—' 'Now!' I insisted; 'I'm a busy man and I must be on my way!'"

"You should have let him go, Barley," grumbled the Director. "Damned impudence of that wizard—cheating on his bill!"

Barley shrugged. "Perhaps so, but at the time my burning desire was to be rid of the place; it stank, and I was rather peeved by the aches and pains in my back from sleeping on the wretched cot which this parsimonious innkeeper had provided for quite a steep charge."

"Frugality is the necessary basis of profit," insisted the accountant. "No doubt," replied Barley, "but it's unpleasant to be the source of the profit oneself." "'Course!" snorted the Director. "Never sleep in one of my own hostels; fit only for the herd."

"In any event," continued Barley, "the innkeeper decided to forego his quarrel and returned to the counter. Reaching into my pocket, I took out a coin and tossed it onto the counter. Then, before the innkeeper could scoop it up, Il Conde's shrunken head thrust itself beside me. His eyes, normally half-closed in reverie, were now wide open; he peered intently at the coin, his lips quivering with excitement. 'Gasp!—a Ruiz!' he cried. 'Been looking for one for years!' The innkeeper made to pick up the coin. 'Unhand that, knave!' shrilled the nobleman, cracking the man's knuckles with his cane. So fierce was his countenance, so menacing the flourish of his cane, that the innkeeper fell back in fright. Not taking his eyes from the coin for a moment, Il Conde said to me, in a quavering voice—'Sirrah, I am an accomplished numismatist, and I *must* have that coin. What will you take for it?'

"You can imagine my irritation. I thrust the coin toward the dotard and snapped, 'You can have it—just pay my bill!' And with that, I stalked out of the inn. Outside, it was raining again and I hurried into the coach. Before long, all were aboard and we set off. The constant rain was a damper on our spirits, and only the tersest of exchanges took place. By midafternoon, however, the clouds began to scatter. The first ray of sunlight pierced downward like an arrow of gold; this shaft was soon followed by a full volley—before long the day was as bright and sunny as you could ask for.

Soon an animated conversation broke out, this time centered upon the person of La Contessa.

"La Contessa's given name, as it developed, was Freya; the oddity of this name for a Grenadine being explained by a trace of Alsask blood in her family. In age somewhere between thirty and forty, her life had been spent primarily in the acquisition of husbands, an enterprise she had elevated to a fine art. Seven aisles had she trod to the tune of wedding marches, and the result of her latest wedding mumbled beside her with toothless gums. While she was too delicate to dwell upon it, it was clear enough that each of her spouses had been of the order of the current one; her husbands seemed to increase in age and wealth as her career progressed. As it was obvious that the seventh was soon to follow his predecessors, it did not take great insight to see that she had her own motives in accompanying Il Conde to Prygg, which focused about the nonagenarian figure of Prince Roman, the extravagantly wealthy cousin of the King of Pryggia.

"And so the day passed. La Contessa seemed to take a kindly interest in the wretched little dwarf. Several times she attempted to draw out from him his life story—peculiar woman!—but the horrid gnome was too shy to respond with more than stumbling half-sentences. Eventually I dozed off for some few hours, only to awaken when the coach came to a halt. Night had almost fallen, but there was still enough light to discern the features of the surrounding countryside. Would it were otherwise!—for we had arrived at the beginning of the next leg of the journey; but a few miles distant loomed the Grimwald, most ancient and somber of Grotum's forests. Shivering a bit, I hurried into the inn.

"This roadside hostel was even more wretched than the last; no one had even bothered to give it a name.

The innkeeper was an obese man of apparently infinite sloth. The accommodations were very simple—no choice provided here! The traveler slept on a pallet on the floor and supped on a thin porridge; nothing else was available. The innkeeper, either through a keen sense for such things or because he had been forewarned by the driver, immediately accosted the wizard and demanded payment in advance. A round of haggling ensued; at the conclusion of which it was agreed that the wizard's apprentice would clean the hostel as payment in kind for lodging; no meal was included in the bargain. Soon the wretch was sent scurrying about by the innkeeper; at the end of his labors, by which time most of us were already asleep, the place looked no cleaner than before. The innkeeper argued that the bargain was forfeit; but the sorcerer countered that the inn was so innately filthy that no amount of cleaning could solve the problem. The argument waxed hotly, but ended soon enough—partly because the wizard was obviously in the right, and partly because the innkeeper's sloth encompassed disputation as well."

"Find out who that man is and fire him!" bellowed the Director; "I won't abide laziness among my employees!" The accountant coughed softly; the others of us said nothing; I thought of decay in the atolls; delusions brought on by misfortune; senility pressing in like the darkness which congealed upon our boat.

After a moment Barley resumed. "The next morning we went on; it was a dreary day—not raining; but the sky was overcast from horizon to horizon. All too soon—it seemed—we reached the edge of the forest—there the coach halted; we heard the driver's voice call out—'All passengers read the sign!' Startled, we leaned out the windows—there, on both sides of the road, were identical signs—

NOTICE

You are about to enter the Grimwald, so named for good reason. The Grimwald is not a subsidiary of the Consortium. The GGNESWC&EE&T Co. assumes no responsibility for losses of property, limbs, lives or well-being incurred by passengers traversing the forest. Passengers continuing onward do so in full knowledge of the situation, and have no grounds for complaint should your pleasant trip be ruined in any of the myriad ways familiar to travelers with experience of the Grimwald. Be warned. Should any passenger, upon due reflection, choose not to continue the journey, you may so inform the driver and he will allow you to disembark. It goes without saying that finding your way back to what passes for civilization in these parts is entirely your own affair. The GGNESWC&EE&T Co. assumes no liability for any mishaps which may occur, these being not unlikely as the northwestern region of Goimria is notorious for its intemperate weather, impure waters, poisonous plants, slavering carnivores, voracious insects, and—at their best—sullen inhabitants. Should you elect to stay on the coach, we hope you enjoy your trip and we thank you for traveling GGNESW etc.

" 'Anybody gettin' off?' boomed the driver's voice. 'Last call!' A moment's silence; the passengers stared at each other; stared at the forest; stared back at the landscape just traversed; shrank into their seats; and were silent. 'Pray for us!' came the driver's voice, and the coach lurched into motion. The forest closed around us."

PART IV

In Which We
Momentarily Suspend
Korzeniowski's Superlative Account
in Order to Resume Our Examination of the
Other Fugitives From Goimric Justice, Discovering
to Our Dismay, as We Do, that Their Social
Villainy Is Becoming Entwined With
the First Horrid Seeds of
Carnal Lust.

*The Autobiography of Benvenuti Sfondrati-Piccolomini,
Episode 3: Umbrellas, Uncles, Urchins, and Urges*

So it was in such a leafy green shroud that I spent
many days thereafter. I remember it, looking back, as
a particularly joyful time of my life. All cares seemed
to vanish as the great forest swallowed us up. Every
day, one after another, was a steady progression along
a narrow and winding trail. Above, the canopy of the
trees shielded all direct sunlight. Everything was bathed
with a dim green glow, which periodically darkened as
storms passed overhead. The foliage was so thick that

the rainfall from the storms we could hear in the sky above never fell directly on the soil. Like so many umbrellas, the great trees diverted the water into a million trickles seeping down the great boles.

At first—fueled, I have no doubt, by the grim reputation of the Grimwald—I found the forest oppressive, even fearful. But by the end of the first day, I had lost all sense of foreboding. In large part, that was due to Gwendolyn. She, who had heretofore appeared so stern and unyielding, seemed to lose her years and troubles the farther we penetrated into the legendary forest. Nothing was said throughout the course of that first day's journey, but I am an artist, with an artist's eye. It became obvious, watching the steady change in her posture as she strode ahead of me, the increasing ease of her movements, that she was more at ease with my company.

Relaxed or not, she set a very rigorous pace. I suspected that she was deliberately trying to exhaust the effete Ozarine urbanite trailing behind her. Had I been a normal Ozarine, I would indeed have collapsed before half the day had past. But my uncles' training stood me in good stead, and by the time she stopped to make camp for the night I was in good shape.

She commented on it, as she put together the makings for a fire.

"You held up pretty well today. For a—" She stopped speaking, made a sour face.

"For an Ozarine?" I asked, laughing. "I grant you, most of my countrymen would be in sorry shape by now. But my uncles kept me in a stern regimen since I was a wee lad."

"I forgot your uncles." She grimaced. "I suppose mercenaries would need to stay in decent physical condition."

I laughed. "In point of fact, my condottiere uncles tend to scorn regular exercise. They claim being in good shape produces cowardice. 'Your fat man's more likely to stay in the fight,' they say, 'seeing as how there's no point in him trying to run.' No, it was my artist uncles who insisted I exercise. The artist's craft can be quite strenuous."

She looked up at me from the kindling, surprised.

"I'm serious. If you don't believe me, try lying on your back on a scaffolding painting the ceiling of a chapel for an entire week."

"I've never thought about it."

"Most people don't. The world thinks artists function on pure inspiration, or some such. Lot of nonsense, that. It's a craft, like any other. At least, that's how I was brought up."

"What kind of art do you do?"

"Anything. Painting, sculpture, whatever pays. My personal preference is wood carving, but there's not usually much money in it."

She dug into her pack and drew out some dried meat. She handed me a small piece, along with some kind of crackers. The crackers were harder than the meat, and I could have carved wood easier than the meat.

"We'll have to live on this while we travel through the forest," she explained, somewhat apologetically. "I know it tastes lousy, and it's more tiring to chew it than it is to walk. But we don't dare hunt anything in the Grimwald. If you see some berries, let me know. It's safe to eat berries."

"Are these dietary regulations due to the danger of snarls?" I asked. She nodded her head.

"I haven't seen any trace of the creatures. I was rather fearful of encountering them, at first, but after a few hours I decided they weren't around."

"They're here, all right. Don't be fooled by not seeing any. Snarls have an uncanny ability to blend into their surroundings. But they're here, never doubt it." And so saying, she lay down and rolled into her blanket. Within a minute, she was asleep. I found her last remark rather unsettling, but after a few more minutes I too fell asleep.

In the days which followed, Gwendolyn and I began talking while we walked. At first, I was preoccupied with trying to figure out how to make a good impression on her. Difficult, that. I was not, if I may say so, inexperienced at what is sometimes called the art of seduction. But I wasn't such a fool, even then, as to think that the ploys and subtleties of Ozarine idle society would do more than irritate Gwendolyn. And I also realized (rather to my surprise) that as much as I lusted for her incredible body, I had begun to care even more for her good opinion. Eventually, I stopped worrying about it and just enjoyed the conversation. Now that she was more relaxed, I found that Gwendolyn's generally fierce outlook on life was leavened by a dry wit. And while she was uneducated by formal standards, she possessed a keen mind and a sharp eye for observation.

Yet, even though she seemed much friendlier than hitherto, she maintained the same relentless pace. I commented on it, after a week of travel, with a jocular remark to the effect that one would think she would have given up trying to wear me down. But she shook her head.

"It's not you I'm thinking about. I've got to get into the Mutt as soon as possible, so I can start warning the underground about the Rap Sheet."

"What is this Rap Sheet?" I asked. "And why are you so concerned about it?"

My question astonished her so much that she actually stopped and turned around.

"You're an Ozarine!" she exclaimed. "You own all the Rap Sheets! Well, at least most of them."

I threw up my hands with exasperation.

"Will you kindly relent with this Ozarine business?" I demanded. "Gwendolyn, I don't own anything except the clothes on my back and the few possessions in my pack. And my easel," I finished, pointing to it slung over my shoulder. "As for the Rap Sheets, it's true that every year the Senate organizes a great parade on Victory Day in which the Rap Sheets along with other great relics and magic artifacts are paraded around to awe the populace. But the truth is I never really paid much attention to the whole business."

"Can you really be such an innocent? It's hard to believe, even for an artist." She frowned. "Oh, stop looking so aggrieved. It's not that I don't believe you, it's just—"

I started to say something, but she held up a hand to quiet me.

"Just give me a moment. I'm trying to make a decision. Meanwhile, let's keep moving."

A half hour later, without turning her head, she began to tell me about her life, a subject she had hitherto avoided completely. I listened, saying not a word, recognizing the acceptance. She spoke steadily for a long time, describing the life of a girl born into abject poverty in a province of Sfinctria, the most powerful—and venal, by all accounts—of Grotum's many realms. A father never known, a mother dead— of exhaustion, essentially—by the time she was six. Her only family a twin brother, her account of whom, as a boy, was filled with affection. Her world, as she grew up, was a fearsome place, full of perils and injustices. The coarse brutality of the Groutch past, increasingly overlaid by the callous rapacity of the Groutch future.

Her incredible size and strength—manifest at an early age—protected her as a girl from the routine dangers of poverty. There was also, whenever needed, the aid of a brother who was an even more fearsome specimen than herself. And another waif, whom she and her brother more or less adopted, whose diminutive size was offset by the kind of ferocity sometimes found in small animals. The three orphans, as children, had formed themselves into a small family, relying on each other for everything and fending for themselves against as harsh a world as I could imagine.

She said little about her brother and the other boy. It was clear enough, though I understood none of the particulars, that there was a great heartbreak lurking beneath her terse account. An estrangement of some sort, apparently, the nature of which she did not touch upon.

By the time she was fourteen, Gwendolyn had come to realize that the evils of her immediate surroundings were but the manifestations of a vastly greater and more impersonal cruelty. By the time she was sixteen, she was a fully-fledged activist in the revolutionary movement of Grotum.

Of this movement, I understood little of what she said. I gained the impression of a far-flung, complex network of organizations, tendencies, individuals and currents, concentrated in the toiling classes, but not without friends in higher places. Wolfgang seemed to occupy some unique position in this movement, from what little she said about him—not really part of it, but held by all Groutch revolutionaries in a weird combination of awe and bemusement.

"Ideological as a Groutch" is, of course, a well-known expression the world over. Listening to

Gwendolyn talk, I began to gain some inkling of the reality captured in the old saw. Yet, despite the manifold and subtle—and, to one of my temperament, utterly confusing—disputes and divisions within the revolutionary movement, there were a few key points on which all were agreed. These can be summarized as:

One, all the realms of Grotum (except, for reasons which were at the time unclear to me, the Mutt) were utterly decrepit and must be overthrown.

Two, the Groutch were a single people and should be united (or, according to some, reunited—the intricacies of this debate completely eluded me!).

Three, neither of these tasks could be accomplished without defeating the imperialist ambitions of Ozarae, which were rapidly coming to dominate the entire sub-continent. This point, at least, I could readily understand.

It was Gwendolyn's assessment—and I gained here the distinct impression, without her saying anything specific, that she herself was a prominent figure in the underground—that the revolution was gaining steadily in strength, while the various regimes of the sundry Groutch realms were ebbing in their ability to repress the movement. An important element in the growing strength of the revolution was the decrepitude and disarray of the ruling classes. Here, her words called to memory something my uncle Rodrigo had once said: "If the rulers of Grotum were a tenth as competent as they are vicious, we'd all be in deep shit."

And *that*, she said, explained the importance of the Rap Sheet which Ozar was bringing to Grotum.

"You *do* know what a Rap Sheet is, don't you?" she asked, stopping for a moment to catch her breath.

I shrugged. "Not precisely. A magic relic, supposedly, which somehow enhances the power of the police.

Geographically, its powers are said to be limited, but within those limits, immense. Beyond that, I really don't know much. To tell you the truth, I always suspected the boasts of the Senate were much exaggerated."

"Would that they were! When the Senate of Ozarae sent a Rap Sheet into the Rellenos, the revolution which was developing there was crushed within two months."

"Yes, I remember that, vaguely. I was only fifteen at the time."

"Do you know what happened?"

"Not really."

"The police and army of the Rellenos—which had been as sorry a bunch of fumble-fingers as you can imagine—suddenly rounded up every single person who was even vaguely associated with the movement. Fifteen thousand, at least. They stuffed them all into a stadium and then butchered them. Two days it took, with the Rellenos army doing the dirty work and the Ozarines directing the operation. The Cruds. In fact, it was Inkman himself who was in charge. Chief of station for the Rellenos, he was then. One of Ozar's top hatchetmen. Now he's here, and he's bringing a Rap Sheet. So, do you begin to understand why I'm in such a hurry to spread the warning?"

She didn't wait for my reply before starting off again down the trail. I thought on her words for some time before asking: "Do you think your movement can protect itself, with your advance warning?"

She shook her head. "I don't know. I'm not very optimistic, to tell the truth. The movement in the Rellenos had advance warning, and it didn't seem to do them much good. The problem is, the Rap Sheet's magic. There aren't all that many real sorcerers in Grotum, despite all the tales you may have heard. Plenty of fakes and frauds, of course, and even a fair number of witches and warlocks. But the Rap Sheet's a Joe relic and that's the so-called 'Old Magic,' whatever that means. The Arcanum, I think the scholars call it. I have a bad feeling it'll take a sorcerer to deal with a Rap Sheet. But the few sorcerers that do exist are no friends of the common people, that's for sure. Reactionaries through and through, the lot of them, so far as I know."

On that gloomy note, Gwendolyn fell silent, and remained silent the rest of the day. Nor did she speak that evening, around the fire. After she finished eating, she curled up in her blanket. But this night, she did not immediately fall asleep. After a few minutes, she rolled over and looked at me.

"Why are you watching me?" she asked. It was a simple question, without unfriendliness, and I decided to answer honestly.

"I watch you every night for a few minutes, before I fall asleep."

"Why?"

"I don't know, really. You fascinate me. I've never met anyone like you, and—" I took a breath. "I find I am very attracted to you."

"As a woman?"

"Yes." After a moment's silence: "I do not mean to offend you."

"I'm not offended. Puzzled, more like. Outside of a few in the movement, who understand me, I've always found that I intimidate men. Or, what's worse, they see me as some sort of bizarre challenge."

She sat up and stirred the fire into life. She motioned to me and I moved over beside her.

"I don't understand your loyalties," she said.

"That's because they are so different from yours," I replied. "You don't really understand, I think, how little being an Ozarine means to me. Just as I don't understand, I think, how you can be so devoted to your cause." I hesitated, groping for words. "My whole life has been—how can I put it? I think only in terms of individuals, specific people. People in general are an abstraction to me."

"That seems kind of narrow."

"It probably is. I'm not boasting about it, it's just the way I am. When I think about it, I actually admire the way you look at things. But I can't feel it myself."

"So why did you agree to help me escape from Goimr?"

"Because it was you."

She fell silent for a moment, then started weeping. I was utterly astonished. She was such a formidable person, that I had never imagined her crying. And even her crying had a kind of basal agony to it. These were not dainty tears dabbed up with a handkerchief, the kind I had seen shed by many a lady. Her sobs were a deep racking, which echoed ancient pain.

"I'm sorry," I said, after she regained control. "I didn't mean to—"

"You don't have to apologize. It's just—when you said, 'because of you,' it reminded me. My brother said that to me, once. After I threw him out—" Her face grew suddenly stiff and hard. "Never mind that. I didn't see him for several years. Refused to see him. But then I was captured by the police—stupid, really, but I was so tired I'd fallen asleep because I'd been— Never mind. Anyway, they had me chained up and were drooling over the prospect of interrogating me. Interrogation, that's what they call it. We lowlifes call it rape and torture. Anyway, that's when my brother came into the police station."

She smiled. "I didn't know whether to be happy or mad! But at the time, I was mostly just laughing to watch the porkers. I think two of them died of fright before my brother even got his hands on them. And, by the smell, all of them had crapped their pants." Her smile became utterly wicked. "I'll say this, their fear was short-lived."

Seeing my frown of puzzlement, she said: "Obviously, you've never met my brother."

"No. Not so far as I'm aware, at least." Suddenly a thought came to me. I suspect my jaw fell. "Wait a minute. Wolfgang called you Gwendolyn Greyboar."

"It's my last name—Greyboar."

"Your brother isn't—*the* Greyboar?"

"You've heard of him?"

"Who hasn't? The world's greatest strangler, my uncles say. They're quite the fans of him, actually. There's some Ozarine strangler who's all the rage in Ozar nowadays, but my uncles sneer at him. 'All your great historic chokesters have been Groutch,' they say, 'and Greyboar's as good as the legends.' They also say that—"

"*I don't want to hear about it!*" she snarled. The iron mask was back on her face. But after a few seconds, her expression softened.

"I just don't want to talk about it. I hate this mystique about stranglers. No different from cheap thugs, as far as I'm concerned, except they're not cheap. Oh, no! Only work for top dollar, stranglers. Exclusive clientele. Professional murderers, that's all they are, with a shiny respectable gloss."

She took a deep breath. "So anyway, here's my brother, gets me out of there. And afterward I told him—'There's people being murdered, raped and tortured by porkers all over Grotum, and you never gave a damn. So why'd you come here?'"

She looked at me. "'Because it was you,' he said."

"I see. I reminded you of him."

"Yes. And no. You're a lot alike, actually, in some ways."

She stirred the fire again. "But then, you've chosen to do something else with your hands." She took my hand and looked at it. "Good hands, you've got. I noticed that the first day we met."

She looked up at me. "There's a kind of shiny patina all over you, very smooth and polished. But I think there's something else inside."

I reached out with my other hand, but she gently fended it aside.

"Please, Benvenuti, don't."

I withdrew the hand, but she kept my other hand in hers. Then she lay on her back and drew me down next to her. After a long silence, she laughed.

"It's not that I'm a shy virgin, you understand? And I admit I find you attractive. You're so impossibly handsome! It's that we're so different, and our lives go in such different ways."

She raised herself up on one elbow and looked down at me.

"I don't think we'd really manage a casual fling of it," she said softly. "And as for anything else—I don't think there'd be anything but heartbreak in it."

I tried to argue with her, but she was a difficult person to argue with. The more so as my conscious intellect thought she was probably right—even if my body was crying out otherwise. I did manage one kiss, and for a brief moment I felt a hint of passion that sent a hot spike through me. But I didn't try to push the matter. Some instinct told me to let it go, for the moment.

When I awoke, the green glow of the sunlight filtering through the trees, I looked up and found Gwendolyn staring down at me. Her expression was unreadable. Then, without warning, she leaned over and gave me a quick kiss. Before I could respond, she rose, took my hand, and, with the fluid grace of a giant cat, hauled me to my feet with one effortless motion. God, the woman was strong!

"Let's go," she said. "We've got a lot of distance to make today. If we push it, we can be out of the forest by tomorrow morning."

The last sentence wasn't said with any great enthusiasm. "I would have thought—"

She chuckled harshly, and set off. "The Grimwald isn't so bad, despite its reputation. And once we're out of the forest, Benvenuti, we'll be in the Baronies—which *are* just as bad as their reputation."

I reviewed in my mind what I knew of the reputation of the Baronies. "Eeek," I muttered.

PART V

In Which We Return
to Korzeniowski's Superlative
Account of the Misdeeds of the Sorcerer
and his Loyal But Stupid Apprentice as the
Desperate Twain Continue their Attempts to Evade
the Forces of Justice; Indeed, Now Compound
Their Crimes with Further Acts of Malice
and Chicanery. Herewith, the Conclusion
of Korzeniowski's tale.

———～～～———

The Last of the Line
By Korzeniowski Laebmauntsforscynneweëld
(concluding portion)

"Going up that road," continued Barley, "was like entering a vegetarian's nightmare, a semi-insane cacophony of ferns and cycads and mosses and vines and—most of all—the trees; endless trees! Huge, but numberless—like an army of leafy kings looming over us in judgment. Impenetrable, silent—but not the silence of peace, no, it was the stillness of an implacable force brooding over the vengeful aspect of its inscrutable intention to prosecute enigmatic purposes aimed at unknowable ends.

"Trees, trees, trees, trees, trees—at their foot, hugging the narrow path, crept the little coach, timid, tentative, a fearful mouse creeping about the catacombs of the Temple—no, not even!—rather, a sightless worm slithering under the shadows cast by the sarcophagi of mummified emperors. It made you feel very small, very alone, very lost—but glad to be lost; hoping not to be noticed by anything—very insignificant, completely insignificant; insignificance defined as never before—and glad of it—wanting to be insignificant!—yearning for microscopic status!—very—"

"*Will* you get on with it, Barley?" growled the Director. "Pretty soon you'll be babbling about the heart of darkness and God knows what else."

"Well, yes,—but! In any event. Around midday a roll of drums—fear! prehistoric the fear and the cause of it—did it mean war?—or peace?—prayer?—well!—we could not tell; but the drum roll passed, fell behind; became distant; more hours passed.

"Just then it happened. It must have been four in the afternoon; the sun's rays filtered through the forest at a pronounced angle, although it was still daylight. The dwarf had been staring out the window all day; long after the rest of us had turned away from the overpowering stillness, he continued to peer into the gloom. Several times he tugged at the wizard's sleeve to point out some feature of the forest that the gnome found of especial interest—he alone of us seemed enraptured, oblivious to the looming sense of disaster. Now again the dwarf tugged at his master's sleeve; nothing to note—but perhaps it was the look in his eyes, impossible to recapture. Whatever it was, I was moved to peer out the window. For a moment I saw nothing; nothing—a gloom; massed trees; immensity of forest. Then—a hint of motion; vagueness—I thought, an animal disturbed by the passing coach; but then, just then—suddenly—like the veil of fog stripped for an instant from the unremarked wave just when it crests; an empty casket just then mysteriously filled—I peered right through the dimness and the shrouding branches, became still—what was it? My blood congealed in my veins.

"The coach came to a sudden halt. The passengers were thrown about in confusion; before we could untangle ourselves the doors were flung wide; the driver and the guard piled in; slammed the doors behind; scrambled into the baggage racks above the seats; cowered behind the luggage. And now—this very moment—it was as if a wind swept away the gloom and for the first time we saw the forest clearly, saw it for what it was. Screams of horror rent the still arboreal air; the passengers swarmed with panic—Sir Carayne shouting at the guard and driver, ordering them to their duty; but they just burrowed deeper into the baggage. There was nothing to be done—we stared at one another with frozen eyes; immobilized—lost, doomed—gripped in terror.

"Just then the wizard looked up from his parchment and peered out the window. 'Forest snarls!' he exclaimed. 'And most magnificent specimens of the breed!' To our astonishment, he opened the door and stepped down. 'Come, dwarf, this opportunity cannot be lost. It is extraordinarily rare that one has the opportunity to examine the forest snarl in his natural state; and there is no other, for the beasts cannot be kept in captivity.' The dwarf, normally so timid, immediately followed his master, almost—I would have said—eagerly. Hastily we slammed the door behind them. The monsters beyond drew near; just then, from the forest, moved a wild and gorgeous apparition of a woman.

"She walked with measured steps, draped in striped and fringed cloths, treading the earth proudly, with a slight jingle and flap of barbarous ornaments, carrying her head high—her hair in the shape of a helmet—her breasts high—her buttocks high—everything high! She had brass leggings, brass gauntlets, brass breastplates, brass bellyband, brass buttplates—a tawny flush on her dusky cheek; a set of six necklaces of beads and cowry shells on her sultry neck—charms, bizarre things hanging from every part of her voluptuous body—you'd hardly think she could walk—but what a body!—did I mention that?—she was savage and superb and wild-eyed and magnificent and unblushing and brazen-faced and immodest and—

"'What a piece!' cried Sir Carayne. A vast and guttural roar rose from the great throats of every snarl lurking in the forest. The knight blanched and fell back; all concupiscence fled from his face—mine too—then—suddenly; she opened her arms and threw them rigid over her head, as though in an uncontrollable desire to touch the sky; the swift shadows darted out from the trees, onto the path, gathering the coach in their embrace. Then, staring directly at the wizard, she asked—'What do you seek?'

"'I myself, madame,' we heard the wizard speak, 'wish to advance my knowledge of the lore of snarls. There is a great mystery which surrounds these beasts, which I have not yet fathomed. It emerges even in the most ancient texts.'

"Silence; then—astonishing! The monsters suddenly circled the dwarf, sat back on their huge haunches, gazed down at the gnome with an intensity impossible to describe. They whined softly in their throats, as if puzzled and confused. For his part, the little runt stared back, completely unafraid—or so it seemed. Then, the woman spoke again. 'If you would know about the snarls, ask them,' she said to the wizard; a motion of her hand—the largest of the monsters left the circle around the dwarf and padded over to stand, like a statue, before the sorcerer.

The giant creature spoke, the voice issuing with a strange timbre—hoarse, bestial, yet not without a palpable strength, an immensity, like the forest itself. 'So—you would know about snarls?'

" 'Certes!' spoke the sorcerer. 'From whence do you come?'

" 'We have always lived in the forest.'

"The wizard cleared his throat. 'Sirrah snarl—'

" 'Forest snarl,' growled the beast. 'I am a forest snarl—not a desert snarl, not a mountain snarl, not a swamp snarl—a forest snarl; my gorge rises when the distinction is lost.'

" 'Most certainly!' spoke the mage. 'As it happens, the sharp distinction between greater and lesser breeds of snarls has long been one of my philosophy's principal tenets.' He cleared his throat again. 'Sirrah forest snarl, I have learned in my studies that there can be more than one meaning to the same word, a different purport poured into the same verbal vessel, if you will—nevertheless, it is possible—'

" 'Cut to the chase,' growled the snarl. A hideous purple tongue licked its immense jaws. 'If you will pardon the expression.'

"Another clearing of the wizard's throat. 'Quite so. Then, let me ask—how long is "always"?'

" 'Wizard, we were here in the time of Joe.'

" 'Blasphemy!' cried out the cleric, who suddenly

lunged from the seat where he had been cowering and
leaned out the window. 'O gross animism! Idolatry! J—
nay, I cannot speak his name—this creature is a
concoction of heathen fantasies! The legend is an
abhorrence before God!' He stretched forth a hand
to the woman. 'Repent, urchin of the forest! Repent!
For while an anarchist beast has no soul and may utter
abominations with wild abandon, you stand in mortal
peril—nay, immortal peril! Take heed! For the wrath
of—'; a snarl glided to the coach and rose up before
the parson; two gruesome paws seized the door. The
monster was mute; but its gaze was enough to send
the parson reeling back, ashen-faced. 'Shut up, you
fool,' hissed La Contessa.

"The wizard made to continue his questioning, but
the woman cut him short. 'Begone, sirrah. The snarls
grow restless; of all human flesh, my friends find that
of clerics sweetest—they say the sanctimony adds flavor
to the meat.' She turned slowly away and passed into
the forest; once only her eyes gleamed back. Then all
was silence; the snarls vanished as if by magic—but
I saw the huge one stop for a moment in front of the
dwarf, and lick his face with that horrid purple tongue.

" 'Come, dwarf,' spoke the wizard. 'We shall pur-
sue our investigations upon some other occasion.' The
two returned to the coach. Meanwhile Sir Carayne, his
courage of a sudden regained, roared at the driver and
the guard. 'Get out, you dogs!' He yanked the shivering fellows out of the baggage rack and booted them
out the door. 'Back to your posts! Knaves! Deserters!'
They made no protest; clear enough it was their only
thought to depart the area at once. In a moment the
coach was clattering down the path at a reckless pace.

"Most of us—you can imagine—were overjoyed to
see the incident past; not so the mage. 'You, sirrah,'
he stormed at the cleric, 'have by your folly impeded

the progress of science!' The cleric, who had been blubbering in terror since hearing of the dietary preference of snarls, burst forth in reply—'My God-given duty it is to forestall paganry! The very mention of J— nay, that cursed name!—uttered, the very name alone is grounds sufficient for inquisition!'

"'Bah!' oathed the wizard. 'Maunderings of a puerile fool! How can one avoid discussion of Joe? Is not every noteworthy geographic feature twixt land and sea named after him? Do we not refer to that great ocean around whose vast expanse almost all civilized lands exist by the name of Joe's Sea? Are not the very mountains which form the spine of Grotum—and upon whose crest, I might mention, perches the Temple of the Ecclesiarchs—named Joe's Mountains?'

"'Not by the Ecclesiarchs!' cried the parson. 'Those mountains are properly named the Prominences of Holiness—and the sea is named the Ocean of Devotion. So hath the church decreed!'

"'Bah!' oathed the wizard. 'None but superstitious mummers use those preposterous names! Joe's Sea and Joe's Mountains—such are the names used by illuminati and common folk alike.' He turned to Il Conde and his wife. 'You are gentle folk. I ask you—what do you call the aforementioned geographic items?'

"'Joe's Sea and Joe's Mountains,' replied La Contessa promptly. 'Everybody does—but I always thought they were just names; do you mean that they are actually named after somebody—I mean, somebody real?'

"'Milady!' wailed the cleric, aghast. 'Think upon your soul! Think upon the gates of Paradise closed before your beseeching pleas! Think—'

"'Oh, shut up, you old bore! I want to hear about Joe. Tell me!'—This last to the wizard; the parson lapsed into a pained silence; his hands covered his ears.

"'In reply to your query, madame,' spoke the

wizard, 'it is difficult to speak with precision. Of all legends and myths, none is so fascinating as that of Joe—none so full of weird portent; none so pregnant with veiled surmise.'

"He paused for a moment; then continued. 'By my studies, I have deduced that he was the first of the Grotum People, that long-since-vanished race of primevals believed to have inhabited this land at the dawn of time. For years, the opinion advanced by Leakey Laebmauntsforscynneweëld—that the Grotum People were an offshoot of the human family which died out without issue—was accepted by all students of paleoanthropology without question. In recent years, however, Leakey's cousin Johanson Laebmauntsforscynneweëld has argued that the Grotum People were, in fact, the direct ancestors of modern humanity, and has even advanced a handful of fossil remains to substantiate his claims.'

"'I myself accept neither of these views, for I tend rather to agree with the more ancient view of the venerable F. Mayer Laebmauntsforscynneweëld that all these purported "vanished species" and "extinct races" are confused myths of deformed, but human, personages. Thus even the existence of this legendary race of proto-humans, these "Grotum People," remains, to my mind, unproved. But this is not the sole mystery surrounding the matter—by no means! For, if the Grotum People did exist, they disappeared most strangely—overnight, it would seem; with no apparent reason. Other than Johanson's questionable fossils, the only record exists in the folklore of primitive savages—and in the shorter tales told by night round gypsy campfires, in the darkness of troglodyte caves, in the tenement cellars of dwarves; and, of course, in the ravings of revolutionists and such-like heteroclites; even there, little is said, for little is known.'

"'On one point all legends agree—the Grotum People were giants, much larger than modern folk; though given, it would appear, to great hairiness and frightful deformities. Beyond that, the stories are obscure, apocryphal, fragmented, contradictory—opaque in all aspects. Only a single substantive scrap of verse remains extant concerning the life of Joe himself; this, a chant sung by the wild men of the Sssuj at the initiation rites of puberty.'"

"Oh, Mrs. Lang—" whispered the Director of Companies; Barley coughed—hurried on—

"'Would milady care to hear this chant?' asked the wizard. 'Certes!' came her answer.

"'I have had my apprentice commit it to memory—no small feat, I assure you!—though less so on this occasion than usual, I will grant the dolt that. Dwarf, recite Joe's Chant!' The gnome sat up straight on the edge of the seat, his legs dangling. His beady little eyes glazed with effort; then, in a shrill voice, the following—

> One day Joe was loping along
> and all the people   came up to him.
> All this loping along   is killing us,
> We need something   to keep us going,
>   they said.
>   So Joe invented food.

> But one day Joe was loping along
> and all the people   came up to him.
> All this loping along   is boring,
> There must be something   else to do,
>   they said.
>   So Joe invented fucking.

> But one day Joe was loping along
> and all the people   came up to him.

Ever since you invented   food and fucking,
there's too many people   and not enough food,
                    they said.
              So Joe invented work.

But one day Joe was loping along
   and all the people   came up to him.
Ever since you invented   work,
   everything's too hard   to keep straight,
                    they said.
              So Joe invented bosses.

But one day Joe was loping along
   and all the bosses   came up to him.
The people won't listen   to our bossing,
      and they tell us   we're full of shit,
                    they said.
              So Joe invented cops.

But one day Joe was loping along
and the bosses and cops   came up to him.
We've got to have some   cover,
   So the people'll stop   calling us hogs,
                    they said.
              So Joe invented priests.

But one day Joe was loping along,
   and all the priests   came up to him.
   We've almost got   everything perfect,
But we still need that   last big push,
                    they said.
              So Joe invented God.

But one day Joe was loping along,
         and God   came up to him.
Ever since you invented   Me,

> *you're nothing but a   dangerous nuisance,*
> *He said.*
> *So God froze Joe in a flash ice age.*

"'How fascinating!' exclaimed La Contessa. 'A crude verse,' grumbled Il Conde, 'utterly lacking in rhyme or cultured meter.' The wizard shrugged. 'As to that, milord, 'tis true enough. But what would you? The savages of the Sssuj are well known to be bestial. Think of the ingratitude with which they have greeted all attempts to bring the benefits of civilization into their midst—merchants and traders broiled and baked—entire armies tossed into the stew pot! And what of the fate of Father Cosmo?—too horrid to contemplate!'"

"Oh, Mrs. Lang—" whispered the Director of Companies; Barley coughed—hurried on—

"Silence followed; the coach clattered and battered down the path—the natural darkness of the forest deepened; twilight drew near; then, just as the last rays of the sun flickered out like emblems of hope snuffed by an immutable fate, we burst out of the forest gloom; a great interminable plain stretched before us—barren beyond belief, but it was a welcome relief from the Grimwald—a cheer went up.

"The coach continued its mad pace down the road, which seemed now to have straightened to an unswerving line, as if drawn by a great rule for an obscure purpose. Suddenly—it was dark now—we stopped; no inn was to be seen. Perhaps, I thought, it is a ways off down the road—it was impossible now to see more than a few feet. But it wasn't so; the driver clambered down, came to the window; 'might's well get some sleep,' he said. 'There's no hostel in these parts—not till we get to the Caravanserai tomorrow; you'll have to sleep in the coach.'

" 'What about our evening repast?' demanded the knight. 'Dunno,' replied the driver indifferently. 'Brought m'own.' He vanished into the darkness. 'Insolence!' bellowed Sir Carayne; he turned fiercely on the messenger. 'You, sirrah! You are an agent of this company—what is the meaning of this outrage?'

"The messenger looked up from his case, now open on his knees; a small sandwich in his hands—clearly he had traveled this route before! 'The GGNESW etc. is in no way at fault,' he sneered. 'You have no grounds for complaint. Shelter is provided by the stout walls of this coach'—not without humor, this man, I now perceived—'and, as for food, you should have thought upon it earlier and brought your own, as I have done; failing that, nothing prevents you from foraging— though, I should tell you, they do not call this region the Drear for nothing.'

"The messenger ate his meal in silence; the rest of us, grumbling, settled down to sleep. There was nothing to be gained by blundering about a pitch-black wilderness hunting for rabbits—so much was clear.

"We set out at dawn the next morning. There was still a long day's journey before us if we were to reach the Caravanserai by nightfall. As the sun rose, we gazed over this new stretch of territory.

"What a cursed wasteland! I still shiver to think of it; behind, on the horizon, the dark mass of the Grimwald could be seen for some little while—ugly as it was, I was almost sorry to see it slip out of sight. Now nothing surrounded us but the Drear. The Drear! Never, I think, have I seen a place so aptly named! Nothing; nothing-*ness*—that's it! It was the most barren desert conceivable, inscrutable in its immensity, but without the searing heat that makes most deserts such a reassuringly palpable experience. Parallels everywhere, the land and the sky, the four points of the compass—a sameness!—to all points and every place between stretched this flat—utterly flat!—spread of naked soil. Hard, crusted dirt; nothing else—quite literally, nothing else; and gray!—not brown; can you imagine that? Gray soil, not brown soil—inscrutable, unknowable—of course, no trees!—but neither was there vegetation of any kind; not a bush, not a shrub, not a flower, not a weed, not a blade of grass. Even the soil itself was of that same opaque uniformity; upon that vast plain not a rock stood higher than a clot of earth.

"'A pleasing symmetry, is it not?' commented the wizard; but his apprentice averted his gaze. No one responded—silence; so it went for several hours. Then, shortly after noon, the first break in the monotony appeared; Sir Carayne, leaning out the window—suddenly he cried—'Look! Up ahead!—a boulder!' We rushed to the window. Sure enough!—ahead, barely on the horizon, a boulder stood by the roadside. Not an especially large boulder, mind you—rather small, totally unremarkable, in fact; but in the midst of that wasteland it was a beacon in the darkness—an oasis— a work of art! We sat back in our seats, laughing a bit—so great the despondency of that place! The coach rolled on; then, suddenly—

"'*Stand and deliver!*'

"The coach screeched to a halt. We rushed to the windows—who had cried out?—we wondered; but nothing; nothing was to be seen but the boulder, next to which the coach was drawn—and it was far too small for a man to hide behind. Except for that, the Drear stretched away in its awful solitude, unbroken in every direction.

"The messenger sighed and resumed his seat. 'It is Rascogne de Sevigneois,' he said gloomily. 'Who?' we demanded. 'Rascogne de Sevigneois, the highwayman;

it can be no other.' 'But there is no one to be seen!' protested Sir Carayne. 'He is a master of disguises,' replied the messenger.

"In confirmation, at that very moment the mysterious voice was heard again. 'It is I, Rascogne de Sevigneois, cunningly disguised as a small boulder!' We rushed to the window anew—sure enough; imagine our astonishment! There—where we had thought to see a small gray boulder—stood instead a horseman— brightly caparisoned in scarlet cloak, emerald breeches, ruffled shirt, floppy feathered hat; a rapier scabbarded to his side. The fellow was short, very muscular; swarthy of complexion; his face adorned by an aquiline nose and dazzling white teeth, grinning at us from beneath a monstrous pair of waxed mustachios. He sprang from his horse and bounded over to the coach. Doffing his hat with a flourish, he opened the door.

" 'Alight, my good people! Commerce awaits us!'

"The driver and the guard—the latter dropping his crossbow as if it were a hot poker—climbed down from the coach and stood to one side; they seemed not overly aroused—plain as day, they had no intention of resisting the brute. 'Knaves!' roared the knight, shaking his fist at the two. Then, glaring fiercely at the highwayman—he flung himself out of the coach, his broadsword clutched in a meaty fist. 'Know, footpad,' he bellowed at Rascogne—the rascal's grin growing more impudent by the second as he bounded about, from level soil to coach top to saddle to ground—'that here you deal not with a brace of scurvy coachmen, but with a belted knight of the realm!' And with that, Sir Carayne swung a terrific blow at the robber. But he misjudged the character of the foe—for in a movement too quick for the eye to follow, the highwayman drew his rapier and deflected the broadsword with the greatest of ease.

"'Aha!' cried the rogue. 'A duel! A merry duel!' He bounded from the ground to the saddle to the top of the coach to the ground to the top of Sir Carayne's head to the ground to the saddle and back to the ground again; his dark eyes gleamed with amusement. 'You seek to undo Rascogne de Sevigneois! *Take, then, varlet, this!*' His rapier blurred—in a trice Sir Carayne was disarmed; his belt sliced in two, causing his trousers to fall; and—imagine his chagrin—there, carved upon his chain mail tunic, the words—'Rascogne de Sevigneois finds thee an ill-bred lout.'

"Discretion overcoming the point of honor, Sir Carayne desisted from further combat. Retrieving his sword, he scabbarded it; then—was forced to clutch his trousers to his waist. The highwayman stretched out his palm; angrily, the flower of the Crapaude tossed over his purse; then—stalked off a ways and glowered at the horizon. Rascogne bounded over to the coach. 'Come, come!' he cried, 'Rascogne awaits!' He held the door open courteously.

"There being nothing else to do, we descended from the coach. The messenger was the first one out, followed by the parson; the wizard and his apprentice came next, the latter toting his gigantic sack; then myself, followed by Il Conde and La Contessa. The latter, however, had no chance to set foot on ground. For, no sooner had her voluptuous figure filled the doorway of the coach than the highwayman's dark features reddened with passion. His eyes gleamed; his teeth sparkled like diamonds. 'Such beauty has not been seen on the Drear in many a day!' exclaimed the villain. La Contessa blushed under his admiring regard. Uttering no further words, Rascogne drew forth a bottle of champagne and two glasses from beneath his cloak; sprang into the coach—the door slammed shut. A boisterous laugh; some murmured words; the popping of a cork; the clink of glasses; some murmured words; a baritone and a soprano voice mingling in gay repartee—then—suddenly the coach was rocking madly on its springs; 'Aha! Furious passion!' came the robber's voice from within.

"At this further outrage, Sir Carayne exploded with rage anew. 'Villain, wouldst do so?' Again he drew his sword and—clutching his pants with the other hand— hobbled to the coach. Rascogne's insolent face appeared above the windowsill. 'Aha!' he cried. 'The gallant knight seeks to throw Rascogne off his stroke! A futile endeavor, clod of a swordsman, I assure you— both my blades are unmatched in their skill!'

"It could not be gainsaid; the coach continued its furious rocking even as the knave effortlessly disarmed Sir Carayne once again, this time carving on the steel of the knight's blade the words—'This rusted kitchen knife is of the same mettle as its owner's member.' Sir Carayne flung himself to the ground, gnawing the earth in bitter humiliation; La Contessa's cries grew louder from within. 'I say,' grumbled Il Conde peevishly, 'I believe that rascal is seducing my wife.' His rheumy eyes squinted suspiciously at the coach, whose bounces now took it quite off the ground. Suddenly a great sigh came from within; all motion ceased; then, a moment later, the highwayman's voice—'Ah, sweet aftermath of love;' the clink of glasses; murmuring voices; then, La Contessa's voice—'Perhaps?' 'Aha!'—this the villain— 'let it not be said that Rascogne de Sevigneois left such a fair lady in distress!' A moment later the coach was back at its rocking."

"Disgusting!" bellowed the Director. "Praise God Mrs. Lang wasn't there to witness it! Her pure soul— perhaps she herself!—her alabaster body—ravished— oh God!" His face filled with horror; though it was difficult to discern his features in the tropical nightfall.

"Yes, well," said Barley, "they're a passionate lot, the Groutch. In any event, this escapade went on for quite some time—there seemed no end to the energy of the twain. Actually, I became quite concerned for the state of the coach, for that dilapidated vehicle was taking a beating which made the rigors of the past days' journey pale in comparison. At length, however, all was done; the coach remained intact. Stroking his mustachios complacently, the highwayman appeared in the doorway; he sprang to the ground—bounded over to us. 'And what have you to offer me?' he purred. From the window of the coach La Contessa's hand emerged, holding a bejeweled purse. 'Here, dear robber.' But the knave would have none of it—'Nay! Nay! Sweet lady, the pleasure of your smile is quite reward enough!' At this, Sir Carayne could contain himself no longer. Once again he hurled himself upon the dastard, hacking and hewing most vigorously with his sword—but in vain; for the scoundrel, leaping and capering about, voicing scurrilous taunts and gibes, committed the greatest indignities with his rapier upon the person of the knight. Again Sir Carayne flung himself to the ground, resuming his trenchwork.

"Rascogne bounded over to me. Without a word, I handed over my purse. The rascal sprang over to the messenger. 'Ah, my good messenger—we meet again! Your purse, if you please.' 'I never carry one, as you well know,' responded the gloomy voice. 'Your satchel, then!' 'It is empty, as you well know,' responded the gloomy voice, showing the bare contents of the case cuffed to his wrist. 'I have afflicted you so much, then?' asked the rogue, grinning from ear to ear. 'For the moment,' responded the messenger, a bit of heat entering his voice. 'But soon you will be apprehended by the Consortium Constabulary!'

"'Ah, yes,' jeered Rascogne. 'The famed and feared

Agent Grimstalk! But, tell me, how long have he and his dreaded cohorts been hot on my trail?' The messenger scowled; said no more.

"Rascogne then leapt to the cleric. 'And you, sir?' The parson spread his hands, smiling in the manner of one weary of the world and its wicked ways. 'Good sir,' he said, 'I am, as you can see, a man of the cloth. Therefore have I taken a vow of poverty; my sole earthly wealth, the poor clothes you see on my back. You may, if your faith be little, search my pockets to verify the truth.' The highwayman snorted. For the first time, his face clouded with anger. 'Ah, villain, wouldst trifle with me? Deceiver of the poor, meddler with their superstitions, well do I know the wealth you have garnered like the faithful reiver your raiment names you!' His sword flicked out; sliced the collar from the cleric's neck—a small torrent of gems spilled out from hidden pouches. 'Be glad, priestly buzzard, that I dispatch you not to that very place you preach of!' The cleric quailed, but Rascogne turned away and sprang over to the wizard and his apprentice.

"And you, sir?'

"The wizard coughed apologetically. 'I have a small purse, sirrah, of great value to me—not, as it happens, for its intrinsic worth, the which is small, but for its value relative to my present state of wealth, the which is meager. This, however, I cede to you—for, in truth, I am a philosophe, and as such my desire for worldly possessions is faint at all times and subject, moreover, to sudden change; such a change, I might add, as the one which has this very moment o'ertaken me.' He handed over his purse. 'You may also,' he continued, placing his hand upon the dwarf's quivering brow, 'take my apprentice to be your servant—and I will aver, sirrah, that though he is stupid and malformed, my apprentice is capable of carrying great burdens and suffering much deprivation as well, docilely and without excessive complaint.' Again, the apologetic cough; a slight straightening of the shoulders. 'Do not, however, I pray thee, take these my scrolls and tablets, nor these my tomes and talismans, nor these my artifacts and relics; for these are my very life and soul, without which I should be as a man lost on a chip in an endless ocean.'

"The highwayman spat fiercely upon the ground. 'A pox on your sheepskins and toys, pedant—products of an unenlightened age! And as for this, your supposed servant—though more likely, judging from his appearance, some evil imp retrieved from a dank and moldy place—I am more moved to skewer him with my rapier, thereby cleansing the earth of one of the many blots upon its surface. But, I will satisfy myself with your purse;' he snatched said object from the wizard's grasp.

"But then—most unexpected! The wretched gnome hopped forward and kicked the robber's shin. Then— kicked it again, and yet again! 'Just you try it!' he shrilled. 'You just try and stick me with that big knife! I have friends! Snarls, they are—and big ones—and one of them's huge! They'll eat you right up when they find out!'

"I was absolutely astonished—first, at the dwarf's unlikely humor; but then—and more so—at the robber's response; for though Rascogne had drawn his blade, and I imagined the apprentice already buried, he stopped; frowned—for the first time a look of something other than utter surety on his face; then— 'Snarls?' he demanded. 'You—a snarl-friend?' 'Well, I am, too!' insisted the dwarf. 'Tell him, master!'

"'Most strange,' muttered the highwayman. He snapped his fingers at the wizard—'Is this true, what he says?'

"'As to that,' responded the mage, 'the snarls did seem preoccupied with him—'

"'The big one licked my face!' cried the dwarf.

"'—but I do not think, at least, judging by the literature—'

"'Enough!' interrupted Rascogne. 'I did not ask for a lecture. Still, 'tis odd, most odd.' He inspected the dwarf closely, frowning all the while; then—'I shall have to think on this,' he announced. Suddenly, his face cleared. 'Ah—but I forget me! Business first! And my business is not finished.' And with that he turned and sprang over to the side of Il Conde, hand outstretched again.

"Il Conde peered up at him, leaning his frail weight upon his cane. 'You are a scoundrel, I believe,' he whined. 'People think I am nothing but an old fool, who can't see his nose in front of his face; but I have been watching you, sirrah, watching you carefully, and it is my firm conviction that you have, very recently in fact, taken liberties with my wife. Five times, if I am not mistaken.' The highwayman grinned impudently. 'Alas,' here Il Conde shook his ancient head, 'I am an old man, feeble in my limbs; I can assure you, sirrah, were I but fifty years younger you would be in a fine kettle of fish—be sure of it! But, as it is—'

"Grumbling, Il Conde brought forth his purse with a trembling hand, veined and liver-spotted with age. The purse was quite large; Rascogne smiled broadly as he emptied its contents into his hand. 'Quite a catch, here!' he cried. 'Doubloons! Dinars! Drachmas! Shekels! Every manner and variety of fine coin! And—but what's this?' He gazed with puzzlement at a small coin, whose worn and shabby surface contrasted sharply with its gleaming fellows. Il Conde peered more closely; suddenly—his entire body became rigid; his rheumy eyes gaped wide. 'My Ruiz!' he gasped, reaching forth to retrieve it from the robber's hand. Rascogne laughed and sprang backward. 'Aha! The octogenarian seeks to regain his lost treasure! Nay, nay, not so, graybeard! Paltry though it is, this little coin as well must join my booty!'

"'Monster! Fiend!' wailed Il Conde. 'Unhand that coin!' The ancient threw himself upon the ruffian, belaboring wildly with his cane. 'My Ruiz! My Ruiz!'

"Then—imagine this! Naturally enough, we thought to see Rascogne deal with the old fool as easily as he had done earlier with Sir Carayne; but it was not so, not at all!—so overwrought was Il Conde at the loss of his prized Ruiz that he wielded his cane with a maddened frenzy that should soon have maimed any but the greatest of swordsmen. Rascogne's grin was soon replaced with astonishment, then, as he gave ground before Il Conde's onslaught, to that intent concentration which is the hallmark of all masters of the fencing art.

"'O doughty dotard!' he exclaimed, parrying the whirling cane, 'O grim gaffer! Well struck—oh, well struck! And yet again!' The highwayman leapt back and forth, his rapier flashing in complex twirls and sweeps; Il Conde's implacable advance continued on tottering legs. 'My Ruiz, my Ruiz,' he wheezed. Never have I seen such a duel! Only Rascogne's genius with a blade sufficed to stave off the oldster's assault; sweat poured down his swarthy, corded neck. He was hard-pressed— more, he was in desperate straits! And now!—Il Conde had him pinned against the side of the coach—there was nowhere to retreat! Now were Rascogne's advantages of sound legs and functioning lungs of little avail—it was sword against cane at close quarters! Slash—stroke—lunge—parry! We were gripped in an intense excitement; the robber was lost!—it was plain to see—the end near, his strength failing at last under the inexorable rain of blows from Il Conde's cane. But then!—I had heard tell of it—dismissed it as a ridiculous fable—Rascogne executed the *dégage sixte-carte du droite arriere à la potage de St. Germain!* Il Conde was disarmed—the highwayman's swordpoint at his throat! The old nobleman wept bitter tears. 'My Ruiz, my lost Ruiz,' he sobbed.

"Rascogne gasped a breath; sheathed his rapier. 'O valiant *vieillard!*' he cried, clasping the ancient to his breast. 'Never have I had such a match! Never such an opponent! Never crossed sword with such a cane!' He released Il Conde and drew forth the contested coin. 'Such art deserves its reward!—here, sirrah, take your coin in token of my esteem.' 'My Ruiz,' cried the nobleman, snatching the coin. He tottered off, clutching the piece. 'My Ruiz, my Ruiz,' we heard his faint whisper.

"Just at that moment a distant cry was heard. 'It is Rascogne de Sevigneois! Hold, villain!' Turning, we saw a large body of horsemen, some twenty in number, appear on the western horizon. They drew their swords; galloped hotly toward us. 'Aha!' cried Rascogne. 'A chase! A merry chase!' With a laugh and a shout, the rogue sprang on his horse and galloped off, flourishing his hat at his pursuers. These worthies pounded past the coach a moment later. Grim of face, stern of demeanor, garbed all in black, their capes streamed behind them as they thundered off in the hunt. In a moment, highwayman and pursuers alike had disappeared over the eastern horizon.

"'It's the Maréchal du Boeuf and the King's Men!' exclaimed the messenger, excitement tingeing his voice. 'Which King?' asked the cleric. 'Nobody remembers,' came the gloomy reply.

"Before long we were on our way. There was no

conversation in the coach; the only sound, Il Conde's murmurs and chuckles as he fondled his precious Ruiz. La Contessa slept in contented exhaustion; while Sir Carayne glowered at her the whole way, picking dirt from his teeth. The messenger's gloomy countenance was as always—but matched now by the cleric and the wizard; the former, raining down heavenly curses—the latter, sorcerous hexes—upon the highwayman. The dwarf, on the other hand, seemed rather cheerful.

"We reached the Caravanserai with the setting sun. Its lingering rays lit up the white stone walls of the oasis. The minarets gleamed for a moment; then, twilight overtook them as well. The gates of the Caravanserai swung wide; before long we had pulled up into the courtyard of the depot—and debarked. The last I saw of the Rebel and his companion was the wizard's back and the dwarf's little legs, twinkling under his great sack, as they vanished into the darkness."

Barley ceased, and sat apart, silent and indistinct, with the poise of a mystic. For a time, no one moved, or spoke; then—

"We have lost the flow of ambition," said the Director of Companies. "We are caught within the tides." Another silence—then: "Curse the Rebel."

I raised my head; the tranquil lagoon at the uttermost end of the earth lapped somber under an overcast night's sky; the future was barred by a black bank of clouds.

Suddenly the native boy put his insolent head up through the hatch, and said in a tone of scathing contempt —"Missus Lang—she alive." He held up a letter.

"What's that?" demanded the Director, leaping to his feet. "Give me that, you savage!" He seized the envelope; tore it open. "A light! A light!" The accountant hastily lit a lamp; held it by the Director's side—he began reading the letter.

"It's from Mrs. Lang!" Never have I heard such joy in a human voice. "She's alive. She—she's coming back to me! She was in Ozar, found out where I am—she's coming to see me!" He read on, as in a frenzy—suddenly, a great groan of anguish. "Oh God, no!" Never have I heard such despair in a human voice.

"What is it?" asked the lawyer. "She—she's remarried," whispered the Director. "She's taken a new husband—how could she?—all these years I waited— the money I spent—" Then, a moment later, another great cry. "A mate! She's taken a mate!—a great horrid savage from the Sssuj!" Never have I heard such outrage in a human voice. "And children! And grandchildren! She's bringing the whole filthy brood here! Oh God!"

He tore the letter in half, clutching a piece in each hand; his eyes rolled wildly—his face gleamed in the lamplight, contorted like a demon. "No! No! I cannot!—instead—yes, I will!" Never have I heard such resolve in a human voice; he ate the letter; then—he was always a man of action—he flung himself headlong into the lagoon; the dark waters roiled for a moment beneath the *Tremolino*'s stern.

"Stop!" I shouted—rushed to the rail; made ready to dive after him—Barley's hand held me back. "Let him go," he said softly; "it's better so." He was right— I looked to the others; all nodded. Slowly we resumed our seats.

Some silent moments later—it was now pitch-black, moonless night—I heard the lawyer say, "Quite a little tale there; by the way, whatever happened to that wizard?" By the dimness of the lamplight, I could barely make out Barley's shrug.

PART VI

In Which We
Resume Our Account of
the Adventures of the Artist
and his Insurrectionary Companion
as They Continue Their
Journey Through
the Baronies.

The Autobiography of Benvenuti Sfondrati-Piccolomini,
Episode 4: Fields, Forts, Form and Function

So it was on such a note of trepidation that we emerged from the Grimwald and set foot in the Baronies.

At first glance, the terrain seemed unremarkable. *Very hilly,* was my first thought. Innumerable hills stretched toward the horizon, each of them surmounted by a weathered rocky tor. Here and there a small wooded copse or a pasture with a stone croft. Beyond that, I had no impression other than the rather barren and rocky nature of the region. Each little peasants' field seemed to be surrounded by stone walls. And I was puzzled by the apparent absence of any dwellings.

When I remarked on the latter, Gwendolyn pointed a finger at what appeared to be, in the distance, some sort of huge gopher hole. "The peasants in the Baronies can't afford huts. They live in holes in the ground."

I made a face. The rapacity of the Groutch Barons was a byword even in Ozar. "Then where do the Barons live?"

Gwendolyn looked at me as if I were a dimwit. "In their castles, where else?"

"What cas—" I broke off, staring at the top of one of the hills. Realizing, for the first time, that what I had first taken to be a crumbling mass of rock was actually . . . had been at one time, at least, an edifice.

"*That's* a 'castle'?" I croaked.

"What passes for one, in the southern Baronies. In some parts of the northern Baronies, the nobility's more sophisticated." She smiled thinly. "This is not, as you may imagine, an area which attracts the world's finest architects."

I stared at the "castle," my eyes probably widening by the second. "Actually," I heard Gwendolyn murmur, "I've been told Gropius Laebmauntsforscynneweëld once passed through here. Rumor has it he was inspired to design something based on one of the Barony castles. Can't imagine what."

"I've seen it," I croaked. "It's in the Imperial Zoo at Ozar. The baboon exhibit." I tore my eyes away from the grotesque pile of rubble masquerading as a castle. "Supposed to have been, anyway. The baboons refuse to use it. When I left, they were talking about turning it into a scorpion exhibit, if they could figure out any way to let people close enough to see the venomous creatures."

"'Venomous creatures' is right." Gwendolyn pursed her lips and nodded toward the nearest castle. "We'll have to be careful here, Benvenuti. Very careful. Each one of those Barons—the best of them—makes a scorpion seem like a house pet."

We were standing in plain sight, on open ground—and easily visible because the sun had risen above the horizon. My feet twitched a little, as if they sought the relative security of the forest.

"Relax. We're safe enough. In the Baronies, you always travel during the period just before dawn and through the morning. Then, although it's a bit risky, you can travel again after the sun's down. During most of the day, you find a place to get out of sight." Again, she nodded at the not-too-distant "castle." "The Barons don't do a lick of work, you know. Exploit the peasants in the afternoon and carouse all through the evening and night. No respectable Groutch Baron rises before noon. Nor do their armed retainers."

My eyes went to the "gopher hole" she had pointed out earlier. "Won't the peasants report us?"

"You must be joking," she said, shaking her head. Then, set off at her usual brisk pace.

The biggest hurdle to our progress—and it was a big one, indeed—was clambering over the rock walls which separated each of the fields. The walls were neither high nor difficult to climb, but there were so many of them that the sheer number eventually became quite fatiguing.

"Too dangerous for us to take the road, I assume," I commented at one point, after negotiating yet another wall.

Gwendolyn was straddling the same wall. I spent a moment envying her leather trousers, which were withstanding the rigors of the wall-climbing far better than my own. I spent rather more time admiring the contents of the trousers.

"*What* 'road'?" snorted Gwendolyn. "It's just a leg, Benvenuti." The second sentence was spoken half crossly, half . . . not.

I grinned. "I'm an artist. Can't separate my appreciation of form from function."

She finished clambering over the wall. "Oh, what a lot of crap. If that's an aesthetic ogle you're giving me, I'll eat these trousers." She set off slogging across another field; over her shoulder: "And if you follow up that train of thought, you're a dead man."

I responded with an innocent smile. I also, I confess, squelched the riposte which had been on my lips—since it did, indeed, "follow up that train of thought."

I saw no reason, however, to refrain from continuing my admiration of the form and function swaying across the field ahead of me. I was by no means a fetishist, but by then I admit to have become quite an enthusiast for leather trousers. Those, at least, which had Gwendolyn in them. Although I will also readily admit that I would probably have felt the same way about any apparel which had Gwendolyn in them. Now that I had spent enough time with the woman to have gotten past the initial impression of her—ah, call it "fearsomeness"—I was finding it quite impossible to ignore the rest. Part of that fascination was simply due to her truly incredible body. Most of it was simply due to Gwendolyn.

This is stupid, I told myself firmly. *A ridiculous—hopeless—infatuation.* Myself cheerfully ignored me.

In an attempt to bring my thoughts onto more practical ground, I spoke again.

"Are you saying there are *no* roads in the Baronies?"

"Nothing more than rutted trails. The Barons cherish their independence, don't you know? Since a real road might imply the eventual possibility of a central authority to build and maintain them . . . they keep them as primitive as possible."

"I'd think they'd at least want to be able to charge tolls," I protested.

Gwendolyn snorted. "They *do* charge tolls. If you're lucky."

The logic of all this escaped me. When I said as much, Gwendolyn's reply was a vigorous shake of the head followed by: "The logic escapes everybody except the Barons. See if they care."

I spent a bit of time admiring the results produced by that vigorous shake of the head. Her hair was every bit as flamboyantly exuberant as her figure. Then: "I'd think some kingdom of Grotum would long since have put paid to this nonsense."

Seeing the frown beginning to form, I added hastily: "Not that I'm advocating imperialism, you understand."

Gwendolyn's frown turned into a somewhat rueful expression. "The Kings of Prygg tried, twice. Those of New Sfinctr, twice also. None of the attempts came to much. There are a lot of barons, and the one thing they are willing to do is fight. And there isn't much here worth conquering anyway. A bunch of surly peasants digging potatoes. About it."

The rueful look stayed on her face. I was a bit puzzled by it. Although I didn't understand that much of Gwendolyn's ideology, I couldn't imagine her feeling much chagrin at Groutch royalty being thwarted.

Something of my curiosity must have been apparent. Gwendolyn paused for a moment, planted her hands on her hips, and swiveled her head to stare off somewhere into the distance to the north. A heavy sigh followed.

"We're not that far away, actually," she said softly. She pointed to the north. "Just two hills over. You'd find the castle where the Comte de l'Abbatoir and his Knights Companion met their end."

My eyes widened. Gwendolyn sighed again. "You're familiar with the incident, I take it?"

I hesitated, finally understanding her odd mix of sentiments. "Um. Yes, of course. It's—ah, please don't take offense—considered the masterwork of the profession. When the report came to Ozar, my uncles spent an entire evening enthusing over the accounts."

Gwendolyn's lips were tight. "Accounts?" she said, emphasizing the plural.

"Oh, yes. A multitude of them, there were. The *Ozarean Times* even ran an article on the front page. Although my uncles spent most of their time engrossed in a much more scholarly version which had been rushed into print by the *Annals of Asphyxiation.*"

Her lips were now very tight. I hesitated for a moment; then, shrugging:

"Gwendolyn, you can hardly object to your brother strangling the Comte de l'Abbatoir and his entire pack of thugs. Even if he did do it for money."

She burst into sudden laughter. "*Object?* When the news came, my comrades and I spent an entire night in wild celebration. The Comte was easily the most vicious baron in the whole of the Baronies—and they're all vicious to begin with." The laugh ended soon enough. "Still . . ."

She gave her head another sharp shake and stalked off. A moment later, we were clambering over another wall and my thoughts were drawn back to more artistic concerns.

I decided to title the painting *Form and Function, a study in leather.*

We stopped at midday when we came upon a dense hedge. I didn't recognize the shrubs, but they were thick enough to make an excellent place to stay out of sight.

"We'll sleep here," Gwendolyn announced, after studying the thicket. "It'll be tight, but there's room for both of us." She gave me an eye which was half cold, half . . . not.

Sometime later, in the half darkness under the thick shrubs, we were more or less falling asleep in each other's arms. There really wasn't much room in that dense shrubbery for two people.

I say "more or less" because I was finding sleep difficult. I trust the reason is obvious.

Gwendolyn started chuckling. The various motions which that process brought in its train made me despair of ever finding sleep. Insofar as the term "despair," in context, isn't completely absurd.

"Think artistic thoughts," Gwendolyn murmured in my ear. "Plan a painting or a sculpture."

"I'm trying," I grumbled.

She chuckled again. "But I warn you. If the words 'leather' or 'form and function' appear anywhere in the title, I'll hunt you down. I swear I will."

PART VII

In Which We Return to
My Ancestors' Chronicle, of Which,
Joyful to Relate, Remains Extant All Portions
Retelling of the Sorcerer's Adventures in the
Famed Oasis, But in Which, Due to Sad
Circumstances Soon To Be Related, those
Portions Recounting the Journey From
the Famed Oasis to Prygg Exist
Only in Truncated and
Misshapen Form.

―᮰᮰᮰―

CHAPTER VII. *A Difficult Decision
Made—Yet Failure Withal. The Dwarf's
Quandary. The Serendipitous Results
Thereof. The Wizard's Praise. The Wizard's
Reproof. Our Heroes' Fortune Restored!*

As the coach for Prygg did not depart the Caravanserai for two more days, 'twas necessary for wizard

and apprentice to obtain lodgings. Fortunately, in the cursed highwayman's bemusement at Shelyid's unexpected tale, he had not thought to inspect the gnome's person. Thus did Shelyid retain the shilling in his waistband, this being the annual allowance permitted to him by his master. The coin proved just sufficient to cover the cost of a small room at the inn for two nights.

Exhausted by the journey, Shelyid curled up on his pallet and promptly fell asleep. Not so the thaumaturge, who was—any fool could see it!—engulfed in a humor both sour and bleak. He paced to and fro until the wee hours of the morn, muttering loud imprecations at the foibles of happenstance, and bringing down many fell oaths, curses, and contumely upon the absent head of a certain Rascogne de Sevigneois. At length, however, this amusement palled, and the wizard fell into silence. Clear it was that he pondered over his present worldly state. As the first light of dawn appeared, he sighed deeply.

"Alas, there is no other way. Shelyid—arise! Arise, I say!"

Grumbling and mumbling, the dwarf rolled over and sat up, rubbing the sleep from his eyes.

"What is it, master?"

"Get up, dwarf. We must discuss our present circumstances, eschewing all pusillanimous melancholy."

"Yes, master!" exclaimed Shelyid, astonishment writ plain upon his face. Rare indeed were the occasions upon which Zulkeh deigned to discuss their common situation with his apprentice. Unheard of, in fact.

The dwarf now awake and attentive, the mage began his exposition of the problem. "Shelyid, we find ourselves in dire straits—this, the result of our recent calamity. I refer, of course, to the reiving of our funds by that insufferable rogue, that leprous villain, that feculent dastard, that heinous rapscallion, that irremissible scapegrace, that—"

"Rascogne de Sevigneois."

"I shall thank you not to interrupt me!—caitiff miscreant, that—well, in any event. We have not a copper to our name, not a sou, not a farthing. True, our passage to Prygg is already paid for, but we shall require further monies to obtain provender—food, drink, and such—the which is necessary even for a thaumaturge of my talents and abilities. Do you find yourself in agreement with my diagnosis of our plight?"

"Oh yes, master!" cried Shelyid, pleased beyond compare at his master's confidence.

"The problem which thus presents itself to us, in all its indignity, is the acquisition of pecuniary resources. This follows, does it not?"

"As night from day, master!" cried Shelyid. Would wonders never cease?

"Fortunately, all is not lost. The Caravanserai is, as you may be aware, notorious not only for its many criminals, prostitutes, and suchlike ethical wantons, but for its enormous traffic in slavery, as well. Indeed, it is the chief slave market of Grotum. The conclusion, I am sure you will agree, is both obvious and inescapable."

"Oh yes, master!" cried Shelyid, overcome with pleasure at his master's bonhomie.

"Excellent!" spoke Zulkeh. "It is settled, then. I shall sell you into slavery at the first opportunity—this very day, in fact."

"*Slavery?*" shrieked the dwarf. "But—but—no! You can't, master! I won't!"

Zulkeh sighed and patted his apprentice's head. "No, no, good Shelyid, do not quail now at the force of logic. I appreciate your loyalty and can only commend you for your selfless desire to share my perils and travails, ill-equipped though you are for the task. But no—a slave you must be."

Of the disgraceful scene which followed these stern but stoic words, we shall exercise our narrative responsibility and draw over it a discretionary veil. For in truth, the gnome Shelyid did comport himself in a most unseemly manner, refusing, in flagrant violation of all custom and reason, to accede to his master's command, even after the forbearant mage had chastised him most soundly. So great, indeed, did Shelyid's intemperance become, that the wizard was required to bring forth from his sack that fearsome instrument which he employed on those (fortunately, quite rare) occasions in which routine thrashings were of no avail.

We refer here, of course, to the "Apt Malediction for the Reprovement of Sullen Stableboys, Impudent Domestics, and Other Artless Imps," the which, as the gentle reader is perhaps aware, has been the subject of great dispute among the savants. For though D.I. Laebmauntsforscynneweëld argued in his definitive *On the Use of False Scrolls* that Zulkeh's application was conditioned by the scroll's thaumaturgic deficiencies, the which rendered it useless for any purpose save the chastisement of drub-deserving dwarf-dolts, to this opinion did Torquemada Sfondrati-Piccolomini take sharp exception in his ground-breaking *Flagellation: The Romantic Face of God's Terror*, claiming instead that the mage opted for said instrument from a keen sense of poetic justice, only to call forth in so saying the intervention of his half brother Draco, this latter advancing in his controversial *Two Jerks Jerking Off* yet the third view that the wizard's use of the scroll was determined neither by goety nor poesy, but by the material substratum of both, in that the scroll was actually not a scroll, but a carved inscription upon an oaken rod.

Be that as it may, the instrument availed its purpose. Thus was propriety restored, following which, wizard and his sullen-but-subdued servant set forth for the great slave market of the Caravanserai. Yet, as the day wore on, it became apparent that the dispute between our protagonists had been needless as well as undignified. For, try as Zulkeh might, he simply could not sell his apprentice. Scrofulous though the average slave was, Shelyid was so grotesque even in this company that no slave merchant would so much as discuss the possibility of purchase.

The closest approach which the wizard enjoyed to success was also the most ignominious. All other establishments on the Boulevard of Bounteous Labor having spurned his offer, Zulkeh advanced upon the very last edifice on that noisome street—the term "edifice" being used very delicately. The ramshackle building— say better, disintegrating hut—did not betray any apparent volume of trade. The only traffic in sight was a large animal urinating next to the rear wall, as if expressing its opinion on the architecture. It might have been a hog, it was difficult to tell.

Above the half-open door—half-open of necessity, since two of the three hinges had fallen loose—was a sign which read:

RIGHT TO WORK INSTITUTE
Herbert & Gertrude Sophist, proprietors
You've got a right to work!
So we'll sell it to you.
Cheap.

Zulkeh strode within, Shelyid in tow. In the gloom beyond, an elderly couple so slender they seemed almost skeletal were lounging on an ancient divan. The male half of the pair was snoring. His female counterpart, eyes widening at the appearance of an actual customer, jabbed him fiercely in the ribs. Given the sharpness of the elbow involved, it was a bit astonishing that no flow of blood ensued.

The man jerked awake. Then, seeing Zulkeh and Shelyid, sprang to his feet. Using, again, the term "sprang" with considerable delicacy.

"Yessair, yessair," he chortled, rubbing his bony hands together with a sound not dissimilar to that made by certain insects. "Yessair, yessair—I've got just what you need!"

He gestured grandly toward the far corner of the shack, where his wife was now occupied hauling forth what appeared to be the only merchandise the establishment had in stock at the moment—a woman whose age was impossible to determine, clad in rags, festooned with chains and shackles, and so skeletal she made the owners seem obese.

"Premium quality house servant!" the man pronounced solemnly. "Not quite suitable fer y'proper carnal abuse—I'll be the first t'admit it, I'm no huckster tryin' to pass off cut-rate merchandise as anythin' more than 'tis—but I'll knock twenty percent off y'price."

Alas, the intended sale turned out to be a skeleton in actual fact. After being dragged halfway across the earthen floor, the arm in the wife's hand came loose at the shoulder and the rest of the body flopped to the ground.

"Vile slave!" the woman snarled. "Wretchit thief! Try and steal from me, would yer?" She proceeded to thrash the corpse with the limb in her hand. Alas, after a single thrash the elbow joint gave way as well, leaving the wife disarmed as well as dispossessed.

"I *told* ye we 'ad to feed 'er more often, Gertrude," hissed her husband. "Onc't a week jest won't—"

Zulkeh cleared his throat noisily. "Sirrah, you misunderstand. I have come here to make a sale, not a purchase."

The mage grasped Shelyid by the shoulder and shoved him forward. "My apprentice. A stout lad, if stupid, and well inured to labor. I warn you I shall not be cheated."

The man—Herbert Sophist, presumably—eyed Shelyid with skepticism. But, unlike all the other slave dealers they had approached that day, he began to examine the prospective merchandise. And if his bony fingers poked Shelyid's ribs with no great vigor, and pried open his lips to inspect the teeth with even less, still and all 'twas at least a semblance of proper slave-dealer custom.

After Sophist was finished he stepped back, planted hands on hips, and announced firmly: "I'll take 'im off yer hands. Nay a problem, sair. Be my pleasure." He eyed Zulkeh for a moment, gauging the possibilities, and then added (not quite as firmly): "Twenty quid. And don't think ye can talk me down, sirrah! I'm being generous as 'tis."

Zulkeh frowned. "I have no intention of talking you down! Your offer is absurd. Thirty quid and not a penny less."

Sophist's eyes widened. *"Thirty?"* he choked.

Before he could say another word his wife shuffled forwardly eagerly and hissed: "Done! Thirty quid it is!" Her hand stretched forth, palm up, like the petal of a Venus flytrap. "Cash now. No credit."

Zulkeh's frown deepened. He stared at the woman's clawlike hand. "There seems to be some confusion here . . ." he muttered.

"No confusion!" snapped Gertrude. "As 'tis, even at thirty quid we'll like as not lose money."

Her husband nodded solemnly. "Indeed so! A dwarf?

Scrofulous as thissun? Th'feed alone'll mos' like bankrupt us afore we kin find some idiot—ah, customer who'll take 'im off our hands."

It was Zulkeh's turn to choke. And choke. Eventually he managed: "Insane! Do I understand you aright? You expect *me* to pay *you* for—for *selling my own merchandise*?"

Hearing these words, Gertrude Sophist began to spittle. "O'course! 'Tis the law!"

"Sairtainly is!" snapped her husband. In the singsong tone of one reciting memorized words: "No dwarven slave may be purchased without payment from the seller, lest the foul notion be established that dwarves are worth anything." In a less stilted manner: "Sorry, sair. No point arguin' th'matter. Thazza direct quote from ye Honorable Judge Greased Hand's decision in th' case o' *The Dreaded Scot vs. the Pewling Dwarf-Lovers' Association.*"

He lifted his nose. "The Dreaded Scot bein', as I'm sairtain yer aware, reckinized 'cross Grotum as th'slave trader's slave trader."

"In the Hall of Fame, 'e is," snapped Gertrude. "Made it on th'first ballot, too."

These words spoken, the mage proceeded to open up to the understanding of Sophists, man and wife, the preposterous and pernicious nature of their logic, reason, rationale, sanity—

But he had barely warmed to the subject before the distaff member of the couple, displaying a vigor quite out of keeping with her anorexic appearance, threw him bodily out of the establishment's doorway. Dislodging, alas, the final hinge in the process, the which produced a shrieking promise from Gertrude Sophist that she intended to sue the mage for every penny he owned in damages.

Shelyid scuttled out of the building, nimbly evading

a savage blow from Gertrude on the way out—so nimbly, indeed, that the hapless woman overbalanced and injured herself on the doorframe, the which mishap produced yet another shrieking promise that she intended to sue the mage for every penny he might *ever* own in damages.

But, by then, Shelyid had hoisted the mage back onto his feet. Master and apprentice hastened from the scene, followed by the shrill curses and imprecations of the Sophists, man and wife, until the cadaverous pair apparently ran out of breath altogether. Which, in truth, did not take long.

Midafternoon, therefore, found Zulkeh and Shelyid trudging back to the inn. Once arrived in their room, the wizard turned to his apprentice and spoke.

"Shelyid, I command you to remain here. You are forbidden to leave this room under any circumstances, no matter how dire or urgent they may seem to you. I now depart, to rendezvous with a certain individual who, such is my hope, may be interested in purchasing your person."

"But we already went to every slave dealer in town, master," protested Shelyid.

"You are too pessimistic, Shelyid. The individual of whom I speak is not a slaver. He owns a circus, and has, I am led to understand, a sizable collection of freaks and sports of nature, to which he may wish to add another specimen." And so saying, the wizard departed, locking the door behind him.

Following the wizard's departure, Shelyid huddled on his pallet, misery writ plain upon his face. Now that his feeble mind was no longer distracted by the sights and sounds of the Caravanserai, it was plain as day that the wretched dwarf's thoughts were focused with undivided attention upon his plight.

"A circus freak," he muttered. "A slave was bad enough, but a circus freak!" Many long minutes of silence followed; then—"People'll laugh at me. Point fingers. Throw food. Probably get better food thrown at you than they give you to eat regular, anyway." Many more long minutes of silence. "And what about upward social mobility?" he called out suddenly, into the gathering twilight.

Many more long minutes passed. Then did a look of discomfort come to sit upon his face. Alas, the dwarf's fears had produced the inevitable biological concomitant.

"Gotta shit," said he. And so saying, rose and minced toward the door, which opened into the corridor where the water closet was located. But at the door he halted, muttering.

"Can't leave the room, master said. Under any circumstances, he said. Besides, door's locked." He turned away, mounting agony writ plain upon his face.

"But I *gotta* shit." He stared at the floor—a wild surmise—but then: "Cripes no, dummy. Issa *Consortium* floor—prob'bly gut ya f'that." Suddenly his legs coiled about each other like vines.

"Gotta shit *bad!*" he wailed. Then did understanding and wisdom come and sit upon his brow. "O'course!" he cried. "The old scroll! S'no good anyway."

And so saying, the dwarf hopped across the room, limbs still entwined. He flung himself upon the wizard's sack, feverishly scrabbling through its contents. At length he emerged, clutching in his hand an old and much-worn scroll entitled *On the Transmutation of Base Elements Into Gold.*

"Master'll never miss't—s'tried it dozens a times, s'never worked." And not a moment too soon did the apprentice spread the scroll upon the floor and attend to his urgent business.

There did Shelyid squat for a time, staring placidly at the opposite wall. Eventually finished with his work, the dwarf rose and buckled his breeches. Then, turning and stooping over, he prepared to pick up the scroll and its contents and hurl them through the window onto the street below, this method of waste disposal being *de riguer* throughout Grotum. But he was of a sudden transfixed. For imagine his astonishment when he perceived that, where should have lain certain objects the precise nature of which we will delicately leave to the gentle reader's understanding, lay instead— *mirabile dictu!*—several large and oddly shaped ingots of gold.

And it was at this very moment that the wizard returned to the room. It required a full ten minutes for Zulkeh to decipher Shelyid's ensuing babble, following which he smiled approvingly and patted the dwarf's head.

"You have done well, Shelyid. I perceive now my past error concerning this scroll. My mistake lay in assuming that by 'base elements' were meant the common metals, whereas in fact were meant base elements, of which, as is well known, there is none baser than dwarf excrement. And there is a lesson to be learned from this, my stupid but loyal apprentice, in that subtlety of mind can be, on occasion, its own undoing.

"Indeed, this stroke of fortune comes at a most opportune moment, for the individual I went to see expressed a total lack of interest in buying you for his circus. All this, however, is now behind us. Armed with this newfound wealth, we are funded not only for our present needs but for some considerable portion of the future as well."

Shelyid's ugly little face crinkled with pleasure. Not so the wizard's—for Zulkeh's benign smile turned in a instant to a fearsome scowl.

"I note also, however," spoke the mage in a stern voice, "that you have grossly defiled one of my scrolls, the which I had faithfully entrusted to your care." And the sorcerer thrashed his apprentice soundly.

CHAPTER VIII. *A Commercial Philoso-*
phy Elaborated. The Wizard Demurs. An
Interview With a Subordinate of the Law.
The Sheriff's Return. The Unsatisfactory
Results Therefrom. The Wizard Seeks
Counsel!

The next morning, with Shelyid in tow, the wizard set
out for the depot of the GGNESWC& etc., desiring,
before making further plans, to assure himself that the
coach to Prygg would depart on schedule the following day. Arriving at the depot, he made his way to the
ticket vendor's window. No sooner had the wizard iden-
tified himself than the ticket vendor exclaimed: "So!
You chose to surrender yourself, did you?"

"I beg your pardon?" queried the mage.

"Sirrah, it has been brought to my attention that
you were among the passengers who arrived in the last
coach from Goimr."

"Indeed so."

"It has also been brought to my attention that the
aforementioned coach was robbed whilst you were
aboard."

"Indeed so—a scabrous event!" The light of understanding dawned in the wizard's eye. "Ah, good sir, it pleases me no end to see the concern with which your company views its customers' woes. An excellent policy, this, to offer recompense to those of your passengers who have suffered indignities while enjoying the hospitality of your firm! Know, my good man, that you are fortunate indeed to find yourself employed by so progressive a—"

"You suffer from a gross misapprehension. It is not you, but we, who are the injured party in this affair, and thus the recipients of restitution."

"I beg your pardon?"

"As a passenger on a vehicle owned and operated by the Great Grotum etc., etc., & etc., you are liable for any damage (physical, financial, mental, moral, emotional, spiritual, natural, supernatural, or immaterial) inflicted upon said vehicle and its contents (animate or inanimate, sentient or senseless) and, by extension, upon the Great Grotum etc., etc., & etc." As the wizard stared on, in a rare speechless moment, the ticket vendor picked up a scroll and began droning:

"For permitting a coach of the GGNESWC& etc. to be robbed, you are hereby fined one hundred and fifty ducats.

"For allowing—"

"Preposterous!" cried the mage, his wits returned. Gesticulating wildly, the thaumaturge thrust his face at the ticket vendor.

"This is absurd! Utterly absurd! You have lost your corporate senses! I am in no fashion responsible for your miserable coach!"

"That statement is not merely incorrect," sniffed the ticket vendor, "it is positively grotesque. You are, in fact, legally responsible in this matter, having made of your own free will a contract to that effect with the Great Grotum etc., etc., & etc."

"Art mad! I made no such contract—I merely purchased a ticket!"

"I see. Obviously you are ignorant of the fact that the moment one consummates any transaction with any subsidiary of the Consortium, one automatically agrees—at that very instant—to the full provisions of the Consortium Cosmological Contract."

"I was not informed of any such provision!"

"To be sure. This point, however, is hardly germane." The ticket vendor resumed his reading of the scroll.

"For allowing a messenger of the GGNESWC& etc. to be interrupted in the performance of his duties, you are hereby fined seventy-five ducats.

"For allowing a servant of the Lord to be slandered and his piety subjected to denigration, you are fined fifty ducats.

"For allowing a belted knight of the realm to have his manhood and noble reputation subjected to gross indignities, you are fined sixty ducats.

"For allowing a female passenger on a vehicle operated by the GGNESWC& etc. to be seduced by a non-paying individual, you are fined forty ducats, per seduction—a total of two hundred ducats.

"For allowing other passengers on the GGNESWC& etc. to be robbed, you are fined thirty-five ducats per passenger—a total of two hundred and ten ducats.

"For—"

"I protest! Why should I be held responsible for other passengers? Why should they not be held responsible for their own mishaps—and mine, for that matter?"

"They have," replied the ticket vendor, "and have been fined accordingly. I might add that two of the passengers, Il Conde de la Manteca and his wife La Contessa—ridiculous titles!—refused to pay the fines, and have accordingly been incarcerated."

"But she's a nice lady!" cried Shelyid.

The ticket vendor sniffed. "Finally, you are fined fifty ducats for allowing yourself to be robbed while traveling on a vehicle operated by the GGNESWC& etc." He laid down the scroll and stared stonily at the mage, palm outstretched. "The total fine amounts to seven hundred and ninety-five ducats, payable in the legal tender of the region, which, in this instance, is the Consortium Ducat."

"I refuse!" bellowed the wizard, beside himself with fury. "O monstrous! O monstrous!"

"Sir," stated the ticket vendor in a voice devoid of inflection or discernible tone, "am I to understand that you are calling into question the philosophy and commercial *weltanschauung* of the GGNESWC& etc., a subsidiary—"

"A pox on your philosophy, sirrah! I shall take this arrant thievery to the law!"

And so saying, the mage strode forth into the street, casting his eyes about for the location of the forces of law and order. Almost immediately, his attention caught by faint wails of agony, he spotted nearby a large gray building built of heavy stone, windows barred, steps blood-stained.

"The Hall of Justice!" he cried, and hastened thence. "Come, Shelyid," he spoke over his shoulder. "You are shortly to witness the manner in which base curs of low degree are called to order!"

Entering the building, Zulkeh saw to his left an old wooden door, upon whose peeling surface was crudely lettered the words: SHERIFF'S OFFICE. He strode within, there to espy a man before him, seated at a large and much-carved desk, belly overhanging belt, booted feet propped up, visage totally obscured by an enormous hat slanted sharply forward.

"Are you the Sheriff?" demanded Zulkeh. The man behind the desk looked up. Faded blue eyes peered at the mage from a face whose every feature was masked by a complex maze of wrinkles, crow's-feet, creases, and the like. A luxurious mustache adorned his upper lip.

"That I am," drawled this worthy. "Sheriff Pike." Then, in a tone which belied the words: "At your service."

"Excellent!" spoke Zulkeh. "I have a complaint which I wish to register with the Law."

The Sheriff spat with unerring accuracy into a nearby spittoon. He sighed wearily.

"All right, all right," he grumbled. "What is it?"

"An abomination! An insolent offense! An outrageous calumny!"

Pike grimaced, or so, at least, one could interpret the heavings of his mustache. "I assumed that. Why else would anyone complain to the Sheriff? *Which* abomination? *What* offense? *Whose* calumny? These are the questions that need to be answered before modern police investigation can get off the ground."

Zulkeh brought himself under control. "I wish to register a complaint against the Consortium. These scoundrels, these—"

"Shove it."

"I beg your pardon?"

"I said 'shove it'!" bellowed the Sheriff fiercely. "I haven't got the time or energy to be bothered by lunatics who want to file a complaint against the Consortium."

Zulkeh gazed coldly at the agent of the Law. "I now perceive the truth. You have been suborned by the Consortium."

Pike's face turned beet-red with outrage.

"Why, damn your insolence!" he roared. "I am a sworn servant of the Law doing my duty! This office as well as the jail which appertains to it is a *bona fide* subsidiary of the Consortium and I am carrying out my responsibilities as a faithful employee of the firm!"

Zulkeh was silent for a moment. "The law in the Caravanserai, do I understand you to say, is owned outright by the Consortium?"

"Lock, stock, and barrel," stated the Sheriff. "Quite a profitable concern, too," he added with some pride.

"Clearly, then," spoke the wizard, "I can expect no justice from these quarters."

"Ruled out right from the start," agreed the Sheriff.

"I must then seek redress elsewhere," mused Zulkeh. "The rot has sunk deeper than I had perceived." He glared at the Sheriff. "Where may I find an attorney-at-law?"

"A what?"

"A lawyer!"

"Oh." The Sheriff shook his head slowly. "Couldn't tell you. There isn't any need for a lawyer in this town. You can say what you like about big city police efficiency, but in my opinion we've brought the science of criminology in this little town to a state of perfection that would be envied in Ozar itself. If anybody has a complaint against the Consortium, they're automatically wrong. If anybody has a complaint against anybody else," he yawned, "who gives a shit?"

The Sheriff rubbed his belly, apparently in an effort to stimulate thought. "You might try the hotel down the street," he suggested. "All sorts of riffraff traveling through the Caravanserai can be found there."

With no further word, Zulkeh stormed out of the Sheriff's office, Shelyid's little legs scurrying to keep pace. Down the street, the mage espied a ramshackle building bearing a much-abused sign on which only the letters ONTHLY RAT S could still be seen. In but a trice, the agitated sorcerer arrived at the hotel and strode within.

Peering about the Stygian gloom of the lobby, the wizard saw, arranged in a manner which defied all geometry and logic, a multitude of couches and divans. These items of furniture ranged, in their degree of corrosion and disrepair, from shabby and soiled to filthy beyond belief and downright dangerous. Despite their, at best, disreputable appearance, each of the couches was occupied by an individual, none of whom, judging from their slouches, seemed to find any great joy in life.

Across the lobby, Zulkeh made out a jury-rigged little counter which he took to be the reception desk. Seated behind the desk, in a posture which matched the decor, was a sallow-faced individual whose thinning gray hair was adorned by a little cap bearing the letters ESK LERK. Advancing upon this fellow, the mage questioned the desk clerk as to the possibility that an attorney-at-law could be found among the hotel's current clientele.

The desk clerk, alas, proved to be an ignorant, slothful, and insolent wight. Ignorant, in that he claimed no knowledge of any characteristic of any of the hotel's residents beyond the adequacy of their purse. Slothful, in that he proclaimed an utter lack of interest in correcting this appalling state of ignorance. Insolent, in that he responded to the mage's vigorous insistence that he do so with a series of exclamations the which ranged from uncouth to downright scurrilous.

No doubt the surly fellow would have been smitten by the mage's wizardrous fury at that point, had not one of the individuals lounging on a nearby divan spoken up. Croaked up, it might be better to say:

"There's a lawyer in the saloon," rasped he, in what seemed to be his last breath.

"Gee," whispered Shelyid, "I thought he was dead." And, indeed, the fellow expired that very moment.

The urgency of his task overriding his urge to chasten the desk clerk, the irate thaumaturge immediately stalked to the saloon adjoining the lobby, guided by the sign appended over the swinging doors: needless to say, ALOON.

Thence did the mage take himself, entering a low-ceilinged room whose atmosphere was most vilely polluted by smoke and the miasma of sundry alcoholic distillations.

"I need an attorney!" he spoke into the murky gloom.

A long-torsoed individual, thin as a rail, perked up at a table in the far corner. "I am here!" he cried, rising to greet the wizard.

"Mustelid's the name, solicitor's the trade." The whiskers beneath his long and pointed nose quivered with the scent of fee.

CHAPTER IX. *A Barrister's Informed Opinion. Sundry Cases of Great Legal Moment Encapsulated. A Youth Intervenes, Hot of Temper and Mien. The Wizard Adjudicates. A Youth Denounces, Hot of Temper and Mien. The Consortium is Recompensed!*

"And thus you have it," concluded the mage. He sat stiffly in his chair, Shelyid standing behind. "And now, sirrah, I will appreciate it if you would unfold before me the manner in which I may obtain full satisfaction from these miscreants, not excluding the extraction of punitive damages for the affront they have committed to my dignity."

Across the table, the lawyer slumped in his chair, utter discouragement evident in both posture and expression. He shook his head mournfully.

"I can't see what's to be done. There's no legal case to be made—you haven't a leg to stand on. The Consortium—its subsidiary, I should say—acted within its legal rights at all times."

"Preposterous!" oathed Zulkeh. "By what legalistic

legerdemain am I held responsible for this so-called 'Consortium Cosmological Contract' by the mere act of buying a ticket?"

"There is no statutory prestidigitation involved," differed the lawyer, shaking his head with some vehemence. "That's the law. I refer you to the famous case of *The Consortium vs. Grandmother Hapless*, in which the decision was written by that most respected jurist, the Honorable Judge Learned Hound. In his opinion, Judge Hound wrote—wait a minute, I have it here in my valise—" Mustelid rummaged around in a briefcase by his feet and brought forth a huge leather-bound book. He laid the tome on the table and rapidly flicked through the pages.

"Here it is. I will quote verbatim:

"'Foolishness 'twould be to demand of any established commercial firm that it limit its transactions with its divers customers merely to the immediate purchase involved at any specific moment in time. For none but reactionary pedants, who fail to grasp the nature of modern industry's rise and growth, can think that any single instance of commercial exchange is but a fleeting node in the complex matrix of modern economic intercourse. Of necessity, both material and moral, all such transactions must be covered by legal bonds which encompass in their implicit nature the whole of modern society's inescapable interdependence.'"

Zulkeh was silent for many long moments, as he examined this logic in his mind. At length, he nodded his head slowly. "The argument is irrefutable, I must admit. However, it remains the case that it cannot be applied to myself, for I was never informed of this provision when I purchased my ticket. Surely the Consortium is under the obligation of informing its customers of the full ramifications of buying a ticket from them!"

"By no means!" countered Mustelid. "The Consortium's long-standing policy of 'Silence is Consent' has been upheld in court. I refer you, in this regard, to that well-known case in the annals of Groutch jurisprudence, *The Consortium vs. Little Johnny Waif.* This case was decided by that other most eminent of Groutch jurists, the Honorable Judge Greased Hand. His opinion concluded with the following impeccable reasoning—" Another quick searching of the pages.

" 'No legally constituted firm of good reputation and proven stability can be held responsible for the time-consuming dissemination of all the picayune details and minutia of its manifold implicit contracts to other parties who may be involved in the endless permutations of such inherent contractual obligations. For, should such a slavishly legalistic doctrine be allowed to prevail, no concern operating along sound commercial lines could long endure, so burdened would it become by foolish and unnecessary paperwork.'"

Again Zulkeh was silent for some time, as he pondered the problem. Again he nodded his head slowly.

"The logic cannot be faulted. It appears, then, that I have behaved precipitously. I shall have to recompense the Consortium."

"Nay, sir, do not so!" interrupted a voice suddenly. Turning in his seat, the mage beheld a youth seated at a nearby table.

"You addressed me, sirrah?"

"I did!" responded the youth, rising and advancing upon Zulkeh's table. "I made my voice known!"

"What else is new?" sneered Mustelid. "Know, good sir,"—this by way of an aside to the wizard—"that this inflammatory stripling is a well-known malcontent, whose irresponsible frothings have plagued fair Grotum since he left the domain of his prominent family's estates."

Favoring the lawyer with fleering nostrils and a gaze in which scorn and contempt commingled in his feverish eyes, the youth spoke again to the wizard.

"Know, citizen, that my name is Holdabrand, and that I hold the Banner of Justice aloft!"

"Such is commendable," spoke Zulkeh, "but what has it to do with me?"

"Forgive, citizen, my intrusion! But I could not help but overhear the poisoned words of this lackey of the moneyed interests! Thus do I hasten to counter his oily filth with the Right!"

The lawyer sputtered, but Zulkeh stilled him with a gesture. Turning back to the youth, he spoke. "Counter it, then, since you have made so bold your claim."

Holdabrand took a chair and spoke in an urgent voice.

"Citizen, you cannot help but have seen with your own eyes how in recent years the fair land of Grotum, once known the world over for its happy and contented people, its stern but fair-minded rulers, its harmony of classes and masses, its simple but righteous ways, its noble customs and traditions—"

"How many more clauses, d'you think?" sneered Mustelid. "Twenty? Thirty?"

The youth glared but drove on: "—has become overrun by this foreign monstrosity, this alien arachnid, this avaricious octopoid, this slimy parasite, this—"

"Forty? Fifty?"

"—this *Consortium*—whose lust for wealth has led it to corrupt and bring down the most ancient and pure mores of our land, whose insatiable rapacity has led it to plunder even the smallest of Grotum's treasures, to exploit even the feeblest of our resources—"

"Sixty? Seventy?"

"—whose lust for domination has led it to suborn all but a handful of Grotum's most venerable institutions, whose unbridled thirst—"

"Enough!" cried out the lawyer. "We're being claused to death! It's all rot—bilge and rot. 'Tis rather by dint of the Consortium's mighty efforts—motivated by self-interest, to be sure, but nonetheless admirable and beneficial—that these backward nations of Grotum stand fair to enter the world of modern industry and progress, to take their rightful place beside all other respected and puissant lands!"

Mustelid thrust his face at Zulkeh and continued in an earnest voice. "Do not allow the ravings of this romantic reactionary to sway your logical faculties, good sir. Fine for him—the scion of a great landowner—to preach airily of the joys of simple Groutch life, he who never labored from dawn to dusk in his father's fields, he whose dronelike existence is made possible by the unceasing toil of his father's serfs, he whose—"

"Damn you, knave!" shrilled the youth. "Have I not shortened my title, renounced certain excessive portions of my inheritance, urged liberalism in our dealings with the peons, even quarreled with my father—why, even in his own drawing room before guests? Have I not devoted my life to the uplifting of that selfsame squalid peasantry whose plight so suddenly grips your heart? Fraud! Impostor! These paeans to so-called progress spring dishonestly from your lips! Fear, greed, and envy—those are your true idols!"

The lawyer leaned back in his chair. "I am not abashed by your fantasies," he sneered. "I have no truck with dreaming fools who spout nonsense to the march of progress without accepting the necessary, if unfortunate, concomitants of that selfsame course of national betterment. And as for 'fear, greed, and envy,' certainly I do not deny them their rightful place in society's onward advance. Was it not the Honorable Judge Learned Hound himself who upheld, in the case of *The Consortium vs. the Maimed and Injured Wretch*, the legal and moral propriety of—and here I quote his exact and immortal phrase—'*Fear, Greed, and Envy, the requisite economic waters upon whose lapping waves the Ship of State serenely sails*'?"

"And well should you mention that corruption in human flesh!" shrilled Holdabrand. "Aye, indeed! That same Judge Learned Hound whose legalistic machinations made possible the devastation of Pryggia's stalwart yeomanry!"

"And glad I am," responded the lawyer with equal heat, "that you have raised this matter! Let us put it to this fine gentleman seated here, to see on which side of this dispute lies reason and the higher justice!"

Turning then to Zulkeh, Mustelid spoke in soft tones filled with great conviction. "Look you, sirrah, the case to which this insolent youth refers is one of the most luminous in the annals—not simply of Groutch jurisprudence—but of Law throughout the civilized world. The decision, jointly written by Judges Hound and Hand, has gained such repute that it is regularly assigned for study at the great School of Law at the University of Ozarae, that most prestigious of all academies. In this most complex and critical case, *The Consortium vs. the Hayseed Malcontents*, ere then murky and confused in the mind of gentility and plebeian alike, the two brilliant jurists charted a course unswayed by any interests save the upholding of Law, Reason, Truth and Justice.

"In essence, the case involved the claim of the Pryggian peasantry that, inasmuch as they had already given over one quarter of their crop to the noble landlords by way of rent, one quarter to the King by way of taxes, and one quarter to the Ecclesiarchs by way of tithe, they should not be required to cede the remaining one quarter to the Consortium by way of interest, as they would then surely starve. In their opinion, Judges Hound and Hand upheld the counterclaim of the Consortium, saying that—I will cite their very words—" A lightning-like flick through the pages. Then:

"*'The legal position of the Consortium is, strictly and constitutionally speaking, unassailable. And, though this will undoubtedly produce mass famine and a peasantry driven into a life of vagabondage, prostitution and cannibalism—a state of misery which, needless to say, we personally deplore and condemn, but also note is illegal and can thus serve as the basis for a profitable new prison industry—it is nonetheless crucial that the State not intrude in this matter, for such intervention would surely become but the first and irremediable step on what the great scholar Hayek Laebmauntsforscynneweëld has rightly called 'the Road to Serfdom.'*'"

Silence filled the room as the wizard considered the question at great length. Indeed, so long stretched his silence that the dwarf Shelyid made so bold as to tug at Holdabrand's sleeve.

"That's awful about the poor peasants," he said.

Holdabrand jerked his sleeve from the gnome's grasp. "I'll thank you to keep your hands off my shirt!" he snapped.

Shelyid drew back, hurt and abashed. But then, his normal timidity apparently overridden by some strong emotion, he tugged once again at Holdabrand's sleeve.

"How much land does your family own, anyway?" he asked the youth.

Holdabrand jerked his sleeve away again, brushing it off. "That's silk!" he snarled. "Not that I'd expect you to recognize it. And it's none of your business how much land we own. Besides, who keeps track of such details? Ask my father's accountants—not that they'd speak to a scrofulous gnome!"

"I'm sorry about the shirt," whispered Shelyid. "It's just—well, I was thinking about all those starving people and—well, since you must own an awful lot of land, maybe you could talk to your father about giving some of it—maybe only half of it—to those people, so they wouldn't have to eat each other and horrible stuff like that. I mean, you don't really probably need—"

"What is this—social philosophy from a subhuman?" sneered the youth.

"But—" The dwarf got no further, for at that very moment his master finally spoke.

"The question is, of course, transparent from the epistemological standpoint. The entire problem lies rather in the ontological ramifications of the case. But here as well, upon reflection, 'tis clear as a mountain stream that both Reason and the Higher Justice lies with the Consortium. For look you, if—"

Holdabrand lunged to his feet. "Then you too are a minion of darkness! I spit upon your Reason and your so-called Higher Justice! Soon enough will the true justice fall down upon your head!" And with that he charged out of the saloon, cuffing Shelyid from his path.

"Impudent youth!" oathed the wizard.

"What would you?" asked the lawyer, spreading his arms. "'Tis the inevitable behavior of these pampered nobles when they are at last confronted with the dictates of progress."

Zulkeh nodded his agreement. "Oft have I noted the parlous state of the modern aristocracy. Most unfortunate. And now, sirrah," he rose to his feet,

"I must be off and finish my business with the GGNESWC& Etc. I thank you for your assistance in clarifying these matters, and I bid you a good day."

The lawyer coughed discreetly. "Good sir, you have overlooked the matter of my fee."

"What fee?"

"Why, the fee for my professional services."

"Nonsense!" spoke the mage. "I merely asked you for some advice. No mention was made of any fee!"

"But my good sir," said the lawyer, smiling like a pool of oil, "have you forgotten so soon my exposition of the Honorable Judge Greased Hand's enunciation of the principle that ignorance of—"

"Are you a subsidiary of the Consortium?" interrupted Shelyid.

"Why, no," responded Mustelid, nonplussed both by the query and its source.

"Well, then," said Shelyid, "I don't see how you could collect anyway because didn't the Sheriff himself say he didn't care about anybody's problems except the Consortium? Didn't he, master? Didn't he?"

"Why yes," mused Zulkeh, "so he did." Then, to the lawyer: "Odd as it may seem, good sir, my stupid but loyal apprentice has for once stumbled upon a truth. I fear you must forget any receipt of payments for your services, if such they may be called."

The lawyer quivered in indignation, his long whiskers and pointed nose thrusting and twitching about.

"But it's your moral obligation!"

"Bah!" oathed Zulkeh. "What boots this sudden philosophical cowardice? Was it not you yourself who so recently demolished the arguments of that foolish stripling, demonstrating with sureness and clarity that no modern society worthy of the name can tolerate the intrusion of haphazard ethical gestures into the workings of its commercial order?" He shook his head sadly. "Fie upon this apostasy! Again, sir, I bid you good day!" And so speaking, the mage strode out of the room.

But Shelyid hung back, and timidly approached the vibrating chord of outrage that was the lawyer. "Maybe," he ventured, "you should get a job working for the Consortium. I'm sure they must hire a lot— a really, really lot—of lawyers," he piped cheerfully. "And sure, probably they wouldn't let you hang out in saloons, and you'd probably have to work in a big room somewhere filled with thousands of other lawyers, hunched over a desk, and sure, probably they'd make you work a lot of hours and you'd get all stooped over and such, but your posture's lousy anyway and besides, you probably wouldn't have time to worry about your health anyway because you'd be worrying all the time about getting fired, and all. But at least you wouldn't—"

He got no further, for Mustelid squeaked in fury and lunged from his chair, aiming a blow at the dwarf.

Shelyid ducked. "I was only trying to help," he whined, and scurried from the room.

Outside the hotel, he espied his master's figure striding toward the travel depot, and hastened to catch up. Once they arrived, Zulkeh thrust his pile of mis-shapen ingots at the ticket vendor. "Here is the gold to pay the fine you have levied upon me."

The ticket vendor glanced coldly at the pile of ungeometric gold bars.

"I regret to inform you, sir," stated the ticket vendor in a voice devoid of inflection or discernible tone, "that this is unacceptable. The GGNESWC& etc. can only accept payment in the recognized legal tender of the region, which, in this instance, is the Consortium Ducat."

"I see. And where may I acquire such specie?"

"You may exchange your gold for ducats at the Caravanserai Moneylenders Association, located two doors down the street."

Arriving at the specified location but a few moments later, Zulkeh and Shelyid passed through a door over which was suspended the traditional and time-honored emblem of the moneylender, an iron fist squeezing blood from a stone. Within, the wizard approached the teller's window and laid his eccentric bullion upon the counter.

"I should like to exchange these for Consortium Ducats."

"Certainly, sir," said the teller, flicking the idiosyncratic nuggets onto a scale with a splayed and callused thumb. "That comes to twenty-four hundred ducats." He laid six stacks of coins upon the counter. But just as Zulkeh reached out to pick up the coins, the tellers removed one of the stacks.

"What do you do there?" demanded the mage. "That is my money!"

"You are grotesquely in error," replied the cashier. "There is a sixteen point six seven percent service charge for processing gold which is not tendered in the form of the officially established Consortium Ingot."

Zulkeh opened his mouth to protest, reconsidered, and stormed out.

Later that night, as our heroes retired to their pallets, the dwarf Shelyid was heard to grumble, "I'll be glad to get out of this place, master."

"Well spoken, gnome. And now to sleep."

PART VIII

In Which, With
Great Horror, We Relate
the Despicable Doings of the
Desperado Sfondrati-Piccolomini
As He Takes It Upon Himself
To Stand Against Custom
in the Baronies.

*The Autobiography of Benvenuti Sfondrati-Piccolomini,
Episode 5: Dirt, Darkness, Droits and Decisions*

So it was in such cramped quarters that I awoke later that day. For a moment—quite a long moment, truth be told—I luxuriated in the feel of Gwendolyn's body pressed against my own. Beyond the thicket in which we were hidden, the sun was setting. The reddish glow within the dimness of the thick shrubbery bathed her in soft and glorious color.

I became so engrossed in the artistic possibilities, in addition to the purely sensual aspects of the experience, that I was quite oblivious when Gwendolyn herself awoke. Her head was nestled on my shoulder,

her face turned toward me, and I suspect she studied me under lowered lids for some time before she
finally spoke.

"I'm not sure whether to be flattered, annoyed,
amused—or all three," she murmured. "I've been ogled
before, but . . . never like this."

I froze for an instant. But then, feeling the gentle
pressure of her hand on my chest and realizing that
she was not really offended, I smiled. "My apologies,
I suppose. But you are both beautiful in your own right
and—" I groped for words. "It would make *such* a
magnificent portrait."

Her initial response was a slight stiffness. But then
I felt her hand slide down from my chest and come
to rest on my ribs, as if instinct was urging her to
caress. The sensation that little movement produced
in me was . . . call it intense.

I believe it was for her, also. At least, the chuckle
which she emitted seemed strained and forced. "So.
What's the title? And I warn you again—no 'leather'
or 'form and function' allowed."

My own response was a bit forced, I suspect. "I was
thinking more along the lines of *Tranquility Where Not
Expected.*"

Her hand on my ribs seemed to tighten a moment,
and not with anger. Again, the sensation that movement produced was . . . intense. Then, she sighed.

"It's too bad, it really is. But it still wouldn't work."

A moment later, with the tigerish energy of which
she was capable, Gwendolyn was up and wriggling her
way out of the thicket. "Come on—we've got to get
moving."

I followed, as quickly and obediently as anyone
could ask. I admit, the sight of her posterior wriggling its way through the bushes ahead of me was a
powerful incentive.

Once in the open, Gwendolyn cast a quick and wary eye over the area. The sun was over the horizon now, but there was still enough light to see by.

"Safe enough," she murmured. "I'd rather wait until midnight, but time is a priority."

A moment later, she was trotting off down a path which could only be called a "country lane" by the most generous definition. "Rutted dirt road" captures more of the reality, understanding that the "ruts" looked to have been made by something other than wheels. Small skids, I imagined.

After a while, once darkness had fallen completely, the little irregularities in the road caused me to trip and stumble several times. The pack I was carrying was not particularly heavy—our food was almost entirely gone, by now—but my special easel was, as always, an awkward thing to carry.

I must have been cursing not entirely under my breath, because I heard Gwendolyn's husky whisper urging me to silence. Then, in a hiss: "Nobody asked you to bring the stupid thing."

Which was true, of course, but still uncharitable. I believed I muttered as much. Gwendolyn's only response was a low chuckle.

We traveled through the night, our progress greatly slowed by the absence of any moon beyond a sliver and the rough terrain. The same darkness, of course, provided us with a certain measure of safety. Near dawn, Gwendolyn found another suitable thicket and we made our daytime lair. These quarters were, if anything, even more cramped than the last had been.

"What?" murmured Gwendolyn, with another little low chuckle. "No complaints?"

Feeling her pressed against me down the entire

length of my body—amazing how thin leather can seem—I believe I managed to choke out a negative reply.

The next two days passed in a similar manner. On the evening of the fourth day, a complication arose.

Just as we were preparing to crawl out of our thicket at sundown, we heard the drumming of horse hooves. We shrank back into the thickness of the shrubbery, holding ourselves utterly still. Despite the lush foliage, we were able to see enough of the barren ground beyond to study ensuing events.

Two children burst onto the scene, clambering over a distant stone wall. They were both girls—although it was hard for me to be certain at first, between their filthy garments and the fact that they were so young. Perhaps fourteen and fifteen years old. The long hair and a certain delicacy of the features were the principal determinants of my judgement.

One of the girls spotted our thicket. She grabbed the other by the shoulder and pointed at it. The two of them began racing toward us. Next to me, I heard Gwendolyn hiss softly.

Long before the girls could reach our shelter, however, they were intercepted by a man on horseback coming from somewhere behind and to the left of the thicket we were hidden in. The man atop the beast was even mangier looking than the "horse" itself, dressed in what seemed to be a pastiche of filthy furs and bits of armor. His head was covered by a helmet which would have given my uncle Giotto apoplexy had he seen the design. A "horned helmet" it was, just like the staple of barbarian imagery—except the "horns" were actually some kind of (mangy, what else?) antlers, and the helmet itself was not a single piece but several poorly-beaten flanges of iron tied together (not well) by rawhide. One of the antlers had come loose, and was flopping around on the man's right shoulder.

The girls veered off and tried to make their escape over another stone wall. But before they could get to the wall, one of them—the younger—had been snared by a noose thrown by the horseman. The other girl made a frantic attempt to pry the noose off her companion. But, whatever the captor's other failings, he was clearly an expert at this endeavor. He had his end of the rope snug to the pommel of his saddle, and was backing up his horse in such a way as to keep the noose tight.

Two more horsemen appeared, leaping their mounts over the same low wall from which the girls had first burst onto the scene. I was surprised to see the relative grace with which the horses managed that leap. But then, reflected that in this terrain the ability to leap low walls of stone was probably the single most prized feature in a "warhorse."

The older girl still at liberty took one look at them and gave up her attempts to free her companion. She began running toward the other stone wall. But, after taking not more than seven or eight steps, she desisted. It was obvious enough that the two new horsemen would reach the wall long before she did.

Disconsolately, she turned back and rejoined her trapped companion. Younger sister, I assumed. They were close enough by then that a certain familial resemblance could be seen.

The man who had lassoed the girl was now on the ground. He was making his way along the rope to the captured girl, expertly maintaining the tension. I recognized the skill, of course. I was a maestro in the use of a whip (if I say so myself—more to the point, my uncle Larue says so). And while a whip and a lasso are not the same, the two devices are similar enough that my uncle Larue had spent some time acquainting me with the art of lassoing. In which art, of course, he was superb—as he was with the use of a bola, or, indeed, any weapon involving the same general principles.

As the man drew near the captured girl, her companion began cursing bitterly. Given the surroundings, I was not surprised to hear such brilliant invective and profanity issuing from the lips of a fifteen-year-old girl.

Eventually, the profanity ceased and the girl lapsed into standard language. "T'ain't right!" she shrilled. "It's not my birthday—Lana's neither! And it's not a saints' day!"

The other two horsemen had reached the scene, and were dismounting. One of them, hearing the girl's protest, laughed harshly. "The Baron decides what's 'right,' girl. Advised by his soothsayer, o' course." He pointed to the new moon, whose dim silhouette could be seen above the horizon. The sun had set, by now, but the area was still half-illuminated by its dying glow. "Th' Baron says 'tis only right that *droit d'seigneur* applies at new moon too, seein' as how the whole business is tied to the lunar cycle and sech."

"T'aint' fair!" shrilled the girl. "T'aint't!" echoed her younger sister.

The man who had spoken advanced and took the older one by the scruff of her tunic. Then, shrugged. "Wha's 'fair' got to do with anytin'? Th' Baron decides what's fair, not you. And he's horny."

"So 're we," chortled the man who had lassoed the younger. He ruffled her hair. "Won't be but a couple o' days, lass. An' y'may as well get used to it anyhow."

Within seconds, the two girls were bundled across two of the saddles and the little party—now remounted—was moseying its way toward a distant hill. Atop the hill, as on all the hills, a castle could be seen. Mangy, of course, insofar as the term "mangy" could be applied to a pile of stone. Until I saw the Baronies, I would have sworn it couldn't.

Once they were out of sight, Gwendolyn nudged me. "Let's go," she hissed. "At least we won't have to be worried about being spotted in *this* Barony tonight. They'll be busy with the girls."

I had been frozen with shock. The casual callousness of her words jolted me out of my paralysis.

"They're but children!" I snarled. "Bad enough, even if they weren't—but this—!"

She gave me a cold look. Her eyes were black even in daylight. In dusk, in the gloom of the thicket, they were pools of eternal night.

"*What?*" she snarled back. "Has the precious Ozarine suddenly discovered that 'oppression' is not an abstraction? Not something to be captured in oils?" She gestured angrily at the distant castle. "You think anything which is going to happen there tonight hasn't happened ten thousand times? Isn't happening this very night, for that matter, in other castles? That—and worse?"

She shrugged her big shoulders, like a tigress shrugging off a fly. "It happens," she continued, her voice filled less with anger now than simple contempt. "There's nothing we can do about it. And even if there were—so what? Save two children out of how many? You can't solve these things one at a time, Benvenuti. And meanwhile, your damn Ozar is coming with the Rap Sheet. I have *got* to get the word out."

She muscled her way past me and crawled out of the thicket. Once in the open, she stood up and glared back down at me. "Move," she commanded. "We can make good time tonight."

I obeyed. But somehow, somewhere, in the short time it took for me to gather up my stuff and make my way out of the thicket, my own decision crystallized.

"Decision" is hardly the word. Some things do not have to be weighed in judgement.

"You go," I said, turning on my heels and heading off toward the castle.

"What are you doing, you idiot?"

I turned and grinned at her. I suspected the expression was murderous. I certainly hoped so.

"Providing you with a distraction."

She stared at me. I sighed heavily. "Go, Gwendolyn. We part ways, here. You're the most magnificent woman I ever met—I'm at least half in love with you, and that's easily the most foolish damn thing I've ever done in my life, not that I regret it—but we part ways here. Our loyalties are too different, just as you say. Oppression as such I can ignore, where you cannot. But—"

I made a vague gesture. "I could never paint a girl again. And I'm fond of portraying girls."

I turned away again. Then, a thought came to me, and I twisted my head back to look at her. "How many was it, that your brother strangled alongside the Comte de l'Abbatoir? Twelve knights, as I recall?"

She nodded mutely. I'm quite sure my responding grin was murderous. I certainly hope so.

"Well, I can't hope to match *such* a feat, of course. But I'll do my best."

A moment later I was striding off, the distant castle serving as my beacon. By now, with the sunset at an end, the castle was nothing more than a jagged shape of darkness against a starry night sky. But 'twas enough, 'twas enough.

Approaching the castle unobserved was child's play, since the Baron had left no one on watch. And a good thing that was, too, as much noise as I was making trying to clamber "silently" over a stony hill in almost complete darkness. Restraining my curses was even more difficult. By the time I reached the "ramparts," my legs were bruised and I was bleeding from several small cuts. My once-fine Ozarine trousers, never designed for such travel at all, were now not much more than tatters.

Long before I reached the ramparts, however, I was assured by the noise coming from the "castle" that silence was a moot point. As much of a racket as the Baron and his retainers were making, they couldn't have heard a bull hammering down a barn door.

I was relieved, as I drew near, that I was not hearing any girlish screams mixed in with the lot. The noise was that of buffoons at their buffoonery, not atrocities in mid-event. I had little doubt, of course, that such noises would soon be occurring. But I had made good enough time that I was almost certain the "festivities" were still just getting under way. There was this much to be said for the wretched terrain of the Baronies—a man on foot could travel almost as fast as a mounted one.

Once at the outer wall of the castle, I paused and studied it as best I could in the absence of moonlight. I found it difficult not to burst into laughter. I was no soldier myself, but having been raised by a pack of condottiere uncles I was quite familiar with the methods of Ozarine fortification. These were quite absent here. The "curtain wall" was a rickety pile of stones, not too carefully fitted. Mortar was, of course, completely absent. Here and there, a desultory attempt to construct something which might be called a "battlement" could vaguely be seen, outlined against the starblaze. But, for the most part, the wall posed no more challenge to an attacker than climbing a pile of stones.

Of course, the ragged nature of the construction *did*

pose a challenge—a hopeless one—to what was left of
my trousers. And my fancy Ozarine shoes were about
the worst possible footwear to use in such a project,
even if I hadn't been encumbered by my pack and easel.
I was tempted to leave the pack and easel at the foot
of the wall. But, after a bit of reflection, I decided that
the pack and easel made a better way to carry my
rapier and whip than anything else would. I could hardly
climb a wall holding them in my hands, after all.

Needless to say, I picked up several more bruises
and cuts on my way up the wall, but the climb itself
went quickly enough. By the time I reached the top,
my principal struggle was mental, not physical. Of the
many lessons my uncles had drummed into me when
it came to the matter of mayhem, the first and foremost was: *never lose your temper.*

So, I paused for a while—not long—atop the wall,
taking the time to regain my composure. By the sounds
coming from within the castle, the festivities were still
at an early enough stage that I felt no compulsion to
rush in. I could hear the girls' voices now, but they
seemed raised more in sullen protest than anguish.
Clearly enough, abuse was such a normal part of their
lives that they simply viewed this latest outrage as
something to be endured.

I used that last thought to steady my nerves and
achieve that state of detached murderousness which
was one more product of my uncles' rigorous training. Ludovigo's, in particular. *Kill as savagely as you
can, boy, as long as your blood stays cold.*

Eventually, I decided it was cold enough. I slid off
the wall and entered the nearest aperture. I'd call it
a "door" except the term would be an insult to doors.

As I made my way through the dank corridors of the
castle, I kept a wary eye out for servants. By now, I'd

seen enough of the Baronies to realize that the Baron himself and his armed retainers would be entirely engrossed with their entertainment. Gwendolyn had never made any mention of a "servant class" in the Baronies, but I assumed such creatures must exist.

As it happens, I ran across only one. A stooped and furtive fellow, clad in rags, rushing from somewhere—the kitchen, I presume—carrying a wooden platter laden with meat. I shrank back into a dark alcove in the rough wall and let him pass. He did not notice me; indeed, he never so much as raised his head from the platter. Servants in the Baronies, I had no doubt, soon enough had any sense of alertness beaten out of them.

His passage did provide me with directions, however. As soon as he was out of sight, I followed him, after depositing the sack and easel in the alcove. I dare say my treads were those of a predator. I certainly hope so. By now, I was pleased to note, my inner soul had achieved my uncles' much-vaunted state of mind. I felt as cold-blooded and deadly as a viper.

The noise increased with every step I took. Soon enough, light began to appear in the corridor—hitherto illuminated by nothing more than an occasional taper in a sconce. The light was spilling around a bend up ahead, along with the sounds of carousal. The flickering nature of it led me to believe that it emanated from nothing more elaborate than a huge fireplace.

I peeked around the corner and—sure enough. Below me, down a short flight of stone steps, was the "baronial feasting hall." Insofar as that term can be applied to something which bore a closer resemblance to a bears' den. Off to my left, set into the stone wall, was a very large fireplace. Logs within it were burning lustily.

The Baron himself, clearly enough, was the man

seated in a large wooden chair at the base of the steps. I deduced he was the Baron because his chair was at the head of the table and was the largest of the eight chairs gathered about. It bore a vague resemblance— very vague—to something you might call a "throne." The fact that the servant had stopped by his chair first to proffer the platter of meat added further evidence to my surmise.

"Table" I said, but the arrangement was actually more complex. Two tables—heavy, clumsy wooden things—had been abutted in an inverted "T" shape. The shorter of the tables made the base of the "T," and it was at the foot of that table that the Baron sat. On either side of that table sat one of his retainers. His chief lieutenants, I assumed. I recognized the man sitting to the Baron's right. He was the one who had led the party which captured the two girls.

The table which formed the crosspiece of the "T" was longer. Five chairs were positioned at that table, each of them occupied by one of the ruffians who passed as "feudal retainers" in the Baronies. One man sat at each end of the table, the other three positioned along its length facing the Baron.

As for the girls themselves, the older one was standing in the middle of the long table at the end, engaged in what you might call a "striptease" if the term weren't too repulsive for the event. She was practically nude by now, her face tight with fear and resentment, being rowdily encouraged by the men at her table.

The younger sister's state of disapparel I could not determine. She was perched on the Baron's lap, most of her form hidden from me by the back of the chair and the Baron's own figure.

I couldn't see the Baron's face, a fact which mattered to me not in the least. I was far too busy gauging the position of the Baron himself, his armed retainers, and their state of inebriation. One man against eight called for a battle plan of some sort.

In my favor were three things: the fact that the men in the feasting hall were not expecting to be attacked, were seated and thus not in good position to resist an attack, and were obviously well on their way toward a drunken stupor. So far along, in fact, that I was sorely tempted to wait until they were comatose from liquor. But . . . before they reached that state, the girls would have been badly abused.

Against me were also three facts: first, that the men were all armed; second, that however crude they might be, they were accustomed to physical mayhem; and, finally, that I was not too well armed myself and had no armor of any kind.

By the time I finished my assessment, the servant had placed the platter of meat on the table and was returning toward the hallway in which I lay waiting. I decided to begin with that happy circumstance, and moved silently back along the stone corridor and into the alcove. There I waited, in full shadow.

The servant scuttled past, his head down and paying little attention. As soon as he moved around the next bend in the hallway, I emerged from the alcove and hoisted the sack and easel back onto my shoulders. Then, I followed him around the bend in the hallway. I would call it a "corner" except that the term would be somewhat ridiculous. Whoever had designed and built that castle, centuries earlier, had obviously never heard of either a plumb bob or a level, much less a T square.

He was not hard to follow. His crude footwork— wooden clogs held onto his feet with leather strips— made quite a racket clumping along the rough stone floor.

Soon enough, I found myself looking into the castle's

kitchen. The servant was there, digging some more meat out of a great kettle on a crude stove while a heavyset female cook clucked at him to hurry up. There was no one else in the room.

I examined the kettle and decided I was strong enough to carry it fairly easily. I thought a big pot full of boiling hot water would even the odds quite a bit. The decision made, I reached over my shoulder, drew the rapier from its hidden sheath in the easel, and strode into the kitchen.

The servant and the cook, as dull-witted as grinding menial labor usually makes people, didn't even notice me until the point of the rapier was at the man's throat.

"*Silence,*" I commanded.

The servant's face grew pale, that of the cook grew red.

"'E's come to kill th'Baron," croaked the servant.

"Kin I watch?" asked the woman eagerly.

Well. That settled one question—whether the Baron's servants would attempt to protect their lord and master. Settled it, at least, so far as the woman was concerned. The man's face seemed to grow even paler, almost ashen, as if the prospect of the Baron's death brought him no pleasure at all.

"Stupid woman," he hissed. "We'll be blamed, wife!"

His words immediately erased the glee in the cook's expression. Her face became as pale as the man's.

I had not foreseen *that* complication. "Why would they blame you?" I asked.

The servant swallowed, his eyes riveted on the rapier. I withdrew the blade a few inches from his throat. After swallowing, he croaked: "Allus blame th'servants, when somethin' goes wrong. Th'other Barons'll say we's done it. Kill us both. Kill half th'peasants on the Barony, too."

Damnation.

Something of my chagrin must have shown. The cook examined me more closely. "Yer not from th'Baronies, sir," she whispered. "Me husband's got th'right of it."

My mind raced, trying to find a way out of the impasse. A thought came to me.

"What happened when Greyboar the Strangler did for the Comte de l'Abbatoir and his Knights Companion?" I demanded. "Were the Comte's servants and peasants slain afterward?"

The servant and his wife ogled me as if I were an imbecile.

"Well, o' course not!" choked the servant. "The great Grey—uh, the vile strangler—slew 'em all, you know, most flamboyant like. Couldna possibly been done by no servants. Nor no peasants, neither."

"Tied they necks into knots, 'e did!" gurgled his wife, glee returning to her face.

I thought on the problem a moment more. This time, with the mind of an artist rather than a swordsman. The solution came almost at once.

"Flamboyance, is it?" I said gaily. "I dare say I can manage that."

I lowered the rapier. Clearly enough, there was no longer any need to threaten them. I glanced around the kitchen, seeing several large and crudely made cabinets. "Do you have flour?" I asked the cook.

She nodded mutely. "Lots of it?" Again, she nodded.

"Excellent. Get it out." I eased the sack off my shoulders and rummaged in it for a moment, before withdrawing the bullwhip. Then, I began removing my blouse.

The husband was gaping at me. "I assume the Baron has enemies," I stated confidently.

The servant seemed to have been struck dumb. But his wife, returning from a cabinet with a barrel in her arms, chuckled harshly. "Plenty!"

"Did he kill any of them? Especially, any that were of approximately my height and build?"

She set the barrel of flour down on a nearby bench, straightened, and examined me closely. "None so purty as you. But Sieur Henri de Pouilleux were as tall, iff'n no so broad-shouldered."

"He'll do. How did the Baron kill him?"

"Stabt 'im inna back, 'ow else? Th'sword went clean t'rough 'im."

"How else, indeed," I agreed cheerfully. "Clean through him, you say? Better and better!"

By now I was bare from the waist up. I seized the husband by the scruff of the neck and shook him a bit, to clear his head. "Come to your senses, damn you! I mean you no harm." I motioned toward the barrel with my hand. "Start smearing that flour all over me. Everything except my hair."

His jaw snapped shut. A moment later, he hastened to obey. While he did so, I turned back to the cook.

"Some meat paste. Cold—lukewarm at least—not hot." Fortunately, she was either quicker-witted than her husband or less confused, so I was not forced to shake her as well. By the time her husband was halfway through the process of coating me with flour, the cook had returned with some greasy meat paste on a wooden spatula.

By then, my plans were made. "Smear it here, and here," I commanded, pointing to a spot just above my kidney and on the corresponding side of my stomach, just opposite. "I rather doubt that's exactly where the Baron stabbed the Sieur, but it hardly matters. I dare say the surviving eyewitness will not remember the fine details."

She smeared the meat paste over the spots indicated. I couldn't see the result on my back, but the one on my belly made quite a gruesome-looking imitation of a wound. In dim lighting, at least—which was all there was in that misbegotten castle.

"And that's it!" I exclaimed softly. "The scene is set."

The cook and the servant were back to ogling me. I gave them a cheerful smile—it must have looked ghastly, my face covered with flour—and dug into my pack again. This time, retrieving a poignard in a sheath which I thrust into my belt.

I gestured at my sack and easel, lying on the floor. "Do watch over them, would you? And I'd suggest you clean up the evidence while I'm gone. This shouldn't take long."

I spun and bounded into the hallway leading back to the feasting hall. I saw no reason for any further delay.

I paused briefly, at the entrance to the feasting hall, simply to assure myself that no great change had taken place. The girl doing the striptease on the table was now completely nude; the sister in the Baron's lap seemed even more unhappy than ever; the retainers drunker. But other than that, the scene remained essentially the same.

All of which, I was delighted to see, came together quite perfectly. I took but a moment to assess the rest of the enterprise, and was then bounding down the stairs. I would say "gleefully," but I assure you I maintained my cold blood throughout. Even my uncles would have approved.

"*Revenge!*" I bellowed. "*Face me, Baron! The Sieur Henri has returned!*"

Bullfighting is, of course, a popular sport in Ozarae. And while my uncles disapprove of the pastime, they did not fail to train me a bit in that art as well. I dare say my rapier went right through the back of the Baron's neck and severed his spine as neatly as any matador could have done.

That splendid enterprise having been achieved, I moved on to the next. Being as I am right-handed, the choice was obvious. Two quick steps brought me past the Baron's skewered form, gushing blood onto his platter. I now stood on open floor to his left. The girl, I was pleased to note, sprang off his lap immediately. The lieutenant seated just in front of me was gaping drunkenly at the Baron's throat, from which a good foot of my blade protruded. The man across from him—the girls' original captor—was staring at me as if he was looking at a ghost.

Which, of course, he was.

"*And you as well!*" I bellowed. "*Vengeance is mine!*" I had no idea, of course, if the lieutenant had played any part in the Sieur de Pouilleux's demise. But it hardly seemed to matter. In the Baronies, I was quite certain, revenge was a sloppy affair.

The lieutenant's mouth opened and he began to squall in terror. The squall was cut short by the tip of my whip, coiling around his neck like a boa. I seized the handle with both hands and, with a great and titanic heave, jerked him right out of his chair and sprawled both him and the table onto the man seated before me. The whole lot ended up in a very nice and tidy jumble.

I am quite a powerful man, as I believe I've mentioned. As the captor more or less sailed across the table, I heard his neck break as cleanly as even my uncle Larue could have asked.

Three down—two, at least, and the third was tangled up—five to go. The problem now, of course, was disentangling the whip. Normally I can accomplish that with a flick of the wrist, but in this instance the whip was enmeshed with two bodies, one of which was writhing on the floor with a corpse and a table on top of him.

I gave a quick glance at the five men at the other table and decided I had time to kill two birds with one stone. As it were. All five retainers at the far table were still seated, like so many statues. Their eyes were wide, their mouths agape, their faces pale. Clearly enough, they had no doubt at all that the ghost of the Sieur was present. If they even noticed the fine spray of flour I was shedding all about, they were too dull-witted to understand what it signified. Or mistook the flour mist, in the flickering light from the fireplace, as a ghostly aura.

I dropped the handle of the whip, knelt, and smote the other lieutenant a mighty blow of my fist. I suspect I broke his jaw. Even if I hadn't, he'd play no role in the ensuing events—other than being a witness when the servants needed one.

That done, it was the work of only a few seconds to retrieve the whip. By the time I advanced upon the remaining five men, they were finally scrambling to their feet. As I had counted on, their state of drunkenness was impeding their reactions as well as compounding their superstitious horror. One of them, I saw with delight—no, two!—had urinated in their trousers.

There seemed no purpose to varying a successful tune. "*Revenge is mine!*" I cried, springing toward them. "*The Sieur Henri!*"

The one closest to me, at my end of the long table, spilled his chair in rising. "Have mercy!" he shrieked, fumbling at his sword.

By then, I had the whip handle in my left hand and the poignard in my right—held by the blade, ready for throwing. For an instant, I hesitated. The man's throat was unprotected, but made a chancy target. The chest—

I decided that his mangy "armor"—lacquered leather strips, with only a scrap of iron here and there—would pose no obstacle to my heavy and finely-made poignard. Neither would the sternum beyond. Not for someone like me, trained by *my* uncles.

Nor did it. The poignard's blade went right through the lot as neatly as you could ask, piercing the heart and not stopping until the hilt struck what was left of the armor. The impact knocked the man flat on his posterior. He sat there, staring at me in shock for a moment. Then, coughed a great deal of blood and collapsed altogether.

Four down, four to go. From here, of course, the enterprise ascended in difficulty. The four survivors were now on their feet, swords in hand. All of them were bellowing with fear, true, but men such as those will react with violence to almost anything. I was counting on their superstitious terror to lessen the odds, and the liquor they'd consumed to dull their alertness—which, judging from the large amounts of said liquids spilling all over the table and floor from upended flagons, was none too "alert."

Still, there were four of them, one of me, and they were armed and armored. Two of them even had the presence of mind to seize the table and upend it, clearing an open space in which to fight. The girl atop the table leapt off nimbly just as it went over, landing on her feet and scampering aside. I heard her shouting something at her younger sister, but didn't catch the words.

The first thing to do, needless to say, was to break up the rough "formation" which the four men were taking. As drunk and terrified as they were, they had enough fighting instinct to form a line.

"A maneuver!" I shouted. "Against de Pouilleux? *Useless! Revenge is mine!*"

To be successful, "maneuvers" presuppose a certain amount of celerity and nimbleness. Neither of which was a strong suit of such fellows—and both of which were a strong suit of mine. (Again, you will recognize, the result of my uncles' rigorous regimen.)

So it was no great feat to scamper around them to the left, double up the whip, and then use it two-handed as something of a flexible club to hammer the man closest to me into a state which approximated senselessness. "Turning their flank," as it were.

My victim seemed a bit shocked by my tactics. Hard to tell, of course. I suspect the man was so stupid that the tactics of a tortoise would have shocked him. In any event, his sentiments were short-lived. A doubled-up bullwhip lashing a man's arms and face—knocking his sorry excuse for a helmet askew in the process—will daze even a genius. His neck then exposed, I danced back two steps, unfurled the full length of the whip, and cracked it once. The armored tip of the weapon opened his jugular vein as well as a razor could have done it.

From there I was expecting the affair to turn desperate. A whip is a dazzling weapon, true enough, but not really very practical in a melee facing determined opponents. It simply requires too much room, either on a battlefield or—more to the point—in a feasting hall. So I abandoned it, but not before one final lash coiled around one of the retainer's legs and, with a jerk, upended him on the floor.

Two left, now, and a third out of the action for at least a moment or so. That left me, wearing nothing but tattered clothes and a coating of flour, unarmed, facing two armored and sword-wielding opponents. As I said, a desperate affair.

Except—

"Facing determined opponents" proved to be a

misnomer. The two surviving retainers, as brutal as they might be, were not the stuff of heroes. They ogled me, ogled the carnage—blood and wine and ale and shattered furniture everywhere—ogled their cursing fellow rolling around on the floor frantically trying to disentangle the whip from his knees . . .

Then dropped their swords and raced for the entrance to the feasting hall, shrieking with terror. I stared after them, too astonished to react immediately.

Along the way, the ruffians passed the two sisters huddled against the wall. The older girl stuck out her leg. A little leg, it was, but it was enough to send the first of them sprawling onto the stone steps. His companion trampled him under on his way up the stairs.

That callous disregard for comradeship proved to be fruitless. When the man reached the stop of the stairs there was a sudden flurry of motion in the darkness of the corridor bend beyond. I saw him stiffen, his head jerking, and heard what sounded like a little gasp. Then he turned and staggered back down, clutching his throat. Blood gushed from between his fingers.

Again, when he reached his still-prostrate fellow trying to rise, he trampled him under. That effort seemed to use up his strength, however, and he collapsed in a heap. His fellow was just getting to his knees, shaking his head to clear the daze, when Gwendolyn came down the stairs and used that great cleaver of hers to sever his spine with one blow. She then stalked over to the man still trying to disentangle the whip from his legs, dropped to one knee, jerked his head back, and practically cut his throat to the bone. All this, somehow, without getting a drop of blood on her.

I stared at her. She stared at me. Then she burst into laughter.

"God, you look ridiculous!"

I spread my arms and studied myself ruefully. "I don't suppose there'd be a laundry anywhere in this castle?" I complained. "What's left of my clothes looks like a butcher's apron. Between the flour and the blood . . ."

Gwendolyn began cleaning her blade on the corpse's clothing. "A laundry?" she chuckled. "Not likely."

She sheathed the cleaver, rose, and pointed to the corpse. "You'll have to make do with odds and ends of their clothing. Your own's pretty well ruined."

I studied the garments in question with considerable distaste, foreseeing a problem with lice. "I'm *not* giving up my shoes," I grumbled. "Not for those things."

Again, she chuckled. The sound seemed oddly forced. When I looked at her, she was shaking her head and her eyes seemed even darker than usual.

"You are absolutely insane, Benvenuti Sfondrati-Piccolomini," she whispered. "Also magnificent."

I moved toward her, wanting an embrace. And so, I think, did she. But she placed a hand on my chest and held me off. "Please," she whispered. "Not now. I think I'm half in love with you myself—more than half, to tell the truth—but it's still insane. Besides, my leather would look silly with flour all over it."

Abruptly she turned away and studied the two girls. The sisters had not left the hall, but they were standing on their feet now. Standing and staring at us, their eyes as wide as saucers.

"Warn your families," commanded Gwendolyn. "You'll have to stay hidden for a while."

They nodded jerkily. Gwendolyn strode over and studied the one surviving retainer closely. Then turned away, apparently satisfied.

"He won't recover consciousness for hours. Plenty of time to finish setting the scene." She studied me again, this time very approvingly. "I wouldn't have thought you could be such a clever bastard. It's almost scary."

She jerked her head toward the entrance. "I assume you made arrangements with the servants? That's the reason for your weird appearance?"

I nodded. By then, the two girls had advanced and were standing not far from Gwendolyn. But both of them still had their eyes fixed upon me.

"Why'd you do it?" asked the older.

Gwendolyn explained. When she was finished, the two sisters were practically hopping up and down in fury.

"You were on a critical mission for *The Cause* and this—this—" The youngest girl was pointing a finger of outrage and accusation at me.

"*J'Accuse!*" shrilled the older, pointing an identical finger.

"Rampant petty-boojoy individualism!" hollered the younger.

"Sabotaging the class struggle for the sake of romantic sentimentalism!" hollered the older.

The two little fingers never wavered in their condemnation. I gaped at them. Gwendolyn burst into laughter.

"Welcome to Grotum, Benvenuti," she gasped. "Where—ah—we take our ideology seriously."

The two sisters lowered their fingers. "Certainly do," they muttered fiercely.

I fear I was still gaping. The youngest sister squinted at me. "What's *his* problem? Is he a halfwit or something?"

"He's from Ozar."

Again, the two fingers. "Imperialist stooge!" shrilled the younger. "The imperialist himself!" countered her older and wiser sister. "In the flesh!"

Gwendolyn cleared her throat. "He *did* rescue the two of you, you might remember."

The two fingers lowered; then, wiped little noses. "Well," said the younger. "That's true." A moment later, grudgingly: "Thanks."

The older was made of sterner stuff. "Still an outrage," she muttered. "I'd call it treason to the revolution except"—she eyed me suspiciously—"you probably never was part of it nohow."

"Certainly not," said Gwendolyn firmly. "Enough of this, girls. Benvenuti meant well, and that's *enough*. You're too damn young to be making ideological pronouncements anyway."

The two sisters transferred their suspicious squints to her.

"Is that so?" demanded the younger.

"And just who exactly are *you*?" echoed her sister crossly.

"I'm Gwendolyn Greyboar. Which is a name I'd just as soon you forgot because—"

She got no further. The suspicious looks had vanished, replaced by—I will swear to it!—the saucer-wide eyes of sheer adulation. Then came the squeals of hero worship.

Heroine worship, I should say. None of those girlish peals of enthusiasm were directed *my* way.

"Gwendolyn Greyboar! I can't BELIEVE it!"

"Right HERE! In the FLESH!"

On and on and on. They even managed to rouse the unconscious retainer. Not for long, of course. I was in quite a foul enough mood by then to have broken a horse's jaw.

And so it was, in the hours that passed thereafter, after we left the castle and the peasants in the area heard the news, that Gwendolyn was surrounded by a mob at all times. Pestering her with questions about the latest news of the revolution; asking her to clarify fine points of doctrine; and, as often as not, just staring at her as if she were an icon come to life.

As for myself, I was largely ignored. Save, of course, for never-ending suspicious squints and the occasional pointing finger of warning and accusation.

About noon the next day, the servant and the cook were seen carrying the surviving retainer in a mule-drawn cart toward the nearest Baron in the area. The retainer had regained his senses, more or less, but his jaw was swathed in a crude bandage.

The servant and cook were playing their part to perfection, according to the peasant who brought the news. Repercussions were not to be feared. Clearly enough, no one in the Baronies not privy to the truth would have any doubt that the spirit of the Sieur de Pouilleux had committed the massacre. Superstition was as common to the area as potatoes.

None of this, of course, allayed the peasantry's hostile attitude toward me. As Gwendolyn and I made to leave the area, the parting words of the common folk were spoken more or less in a chorus.

"Dump the imperialist, Gwendolyn! Beware the Ozarine snake!" And so on, and so forth. Quite tedious, it was.

Once we were finally out of sight, I gave vent to my spleen. At some length, as I recall.

When I was done, Gwendolyn smiled. Then, stopped me in my tracks with a hand on my shoulders. "Don't pout. For whatever it's worth, *I* don't think you're an imperialist snake. A dinosaur, maybe, but not a snake."

"Well, that's something," I muttered. "Progress of sorts, I guess."

I started to say something else but was cut off by

a fierce kiss. A quick one, true, but fierce. The sensation which went down my spine was equally fierce.

"Be quiet," she whispered. "Let's just get to the Mutt. Then . . . we'll see what happens."

As usual, the damn woman was decisive and quick-moving. I hadn't time to recover from that incredible kiss before she was striding off. "Now, move! No time for your sluggard Ozarine ways, Benvenuti the Gallant! You've just made the Baronies even more dangerous than usual."

That night, as we lay together in another thicket, Gwendolyn's hands upon me were softer than they had been before. Almost caressing, now; and my own, the same. The touches were not those of lovemaking. The tight quarters would have made that quite impossible, leaving aside anything else. But if she—and I, for that matter—still thought our feelings for each other were well-nigh insane, neither of us would any longer pretend they didn't exist.

When we emerged from the thicket at sundown the next day, Gwendolyn studied me for a moment. The furs and assorted leather rags I was now clad in seemed to meet her approval. But when her eyes fell upon my feet, she chuckled and shook her head.

"When we reach the Mutt, we really have to get you a decent pair of boots. Those—things—you're wearing are almost worn out, and besides, I'd be too embarrassed to be seen with you. Me, Gwendolyn Greyboar, cozy with an Ozarine down to his pointed patent leather shoes! No, it just won't do."

PART IX

In Which, Sad
to Relate, Our Narration
of the Further Adventures of
the Wizard and His Loyal But Stupid
Apprentice is Cast Into Disarray
By a Truly Unfortunate
Chronicler's Mishap.

—◆—

CHAPTER X. *The Dwarf's Question. The
Wizard's Reproof. The Dwarf's Question.
The Wizard's Reproof. The Dwarf's Question.
The Wizard's Bemusement. The Dwarf
Is Dispatched On a Perilous Journey—
Into the Very Darkest Interior of the
Sack! Adventures Too Overwhelming to
Relate In Detail! Alas! Suffice It To Say—*

"Why did he say that, master?" queried Shelyid, as the
coach lurched into motion. His question was in regard

to the driver's announcement that passengers should bring their own provisions for the first two days of the journey, as no roadway inn could be constructed in the Drear.

"Bah!" oathed Zulkeh. "More to the point, gnome, is the question: Why did he say that three seconds before departure, thus ensuring that no time would be available for the acquisition of said necessities? An outrage!" He fell into a brooding silence, which lasted the length of the coach's voyage through the gates of the Caravanserai and out into the Drear beyond.

Then did the dwarf speak again.

"But why did he say that, master?"

"What?" demanded Zulkeh, frowning fiercely at the runt. "Why did he say that? Because he is a churl, dolt, employed by a churlish firm!"

"But *why*, master?" persisted Shelyid.

"Why? Why? Why?" cried Zulkeh, his wrath now steeping to the surface. "Wherefore am I plagued by these imbecile inquiries? I have already explained why, diminutive cretin!"

"B-but," stammered the dwarf, "why *can't* they build a roadway inn in the Drear, master?"

Zulkeh leaned back in his seat, clearly taken aback. "Why, because—" A moment's silence. "Quite amazing. I don't know the answer to that question. Most amazing." He stroked his beard thoughtfully, gazing out the window onto the barren vastness of the Drear.

For many long minutes did the wizard muse after this fashion, until the Caravanserai had long since disappeared below the southern horizon. At length, Shelyid became so bold as to make a whispered suggestion to his master.

"Maybe you could ask one of these people on the coach, master. They've probably lived here for years."

"Bah!" oathed Zulkeh. "Am I to waddle about in the

swamp of empiricism, like a child in his sandbox? No, dwarf, the truth is found in books. The question is—which book?"

More long moments of silence. Then did the gleam of understanding come into the wizard's eyes.

"Of course!" he spoke. "Shelyid, fetch me the *Chronicle of Edward the Confusor*."

Shelyid blanched. "B-but . . . but." He gulped. "Do I have to, master?" This last in a piteous wail.

A frown gathered on Zulkeh's brow as quickly as the storm clouds of the north amass themselves about the awesome granite slabs of Mount Pud. "Do you question my command, gnome?" he demanded.

"N-no, but—but—" stammered Shelyid.

"Silence!" stormed Zulkeh. "Perform your duty as I bade you!"

Realizing that all resistance was useless, and quite obviously regretting the innocent question which had led him to such a pass, Shelyid sighed, gathered up his courage, and went to seek out the appointed tome in the wizard's sack.

Now, the gentle reader is no doubt perplexed by this attitude on the part of the dwarf. Of course, it will have become transparent to the gentle reader through his perusal of the preceding pages of this chronicle that the dwarf Shelyid was not, shall we say, blessed with leonine audacity. Nonetheless, it must appear bizarre that Shelyid should exhibit such cravenness when faced with the routine task of extracting a volume from a sack.

Ah, dear reader, do not so malign the poor dwarf! His fear was well-founded. For remember, this was no ordinary sack! No, no. Any comparison between the wizard Zulkeh's sack and the traveling pack of any common voyager would be mistaken in the extreme.

For *this* pack was a wizard's pack, and that of a

well-traveled and prodigiously learned wizard to boot. Thus not only was it voluminous—nay, huge—nay, elephantine—in its proportions, containing as it did every single item of every bizarre description which the mage had accumulated in his long and varied lifetime; not only was the internal ordering and arrangement of that multitude of sorcerous materials mazelike in its dimensions; not only was it filled with many a noisome specimen, many a sharp instrument, and many a perilous artifact; not only was all this true, but Shelyid must have known as well, dim-witted though he was, that the many days of arduous and jostling travel would inevitably have rearranged the objects of the interior into a new kaleidoscope in which he stood a fair chance of losing his way for days, and would as well have brought to sullen life the divers intelligences (not all of them animate) which lurked therein.

Mind you, in most instances no problem was posed in extracting the object of Zulkeh's desire from the pack. For the wizard, like all professional men—though he would have bitterly challenged this statement—relied for the most part upon only a small portion of his accumulated treasures. For just as a scholar may have shelf after shelf in his library lined with the most obscure tomes, journals and scrolls, yet does he still rely for the most part on a handful of essential works: the encyclopedias, the classics, and so forth. So it was also with the wizard, and when Shelyid had packed up the sack, he had taken great care to place these items of common usage at or near its surface. But now, it seemed, his preparations had been in vain. Into the heart of the interior must he go!

And so it was that Shelyid went into the sack, in that bouncing coach on its way to Prygg, and did not emerge for many hours. Alas, dear reader, our tale lengthens overmuch already, and so we cannot chronicle Shelyid's adventures that day. Alas! For verily those adventures were epic in their scale!

Suffice it to say that many a time did Shelyid lose his way and tremble in fear lest he starve before finding the book and blessed egress. Suffice it to say that the rearrangement of the interior of the sack would have provided more than ample evidence for Shelyid to have from its study, had he the wits, derived brilliant treatises on heretofore unknown aspects of Brownian motion and entropy. Suffice it to say that he nearly became asphyxiated on the fumes of the noxious ragweed specimen with which the wizard bribed the lower classes of demons whom he conjured up on occasion. Suffice it to say that for many terrifying moments was he locked in mortal combat with the normally lethargic Great Newt of Obpont, now risen from its torpor and filled with the venomous rage which is that beast's distinguishing characteristic—a combat made more difficult for the gnome by his knowledge that the wizard prized the monster highly and would thus overfill with spleen should Shelyid, in his frenzied efforts to prevent his devourment by the amphibious carnivore, cause the creature to come to harm. Suffice it to say that at length the dwarf succeeded in bottling the vicious predator in an unused vial, only then to fall into a pool of that unnamed and unnameable fluid whose presence in various pockets and folds of the sack was made necessary for the sustenance of that very amphibian horror of which I have just spoken—and of that fluid itself, of its nature and its effects upon the human much less the dwarf body, I will say nothing, lest the gentle reader discontinue in his nausea the further perusal of our tale. Suffice it to say that at length the dwarf found the book in question, seized it by frontal assault, and escaped at length the maddened pursuit of the band of club-wielding imps for whom, alas, the tome was their tribal totem. Suffice it to say that as the sun began its descent over the western horizon, Shelyid emerged from the sack, book in hand, and handed it over to his master. Surfeit it to say that that that that that that that—

CHAPTER XI. *In Which the Wizard Acquaints Himself With His New Traveling Companions, the Florid and Well-Dressed Man of Some Middle Years, the Imperious Dowager La Madame, and the Warden and His Young Prisoner, Newly Convicted of Stealing Bread From Mother Edna's Bakery (a Subsidiary of the Consortium). A Dialogue Between Zulkeh and the Youth, With Our Hero's Remonstrances Concerning Law and Reason Countered by the Unrepentant Miscreant's Discourse on Poverty and Its Effects. A Visit From the Forces of Law Themselves, and Their Representative's Unfortunate Experience With La Madame's Dog. A Villain Strikes Again! Pursuit. A Villain Strikes Again!*

It is with great regret that I must now inform the gentle reader of a most unfortunate episode in the history of my ancestors' compilation of their chronicle. Or rather, two unfortunate episodes.

The gentle reader will perhaps have noticed two recent oddments in our chronicle, to wit, that the preceding chapter ended in a somewhat peculiar manner, and that the chapter heading above is unwontedly fulsome and verbose. This results from the fact that the chapter heading was not written by Alfred CCLVI, but by his successor, the notorious Alfred CCLVII. For know, gentle reader, that Shelyid's odyssey in the wizard's sack, recounted in the previous chapter, had as one of its unforeseen effects the untimely demise of the great Alfred CCLVI. For though my ancestor faithfully mentioned the dire effects of the unnamed and unnameable fluid which filled various niches of that sack upon the human and dwarf body, he neglected to consider the possible effects upon the louse body. And, as it happens, these effects are most disastrous in their effects and most precipitous in their onset.

Shortly after the encounter with the unnamed and unnameable fluid, Alfred CCLVI was smitten by a most terrible seizure, the which not only caused his mandibles to vibrate like a tuning fork and his appendages to quiver like stalks in the breeze, but also made it quite impossible for him to continue in his duties, inasmuch as his every heroic attempt to do so—and there were many!—led to so much nonsensical gibberish.

Thereafter, though his mandibles and appendages ceased their disorderly motion, Alfred CCLVI fell into a deep lassitude. Try as he might, and despite the exhortations of the many members of our lousely clan which gathered about, he was unable to take pen in foreleg until the excitement which ensued following the reappearance of the villain Rascogne de Sevigneois. Then, most nobly, did Alfred CCLVI rise and scribble the accounts of that episode, upon the completion of which he dropped dead.

The chapter heading was thus written by his

successor, Alfred CCLVII, of whose eccentricities we will become all too shortly acquainted. But before I take up that regrettable piece of my clan's history, I will present the final pages of the illustrious Alfred CCLVI's career, that his name might shine forth in history. Only this portion of the chapter exists.

"Halt!"

The coach screeched to a halt. The occupants peered out the window, there to perceive a body of horsemen.

"It's Sheriff Pike and the Posse!" exclaimed the florid and well-dressed man of some middle years.

"And who are they?" demanded the imperious dowager La Madame.

"The local law enforcement agency, Madame," explained Zulkeh, "if such they can be called."

"And what do they wish?" demanded the imperious dowager La Madame.

Her answer was provided by the Sheriff himself. "We're looking for Rascogne de Sevigneois, the notorious highwayman! Do not move until I've inspected the coach!" The Sheriff trotted his horse over to the coach window in order to search the interior. Pushing down the peak of his pique hat to cover his widow's peak and peeking through the window, Pike's pique peaked as La Madame's peke bit him on his peak of a nose.

"How piquant!" exclaimed the imperious dowager La Madame.

[*Chronicler's note: These last sentences—grotesque and baroque—were, of course, the penultimate symptom of Alfred CCLVI's fatal condition, which even now approached its sad end.*]

"Vicious beast," growled the Sheriff, but he forbore further quarrel.

"The highwayman's not here!" he announced to the Posse. Then, to the driver: "You may be off!"

But, just as the coach began to move, a new voice cried out.

"Stand and deliver!"

The coach stopped again. The passengers leaned out the window. Imagine their astonishment when they perceived that where had seemed to stand the Sheriff and the Posse, stood instead, none other than Rascogne de Sevigneois himself.

"It is I, Rascogne de Sevigneois, cleverly disguised as the Sheriff and the Posse! Descend and be robbed!"

The driver, guard, and all the passengers climbed down from the coach.

"Why is the youth so illy treated?" demanded the highwayman, seeing the prisoner shackled to the warden. Upon hearing the explanation, Rascogne smiled at the youth and said, "Fear not! I shall not permit such injustice to continue!"

It took but a moment for the rascal to strip the passengers of their wealth. Upon seeing the wizard and Shelyid, he said, "So! We meet again!" Here the impudent rogue seized Shelyid by the nape and suspended him in midair, turning the gnome this way and that. The dwarf did protest this treatment—indeed, he swung his little fists most energetically at the highwayman, but all to no avail.

"A snarl-friend, eh?" mused Rascogne, inspecting the dwarf from every angle. "Most strange, most strange."

He deposited Shelyid back on the ground. Then, looking about at the other passengers, he demanded: "But where is La Contessa and her decrepit but doughty spouse?" He stroked his mustachios. "I confess I was much taken by the fair lady."

Shelyid, his indignation replaced by concern, cried out, "Oh, it's horrible! They threw her in prison—her and Il Conde both, because he wouldn't pay the Consortium's fine!"

"*What?*" demanded Rascogne. "O infamous deed! And where are they held? In the Caravanserai gaol?"

Shelyid nodded.

Rascogne's face flushed with anger. A most ferocious smile, like unto a wolf's, spread across his features. He stroked his mustachios vigorously.

"Well!" he exclaimed. "We shall have to deal with this—*most certainly!*"

Just then a cry was heard. "It's Rascogne de Sevigneois! After him, men!" Turning, all saw that a sizable body of men had appeared on the eastern horizon.

"It's the Hue and Cry!" exclaimed the driver.

Rascogne bounded onto his horse. "A chase! A merry chase!" he cried gaily, and galloped away over the western horizon. A moment later his pursuers pounded past the coach, a motley horde of ruffianly bounty hunters seeking the reward for the highwayman's head.

"Ah, malediction," spoke Zulkeh. "The villain has struck again!"

Suddenly the florid and well-dressed man of some middle years pointed to the northern horizon. "Look!"

Turning, all saw Rascogne de Sevigneois furiously galloping toward the coach, pursued now not only by the Hue and Cry but also by the Lynch Mob and the Band of Outraged Fathers and Husbands. The highwayman pounded up to the coach, cleaved the manacles binding the youth with one blow of his sword, swept the erstwhile prisoner onto his saddle, and galloped away over the southern horizon. A moment later his pursuers mounted past the coach, leaving the dust of a small army in their wake.

"Ah, malediction," spoke Zulkeh. "The villain has struck again!"

◆◆   ◆◆   ◆◆

Such were the last words penned by the illustrious Alfred CCLVI, to whom we bid a sad adieu. Sad, first, for the untimely passing of this great chronicler in the prime of his powers. Sadder still, for his demise led to the succession of Alfred CCLVII.

Every great line has blots on its escutcheon, and Alfred CCLVII is one of the greater ones on the noble clan of the Alfredae. To begin with, Alfred CCLVII was a mere apprentice at the time of his ascension to the inkwell. Heretofore, under the tutelage of Alfred CCLVI—who was known not to be overly admiring of his student—he had been restricted to the writing of chapter headings. This necessary, but of course not sufficient, aspect of the chronicler's trade, was known by all Alfredae to be his sole skill, in which, truth be told, he was not skillful.

And here lay the first of his two great faults. Of the second of these, his grotesque egomania, I will speak in a moment. But the first of his faults was perhaps even worse. For Alfred CCLVII was given, even in the writing of chapter headings, to verbosity.

Know, gentle reader, and I speak here as an experienced and accomplished chronicler in my own right (as the gentle reader has already had occasion to judge, from his perusal of these preceding pages of our tale), that of all the sins and foibles which afflict the writer—be that writer a scribe or a scribbler, a diarist or a dramatist, a narrator or a notary—there is none so foul, so odious, so disreputable, so arrant, so untoward, so deplorable, so infamous and so peccant as verbosity, yes, I say again, *verbosity*, that malignant cancer of the narrator's craft, which, under its many names—whether those be the names preferred by the educated gentility: wordiness, long-windedness, prolixity, superfluity or garrulity; or yet those more exact and fine-focused terms which are the natural optation of the scholar, the rigor of whose training in the necessity of precise meaning naturally leads them to such labels as: longiloquence, largiloquence, grandiloquence, multiloquence, polylogy and rodomontade, not to mention the yet-more-technical terms of the specialist: nimiety, pleonasm and amphigory (or amphigouri, as the purists insist); or those euphemisms which are, not surprisingly, the terms of choice of the verbose themselves, I speak here of: circumlocution, loquacity and eloquence; or even, for we should not in natural pride of our intellect and refinement ignore their cultural contributions, meager and crude though these be, the coarse epithets which are oft heard from the lips of the uneducated and unwashed: chatter, jabber, prattle, gabble, babble, blabber and blather—wreaks the greatest havoc of all the literary vices upon the heart of literature and narrative itself, that heart being, although most (even exceptionally well-read) literates are unconscious—say rather, not fully conscious—even of its existence, much less its centrality, the fundamental bond of trust which develops 'twixt writer and reader as these twain intersect, though indirectly and at a distance (a distance measured not simply in space but in time), without which education itself becomes an impossibility, for the reader becomes wearied and overtaxed, and thus loses his concentration, indeed, even his interest, while—what is worse!—the writer loses all sense of the purpose of his craft, the which is not to aggrandize himself, in a frivolous display of empty virtuosity, but to impart to the reader the pith and the meat of the tale which he tells, and in so doing, loses all grasp on reality and reason, falling thus further and further into the fell sway of those psychologic disorders which we know as solipsism and egomania.

Even so was Alfred CCLVII struck down by his vice.

For not only did this callow youth know nothing of his
trade save the writing of chapter headings, but once
come to the Alfredship, he proclaimed his very vice
a virtue! It was astonishing! This crazy little louse began
strutting about, telling one and all that chapter headings were the essence of narrative, indeed, all of narration that was significant!

And so—here I come to the heart of the matter—
it is with great regret that I must inform the gentle
reader that the next few chapters of my ancestors'
chronicle exist, alas, only in the form of chapter headings. But do not despair! For the Alfredae were and
are a stern breed. Once it became apparent that the
newly-penned Alfred was a madlouse, the clan did meet
in full assembly and with no further ceremony did seize
the apostate and maroon him on a passing peddler. And
so was Alfred CCLVII succeeded by Alfred CCLVIII,
of whose narrative skills nothing but praise can be said,
as the gentle reader will soon learn for himself.

In the meantime, however, I must ask the gentle
reader's indulgence. Glean what can be gleaned from
the chapter headings and then, in the next portion of
our tale, glean what can be gleaned from an extrane-
ous source, the which was most cleverly obtained by
my ancestors through mechanisms which remain, to this
day, a deep secret of my clan.

CHAPTER XII. *In Which Our Heroes Continue Their Journey Through the Drear, Heading North by North-West, to the Still Distant City of Prygg. Zulkeh Denounces the Highwayman. Further Broodings of the Mage, and Shelyid's Fears and Remembrances Thereof. A Quarrel Between the Imperious Dowager La Madame and the Florid and Well-Dressed Man of Some Middle Years. The Wizard Adjudicates. A Quarrel Between the Wizard and the Imperious Dowager La Madame. A Quarrel Between the Wizard and the Florid and Well-Dressed Man of Some Middle Years. Arrival at* Sigh *of Relief (a Subsidiary of the Consortium), the Roadway Inn Located on the Northern Edge of the Drear. The Consortium Levies a Heavy Fine on Our Heroes For Allowing a Coach Operated by the GGNESWC& Etc. to be Robbed (Second Offense). The Wizard Instructs the Dwarf to Utilize the Gold-Making Scroll Anew. The Dwarf Demurs, the Rascal Impudently Recounting a Past*

Beating For This Selfsame Deed. The Mage Explains to his Stupid but Loyal Apprentice the Philosophical Distinction Between Essence and Appearance, in the Course of Which Sublime Lecture Many Ethical Subtleties Are Developed. The Dwarf, Reassured, Utilizes the Gold-Making Scroll. Our Heroes' Fortunes Are Restored! The Dwarf is Praised For The Deed. The Dwarf Is Soundly Thrashed For Rebellious Impertinence in Doing the Deed.

CHAPTER XIII. *A Journey Resumed. The Coach is Halted by a Band of Armed Horsemen. They are the Noble Royal Commandos of Goimr, Seeking the Subversive Sorcerer Who Has Driven the Former King to Madness. Zulkeh and Shelyid Are Arrested! Shackled, Chained and Gagged, Our Heroes are Dragged Through the Drear Toward Goimr. En Route, the Company Arrives Upon a Gibbet, From Which Swings the Grotesque and Decayed Corpse of a Hanged Man. Our Heroes are Taunted by Their Captors, Who Predict a Like Fate for Them! The Company Makes To Depart, But Are Halted by A Voice in the Wilderness. "Stand and Deliver!" All Are Astonished To See That, Where Had Seemed to Swing the Grotesque and Decayed Corpse of a Hanged Man, Swung Instead a Much Alive and Gaily Dressed Highwayman, Clutching his Horse Between His Legs! "It is I, Rascogne de Sevigneois, Cleverly Disguised As a Hanged Man! Release Your Prisoners!" The Commandos Demur, Scoffing at This*

Demand From a Lone Man. The Lone Highwayman Demurs, Announcing That He Has Confederates. Sure Enough, Where Had Seemed to Stand a Gibbet From Which Depended a Rope, Stand Instead, Il Conde and La Contessa. A Fierce Melee Ensues. Rascogne Skewers Multiple Commandos With the Greatest of Ease. Il Conde Bludgeons Several More With His Cane, Feverishly Searching For Rare Coins. La Contessa Proves Astonishingly Adept As a Cutthroat, Flaunting Her Magnificent Cleavage All The While. A Massacre Most Foul! The Noble Company of Commandos Butchered To the Last Man! Our Heroes Are Freed and Flee Into the Mountains With the Villainous Highwayman and His Accomplices.

CHAPTER XIV. *A Bandit Camp in the Mountains. The Wizard Admonishes His Rescuers With Subtle and Intricate Lessons on Ethics and Legality. Rude Replies. Shelyid Learns From La Contessa of Rascogne's Bold Rescue of Her and Il Conde From the Caravanserai Jail. She and Her Husband Have Decided to Join the Highwayman in a Life of Crime—She, From Love of the Scoundrel, Her Husband, From Love of the Rare Coins Which the Rogue's Trade Brings In Such Great Profusion. A Visit From the Big Banjo, Old Friend of Rascogne de Sevigneois. He is Seeking Material For a New Opera. The Big Banjo is Delighted With Rascogne's New ménage a trois, Finding in This Peculiar Arrangement Most Fertile Ground For a Popular Tragedy Filled With Great Emotion and the Littering of Many Corpses About the Stage At the Final Curtain. Rascogne Scoffs at the Big Banjo's Sublime Artistic Proposal, Advocating Instead the Dull Maintenance of a Most Pleasant Arrangement*

Satisfactory To All Parties Involved. The Big Banjo Approaches Il Conde With the Selfsame Libretto. Il Conde Demurs, Allowing That If He Were But Fifty Years Younger He Would Cheerfully Satisfy the Composer's Desires, For He Suspects the Highwayman of Taking Liberties With His Wife, Several Times a Day, In Fact, If He is Not Mistaken. Alas, At His Age A Man Has Energy For But One Passion. And There Is No Denying the Scoundrel Rascogne de Sevigneois Amasses Coins At a Prodigious Rate, Of Which All Those Of Value to the Numismatist Are Immediately Handed Over to Il Conde, Who Stands Fair to Become the World's Recognized Numismatist Supreme As a Result. Disgruntled At This Uniform Disrespect for the Necessities of Art, the Big Banjo Departs, Seeking More Tragic Sensibilities Elsewhere.

CHAPTER XV. *The Wizard Determines to Leave the Camp of Rascogne de Sevigneois, Explaining to Shelyid the Continuing Necessity To Consult the Witch Magrit That He Might Determine the Identity of His Enemies, the Uncovering of These Dastards Being Essential to the Thwarting of Their Scheme to Thwart the Thaumaturge in His Efforts to Uncover the True Meaning of the Dream of the (Now Deceased) King of Goimr, the Discovery of This True Meaning, In Its Turn, Being Essential to the Mage's Determination to Forestall the Catastrophe Which Even Now Looms Over All of Civilization, Even as the Mighty and Forward Rushing Tidal Wave Looms Over the Sleeping and Unaware Inhabitants of the Island Paradise. The Dwarf Argues With the Wizard, Announcing That He Has Discovered in His Runtish Soul the Burning Desire to Become a Highwayman. Indeed, the Gnome Cavorts About in a Most Unseemly and Ridiculous Manner, Displaying With a Small Poignard the*

Novice's Skill He Has Learned in Sword-play From the Rascally Rascogne, Who Has, The Mage Now Discovers To His Great Displeasure, Been Usurping the Wizard's Monopoly Over the Dwarf's Education. After a Most Disgraceful Scene, the Proper Relation Between Master and Servant is Restored. Our Heroes Depart, Shelyid Blubbering Great Tears at His Parting From the Highwayman and La Contessa. An Adventurous Trek Through the Mountains, Northward Toward the Still Distant City of Prygg. Several Days Into Their Journey, They Rest For the Night in a Great Cave. Alas, the Cave is Inhabited By Trolls, Which Pounce on the Dwarf Whilst the Wizard Is Absent, Searching for Fell Herbs on the Mountainside Below. Hearing the Alarum, Zulkeh Races to the Scene. He Is Trampled By Trolls Fleeing the Cave in Utter Terror. Entering the Cave, Zulkeh is Presented With a Mystery. Nothing is Within the Cave to Have Caused This Unwonted Troll Stampede Save the Swooned Form of Shelyid, Clutching in His Little Hand the Dagger Given Him by Rascogne. The Wizard Revives His Apprentice and Discusses the Paradox. Shelyid Proudly Proclaims the Trolls Fled From the Most Fearsome Manner In Which He Displayed His Poignard. The Mage Disputes This Absurd Claim, Recounting for the Gnome's Edification The Slavering Fury Of Trolls And These Monsters' Utter

Disregard For Pain and Wounds. The Wizard Ponders on This New Paradox Long Into the Night, Taking the Opportunity to Educate the Dwarf Not Only On Trolls But On All Other Manner of Fearsome and Unnatural Monsters, Among Which He Touches Upon, If Only In Passing, Such Creatures As Vampires, Ghouls, Ghasts, Goblins, Hobgoblins, Orcs, Wargs, Werewolves, Ettins, Not To Mention the Divers and Sundry Breeds of Demons, Daemons, Devils and Demodands. Shelyid, Most Unlike Himself, Cannot Sleep. The Next Morning, the Journey Continues. The Crest of the Mountains is Reached. Below Lies the Land of Pryggia, Upon Whose Northern Coast Lies the Less Distant Than Before City of Prygg Itself. Atop the Mountain, Our Heroes Encounter the Legendary Sage of the Mountains. He Summons Shelyid to His Cave. Shelyid Approaches the Entrance. From Within, Unseen in the Darkness, the Sage Whispers the Secret of Life. So Eager Is the Dwarf to Impart This Secret To His Master That In His Haste He Slips On the Rocks and Falls On His Head. Shelyid Cannot Remember the Secret of Life! The Wizard Is Most Displeased. He Rebukes the Dwarf Soundly, Indeed, Very Soundly, Indeed, Not To Put a Gloss On the Matter, Supremely Soundly—Alas, To No Avail. Our Heroes Begin Their Descent From the Mountains Into Pryggia. Along the Way They—

It was even at this moment that the lunatick Alfred CCLVII was seized and deported. A crash program to train his young successor was immediately set under way, but this youth, valiant though his efforts and great though his innate talents, was not deemed capable of taking the Pen of Pens in foreleg until the arrival of our heroes in Prygg itself.

To that narrative we will turn in due time, but first we will seek to supplement our knowledge of the preceding portion of our tale through the introduction of material hitherto most secret, obtained only, as I said before, by hidden methods which remain to this day the closely-guarded privilege of my clan.

PART X

In Which the Persons and Activities
of Our Heroes Come to the Attention of
Those Authorities Of Puissant and Mighty
Ozar Upon Whose Shoulders Rests the Grave
and High Task of Defending Ozarae And Its
Interests Against Subversion and Insurrection.
Taken From the Minutes of the Senate Committee
Armed and Brevetted to Investigate Odious
Unconscionable Sedition, Obtained by the
Alfredae Through Means Which Remain
To This Day the Well-Hidden Secret
of Our Noble Clan of Chroniclers.

*Minutes of the Monthly Session of the Ozarean Senate
Committee Armed and Brevetted to Investigate Odious
Unconscionable Sedition. Convened on the 28th day of
October, Year of the Jackal. Chairman of the Committee: His Puissance the Senator Whelm, Imperial Republican Party. Meeting in Full and Open Session, All
Members Present. His Puissance the Senator Whelm
pounds his gavel.*

Chairman Whelm: I hereby declare this session of

the Committee open. All persons will come to order.
Puissant colleagues, distinguished guests, this session of
the Committee will concentrate its attention upon the
nefarious activities and schemes of a newly discovered
plotter against the well-being of Ozarae and its
interests. *(Murmurs in the chamber. Chairman Whelm
raps his gavel.)* Order! *(Order is restored.)* A new
threat to our peace and prosperity has been brought
to my attention. So grave did the menace posed by
this heretofore unknown subversive seem to me, that
I determined at once to bring the attention of
the entire Committee to bear upon him. Let me
begin my remarks by informing the Committee that
the great and long-standing friend of the Imperial
Republic of Ozar, King Roy of Goimr, is no longer of
this world. *(Great hubbub erupts in the chamber.
Chairman Whelm raps his gavel.)* Order! Order!
(Order is restored.) Yes, sad to say, that peace-loving
monarch, trusted friend of our nation, who was always
ready to assist our commercial and industrial enterprises in their endeavors to uplift his backward country, has been most foully undone. He was driven to
madness by the schemes of a sorcerer of his own
capital, one Zulkeh of Goimr by name. But rather
than tell the story myself, I would like to call to the
stand one of our distinguished guests. *(A man of easy
grace leaves his place in the visitors' gallery and takes
a seat at the witness table.)* This gentleman, yclept
Gerard, was formerly the Chief Counselor to the
Throne of Goimr. Upon the King's descent into insanity, Gerard was one of the notables of the realm who
took matters into their capable hands and established
a new provisional government. May I introduce the
new head of the state of Goimr, First Clerk Gerard.
(Polite applause.)

First Clerk Gerard: Thank you. May I extend to the honorable Committee the greetings of the new provisional government of Goimr, of which I have the honor to be its First Clerk. Let me say here that the new government of Goimr intends to continue the enlightened policies of the former government with regard to cooperation with Ozar's legitimate interests. Indeed, we are determined to go further than the late lamented King in this respect. We are firmly determined to bring the now-Republic of Goimr fully into the modern world.

Senator Bourse: Senator Whelm, I would like the floor.

Chairman Whelm: The chair recognizes Senator Bourse, of the Imperial Democratic Party.

Senator Bourse: First Clerk Gerard, I would like to say that your initial remarks have been most gratifying. In these times of turmoil, we are naturally concerned upon hearing of the collapse of yet another government, especially one of such long-standing stability and servil—amity—with the legitimate needs and interests of the Imperial Republic of Ozar. In this regard, do I understand that the Kingdom of Goimr is now replaced by a Republic?

First Clerk Gerard: That is so, Senator.

Senator Bourse: I see. Naturally, I myself advocate the republican system. Indeed, I yield to none in the depths of my love, my adoration, for democracy. Yet— I must speak frankly—it is a fact, albeit regrettable, that the replacement of monarchies by republics has frequently been accompanied by great disorder and tumult. For all too often the lowlifes of a new

Republic confuse freedom with license, especially as the economic dictates of modern society gain their full sway, unhampered by now-discarded feudal impediments.

First Clerk Gerard: Puissant senator, I believe that you need have no fears in this regard regarding the new provisional government of Goimr. To begin with, let me assure you that the ascension of the new government did not take place through disreputable riot and revolution, but through the most precisely legal and legitimate means. The King of Goimr having been determined an insane man, the Council of State declared him unfit for regnancy and placed him in an asylum, where, I regret to say, the poor man hanged himself in his sleep. We then examined his heirs, down through all collateral lines to three generations, both male and female, to find an heir who would satisfy the basic requirement of rulership according to the ancient laws of the Kingdom of Goimr. Regretfully, not one of them could satisfy this basic requirement.

Senator Bourse: And what is that requirement?

First Clerk Gerard: Being able to count your fingers.

Senator Bourse: Not one of them could count their fingers?

First Clerk Gerard: I'm afraid not. The Heir Apparent failed the examination completely. In fact, he dropped dead from the strain. We sought to test the other boys of the royal family, but the little rascals had all burned to death in the great fire which destroyed the royal palace because they were playing with matches. We had hopes for the distaff members of the family, but the clumsy girls had apparently cut off their fingers in a series of kitchen accidents just before the fire. An unfortunate coincidence, since it's possible that one of them might have been able to count her fingers, if they'd had any left. In fact, it seems certain that at least one of the princesses would have passed the test. For would you believe that, after we placed the girls in the care of the Abbess of the Convent of the Ladies in Peace, the clever little hoydens managed— even without fingers!—to hang themselves.

Senator Bourse: All of them?

First Clerk Gerard: Every last one. Distressed, no doubt, at the untimely death of their brothers. It was at that point that the Council decided we had no choice but to replace the kingdom with a new provisional government. At each step of the process, I should like to say, we consulted closely with the leaders of the Armed Forces and the Ecclesiarchy, as well, it goes without saying, as the Ozarean Consul and the Regional Vice-President of the Consortium. I might also mention that we were greatly assisted in this difficult time by the energetic efforts of your—ah— representative, Rupert Inkman.

Senator Bourse: Well, this is certainly encouraging. And what is the name of your new government?

First Clerk Gerard: Attila the Junta.

Senator Bourse: Most reassuring, most reassuring! I believe I speak for every member of the Committee here. (*Cries of "Quite right" and "Hear, Hear!"*) Indeed, if I may—

Chairman Whelm: Pardon my interruption, esteemed colleague, but I would like to get on with the business at hand, which is the investigation of the knavish sorcerer Zulkeh. I believe that First Clerk Gerard has more than satisfied the Committee's concern regarding his reliability as a witness? (*Cries of "Quite right!" and "Hear, hear!"*)

Senator Bourse: I stand corrected and yield the floor. Will the Puissant Chairman continue the investigation?

Senator Whelm: I thank the esteemed Senator from the Imperial Democratic Party. First Clerk Gerard, as I understand it, the unfortunate train of events which led to the demise of the Kingdom of Goimr was set in motion by this sorcerer, Zulkeh of Goimr?

First Clerk Gerard: Quite so, Honorable Chairman. The wizard Zulkeh was summoned to the palace at the request of the King, whose peace of mind had been disturbed by a ridiculous dream. I instructed this so-called wizard, in no uncertain terms, to quiet the King's fears. Instead this fiend, seeing in the King's unstable frame of mind a chance to strike a mortal blow at the tranquility of the Realm, chose to interpret the King's dream in such a way as to inflame His Majesty's morbid temperament to the point of madness.

Chairman Whelm: What did he say to the King?

First Clerk Gerard: The villain told the King that his dream foretold the utter and complete destruction of his kingdom, his palace, his dynasty and his Royal Person, this ruination to encompass the entire male line of the Royal Family down to three generations, and possibly—on this point the scoundrel feigned uncertainty—the entire female line as well. (*Great hubbub fills the chamber. Cries of "O foul deed!" and "Damnable Treason!" Chairman Whelm pounds his gavel many times.*)

Chairman Whelm: Order! Order! Order! (*Order is restored.*) I believe the Committee can now see for themselves the danger which this sorcerer presents. In one stroke, he overthrows the government of one of our most long-standing and reliable allies on the all-too-often unsettled sub-continent of Grotum. Nor was this the last—nor even the greatest!—crime committed by this demon in human flesh. Nay, esteemed colleagues, prepare yourselves for a long and weary session. For I assure you, we have only begun our investigation. Many witnesses are still to be called. But for the moment, I would like to extend my thanks, and that of the Committee, to our distinguished guest. First Clerk Gerard, I thank you again, and you may resume your seat in the gallery. (*Vigorous applause fills the chamber. First Clerk Gerard takes his seat in the gallery.*) And now I would like to call to the witness stand the esteemed Director of the Ozarean Republic's Commission to Repel Unbridled Disruption, the Angel Jimmy Jesus. (*Vigorous applause fills the chamber. The Angel Jimmy Jesus takes his seat at the witness table.*)

Chairman Whelm: For the official record—although it's hardly necessary in your case!—will the witness please identify himself?

The Angel Jimmy Jesus: Certainly. I am the Angel Jimmy Jesus, Director of——, assigned to all work involving——.

Chairman Whelm: Thank you. And will you now

inform the Committee as to the nature of the work you have been co-coordinating for the past period?

The Angel Jimmy Jesus. Yes, sir. At the request of the Chairman of this Committee, and pursuant to all regulations governing the activities of the——, I have launched an investigation into the history of the individual known as——.

Senator Patellarasa: Puissant Chairman, may I have the floor?

Chairman Whelm: The floor is given to Senator Patellarasa of the Liberal Party (Hand-Wringing Faction).

Senator Patellarasa: The Angel Jimmy Jesus, I wish to assure myself that the suspect's right to privacy and freedom from inquisitory harassment were respected in the course of your investigation, as laid out in the Citizens' Privacy Code.

The Angel Jimmy Jesus: Senator Patellarasa, the investigation into the person of——was conducted at all times within the guidelines of the Citizens' Privacy Code, as well as, I might add, the specific regulations governing my organization, the——, even though, I might add, the subject is not actually a citizen of——. In proof of my assertion, I present the following documentation. *(The Angel Jimmy Jesus hands a folder to the secretary of the Committee, who presents it to Chairman Whelm.)*

Chairman Whelm: After examining the contents of this folder, I inform the Committee that it contains documentary proof that an anonymous message warning the suspect that he was under investigation by Ozarine authorities was scrawled on the underside of a manhole cover within a fifteen mile radius of the suspect's last known residence. I believe, and I am sure the Committee will concur, that this more than satisfies the provisions of the Citizens' Privacy Code.

Senator Patellarasa: One moment, please. I would like to know the exact content of the message.

Chairman Whelm: The message reads: "We're watching you." As this message clearly identifies both a subject and an object, as well as specifying the precise relationship between the two, I believe that it more than satisfies the Code. Senator Patellarasa, do you not agree?

Senator Patellarasa: Not entirely. I— (*The chamber erupts in jeers and catcalls.*)

Chairman Whelm, pounding his gavel: Order! Order! Order! (*Order is restored.*)

Senator Arbeitmachtfrei: Puissant Chairman! I demand the floor!

Chairman Whelm: I recognize the Senator from the Sons of Ozar.

Senator Arbeitmachtfrei: I denounce this interference with the sword of justice! I denounce this attempt on the part of the Liberal Party (Hand-Wringing Faction) to handcuff the authorities! I denounce the Citizens' Privacy Code as a stain on the Ozarean spirit!

Senator Patellarasa: And for my part, I whine in protest at— (*The chamber erupts with insults directed at Senator Patellarasa's ancestry and manhood.*)

Chairman Whelm, pounding his gavel many times.
Order! Order! Order! *(Order is restored.)* Senator
Patellarasa, you are out of order! And let me say for
the record that while the Senator from the Sons of
Ozar at times advances his opinion in somewhat more
rigorous terms than would most others—

Senator Arbeitmachtfrei: To the ovens! To the ovens!

Chairman Whelm:—that many of us, indeed, I will say
most of us here, share his concern with the weight of
pettifoggery and red tape which has come to overbur-
den our finest investigatory agencies. With that in
mind, let us proceed with the report of the Angel
Jimmy Jesus. *(Cries of "Quite right!" and "Hear,
Hear!")* The Angel Jimmy Jesus, you have the floor.

The Angel Jimmy Jesus: The principal purpose of our
investigation has been to establish the history of the——,
with particular regard to any of his associations with——. I
am pleased to say that our investigation has turned up
much information. This information, as will become
apparent, fully justifies the great concern which the
Committee and my own organization the——has
taken in the activities of the——. As the Committee
has already heard the testimony of——, which recounts
the criminal actions of——in the city of——, I would
like to concentrate my testimony on the actions of——
following his escape from justice in the city which I
have not mentioned.

Chairman Whelm: Certainly, certainly.

The Angel Jimmy Jesus: Thank you, sir. As will become
clear, the suspect——has in a short time compiled a
truly impressive record of criminal wrongdoing. Indeed,

both my own organization, the———, as well as such other investigatory agencies as———,———,———, and———have been hot on the trail of the miscreant and his confederates—

Chairman Whelm: Confederates? Do I understand you to say that the villain is part of a cabal?

The Angel Jimmy Jesus: Yes, sir. He has been associated for some years with a dwarf of unknown and suspicious origin— *(Cries of "A dwarf!" and "How disgusting!")* —and has in the more recent period been acting in league with a notorious highwayman and that latter's own criminal gang, which consists of two renegade nobles from Malata. The offenses of this subversive—I leave out of consideration the suspect's crimes in Goimr, which have already been recounted—are positively legion: 1) calling into question the commercial philosophy and *weltanschauung* of a subsidiary of the Consortium; 2) ridiculing a man of the cloth; 3) proselytizing Joesy; 4) associating with a notorious highwayman under the guise of being robbed; 5) calling again into question the commercial philosophy and *weltanschauung* of a subsidiary of the Consortium; 6) exhibiting disrespect for the legal profession; 7) participating in the escape of a felon under the guise of being robbed; 8) calling into question yet again the commercial philosophy and *weltanschauung* of a subsidiary of the Consortium; 9) participating in his own escape from lawful capture by representatives of the provisional government of Goimr with the assistance of a notorious highwayman; 10) participating in the slaughter of said legal representatives of the provisional government of Goimr with the aid of— *(The Angel Jimmy Jesus is interrupted by a cry from the visitors' gallery.)*

First Clerk Gerard: What's this? What's this? Are you saying the fiend has murdered our noble commandos? *(Great hubbub erupts in the chamber. Chairman Whelm pounds his gavel vigorously.)*

Chairman Whelm: Order! Order! Order! *(Order is restored.)* First Clerk Gerard, I must reprimand you for disrupting the session! Guests in the visitors' gallery are not permitted to speak!

First Clerk Gerard: My apologies, Puissant Chairman. It's just—the sudden shock—

Chairman Whelm: Yes, yes, I understand. Nevertheless, the formalities must be observed. I take it from your reaction that this is the first you have heard of the fate of your commandos? Go on, man, you may speak.

First Clerk Gerard: Thank you, sir. Yes, yes, it's true that our commandos were long overdue, but we had thought they had deser—uh, well, that is to say, the salary of our soldiery is perhaps not—we are a poor country—for that very reason, in fact, do I require the assistance of the—well, I will speak of that later—The Angel Jimmy Jesus, do I understand you that our noble commandos were slain?

The Angel Jimmy Jesus: Butchered like sheep.

First Clerk Gerard: All of them?

The Angel Jimmy Jesus: Does a pack of wolves spare the littlest lamb of the flock?

First Clerk Gerard: O horror! O murder most foul!

(Hubbub and uproar. Chairman Whelm gavels ferociously. Order is restored.)

Chairman Whelm: First Clerk Gerard, the entire Committee is in deepest sympathy with your distress. At the same time, it is essential that we press on, precisely in order to bring this criminal to justice in the swiftest manner. With that in mind, I would like the Angel Jimmy Jesus to continue his testimony.

The Angel Jimmy Jesus: Certainly, sir. In the interests of that selfsame swift justice, let me wrap up this well-nigh endless list of crimes with the latest and most heinous depredation of the suspect—nothing less than debasement of the currency. *(Tremendous uproar in the chamber. Chairman Whelm pounds his gavel many, many, many times. Order is restored.)*

Chairman Whelm: Do I understand you to say that the suspect is guilty of counterfeiting?

The Angel Jimmy Jesus: With all due respect, Puissant Chairman, it is difficult to give a precise answer to your question. We find ourselves here in a gray area of the law. I did not state, you will perhaps notice, that the suspect has engaged in counterfeiting. I stated that he was guilty of debasing the currency. Our legal experts are even now working night and day to determine if actual counterfeiting, as covered by the various statutes of Ozarae or any of the countries of Grotum, can be charged as well. The matter remains unclear.

Chairman Whelm: I admit to being a bit confused. Did, or did not, the suspect pass bad money?

The Angel Jimmy Jesus: The question cannot be

answered so simply, sir. The suspect purchased a number of services and goods from various subsidiaries of the Consortium, which he paid for by presenting gold tender. Our suspicions became aroused after we noticed that, on every occasion, this gold tender was presented in the form of oddly-shaped ingots. The gold was then subjected to careful examination by our best experts.

Chairman Whelm: And the result? Was it real gold?

The Angel Jimmy Jesus: In its content, the gold proved on every occasion to consist of pure, twenty-four-carat gold.

Chairman Whelm: Wherein, then, lies the debasement of the currency? I must say, the Angel Jimmy Jesus, it seems to me that, in your admirable efforts to apprehend this rogue, you are here adding a rather flimsy charge to what is already a long list of capital crimes.

The Angel Jimmy Jesus: I understand your point, sir, but as I hope to make clear, it is our suspicion that the suspect is in fact engaged in a crime of monstrous proportions, so monstrous that it has as yet no name in the statute books. For our experts pursued the matter further and examined the external form of the ingots, with a particular eye to determining the method of casting involved. As you may know, the Consortium retains a legal monopoly throughout Grotum on all casting, smelting or forging of gold bullion. It was thus our thought that the suspect might be guilty of illegal gold-casting, if not of actual counterfeiting.

Chairman Whelm: I see! And your investigation showed that the suspect is running an illegal gold-casting operation?

The Angel Jimmy Jesus: I regret to say that it is not so simple, sir. The statutes specifically forbid the unauthorized casting, smelting or forging of gold. The gold distributed by the suspect, however, was procured by a hitherto unknown method, which, I am sorry to say, is not forbidden by any statute.

Chairman Whelm: A new method of making gold? What is it?

The Angel Jimmy Jesus: Transmutation, sir. Transmutation. (*Stupendous hubbub explodes in the chamber. Chairman Whelm pounds his gavel innumerable times. Order is restored.*)

Chairman Whelm: Indeed! Well, I must say this is most irregular. I can assure you that my colleagues and I will see to it that statutes are passed which regulate this new method of gold-making, placing it in authorized and responsible hands. But until such statutes are on the books, I must tell you that with the best will in the world I cannot see the validity of your charge that the suspect is debasing the currency. After all, gold is gold. As the old saying goes, gold has neither lineage nor need of one. It is purity itself.

The Angel Jimmy Jesus: Precisely, sir! And there lies the villain's depravity! For he has struck at the very linchpin of modern civilization—the purity of gold.

Senator Sahib: Mr. Chairman! Mr. Chairman! It is imperative that I be given the floor!

Chairman Whelm: The Chair recognizes the Senator from the No-Bullshit Imperialist Party.

Senator Sahib: Thank you. Puissant Chairman, I must insist that the Committee go into closed session. All guests and visitors must be removed, with the exception, of course, of our witnesses. *(Senator Bourse seconds the motion.)*

Chairman Whelm: All in favor? *(The Committee votes overwhelmingly for the motion.)* Sergeant-at-arms, clear the room. *(The room is cleared.)*

Senator Sahib: Let me explain to the august Senators of our Committee that I insisted on closing this session in order to forestall public panic. I believe I have grasped the essence of the Angel Jimmy Jesus' testimony. And if my surmise is correct, then I agree completely with the esteemed Director that we are faced with an unprecedented threat to the security and well-being of our glorious empire. With your permission, Mr. Chairman, may I conduct the further questioning of the witness?

Chairman Whelm: Certainly.

Senator Sahib: Thank you. The Angel Jimmy Jesus, a question has remained unasked. You have stated that the suspect has created gold through transmutation—that is to say, by the magical transformation of something else into the noblest of God's substances.

The Angel Jimmy Jesus: Yes, sir.

Senator Sahib: And what was that something else out of which the gold was transformed?

The Angel Jimmy Jesus: Dwarf shit.

Senator Sahib: I beg your pardon?

The Angel Jimmy Jesus: Dwarf shit.

Senator Bourse: Not regular shit? I mean, normal people shit?

The Angel Jimmy Jesus: Dwarf shit. *(Stupefying hubbub erupts in the chamber. Chairman Whelm pounds his gavel an innumerable number of times.)*

Chairman Whelm: Order! Order! Order! Order! *(Order is restored.).* Senator Sahib, I give you back the floor.

Senator Sahib: Thank you, Mr. Chairman. The Angel Jimmy Jesus, I now require the answer to several questions. First, how much of this—tainted—gold has been placed into circulation?

The Angel Jimmy Jesus: It is difficult to say, Senator. We first became aware of the situation but recently. Over a considerable period, the suspect has remained at large, along with his dwarf accomplice, and has pursued activities which do not appear to have been restricted in any way by lack of funds. Given that dwarves shit quite regularly, once, sometimes twice a day, we can only conclude that a large amount of this, as you aptly put it, tainted gold is now in general circulation. I might also add that, given the velocity of modern currency exchange, it is well-nigh certain that at least some of this gold has long since departed Grotum and is to be found here in the Ozarine heartland as well.

Senator Sahib: My second question, then: Is there any way to distinguish this horrid dwarf gold from normal gold, once it has been turned into coinage and has entered the global monetary system?

The Angel Jimmy Jesus: No, Senator, there is not.

Senator Sahib: I feared as much. My third question: Has either your Commission or the Consortium managed to discover the exact process whereby this dwarf gold is produced?

The Angel Jimmy Jesus: No, Senator, we have not.

Senator Sahib: Have you attempted to do so?

The Angel Jimmy Jesus: Certainly. In fact, we've given it top priority. We have established a special secret laboratory—far removed from any population centers, needless to say—which is working night and day to discover the technique. Pursuant to that end, we have obtained a sizable number of dwarves and have subjected their defecatory products to exhaustive and rigorous scientific examination.

Senator Sahib: And the result?

The Angel Jimmy Jesus: We've got a lot of dwarf shit on our hands.

Senator Sahib: My fears deepen by the minute. I assume, since you have been unable to determine the method by which this dwarf gold is produced, that you have also been unable to determine anything else about its properties.

The Angel Jimmy Jesus: That is correct, sir.

Senator Sahib: I tremble for the State. My last question: How long will this dwarf gold remain in that form? Do we have any reason to believe, based on solid scientific data, that this dwarf gold will not, at some uncertain future date, suddenly transform itself back into dwarf shit?

The Angel Jimmy Jesus: No, Senator, we do not. (*Indescribable chaos erupts in the chamber. Chairman Whelm pounds his gavel a multitude of times. Order is at length restored.*)

Senator Sahib: Esteemed colleagues, you now grasp the full extent of the crisis. It would be bad enough if the loyal citizenry of Ozarae were to discover that some of the gold in circulation resided once in the bowels of a cruddy little dwarf. But this! At any moment, the most delicate financial transactions, the most pivotal commercial exchanges—all of domestic and foreign trade alike!—could be suddenly brought to ruin by the emergence of dozens, hundreds, thousands, of little piles of dwarf shit everywhere—in the bank vaults, in the cash registers, why—even in the pockets of the very Senators sitting around this room! (*Great hubbub erupts.*)

Chairman Whelm, wielding his gavel. Order! Order!

Senator Vichyssoise: Mr. Chairman! I require the floor!

Chairman Whelm: The Chair recognizes Senator Vichyssoise of the League Larvaliste.

Senator Vichyssoise: Esteemed colleagues, I submit that we now have no option but to collaborate with the proposal which has often been placed on the floor by Senator Arbeitmachtfrei with respect to the dwarf menace. All dwarves must be immediately exterminated.

Senator Patellarasa: Mr. Chairman, I whimper for the floor.

Chairman Whelm: The Chair faintly discerns the wavering figure of Senator Patellarasa.

Senator Patellarasa: Esteemed colleagues, I must take exception to Senator Vichyssoise's proposal. We are confronted here with a moral quandary. Does the good of civilization as a whole outweigh the drama and pathos of the mass slaughter of millions of dwarves— all but one of them innocent of any wrongdoing? *(Jeers and gibes erupt in the chamber.)*

Chairman Whelm: Order! *(He pounds his gavel.)* Senator Patellarasa, I warn you that the Committee, famed though it is for its tolerance and willingness to examine all sides of an issue, is rapidly losing patience with your usual pussyfooting drivel.

Senator Patellarasa: Mr. Chairman, the Liberal Party (Hand-Wringing Faction) cannot in good conscience acquiesce without protest in the prospective massacre of multitudes of law-abiding citizens, even if they are a lot of cruddy little dwarves. I must warn you that if Senator Vichyssoise's proposal is adopted we shall certainly organize a candlelight vigil—in which we will undoubtedly be joined by the Well-Meaning, Bleeding-Heart and Knee-Jerk factions of the Liberal Party, as well as the Sociable Democrats. *(Taunts and jibes fill the chamber.)*

Chairman Whelm: Order! Order! *(He bangs his gavel. Order is restored.)* Senator Patellarasa, you may resume the floor—but I warn you, get to the point!

Senator Patellarasa: I shall do so, Mr. Chairman. But I say again, I cannot let pass the opportunity to dwell on the savagery of the action under consideration. You must understand the full ramifications! We'd have to chop up the whole lot of them, even the little baby dwarves. For they all shit quite regularly, you know, once, sometimes twice a day. It is this ethical— *(Jeers and taunts erupt in the chamber.)*

Chairman Whelm: Order! Order! *(He bangs his gavel. Order is restored.)* Senator Patellarasa, that's about enough. The time of this Committee is valuable and not to be wasted with a lot of puling nonsense about widdle-biddle itsy-bitsy eeny-weeny dwarf babies. I mean, who gives a fuck? You are no longer recog—

Senator Patellarasa: But Mr. Chairman, there's big money to be made here! *(For the first time in living memory, total silence erupts in the chamber.)*

Chairman Whelm: The Senator from the Liberal Party (Hand-Wringing Faction) is commanded to explain his last remark.

Senator Patellarasa: Puissant Chairman, esteemed colleagues, in your haste you have—as is so often the case with conservative attempts to deal with symptoms rather than causes—overlooked the obvious. We do not know, as yet, that this new method of producing gold is temporary. For all we know, it may well be permanent. Before taking any precipitous action, we must find out! For if this new method of gold-making results in permanent gold, think of the prosperity for the many—and the fortunes for the few! Think of the countryside dotted with hundreds, even thousands, of little gold factories, inhabited by thousands, even millions, of little dwarves crapping away for the enrichment of all society! Of course, they'd have to be regulated and such, but—

Senator Arbeitmachtfrei: Treason! Treason! If you think for a minute we'll put up with gold made out of dwarf shit, you're—

Senator Sahib: Shut up, you clown! When we need you, moron, we'll call on you. You stupid jackass, gold already comes from dwarf shit, or the nearest thing to it. Everybody knows that all the gold mines are already worked by dwarves. Never let the scummy little bastards up after they're sent down, of course, they'd steal you blind if you did. So they're already down there digging up the gold and crapping all over the place. They shit quite regularly, you know, once, sometimes twice a day. So what? That's why we have processing plants. Personally, I think Senator Patellarasa's hit on something here. *(Cries of "Quite right!" and "Hear, hear!")* Esteemed colleagues, I move we adopt a multipartisan solution to the problem. Our policy: First, underwrite a top-priority crash program to discover the secret of dwarf-gold production. Second, shackle the lazy little crappers to the toilet bowls!

Chairman Whelm: Colleagues, what is your pleasure? *(Senator Arbeitmachtfrei votes against the motion; all others vote in favor.)* Colleagues of the Committee, I have but one thing to add to the motion which we just adopted. I believe it goes without saying that, in addition to the steps adopted, we must place a top priority on the quickest possible apprehension of the suspect Zulkeh and his dwarven accomplice. *(Cries of "Quite right!" and "Hear, hear!")* All in favor? *(The motion passes unanimously.)* Excellent! The Angel Jimmy Jesus, you are hereby invested by this Committee with the fullest authorization to deepen and expand your manhunt for the selfsame miscreant and all who might aid or abet him.

The Angel Jimmy Jesus: At your service, sir.

Chairman Whelm: Well, then! Esteemed colleagues, I believe we've done another good day's work. I hereby declare this session of the Committee—

Senator Bourse: One moment, please! Puissant Chairman, there is one last item of business I would like to take up.

Chairman Whelm: And what is that?

Senator Bourse: I believe the Committee is entitled to hear a report from the Angel Jimmy Jesus concerning the current situation with the Rap Sheet in Grotum. *(Many cries of "Quite right!" and "Hear! Hear!")*

Chairman Whelm: Well, I'm not sure—imperial security—

Senator Bourse: Puissant Chairman, I must insist! The decision to send the Rap Sheet to Grotum was hotly debated in this very chamber. The final vote was not unanimous, even despite the great pressure from the Nabobs. Indeed, had the Director of Companies not been so insistent I would have voted against the proposal myself. At the very least, therefore, I believe this

Committee is entitled to a report as to the current status of the project.

Chairman Whelm: Very well. The Angel Jimmy Jesus, can you inform the Committee with regard to the point raised by Senator Bourse?

The Angel Jimmy Jesus: Certainly, sir. Pursuant to the authorization given by this body, I immediately organized the dispatch of our third Rap Sheet to Prygg, under the direct supervision of one of my most capable and trusted lieutenants, Rupert Inkman. *(Cries of "O fell and mighty operative!" and "The savior of the Rellenos!" fill the chamber.)* Agent Inkman reports that the Rap Sheet is in position and we are on the verge of launching our final campaign to destroy the revolutionary movement throughout Grotum. Indeed, the announcement of the campaign will be made very soon, at the culmination of the festivities surrounding the upcoming wedding of the Princess Snuffy and the Honorable Anthwerp Freckenrizzle III. It seemed to Agent Inkman and myself that this social occasion, embodying as it does the unity in action of Ozarae and Prygg, was the perfect occasion for making public our plans. Needless to say, all police and military forces throughout Grotum are now on full alert status and will throw themselves into action at the stroke of midnight, October 31, simultaneously with the public announcement of the campaign. *(Cries of "Bravo!" and "O shrewd stroke!")* I might add that the fact that our campaign will begin on Halloween has the additional advantage of making full use of the well-known superstitious proclivities of the Groutch masses.

Senator Bourse: Excellent! My principal concern, however, is not with the actual plan of operation. I would not presume to interfere with your expertise in these matters. And I am certainly gratified to hear that our noble Agent Inkman is in direct charge. Why, the man's name alone strikes fear into the heart of subversives the world over. (*Cries of "Ozar's finest!" and "The iron heel!"*) My concern is rather with the security of the Rap Sheet itself. Should, by some mischance, the Rap Sheet be—well! Its loss would be irreparable. Our other two are already committed, the one to the Rellenos and the other to Ozar itself. We will not be able to replace the Rap Sheet now in Grotum, should it be lost. That was always my great concern, and the reason I agreed with such reluctance to this project.

The Angel Jimmy Jesus: I believe you may rest easy here, Senator. I assure you that the security for the Rap Sheet is insurmountable. I cannot, of course, go into the details. But let me simply say that the security for the Rap Sheet could only be overcome by a combination of brains and brawn which—certainly the brains!— is far beyond the capacity of the Groutch rabble. Finally, even if by some impossible stroke of blind luck the Rap Sheet were to be taken from us, its loss would only be temporary. I hesitate to say the following, but I will trust the discretion of the Committee. Know, Senators, that despite his own great misgivings regarding our project, that God's Own Tooth consented to apply his immense magical powers and has incorporated Rupert Inkman's soul into the Rap Sheet. (*Cries of "O mystic power!" and "Ozar's grandeur swells!"*)

Senator Bourse: I confess I am not quite sure what that means.

The Angel Jimmy Jesus: What it means, Senator, is that

so long as Rupert Inkman exists, he can call the Rap Sheet to his presence, whatever it is.

Senator Bourse: But what if he's killed?

The Angel Jimmy Jesus: I said, "so long as he exists," Senator. Rupert Inkman can be killed, but his body will be revivified by the power of the Rap Sheet. Indeed, any part of his body will serve. So you can see the trap which lies here for our opponents. Should they, by some unimaginable means, obtain the Rap Sheet, we will simply get it back—with their names emblazoned on it! Even if our opponents should kill Inkman in the process. So long as Rupert Inkman exists, the Rap Sheet is ours—so long as even a finger bone remains. *(Cries of "Bravo!" and "incomparable cunning!")*

Chairman Whelm: Senator, are you satisfied? *(Senator Bourse nods his head.)* I then declare this session of our Committee meeting at a close. *(Chairman Whelm bangs his gavel. The members of the Committee file from the chamber.)*

PART XI

In Which the
Artist Arrives in That
Disreputable Realm Called
the Mutt And, Though Discovering
For Himself the Nature of That Disrepute
is Given Neither to Reproof Nor
Demurral, Thereby Confirming
His Own Most Odious and
Disreputable Nature.

*The Autobiography of Benvenuti Sfondrati-Piccolomini,
Episode 6: Boots, Beer, Banners and Beds*

So it was on such a wretched pair of patent leather shoes that I arrived in the Mutt.

Indeed, my first action upon reaching the Dog-house—for such is the curious name of the Mutt's capital, insofar as the term "capital" can be applied to the chief town of that country—was to locate the shop of a bootmaker and limp therein.

Entering the shop, I approached the bootmaker at his bench. He looked up at the sound of my approach.

A huge grin split his wizened old face. I began to smile myself, pleased at this amicability toward a customer, an attitude sadly lacking in all too many Ozarine establishments.

I soon discovered my error.

"Gwendolyn!" yelped the oldster. He charged past without so much as a glance in my direction and flung himself into Gwendolyn's arms. She picked him up, for all the world like a wrinkled babe, and planted a big kiss on his bald head.

"Hello, Mishka. Long time."

"Much too long." Now back on his feet, he looked up at her with a hurt expression.

"The word is you came through here three months ago. Is it true? And why didn't you stop by for a visit? Distressed, I was, at the news."

Gwendolyn shook her head. "I had no time for visits, Mishka. I was on a mission from—"

The old man held up his hand abruptly. "'Nough said! I don't want to know the details. 'What you don't know, the porkers can't screw out of you,' as they say." He laughed. "Not that I've had to worry much about porkers since I retired and moved to the Mutt! But still, you never know."

I looked around his shop, which had about it all the signs of a busy establishment.

"Doesn't look like much of a retirement," I said.

The old man peered at me, scowling. I'm afraid my Ozarine accent was just as thick as ever, even though I'd been speaking nothing but Groutch for weeks. I'm good at learning languages, and I'd become quite fluent in Groutch, but I just don't have the ear for speaking without an accent.

Still scowling, Mishka darted a sharp look toward Gwendolyn.

"Relax, Mishka," she said. "I'll vouch for him."

"He's a sympathizer?" he asked.

Gwendolyn shrugged. "Yes and no. He's not really involved in politics. He's an artist. I met him in Goimr."

Mishka was still scowling. Gwendolyn scowled back.

"Impossible old man! I told you I'll vouch for him."

Mishka looked away. "Well, your word's as good as gold, of course. But still, I just don't understand why you've got him around."

"It's personal, Mishka."

The old man suddenly grinned.

"Well! Well! That's all different, then!" The next thing I knew, Mishka was vigorously pumping my hand.

"Wonderful, wonderful," he prattled, "I've always said you were too intent on the cause, Gwendolyn. It's not good for the soul, you know, never taking the time out to smell the roses and such, and shouldn't I know?"

He continued his vigorous handshake.

"Pleased to meet you, young man. Very pleased, even if you are an Ozarine oppressor. My name's Mishka, by the way. Mishka the bootmaker."

"Benvenuti Sfondrati-Piccolomini."

Gwendolyn interrupted. "He needs a new pair of shoes, Mishka. Proper Groutch boots, if you would."

Mishka looked down at my feet, still shaking my hand.

"And will you look at those monstrosities!" he cried. "A wonder the man's not a cripple! All the way from Goimr, you say you've come? In those things?"

I nodded. Mishka released my hand and began busying himself in stacks of leather, muttering about "mad dogs and Ozarines."

I cleared my throat. "Uh, Sirrah Mishka, before you get started, I'm afraid I have very little money left. So if—"

I stopped, struck dumb by the ferocious glare the

old man was bestowing on me. I looked to Gwendolyn for assistance.

"Money's not the custom in the Mutt," she said. "Quite disapprove of money, people here." She looked at Mishka. "Oh, stop glaring, Mishka! The man's new here—how's he supposed to know? I assure you, he's not a Consortium agent."

The old man was still glaring. "A Consortium provocateur came through here not long ago, you know? Tried to give money to children, he did, the scurvy knave! Proper boys and girls, though, well brought up, so they turned him in and the General called out his dogs." A wicked laugh followed. "Squealed like a pig, the rotten collaborator, when Fangwulf pulled him down. Didn't get more than half a mile, he didn't, even with the General's usual generous head start."

"You'll have to make allowances for Mishka, Benvenuti," said Gwendolyn. "When he said earlier that he was retired, he meant from the struggle. Old habits die hard, especially his."

Mishka's glare eased. "Well, I suppose so. Have to make allowances, I guess, for honest strangers, even plundering Ozarines." His glare briefly returned. "But no more talk of money, d'you hear? I won't have it! This is a respectable establishment!"

"By no means!" I exclaimed, fending off his glare with my hands. "But how—" Again, I looked to Gwendolyn for assistance.

"See if you can do him some service or other," she said. "How about the sign over his door? Thing's so weathered you can hardly read it. Can you make him a new one?"

I went outside, looked at the sign, came back.

"Certainly. But I'll need some fresh wood."

Mishka disappeared into the back of his shop. A moment later he reemerged, carrying a nice slab of oak.

"How about this?" he asked. "Ingemar the cabinet-maker gave it to me a few months ago. I've been meaning to use it for a new sign, but I never got around to it. I've even got some paint, but I'm not much of a painter, actually. Are you?"

I managed to make some modest but reassuring noises, while digging in my pack for my woodcarving tools. And so did the time pass pleasantly, with me carving and painting Mishka a new sign, while he busied himself with my boots. As he worked, Gwendolyn told him of our adventures, leaving out, I noticed, any mention of Wolfgang. This odd reticence left great holes in the narrative, but Mishka didn't notice them, so upset was he when he heard of the imminent arrival of a Rap Sheet in Grotum.

"We're doomed!" he cried, over and again. "Doomed! It'll be the Rellenos all over again! The streets awash in blood! The executioners collapsing from exhaustion! The racks splintering from overuse! The whips worn to a nubbin! The dungeons bursting at the seams! Even here! Even the Mutt!"

But he only stopped working once, looking up at Gwendolyn intently.

"You've got to tell the General right away. Everyone else, too, of course. If you get the word out at the Free Lunch it'll spread quick enough, sure, but you've still got to tell the General right away. Maybe he can think of something."

"First the Free Lunch," responded Gwendolyn. "Then I'll talk to the General."

Mishka made as if to argue, but then went back to his work. He finished with my boots at almost the same time I was done with his sign.

Mutual admiration followed.

"What a sign! What a sign!" exclaimed the old man, as I tried on my new boots. A perfect fit, they were, and very comfortable. Not fashionable, I admit. I noticed the old man was rummaging around again in his stacks of leather.

"Just give me a little time," he muttered, "I'll have another pair of boots ready."

"What for?" I asked. "These are perfect."

Mishka looked up, surprised. "Of course they're perfect. Am I not Mishka? But a sign like that! It'll be the best sign in town! Calls for two pair of boots, at the least."

I waved him off. "Nonsense. The sign was a trifle, I assure you."

Mishka wrung his hands. "Well. Well."

"Relax, Mishka," laughed Gwendolyn. "Benvenuti's an artist, doesn't have any proper sense of value. Leave it be. He's happy with the deal, and besides, we've got to be off to the Free Lunch."

"Oh, yes! I forgot. Well, then, at least let me obtain a cab for you. I insist!" he cried. "Such a great sign!" He rushed out into the street and began a fierce whistling.

A minute later he reentered the shop, a burly man in tow.

"Look who's here, Gwendolyn!"

"Mario!"

The beefy newcomer swept his cap off his bushy head and stretched out his arms. Big as he was, he was almost dwarfed in Gwendolyn's embrace.

"Take us to the Free Lunch, if you would, Mario. Oh, let me introduce you to Benvenuti Sfondrati-Piccolomini."

Mario and I shook hands and exchanged pleasantries. He did not, I was relieved to note, seem to take offense at my Ozarine accent.

A minute later, Gwendolyn and I piled into the back seat of the cab, stowing our packs and my easel in the back. Mario eyed the easel with curiosity, but refrained from comment. He slapped his horse's rump with a short whip and we jolted out into the streets of the Doghouse.

Within a few blocks, I had come to the conclusion that this was the oddest town I had ever seen. There seemed no rhyme or reason to anything about it—neither the layout of the streets, nor the mixture of the buildings scattered about. Despite its relatively small size, the town positively shrieked "polyglot" in a way in which even the great and cosmopolitan imperial city of Ozar didn't. Still, the relations of the numerous inhabitants seemed quite cordial.

The Doghouse is not a big town, however, so it was not long before Mario reined in and wheeled the cab through a narrow gateway into a large walled court-yard.

Along one wall was a livery tending to the needs of the horses. On the opposite wall, under a well-weathered colonnade, stood a stout door, much abused by time and circumstances. The door's green paint was peeling off. Numerous cuts, gashes and nicks in the wood of both door and frame gave evidence that the customers were not a particularly sober and upright sort.

Above the colonnade stood—or rather, leaned slightly askew—a sign (very badly lettered) which proclaimed:

THERE AIN'T NO SUCH THING AS A
FREE LUNCH

Gwendolyn and I grabbed our belongings and followed Mario inside. The place, to all appearances, was a classic provincial alehouse: numerous tables and chairs, a long, long bar, a few small windows high in a back wall, and several curtained alcoves or private rooms. Behind the bar was a small kitchen from which emanated a variety of amazing smells. The air was thick with tobacco and cooking smoke, not to mention alcohol vapors. A subdued hubbub filled the room, which soon changed to cries of loud greeting when the customers spotted Gwendolyn. We took our places at the bar. The tapster, a fat and placid-looking man, made a slow but inevitable progress up the long bar, like a stout ship moving through a canal, propelled by ritual wipes of the counter with a towel.

"'Lo, Mario. 'Lo, Gwendolyn. Long time. And who's your friend?"

Gwendolyn introduced me. "And this is the Tapster, Benvenuti. What's the free lunch, today? Arsters? Arsters and beer?"

"'Course it is," snapped the Tapster. "Just like it's been for the past twenty years and more."

"I'll have some," said Gwendolyn. The Tapster eyed me.

"I'll have oysters and beer, also." The gathering fury on his face warned me. "Arsters, I mean! Arsters!"

He waddled off, wiping the bar, then passed through a curtain into the kitchen.

"What is it about shellfish," I complained to Gwendolyn, "that people will commit mayhem over pronunciation?"

She and Mario frowned at me, like bishops regarding a heretic.

"A quahog is a quahog, a clam is a clam, and an arster is an arster," came their joint pronunciamento. I sighed, but let it go. I'm bold, but I'm not crazy.

The Tapster returned, bearing great pots of ale and a platter full of mollusks.

Famished, I started to dig in, then hesitated.

"Uh, tapster, a question. What about—?" I avoided the obscenity. "What I mean is, the sign above says there is no free lunch."

"Well, of course there isn't! What are we—witless nihilists?"

"He's new," said Gwendolyn, devouring her "arsters."

"Oh. Well, then, young man, let me explain the customs of the Mutt. In this happy and prosperous little place, we handle the exchange of goods and services rather differently from those benighted lands groaning under the yoke of"—here, a tight jaw, a grim lip, jowls quivering with contempt—"money. Keeps the Consortium off our backs, you understand? Not to mention the usurers and the rest of the world's drones. So it's like this. You come in here looking for something to eat and drink, but naturally I can't sell it to you because if I did, before you know it I'd be a subsidiary of the Consortium—whether I wanted it or not—and the next thing you know all of my customers would boycott the place and the next thing you know I'd be run out of town on a rail, if I was lucky and the General's dogs were in need of a rest. So we can't have that. So instead I give everybody a free lunch. Booze is on the house too, of course."

He proceeded to give the counter a solemn wipe of his cloth.

"Now, of course if people didn't help me out, I'd soon be starving on the street. And then they'd miss out on their free lunch. So out of the goodness of their hearts they provide me with the various services which I require. Everything make sense?"

I thought it over. "Yes, I think so. Your system reminds me a bit of a book written by one of my relatives. Proudhon Sfrondrati-Piccolimini, you may have heard of him? If I recall, he argues—"

"The man's an idiot!" cried the Tapster. "All that

nonsense about the people's bank and such! No, no, young man, you're quite mistaken in all this!"

There followed a lengthy discourse on the competing theories which guided, or failed to guide, the daily life of the Mutt. It all went over my head, other than a general sense that people here seemed well enough pleased with their arrangements. And the beer and oysters were excellent.

When we were finished, Gwendolyn asked if there were some service she could provide for the Tapster, but he waved it off. He seemed rather offended, in fact.

"What?" he demanded. "Am I an ignoramus? A provincial cloddy, doesn't know a use value from an exchange value?" He sucked in his paunch, more or less, and assumed a pose of stern wisdom.

"I assume you're here on movement business?"

Gwendolyn nodded.

"Well, then, that's settled! Is there any greater use value for one's labor that to strive for the overthrow of the established order? 'Course not! So I feel the beer and arsters have been made good already."

The look of stern wisdom was now bestowed upon me.

"Don't know about him, though. Is he here on movement business, too?"

Gwendolyn started to explain my role in our escape from Goimr, but I interrupted.

"Nothing that could match this fine brew and—arsters. I've a bit of a knack for signs, however. I believe yours could use some improvement?"

A bit of friendly haggling ensued—although I'm not sure the word "haggling" fits a discussion in which the perverted concept of money never reared its head. At the end, it was agreed that I would fix up various unsightly aspects of the Free Lunch. Beer and arsters, needless to say, remained on the house.

There was one awkward moment.

"And will you be needing one room, or two?" asked the Tapster, his face bland and unreadable.

A moment's silence followed.

"Two rooms," I said quickly. Gwendolyn took a deep draught of ale. We sat side by side for several minutes, saying nothing.

"I'll be going," announced Mario. "I'll spread the word you're here, Gwendolyn. From what little Mishka told me, I gather you'll need to be talking to people."

"Thank you, Mario. And can you get word to the General? I'll need to see him soon."

"Certainly. I'll warn you, however, that you probably won't get many people here this afternoon. There's a new civil war scheduled for four o'clock, and the betting's been pretty fierce. Not many people'll want to miss it."

"Really?" Gwendolyn's interest was aroused. "What are the odds?"

"The Oligarchy's favored. The Republic's considered a serious contender, though I don't for the life of me understand why. The Aristocracy of the Robe is thought to have a good chance. The Aristocracy of the Sword's weak. And the Democracy's a joke, of course."

"How about the Monarchy?"

Mario smiled, rubbed his nose. "Well, now, there's what's interesting. I've a feeling—let's just say I'm betting on the Monarchy, and leave it at that."

"You know something?"

"Just a feeling, just a feeling."

Gwendolyn frowned, then smiled. "What the hell? Life can't be all business. Let's go! Like to watch a proper civil war, Benvenuti?"

Actually, the prospect of fratricidal slaughter didn't seem too attractive on such a fine afternoon, but I noticed that the patrons of the tavern were already streaming out, gabbling with excitement. Odd place, the Mutt.

Not much later, Mario pulled his cab over to the side of a street near what seemed to be the center of the Doghouse, if such a strange town could be said to have a center to it. At least, there was a very large square, around which a multitude had gathered, lining the sidewalks and perched on the surrounding rooftops.

Not more than a minute after we arrived, a disordered and shabby-looking mob entered the square from the north, chanting the praises of freedom and democracy. They were greeted by shouts of derision from the onlookers.

Derision which was well deserved, let me say, for it was not a moment later that a much more prosperous-looking and well-ordered mob poured in from the east and rapidly set the Democracy to flight with a few well-delivered curses and blows.

"This isn't a democracy, it's a republic!" was the battle cry of these newcomers.

But the victory of the Republic was short-lived, for it was but a minute or so later that four more columns of combatants entered the fray, and the advocates of the Republic were soon set into flight no less undignified than that of their scruffier cousins of the Democracy.

From the south marched two columns, one consisting of men dressed in aristocratic finery, the other of men in robes. Above the first column floated a banner depicting an eagle clutching a sword. Above the second, a banner depicting an owl clutching a quill pen.

The two columns fell to blows before they even reached the square.

"Power to the pure of blood!" cried the eagle-bannered ones, whom I deduced to be the Aristocracy of the Sword.

"Power to the keen of mind!" came the response, from those I took to be the Aristocracy of the Robe.

It was quite the affray. Evenly matched, at first, polo mallets against heavy ledgers, but then the Aristocracy of the Robe unleashed their secret weapon. Bottles of ink were hurled at the Aristocracy of the Sword, who soon fled in a panic, screeching in dismay at the ruin of their finery.

The crowd of spectators roared their approval of this cunning stratagem. The Aristocrats of the Robe, now in possession of the Square, strutted about, proclaiming the enactment into law of a multitude of measures, none of which I could comprehend because of the complexity of the language involved.

"I thought my Groutch was good," I whispered to Gwendolyn, "but I can't understand anything of what they're saying."

"Who can? Lawyers and bureaucrats, the lot of them. Boring sods, the Aristocrats of the Robe. Although I admit the ink bottles were a stroke of genius. Won't work against—and here they come! The Doges!"

Sure enough, into the square from the west came a small body of men—hardly a column, so few in number they were. Their garments were luxurious. Rings glittered on every finger. The Aristocracy of the Robe cried out their displeasure and swarmed toward them, waving their staplers and quills in a most martial manner. But the Doges stood their ground.

"Oligarchy!" they bellowed. "Money rules the world!" And so saying, they hauled forth large sacks and began strewing gold coin about with great vigor. More than a few Aristocrats of the Robe broke ranks, then, scooping up handfuls of coins and taking their side by the Doges, bowing and scraping. Several Aristocrats of the Sword came charging back into the square and did likewise. Then, but moments later, a veritable horde of people came pouring into the square, among whom I recognized many Democrats and Republicans. These, too, collected their coins and flocked to the rapidly growing forces of the Oligarchy. The remaining Aristocrats of the Robe croaked in despair and retreated.

"Well," I said, "it looks as if the Doges are going to carry the day."

Gwendolyn and Mario looked at me like I was a cretin.

"Nonsense!" snorted Mario. "Always looks that way, early in a civil war. Money'll collect a horde about, but they've no discipline. No stomach for the long struggle."

It could not be denied. For at that very moment entered—by surprise, leaping out of doors and windows from a large adjacent building—the resolute warriors of the Monarchy, led by the King himself.

"O noble stroke!" cried Mario. Gwendolyn was clapping her hands with excitement. The crowd was roaring with vast approbation.

A great howl of fear and fury rose from the motley ranks of the Oligarchy, as the champions of the Monarchy lay about them with rigorous blows of their scepters. "Divine right! Divine right!" bellowed the newcomers.

But then, just as the forces of the Doges seemed on the verge of collapse before the disciplined onslaught of the Monarchy, another great roar from the crowd indicated the advance of yet another party into the fray. "The Rabble! The Rabble!" came the cry from many voices.

A disorganized but energetic crowd poured into the square, brandishing torches and nooses, hallooing various war cries, of which "Anarchy!" and "Chaos and Confusion!" figured prominently. These new arrivals attacked everyone else indiscriminately.

From that point on, I lost all sense of the ebbs and flows of the civil war. It was too confusing for a novice, the more so as the square was soon invaded by a multitude of small columns, who did not seem to have much effect on the action but who certainly made a disproportionate amount of noise. Among these new arrivals, I gathered from the knowing remarks made by my two companions, were included such forces as the Tyranny, the Theocracy (these fellows much divided amongst themselves—spent most of their time attacking each other with miters and censers), the Big Brotherhood, the Autocracy, the Red Terror, the White Terror, the Green Terror, the Pacifists (singularly ineffective, this bunch), the Militarists (only a few here), the Colonels (fewer), the Generals (fewer still), the General Staff (a handful), the Generalissimo (one only—a skeletal old man, his face creased with infinite corruption, roaring over and again: "Unleash me!" "Unleash me!"), and a host of other little groups whose names and ideologies meant absolutely nothing to me. One such group advocated government by mass drunkenness, which they promptly enacted on the spot, to the great approval of the crowd. Another group advocated government by mass orgy, which they promptly enacted on the spot, to the even greater approval of the crowd.

My most vivid memory, however, was of a man painted all over his body with gold. He rode in a small cart, stiffly erect, vastly dignified. His two adherents alternated between pushing the cart and lying underneath its wheels, crying out: "All abase themselves before the Reincarnated Emperor of the Grinding Hegemony!" As the trio made their way around the

square, the cries of the faithful got weaker with
every passage of the cart over their bodies. In the end,
the Reincarnated Emperor of the Grinding Hegemony
was forced to dismount and haul the cart away himself, leaving the prostrate bodies of his loyal follow-
ers behind in the square. Judging from the expression
on his gold face, he was exceedingly disgruntled.

After I gave up trying to follow the progress of the
civil war, I spent most of my time observing the
onlookers. Clearly, this was a great social event for the
inhabitants of the Mutt. Not only were the residents
able to follow every nuance of the struggle, commenting
on every twist and turn with that peculiar language
which is shared by every devotee of a sport, and which
is utterly incomprehensible to those ignorant of it, but
they were enlivening their entertainment by a vast
consumption of food and beverage as well. Across the
square, I could discern the figure of the Tapster
manning a portable refreshment cart, around which
swirled at all times a small mob. Even across the great
din, I could hear his voice: "Beeeeer! Beeeeer! Beer
and arsters! Free beer and arsters!"

Suddenly, a great cry drew my attention back to the
civil war. In the center of the square, there was a sudden
swirl of movement. In a moment, the confused mob of
combatants resolved itself in its component parts, with
various political trends fleeing in all directions.

"Treason! Treason! O foul treason!" came the cry
from many throats in the square, along with: "O damnable King! O duplicitous royalty!"

From the spectators came an excited roar, as an
understanding of the recent developments swept the
crowd. Beside me, Mario was capering about in glee.

"I knew it!" he howled. "I knew it! There's nothing
like the Monarchy for a stab in the back! O cunning
stroke! O shrewd stratagem!"

"What's happened?" I asked Gwendolyn. She was almost as gleeful as Mario. She grinned at me, and put her arm around my waist. Not bashful, I followed suit. Then, for all the world like two teenagers enjoying an outing at the carnival, she filled me in on the developments of the civil war.

"The King's betrayed his alliance with the Oligarchy and the Aristocracy of the Robe. Threw in his lot with the Rabble and what's left of the Republic. Caught his allies totally by surprise. They've been routed—look!"

Sure enough, even at that moment were the Doges and the Bureaucrats fleeing the square, not without belaboring each other in the process, each blaming the other for the disaster. Inkpots were tossed, coins flung. Fierce weapons, I discovered, doubloons hurled at close range. But all this was but aftermath. The civil war itself was over.

The King now advanced to the center of the square. A tall man, he was, very regal looking. Arrived at the center of the square, the King summoned a herald, who blew a fanfare. The herald then bellowed, in a great voice which could be heard in every corner of the square, the following:

"Glory be to God and the Right! The legitimate King has triumphed in the field of battle! Let the word go forth to all the towns and villages! The Mutt is now declared a Monarchy!"

A great chorus of cheers came from the spectators. The herald continued.

"Let the word go forth to all the hills and dales! The King, in his graciousness, proclaims that his rule will be governed by the needs of the common folk! For he is not unmindful that, at his greatest hour of need, it was the Rabble which gave him victory! In this light, the Rabble is given leave to pillage the town!"

At these words, the Rabble advanced upon the crowd lining the square, nooses and torches held high. But as they neared the spectators, the nooses and torches were suddenly discarded. As if it were a signal, the distance between Rabble and crowd dissolved as the two groups greeted each other with much slapping of backs and general hilarity. A mad rush followed toward the Tapster's beer cart, as, for that matter, toward the many pubs and alehouses which lined the square. This rush was led by the Generalissimo, still crying, "Unleash me! Unleash me!"

Within a minute, the various contenders for state power were reentering the square. Distinctions between Democrat and Republican, Doge and Aristocrat, were lost in a general wave of gaiety. The only exception to this universal good feeling came from one of the former cart-pullers. "Next time," I heard him grumble as he rose to his feet, withdrawing a leather shield from under his shirt, "I get to be the Emperor of the Grinding Hegemony."

"It's such a nice evening, let's walk back to the Free Lunch," suggested Gwendolyn. I readily agreed to her proposal, and so off we went, hand in hand.

"That was such fun," she chuckled. "I haven't been to a Mutt civil war in ages."

"It's not quite how I had envisioned a civil war."

She smiled. "It's a great place, the Mutt. Wolfgang calls it the one oasis of insanity in the whole of Grotum. It's been a refuge for centuries. What few revolutionaries make it to old age always retire here."

"I should think the other realms of Grotum would take offense and invade."

"Oh, they do. Try to, I should say. But no one's ever been able to defeat the Mutt in a war of invasion. Not with the people up in arms, and the dogs, and the Kutumoffs to lead them."

I stopped and looked around. "*This* is where General Kutumoff lives? Is he the General you keep talking about?"

"Of course. He doesn't actually live in the Doghouse, although he's got a mansion in town. Mostly he stays in his shack in the woods, out on his estate. You've heard of him?"

"Heard of him? My uncles never stop talking about him! The world's greatest general, they say. Rodrigo and Ludovigo even served under him. Brag about it all the time. I knew the General was Groutch, but I somehow thought he was the commandant of one of the major Groutch armies."

"Your uncles served with the General?" she asked. I nodded. She pursed her lips thoughtfully. "I never heard of Ozarines serving with the General. Plenty of them hang around, of course, but to actually serve with him—! Well, anyway. You'll be meeting the General soon enough. I have to talk to him. If you want to come along, that is."

"Wouldn't miss it. My uncles would kill me if I did."

When we got back to the Free Lunch, night had fallen. We enjoyed some more beer and "arsters," and then made our way upstairs to our rooms. Both of us were very tired. There was another awkward moment in front of our respective doorways, where I felt like a fumbling schoolboy for the first time in years, not sure what to do. After a brief hesitation, Gwendolyn just smiled, said, "Goodnight," and went into her room. I remained in the corridor for a minute, staring at her closed door, feeling immensely frustrated. Then I went into my own room and tried to get to sleep. Not with any great success.

PART XII

In Which We Present
a Stirring Narration of the Exploits
of Our Heroes in the City of Prygg, the Which
Include Not Only a Daring Confrontation With the
Foul Witch Magrit and Divers of Her Villainous
Associates, But Other Impressive Deeds,
As Well, Both Fair and Foul.

―∾∾―

CHAPTER XVI. *A Wizard's Stealthy Cunning, Undone by a Clumsy Dwarf. A Wizard's Subtle Subterfuge, Undone by a Witless Gnome. An Impudent and Motley Crew's Disrespectful Ditty. A Mage in Foul Humor. A Gnome's Nature Dissected, A Dwarf's Character Denounced. But the Road Forward Gleaned! A Grim Resolve Made!*

Wizard and apprentice carefully picked their way through the streets of Prygg, hidden by the dark of night. Truly the mage listed among his many attributes the art of stealthery! For none living—no natural creature, at the very least—could for an instant have discerned his shadowy form gliding soundlessly through the gloom.

Alas, 'twas otherwise with his dwarfish companion. For the diminutive clod staggered to and fro beneath his enormous sack, raising both in voice and body the most horrendous din in the quiet streets of Prygg.

"Silence, dwarf!" hissed Zulkeh. "With your fatuitous clangor you shall arouse my enemies, ere now lulled into lassitude by the cunning of my trickery!"

"But, master," whined Shelyid, "I can't help it. The sack's *heavy*. And I can't *see*."

"Bah!" oathed Zulkeh. "Is the furtherance of science to be undone by the frailties of such as you? Again, I command you: desist from this vociferous conduct!"

But 'twas in vain. Threaten as he might, the wizard was unable to enforce furtiveness upon his ward. At length, he desisted in his efforts.

"Clearly," grumbled the mage, "I shall have to adopt an alternate course. No hope of escaping the notice of my enemies in the streets, burdened as I am with this dwarven lummox. So be it! We shall establish quarters for the night, and begin anew by utilizing my powers of disguise and misdirection." And so saying, the wizard sought out a nearby hostel, Shelyid caroming behind.

Later that night, after acquiring a room in the hostel, Zulkeh instructed his apprentice in the methods of disguise and misdirection.

"Know, dwarf," spoke the mage, "that disguise and misdirection are but two faces of the same coin. The cunning of the one stands in profound dialectic with the craftiness of the other. With this truth foremost

in our minds, we stand fair—even this very night!—
to advance greatly in our quest. For look you, gnome,
what transpires this very moment in the common room
on the floor below? In an establishment, I might add,
which I chose for our lodgings due to its very noto-
riety as a hotbed of carousal and debauchery."

"A lot of local folks are getting drunk," replied
Shelyid promptly.

"Precisely so! And while this behavior is unseemly
and disreputable, yet does it present us with the ful-
crum with which to apply the lever of my subtlety. For
look you, runt, what do plebes do when they become
inebriated?"

"Well, they do all kinds of things, master. They have
a good time, they joke around, they play games, they
urinate a lot, they get—well, I mean, they—at least
they try to, you know, I mean with people usually of
the opposite sex, although not always, and they—"

"Bah!" oathed the mage. "I did not request a catalog
of all mortal and venal sins! The point, my stupid but
loyal apprentice, is that they engage in discourse."

"Oh yes, master! They always talk a lot, I mean a
really lot, and they usually repeat themselves all the
time, especially after they've had a lot—"

"Bah!" oathed Zulkeh. "I did not request a demonstration! Suffice it to say that it is the inevitable characteristic of the lowlife in his cups to babble freely
of all manner of things, the which include secrets
which would normally be kept closely hidden. I trust
that our course of action should now be clear in your
mind, even given your limited intellect?"

"Oh yes, master! You're going to go down into the
pub disguised like a common workman and get drunk
and hang out with the people there and get slobber-
ing drunk so you can worm your way into their confidence because they'll see you're just an ordinary guy,

especially after they see you pissing about a gallon and
falling down a few times and maybe even barfing once
or twice. O master, you are the cleverest and most
cunning of wizards!"

"Bah!" oathed Zulkeh. "Impudent dwarf! Cretinous
midget! How could you conceive such a preposterous
idea? To begin with, 'twould be utterly beneath my
dignity to conduct myself in such a manner. And
moreover, 'twould be futile as well. For not even the
common souse could be so dim-witted as not to detect
my superior character—the lofty brow and piercing
glance would alone give me away. No, Shelyid, 'twould
be ridiculous for me to attempt to pose as a lowlife
when I have the ultimate lowlife as my apprentice."

"Me?" gasped Shelyid. "You want *me* to go down
to the pub and get drunk with the people there?"

"Of course! The plan is ingenious! Meanwhile, utilizing my powers of disguise and misdirection, I will
insinuate myself into an obscure corner of the common room, unnoticed by all, there to observe and
overhear the loose words which your carousal with the
plebes will cause them to guardlessly utter."

Shelyid slumped to the floor. His ugly little face
became more unsightly still, his features squeezed into
a ball, great tears wending down his cheeks.

"Oh please, master," he sobbed, "don't make me do
it."

"Why ever not? And whence this grotesque display?
I should have thought you delighted at the prospect!
Many is the time I have espied you gazing longingly
at the boisterous crowds in alehouses."

"But, master," snuffled Shelyid, wiping his nose with
his sleeve, "sure and I'd like to have fun in the pubs
like real people do, but that's the thing. I'm not a real
people. I'm a dwarf. I'm a really ugly, hairy little dwarf.
They'll be mean to me. Real people are always mean

to me. Real mean. They kick me, they hit me, and even when they don't, they curse at me or they make fun of me. They always do. Well, La Contessa was nice to me. And Rascogne wasn't so bad after a while—actually, he was really nice, too, except I wish he would have stopped picking me up all the time by the scruff of the neck and turning me this way and that and looking at me over and saying"—here the gnome's voice dropped to a baritone—"*a snarl-friend, eh? Most strange, most strange*—but they're the only ones." The dwarf snuffled again. "For that matter, you're not usually very nice to me, and you've known me all my life."

"Bah!" oathed the wizard. "I have no time for this puling drivel! Do as I command you, unworthy gnome—and be quick about it. For even as I speak, time wanes!"

And thus it came to pass that our heroes descended into the common room. The cunning wizard allowed some moments to transpire, following the first tentative steps of the dwarf into the boisterous environs of the pub. Then made he his own entrance, passing beneath a placard which announced the name of the tavern: The Swill As You Will. Shoulders hunched, his cloak drawn about him, hat pulled low over his lofty forehead, the mage quickly but unobtrusively found himself a seat in a dim and unoccupied corner of the tavern.

Meanwhile, Shelyid advanced to the center of the room, his mincing gait bespeaking his unease and trepidation. There did he stand for some few moments, peering about. The room was quite full of carousers, but his attention was almost immediately drawn to the big table along one side. For there sat the very epicenter of the carousal—six lowlifes, well into their cups, noisy and boisterous in the extreme. From their

garments, rough-knit and soiled; from their hands, callused and scarred; from their faces, coarse-featured and
weathered; from their voices, rude and profane; indeed,
from every aspect of their personae, 'twas clear as
day that here was the very archetype of the brutish
proletariat.

"Well," muttered Shelyid, "might's well get it over
with. Big as they are, least it'll be quick."

And so muttering, the gnome advanced to the table,
squared his shoulders, and piped up: "Can I have a
drink with you guys?"

The boistering ceased. Six pairs of bleary eyes
focused on Shelyid.

"A very little man!" cried one.

"Nay," said a second, peering closely at the dwarf,
"say rather a very little youth."

"Preposterous!" cried a third. "There's no youth so
hairy in all the world."

"Nor so homely," added a fourth.

Before the fifth and sixth could add their opinions,
Shelyid cut right to the quick.

"Actually, I'm a dwarf. I'm a very ugly dwarf, and
the reason I'm so hairy is because I suffer from that
most dread of nervous conditions, *hysteria follicularia*,
the uncontrolled growth and spread of hair upon the
body."

"What?" cried one.

"That old wives' tale!" bellowed a second.

"'Tis true, then," interjected a third, "the superstition
lives on!"

"And in these modern times!" added a fourth.

"Infamous!" and "Disgraceful!" came the voices of
the fifth and sixth.

"Why do you think that?" demanded the first.

"W-well," Shelyid stammered, "it's just true, that's
all. I've always had it."

"What nonsense!" sputtered the second. He reached down a meaty hand and hauled Shelyid up to the bench. A pot of ale was thrust into the dwarf's hands.

A very large finger, belonging to the third, wagged before the gnome's nose. "See here, young man," pontificated this worthy, "it may be true you're a dwarf—"

"Difficult to say," opined the fourth.

"Most difficult," agreed the fifth. "For who is so wise as to distinguish, with unerring precision, between a little man, a dwarf, a gnome, a midget, a shrimp, a runt, a pygmy, a Lilliputian, a chit, a fingerling, a pigwidgeon, a mite, a dandiprat, a micromorph, an homunculus, a dapperling, a small fry or someone with bad posture, weighted down with the cares of the world?"

"Not us, that's for sure," concluded the sixth, "for are we not uneducated, untutored, unlettered and ignorant?"

"Rude, crude, lewd and uncouth, that's us!" cried the first. This was apparently in the nature of a yahooish toast, for the six rowdies guzzled their pots in unison, Shelyid timidly joining in.

"Now then," spoke the second, waving to the barkeep for more pots of ale, "who told you that?"

It took a moment before Shelyid, his head swimming with the unaccustomed effects of the evil brew, grasped that the question was directed at him.

"Who told me what?" he asked.

"That you were afflicted with that most dread of nervous conditions, *hysteria follicularia*," explained the third.

"Oh. Well, actually it was—I mean, well, I shouldn't really say."

"Must have been a wizard," opined the first.

"Goes without saying," agreed the second.

"Even old wives don't believe that fable any more," added the third.

"Even ancient wives," contributed the fourth.

"Even crones rotting in their graves." This from the fifth.

"Even old husbands," concluded the sixth.

"You mean it isn't true?" queried Shelyid.

"'Course not!" bellowed the first.

"Bilge and rot!" added the second.

"S'natural for some people to be extra hairy like," slurred the third.

"S'no crime," came the thick-tongued voice of the fourth.

"Was not Joe himself called 'Old Shaggy'?" commented the fifth.

"Here's to Joe!" roared the sixth. This was apparently in the nature of a bumpkin toast, for the six rowdies guzzled their ale pots in unison, Shelyid joining in, with somewhat unseemly haste, if the truth be known.

This ceremony concluded, the first wiped ale foam from his lips and asked: "So, where are you from, short one? Goimr, I expect, judging from your accent, your clothes, and your hesitant and dispirited sense of self-worth."

"A dismal lot, your Goimrics," commented the second.

"Can't hardly blame 'em," remarked the third.

"True," said the fourth.

"Better yet than being Kankrese," countered the fifth.

"Being a trilobite on the ocean floor's better than being Kankrese," added the sixth.

"But trilobites're extinct," protested Shelyid.

"Exactly his point," said the first. "And you haven't answered my question, lad."

Shelyid fumbled for words. 'Twas clear as day that the two pots of ale he had already consumed were taking effect upon the never-too-quick-witted gnome. Perhaps it was dawning on him that he was supposed to be obtaining information from lowlifes, not the other way around. Certain it is that this thought would have pierced through to his brain like a poker, had he caught a glimpse of the ferocious glare bestowed upon him from beneath the wizard's floppy hat. In any event, the dwarf made a valiant attempt at turning the tables.

"Yes, I'm from Goimr. Boring place, I agree, not worsh—worth—talking about. Prygg's a much more interesting place. Must be a lot of hidden secrets and such in a great city like this. You guys lived here all your life, I bet. Bet you know all the secrets there are in this town."

" 'Tis clear," said the second, "that among this wee fellow's strengths, subtlety does not find its rank."

"Most maladroit attempt to pry information out of drunken sots I've ever seen," agreed the third.

"Not so!" disputed the fourth. "I am reminded of the occasion when we were blessed by a visit from Rupert Inkman."

"True, true," admitted the third, "I had forgot me. Sorry, lad,"—this to Shelyid—"you'll have to take second place."

"There's no comparison at all!" roared the fifth. "Why, I think this little chap's done quite decently— s'been polite, s'drank two rounds already, s'not snarled or yapped or threatened or done nothing 'cept fumble s'first effort to pry information out of sodden louts like us." He slapped the dwarf's back in a comradely manner.

" 'S'true!" cried the sixth. "Nothing at all like the cadaverous Crud. Let me remind you, fellow sods, that when Rupert Inkman paid us a visit he conducted hisself altogether different from this small not-yet-master spy."

"Can't be denied," concurred the first.

"Did the Crud share in our slops?" demanded the second.

"Nary a drop!" bellowed the third.

" 'Twas the thumbscrews gave him away," pointed out the fourth.

"Especially when he tried to apply 'em to us," howled the fifth.

"Here's to thick thumbs!" boomed the sixth, rising to his feet, ale pot in left hand, right hand outstretched, thumb sticking up like a potato. His sodden compatriots lurched to their feet and assumed a similar pose, six thumbs standing forth. And then, staggering to his feet, Shelyid joined his little thumb to the cluster, a sapling among great oaks.

"Here's to thick thumbs!" roared the motley crew. This was apparently in the nature of a yokel toast, for the disreputable half dozen guzzled their ale pots in unison, Shelyid joining in, with most untoward gusto, if the truth be known.

"And now, lad," demanded the first, "who is it what's put you up to this foolish poking and prying?"

"Speak up, now," urged the second, refilling Shelyid's pot. "You're among friends."

Shelyid stammered and stuttered. He glanced into the wizard's corner, as if for assistance, only to look hurriedly away. For veritably the mage's glare was now like unto the fiery furnace.

"Don't badger the poor little chap!" protested the third. "He hasn't even had time to drink his pot!"

"An outrage," agreed the fourth.

"An abomination," concurred the fifth.

"Here's to drinking our pots!" bellowed the sixth. This was apparently in the nature of a ragabash toast, for the six great brutes guzzled their ale pots in unison, Shelyid joining in, with positively disgraceful zest, if the truth be known.

"I have been rude to our tiny guest," admitted the first remorsefully, belching for emphasis.

"Unmannerly," added the second.

"And in a most disneedly fashion," reproved the third.

"For the answer's plain as day!" cried the fourth.

"S'no reason to pester the wee one," agreed the fifth.

"S'a wizard has put the poor boy in the pickle," concluded the sixth, shaking his head solemnly.

At the mention of the word, Shelyid's head popped up from the ale pot in which it was buried, worry writ plain upon his face. He glanced into the mage's corner, as if for assistance, only to look immediately away. For veritably the mage's glare was now like unto the volcano eruptant.

"Apologies having been properly extended to the injured party," stated the first, "I believe the time has now come to ask the question which is uppermost in our minds."

Here the six drunkards turned, as one man, and peered into the corner where sat the thaumaturge.

"I say, mates," boomed the second, "who is that ridiculous fellow who has been sitting in the corner for some time now in a transparent attempt at disguise and misdirection?"

"The one with hunched shoulders," said the third.

"His cloak drawn about him, his hat pulled low to conceal his lofty forehead," added the fourth.

"Though not his piercing glance, which flames at this very moment like the molten basalt of creation," specified the fifth.

"Here's to the molten basalt of creation!" roared the

sixth. This was apparently in the nature of a riffraff toast, for the six rowdies guzzled their pots in unison, Shelyid joining in, with a zeal which can, under the circumstances, only be described as a public scandal.

"A sorcerer," pronounced the first.

"From Goimr, 'tis clear," added the second.

"Most wretched wizards in all Grotum," commented the third.

"Not so!" countered the fourth. "'Tis a truth beyond dispute that of all piss-poor prestidigitators, 'tis those of Kankr who excel all others in the fumble-witted scale of misbegotten magery."

"Preposterous!" snorted the fifth. "'Tis true that your Kankrene conjuror is an incorrigible maladroit, this I admit. 'Tis true as well that your Goimric goetic is a bungling buffoon, this goes without saying. Yet still do these shine as veritable Magi in comparison to the feckless rattlepates who adorn the pantheon of Sfinctrian necromancy."

"What nonsense!" bellowed the sixth. "'Tis a fact known to babes in swaddling clothes that the faculties of all Groutch incantators are of such base degree that 'tis impossible, as a practic art, to discern amongst them the lowest from the low. Easier to rank the art of a pile of fruit flies!"

Now spoke the first. "In general, I would agree, yet there is one exception must be made."

"Most true!" cried the second. "For even here in Prygg itself does there reside a thaumaturge of undisputable acumen and merit!"

"Aye," agreed the third. "Our very own Magrit."

"Proper witch, she is," intoned the fourth piously.

"Here's to Magrit!" roared the fifth. This was apparently in the nature of a scalawag toast, for the six scoundrels guzzled their pots in unison, Shelyid joining in, with a ravenous fervor which, it can hardly be doubted, caused the angels to ring the dome of heaven with a united peal of outrage.

"I grant you that single exception," admitted the sixth. "She's not one to stutter up her cantrips, mal-administer her potions, bungle her exsufflations or muddle her demonography!" He took a deep draught of ale. "Nor, I might add, is she one to sneak about alehouses in a foolish attempt to inveigle privy information from a motley crew of drunken lowlifes such as us—rude, crude, lewd and uncouth though we be"—here there took place a clinking together of ale pots, in which, grievous to relate, Shelyid's pot was not found absent—"but who are still, I estimate with my primitive brain untutored in the mathematic skills, approximately thirteen orders of magnitude more clever than yon wizard of Goimr. Taken together, that is—alone, I reckon the slowest wit among us is not more than eight orders of magnitude smarter." He mused briefly; waved a huge magnanimous paw. "I will give him seven."

Then, like the stalking lion discarding all stealth and leaping forward in his fury, did the mage charge forth into the center of the room. His eyes glowed like coals, smoke and lightning issued from his ears.

"O infamy!" he raged. "O base impudence!"

"Impudence, is it?" roared the first, slamming his great fist onto the table. "And who are you, sirrah, to call us impudent?"

"I bear the dreaded name Zulkeh of—"

"—Goimr, physician," concluded the lowborn in one voice.

"Author of *Reason's Absolute Idea*?" asked the second.

"*The Speculative Logic*?" queried the third.

"*The Phenomenology of True Truth*?" This from the fourth.

"They number among my titles," spoke the wizard in a majestic tone.

"And are you not as well the originator of the Theoretical Theorem, that all facts derive from theory?" boomed the fifth.

"That I am!"

"And—this last but not least," demanded the sixth, "are you not also the author of *The True Law of Gravity, Properly So-Named Only By Myself?*"

"Quite so!" spoke Zulkeh. "And may I say I am pleased, albeit surprised, to find that my fame has penetrated even into the—"

But his speech was cut short, for even at that moment did the motley crew erupt into gargantuan laughter, slapping their backs and pounding their fists onto the table, rocking back and forth in mad abandon upon their chairs, several, indeed, collapsing onto the floor in most unseemly mirth. Grievous to relate, into this grotesque revelry did the now-utterly-inebriated Shelyid throw himself without a thought, behaving in a manner which, were there justice in the world, should have seen him burned at the stake.

"Ho! Ho!" gasped the first, as his rollicking humor flung him to the floor, "my graveness pulls me down!"

"Ha! Ha!" shrieked the second, his ale slopping across his noisome workhabit from the shaking of his shoulders, "perceiving the True Truth, my brew unfolds likewise in accordance with the foamy logic of its essence!"

"Hee! Hee!" giggled yet the third, draining his mug in a single quaff, "my own brew, closer to the speculation that is its proof, finds its Absolute Reason in the Idea of my gullet!"

Great was the mage's wrath. "This is an outrage!" he cried, gesticulating wildly.

"An outrage, is it?" demanded the fourth, clutching

his heaving ribs. "How so?" he gasped. "Have we not caught the germ of your thought, stripped it like a seed from its husk, and shown it to the world as its own true kernel?" And at this latest uncouth witticism, the entire party of rogues exploded into a veritable hurricane of laughter.

This most disreputable scene was now brought to a positively disastrous state of affairs. For 'twas at this very moment that the dwarf Shelyid, his normal lack of wits compounded by gross inebriety, chose to rise in defense of his mentor.

"Should't make fun a th'master," protested the gnome. "Hissa mighty mage, th'master, an' hissona great 'n' dangerous kest—quest." He took another draught from his pot, spilling a good half of it down his tunic. "Me too!" he added proudly. "I'm 'nis 'prentice." The diminutive numbskull peered owlishly at the party of louts. He placed a finger before his lips. "Shhh!" he hissed. "Gotta keep kite—quiet. We got enemies, y'see. 'N' thass why—"

"Silence, cretin!" spoke the mage, wroth with wrath. He waved his arms wildly. "Be silent, I say! Enough harm have you done, you unspeakable dolt!"

"Cretin, is he?" roared the first.

"Unspeakable dolt, is he?" bellowed the second.

"'Tis a damnable lie!" cried the third.

"'Tis a decent little man!" averred the fourth, clapping the dwarf's shoulder.

"A right and proper shorty!" concurred the fifth.

"Here's to all shrimps!" hallooed the sixth. This was apparently in the nature of a canaille toast, for the six vulgarians guzzled their pots in unison, Shelyid joining in, with a passionate ardor so utterly inappropriate to the situation that even the lambs of the field, should they have been witness, would have bleated for his blood.

"You seek the witch Magrit!" boomed the first.

"A mystery has befuddled his mind!" cried the second.

"But 'tis not for lack of his science!" pronounced the third.

"Nay—perish the thought!" protested the fourth.

"Not he—not such a prodigy among philosophes!" concurred the fifth.

"Verily, the answer lies elsewhere!" concluded the sixth.

As one man, the roughnecks leapt to their feet and cried out in unison:

"He has enemies, don't you know!"

Then, spreading into a ragged line, the six hurly-burlies linked arms and elbows and began a most uncouth dance, accompanied by the following doggerel verse:

> It's enemies brought him low, don't you know,
>   don't you know?
> Enemies what's brought him low, don't you
> know,
>   don't you know?
> Hid the truth from his cunning, don't you know,
>   don't you know?
> Hid theyselves from his cunning, don't you
> know,
>   don't you know?
> And that's why he's here, don't you know,
>   don't you know?
> A-looking up old Magrit, don't you know,
>   don't you know?

At any rate, this tiresome and disgraceful ditty went on for some little time, showing on the part of its authors neither couth nor urbanity. Even worse was the spectacle presented by the treasonous dwarf

Shelyid, who not only attempted to join the dance—
in which enterprise he failed due to his by-now-total
state of drunkenness—but even, sprawled on the floor,
attempted to learn the words, and then!—when he
failed in this enterprise as well due to his sodden
incapacity to form any words beyond mush—still
managed to beat time to the tune with his ale pot. A
sad and sorry sight, indeed!

As for the wizard himself, it is not inaccurate to state
that this proved to be one of the rare moments in his
life when he was actually speechless, so great was his
indignation. It goes without saying that this atypical
speechlessness was all that saved the six lowlifes from
the most gruesome of fates. For had the wizard been
able to form coherent phrases, there is not the slightest
doubt that the hexes and spells which would have
issued from his lips should have brought down upon
the half-dozen hooligans a termination so hideous as
to have served generations of proletarian mothers in
cautioning their children on the dangers of insulting
a sorcerer.

As it happens, however—and in this we see that
primitive cunning so often evidenced by the lower
classes—'twas at this very moment that the gargoyle
group announced, again as one man, that it was time
to turn in for the night. No sooner said than done, the
loathsome gang staggered out of the tavern into the
darkness of the streets beyond. Yet did the sixth of the
motley and disreputable crew pause upon the threshold,
and, gazing back within, wave a thorny finger in the
direction of the street to his left, announcing: "You'll
find the witch Magrit down this street—two blocks,
turn left a block, right three blocks, and there she is—
an old great gray house, tall and turreted about. You
can't be missing it." And so saying, he followed his
brethren.

These events recounted, the gentle reader may imagine that it was in no great humor that the wizard returned to his rooms above, dragging his apprentice by the scruff of the neck. Therein he stormed about, casting down curses upon lowlifes in general, a half-dozen lowlifes in particular, and one specific dwarf.

Especially, one specific dwarf.

Indeed, indeed, he waxed most eloquently upon the subject of this one specific dwarf, cursing not only the fate which had saddled him with the witless and unworthy gnome, but every habit, attribute, characteristic, feature, foible, trait, earmark, peculiarity, particularity, singularity, lineament, quality, property, idiosyncrasy, mannerism, tendency, detail, aspect, streak, stripe, crasis, diathesis, disposition, affectation, temperament, bent, bias, warp, woof, twist, turn, leaning, inclination, propensitude as well as propensity, propendency, propension, proclivity, predilection, and predisposition, forgetting not humor, mood, temper, tone, vein, grain, cast, cue, heart, mettle, and spirit, the which, taken together, summarized the persona of this specific dwarf, even including in this condemnation certain descriptions of the gnome which, fairness requires me to say, were something of an exaggeration, of which "cloven-hoofed" was perhaps the least ill-tempered.

No doubt this lecture would have greatly enlightened the wretched dwarf, opening up to his understanding many aspects of his character which the dull-minded runt had not hitherto grasped. But alas, the wizard's efforts were in vain, for the dwarf Shelyid had long since fainted away, whether in awe and wonder at the wizard's psychologic facility, or from the unaccustomed effects of many pots of ale, it is difficult to say.

PART XIII

In Which We Return to the
Autobiography of the Malefactor
Sfrondrati-Piccolomini, this Portion
of Whose Story Consists of a Crude and
Unscrupulous Attempt to Win the Favor
of the Reader, by Means of Mawkish
Romance and Melodrama.

The Autobiography of Benvenuti Sfondrati-Piccolomini,
Episode 7: Signs, Signals, Sighs and Sorrows

So it was on such a note of frustration that I awoke the
following day. Gwendolyn and I saw little of each other.
She spent the whole day sitting at a table in a corner
of the Free Lunch, talking to an endless stream of
people who came in and out of the alehouse. All of
them ambled in with a smile and left in a hurry, great
frowns on their faces. I made it a point not to overhear her conversations, but it was plain enough even
to one of my limited grasp of politics that she was
energetically spreading the word through the revolutionary network. And I couldn't help but overhear some

of the comments made by people as they left the alehouse, among which "A Rap Sheet!" and "We're
doomed!" figured prominently.

I couldn't help but overhear, I say, because I myself
spent the morning perched on the colonnade in the
front of the Free Lunch. As I had promised the Tapster,
I repaired his sign. When I was done, if I may say so
myself, I had turned the thing into a work of art.

Then, partly because I had nothing else to do and
partly because my artist's instincts, once aroused, are
difficult to control, I started working on the entire
colonnade. The underlying construction of the colonnade was sound enough, but whoever had built it had
absolutely no sense of decoration and what little they
had was long since eroded by the elements.

So there I was, happily painting and carving away,
when I heard a loud voice below.

"That's enough, Benvenuti! Enough!"

I looked down. It was the Tapster.

"Look at it! It's a work of art, now, for the love—
gargoyles, even." He shook his head, jowls quivering.
"You couldn't eat and drink that much in a lifetime."

I climbed down off the colonnade. A lengthy
debate followed, at the conclusion of which I managed to convince the Tapster that since I myself
considered his beer and "arsters" a form of art in their
own right I considered us to have made a reasonable
exchange of use values. The clincher—a shrewd move,
this, though it pained me deeply—was my insistence
that I was deeply in his debt for correcting my pronunciation with respect to edible mollusks.

"Well, that's true," he mused, "seeing as how I not
only did you the great service in its own right but
probably saved your life, in the bargain. Most people
aren't as tolerant as myself, you know, when it comes
to the proper name for arsters."

In the end, he was mollified. But he still insisted that I'd done enough. And so there I was, it being only the early afternoon and with too much time on my hands.

After enjoying an enormous lunch—the Tapster insisted on heaping my platter time and again—I approached Gwendolyn at her table.

"I'm sorry to interrupt," I said—and no sooner did these accented words issue forth from my lips than I was greeted with a sea of hostile and suspicious faces from the people gathered about the table—"but I just wanted to tell you I'm going to wander about the town for the rest of the afternoon. I'll see you tonight."

Gwendolyn smiled at me. Then, noticing the expression on the faces of the others at the table, she scowled.

"And what's your problem?" she demanded of them. "So he's an Ozarine—so what? He's with me. I vouch for him."

The frowns eased, but did not vanish. Gwendolyn slammed her fist onto the table. Everyone jumped a foot in their seats.

"What is this?" she roared. "Bigotry? In the movement? I won't have it!"

I managed to keep from smiling. This, coming from Gwendolyn!

The frowns were replaced by looks which combined shamefaced guilt and not a little trepidation. This latter was not surprising. Gwendolyn in a fury is not a thing to be taken lightheartedly.

"I'll probably be tied up most of the night, Benvenuti," growled Gwendolyn, her fierce gaze not on me but on her comrades. "There's still a lot of the comrades I have to talk to, and then"—her voice here resembled a great feline's—"there's perhaps a little matter of political re-education to be dealt with."

I left the room, then, trying not to laugh at the expressions I left behind.

The rest of the day passed pleasantly enough. It's an odd place, the Doghouse, but not without its own charms. The artwork, I found, had a crude but strangely appealing quality to it. There was one figurine in particular that I found attractive. It was made of terra cotta, unpainted, depicting the bust of some very rough-looking man. More like an ogre than a man, really, with his beetling brows, great hook of a nose, and deep-set eyes. Some of that was due, I was sure, to the crudity of the craftsmanship, but I felt, without knowing why, that it was not unlike the original model. But what struck me about it was that, even despite the obvious lack of skill of the artisan, the figurine somehow managed to capture a hint of a great spirit lurking within that horrid exterior. It was really a fine piece.

I noticed it in one shop, and then began seeing it in several others. Eventually, I found myself so taken by the thing that I determined to obtain one, so that I might make my own carving. I retraced my steps back to the first shop, whose figurine had been of the best quality, and effectuated an exchange of services with the proprietor. It was not difficult. My travels about the town had made it clear to me that if I should ever decide to become a sign-maker I could easily set myself up in the Doghouse and enjoy all the simple bounties of its life.

And so it was that I returned to the Free Lunch, gay as a lark, and walked into a most painful episode.

By the time I got back it was very late. Gwendolyn was sitting at the same table, but the crowd of the day was gone. Only one person was sitting there with her. I did not pay much attention to him, so happy was I to see her again. A general impression of great height—obvious even seated—and a luxuriant beard, was all that initially registered. Gwendolyn glanced at me as I approached, then looked back to the man. Something in the set of her shoulders—a rigidity, perhaps—stilled the affectionate greeting that I was about to utter.

"Have a seat," she said. Her voice seemed distant. She motioned back and forth. "Roach, this is Benvenuti Sfondrati-Piccolomini. Benvenuti, meet The Roach. He's an old friend of mine, just got here. I wasn't expecting him."

The man stood up politely. A large, long-fingered hand reached out. I shook it. For the first time, I looked at him closely. Extraordinarily tall, he was. Middle-aged, rather slender, although obviously sinewy. His face was difficult to discern, so covered it was with an immense beard. His hair and beard were streaked with gray. I got an impression of a great prow of a chin buried somewhere beneath the hair, but I was more struck by his eyes. Somewhat deep-set, light-colored, and very hard to read. His clothes were those of a workman, very nondescript except for the most immense and striking set of boots that I ever saw in my life. The Boots, I was later to learn.

"Which branch?" the man asked, after he resumed his seat. His voice was a pleasant tenor.

I began to explain where my immediate family line fit on the complex hereditary tree of the Sfondrati-Piccolomini clan, but before I got very far into it he began nodding his head.

"Yes, yes, I know it." A look which combined amuse-ment and a certain respect. "An odd lot, not at all like most of those pedants. When I was in the Ozarine, I spent some pleasant afternoons quaffing ale with an Idomeneo Sfondrati-Piccolomini. A cousin of yours, he must be."

"Second cousin. I've only met him once. My uncles sent me to bail him out of jail."

The Roach emitted a great baying laugh. "I can believe it! He never had the proper respect for his patrons, that lad. 'Rich slobs couldn't tell a work of art if it bit them on the arse,' he'd always say."

My initial warmth toward the man, however, began ebbing as the night wore on. Soon enough, I came to view him with a great coldness. The fault was not his, actually. Indeed, it was part of the growing horror of the scene, that I knew him to be a man whose acquaintance I would have enjoyed, perhaps even cherished, under other circumstances. Under that rough and bristly exterior I could detect a great, somehow gentle, self-confidence—a quiet dignity, a sense of his place in life that it is given to very few people to possess in this world.

But the fact is, the circumstances were as they were. Nothing was said, neither by he nor by Gwendolyn, and they never so much as touched each other once. But I am not a fool. I will admit I stayed at the table well past the time I should have made a graceful exit. The Roach seemed oblivious to the situation. But I am an artist, with an artist's eye, to whom the tension in Gwendolyn's posture was obvious. So stay I did, trying to forestall the inevitable, until my stern upbringing came to my rescue.

"When it comes to romance and heartbreak and all that," my uncles had told me more than once, "try not to be a complete jackass."

And so I finally rose from the table, bid them goodnight, and made my way to my room. Sometime later, I heard Gwendolyn and The Roach moving through the corridor and into her room. The indistinct murmur of their voices came through the wall for a few minutes, followed by silence, followed, some minutes later, by sounds which I did my best to ignore. Eventually, I managed to fall asleep.

When I awoke, my body feeling ill-used and my soul worse, I lay in my bed unmoving. After some time, I realized that I was hearing a conversation coming from Gwendolyn's room. I could not hear the words, but I seemed to detect an undertone of anger in The Roach's voice and a coldness in Gwendolyn's. For a moment, the temptation to press my ear against the wall and eavesdrop swept over me like a tidal wave. But I resisted it, springing to my feet and charging downstairs after hurriedly making my ablutions and throwing on some clothes.

Good as they were, I was getting a bit tired of beer and arsters, so I wandered down the street and had breakfast at a nearby restaurant. When I got back to the Free Lunch, Gwendolyn and The Roach were finishing a platter of arsters at the table in the corner. After a moment's hesitation, I decided that avoiding them would be undignified. So I made my way over and accepted The Roach's invitation to sit.

A somewhat strained silence followed, which Gwendolyn broke by saying: "I have to make arrangements to go visit the General. I'll be back shortly."

After she left, the silence returned. I was trying to think of some pleasantry to break the awkwardness when The Roach suddenly exclaimed some meaningless noise. He stood up abruptly and glared around the room. His great beard bristled fury at the universe.

"Absurd situation!" he exclaimed. Then, glancing down at me, he said: "Come on, Benvenuti, let's go outside."

I followed him out of the tavern, not sure what to make of things. He began pacing restlessly back and forth in the courtyard, staring down at the pavement. I soon gave up trying to match his immense strides, and stood unmoving. After a minute or so, he looked over at me and motioned with his head toward a bench against the wall.

Once we were seated, he leaned back against the wall and emitted a great sigh.

"Had I realized the situation soon enough," he said suddenly, "I would have gone elsewhere to spend the night."

"I don't see why," I said, very stiffly. "I have no claim on Gwendolyn."

"Who does?" he demanded. "No man has any claim on any woman. Certainly not Gwendolyn."

He looked over at me, and then burst into a barking laughter.

"Ah, and will you look at those square shoulders! A Sfondrati-Piccolomini of the old school! Face the ovens of hell with a stiff upper lip."

My upper lip was stiff. "I assure you, sirrah, that your concern is misplaced. I hold the lady in the highest esteem, but—"

His laughter became positively canine. When the grotesque mirth ebbed, he shook his head and said:

"I don't think there's anyone in the world who can be such a jackass as a man trying not to be a jackass."

I let this unseemly comment pass. My upper lip, I believe, now resembled the prow of a war galley. Suddenly, I broke.

"I—I just—" I stammered. "I'm only trying—what I mean—" I took a breath. "It is true what I said. There has been nothing—well, nothing serious— between Gwendolyn and me. That is, well, of a physical nature."

Again, that barking laughter.

"Think I give a damn where your pecker's been?" For some reason, this crudity was not offensive, coming from him. When I looked at him, he was gazing at me with a strange look in his eyes. But then, as I've said, his eyes were hard to read.

"This is not about you and me," he said quietly. "Nor, to be honest, do I care a fig about your relationship with Gwendolyn."

He looked away for a moment, and then continued.

"Gwendolyn and I have known each other for many years. During those years, we have been friends and comrades-in-arms. And, whenever the occasion permitted, we have been lovers. It is a hard world we live in, she and I, with few enough of life's joys and comforts." A hint of sorrow came into his voice. "I have thought sometimes, if—well, no point in that." His eyes grew distant, as if gazing at an unreachable horizon.

"During those years," he continued, "neither of us has ever asked any questions of each other. The truth is, for all that I love the woman, and I believe she loves me, there is no great passion in it."

He stared down at his long fingers, restlessly intertwining. "Passion is not something that I can give her. It's the legacy of my own line. Goes all the way back to the first Roach, that." Bleakly, but with great pride: "Our passion is directed elsewhere."

He took a deep breath. "You are something new to her. Quite new, and she doesn't know what to make of it. I'm not certain—who knows, really, what moves another?—but I think you stir up in her all the feelings of a young womanhood that she never had. She was thrown into the revolution at such an early age. Took to it, too, like a fish to water. Little enough chance, she's ever had, to enjoy her life. And most men are too intimidated by her to do more than stare from a distance."

That brought a smile to my lips. "It's a bit

disconcerting, when it dawns on you the lady could bend you into a pretzel."

The Roach shook his head. "It's not even that. It's the fierceness in her soul. She could be a third her size, and she'd still terrify most men."

I thought about that, and nodded my head.

The Roach scratched his beard. Even a hand his size almost disappeared in the great mass of hair.

"Anyway, the point I'm trying to get to is this. It was not until this morning, after listening to her talk about you through most of the night, that I finally realized what was going on. Of course, then I was furious." His beard bristled. "I don't like being used."

"How are—oh. You think she's trying to make me jealous?" I frowned. "I don't think—no, I don't believe that. It doesn't seem—"

"You idiot," he said. "Of course she's not trying to make you jealous! What is she, some schoolgirl playing children's games? No, she's trying to drive you off, that's what. Doesn't realize it, of course. But that's what it is, sure as I'm sitting here. And she used me to do it, and I am not pleased."

He stood up abruptly. "I'm not sure why I'm talking to you about this," he said, looking away. "Partly it's because I refuse to be a part of it." Again, the bristling beard. "Damn the woman! Let her solve her own problems!"

He looked down at me. "You really don't understand, do you? Not surprising, you're so like her. I can tell, even on such short acquaintance. Well, lad, I've done my duty by my own lights. I told Gwendolyn this morning that it'd be pure and simple movement business between us until she straightens out the knots in her own love life. I am not a tool. If she wants to chase you off, fine. Let her do it.

If she doesn't, that's fine also. I will tell you, for whatever it's worth, that I think you're both fools—you more than she."

He bestowed a world-class glare on me.

"Damn all romantics, anyway! Do you really think you're prepared to give up all your dreams and ambitions?" He laughed, not very pleasantly. "Don't deny it. Your branch of the Sfondrati-Piccolominis all have that madness. Want to shape the world's great art, you do. Statues in the park, paintings on the great cathedrals, only the finest gold filigree! Can you picture Gwendolyn in a noble's salon, arguing over the latest style?"

I avoided his eyes.

"Not likely, is it? And what about you? Are you ready to give that up? I don't mean the company of the rich—I know that doesn't mean anything to you. But if you want to muck around in fine art, you've no other choice, Benvenuti. Precious few patrons you'll find, in Gwendolyn's world."

I was silent.

"Romantics! Stubborn and stupid, like no mule even dreams of being."

At that moment, Gwendolyn came striding into the courtyard. When she saw us, she hesitated, then continued on into the tavern without a word or a glance.

My eyes followed her all the way in. When I looked back at The Roach, his expressionless gaze had returned.

"What the hell," he said. "Whoever said life was easy?" He turned and followed Gwendolyn into the Free Lunch. I remained in the courtyard, seated on the bench. My thoughts were hard to describe. Stupid. Stubborn.

Some time later, Gwendolyn reemerged into the courtyard. The Roach followed a few steps behind, then stopped. Gwendolyn turned back to face him.

"You're sure you won't come?"

The Roach shook his head. "There's no need, Gwendolyn. You can fill the General in on the situation, and I need to get to Blain as soon as possible. Except for Prygg, the initial blows will land there the hardest. And the comrades in Blain have the best contacts with Pryggia."

She hesitated.

"Go," he said gently.

PART XIV

In Which Our
Heroes Complete the
First of Their Self-Appointed
Tasks, Falling Thereby Into the Most
Unseemly and Questionable Company,
At Great Peril To Their
Good Reputation.

～～～

CHAPTER XVII. *A Search for a Secret Door, Thwarted by a Clumsy Dwarf. A Surprising Entrance Found, Thanks to a Clumsy Dwarf. The Secret of Its Entry Sought By the Mage's Lore, Undone By a Doltish Apprentice. A Stairway Leads Up!*

The following day, under cover of a heavy rainfall, wizard and apprentice set out on their mission. Guided

by his cunning, Zulkeh quickly found the location of
Magrit's house. It was much as described the evening
before: a gray, dilapidated building, four stories in
height, surmounted by a profusion of turrets, crenelets,
and whatnot architectural monstrosities. Even from a
distance, the main entrance was plainly evident: a large
wooden door, painted yellow, facing directly onto the
street.

"Seek we now another entry," whispered Zulkeh to
his apprentice. "Quiet now, Shelyid! Enemies lurk all
about!" And so saying, the mage circled the block and
came up to the rear wall surrounding Magrit's domicile.

"Doubtless there is to be found a secret door in this
wall," spoke the mage. "Search now, dwarf, and be
quick about it!"

Alas, the dwarf's efforts at finding the concealed
entrance were sorely hampered by the overhang of his
sack, the which prevented him from approaching the
wall closer than two arm-lengths away. Shelyid began
to whimper and complain.

"But master, I can't see anything and I can't even
get close to the wall."

"Clumsy dwarf!" oathed Zulkeh. "Is the advance of
science to be thwarted by the stubby limbs of such as
you? Stretch your joints, dolt! Again, I command you:
find the secret door!"

Grumbling but obedient, the dwarf made a valiant
effort to reach the wall. But in his clumsiness he
stepped upon a wooden storm drain grate, the which,
overcome by the bantamweight gnome and the heavy-
weight sack, broke beneath his feet.

"Help, master! Save me!" shrieked Shelyid, as he
plummeted into the hole. In an instant he was gone.

"My sack!" cried Zulkeh, and leapt after the gnome.

The gentle reader may imagine the difficult moments
which ensued, what with wizard and apprentice swept

along down a storm drain torrential with rainfall. Fortunately, though much battered about, our heroes quickly came to rest upon a ledge within the sewer below. All was as dark as a cellar at midnight. But it was only a moment before Shelyid produced a taper from the sack, the which soon produced enough light to see a few feet.

"Diminutive clod!" oathed Zulkeh. "Did I not entrust you with the safekeeping of my thaumaturgic possessions?" He cuffed the gnome soundly.

"Yet all was not in vain," continued the wizard. "For look you, wretch of an apprentice!" His finger pointed to a large gate in the wall next to Shelyid. Through the gate could be seen a passageway beyond, which was dry as a bone. "No doubt yon passage leads direct to some hidden entry into the witch's quarters. Seek we now the trick of its opening."

For long moments did the wizard remain poised in silent stillness, examining the iron gate with that degree of concentration which is the unique attribute of great sorcerers, a depth of perceptive focus which is as far beyond the understanding of common folk as is the eagle's power of flight to frogs in the fen. Meanwhile, Shelyid shivered and hugged himself, looking both bedraggled and woebegone.

At length the mage spoke.

"Know, my stupid but loyal—I graciously leave aside the scandalous events of the evening past—apprentice, that the problem which presents itself to us at this moment is of the deepest intricacy."

"What problem's that, master?" queried Shelyid.

"What problem, you say? It is obvious, lummox! In what manner—and by what means?—are we to open yon secret gate which leads to yon secret passageway which, in turn, leads to yon, not as yet seen, secret door?"

"Why don't we—"

"Quiet, if you will! I must concentrate my full attention on the task, undisturbed by the idle ramblings of an ignorant gnome." Abashed, Shelyid fell silent.

"Of course," mused the mage, "the obvious approach would be the utilization of either the Tomb Robber's Cantrip or the Grave Despoiler's Cantation. But the first runs the risk of arousing the pharaohs from their necrotic sleep, and the second, as is well known, will summon every zombie within miles. The pharaohs, of course, can be encapsuled in a cartouche, and even a mage much less puissant than myself can thwart any number of zombies. But the use of the cartouche will release great goetic energies, which Magrit—the noxious harridan!—will be sure to detect. And, as all experience attests, thwarted zombies would raise so great a din of protestation as to awaken every deaf mute in the city. No, no, 'twill not do." And again the wizard fell to musing.

"But, master," whispered Shelyid timidly, "I think if we—"

"Did I not bid you to be silent?" demanded the mage. Then, seeing the hurt reproach on his apprentice's face, the wizard sighed deeply. "My loyal but stupid apprentice, you do not begin to grasp the difficulty. It is utterly pointless for you to fumble about in your feeble mind for the solution to the problem."

Here the wizard wagged a solemn finger at the dwarf. "Know, Shelyid, that for eons the greatest minds of mankind were united in the opinion that secret doors and passageways, buried entries and the like, were impenetrable to any not privy to their secrets. 'Twas only the supreme genius of Schliemann Laebmauntsforscynneweëld which finally proved this universal belief incorrect, when he opened up to the world's understanding the hidden treasures of the lost and fabled cities of antiquity. His example before them, other members of the clan have since followed in his footsteps, of whom the great Breasted Laebmauntsforcynneweëld is perhaps the most notable."

The mage settled himself comfortably, preparing, 'twas clear as day, for the pleasure of a learned lecture. It seemed, on the other hand—judging, at least, from the furrow on his brow, the clutching of his shivering limbs to his body, the wrinkling of his nose at the noxious odors emanating from the proximate sewer—that his apprentice did not fully share the wizard's anticipation of the didactic prospect. But the mage took no heed, being totally engrossed in the pressing subject at hand.

"Sad to say, however, the prodigious progress made by the descendants of Schliemann in advancing the lore of secret doors, buried treasures and such, were not matched by any comparable feats emanating from their rivals in the normally noble, but in this instance sadly remiss, clan of the Sfondrati-Piccolominis. This peculiar archaeologic imbalance 'twixt the great clans—well-known to the world's cognoscenti—has itself been the subject of much scholastic inquiry and debate. Indeed, 'twould be the proper subject of a profound dissertation on some future occasion—remind me of this point, gnome!—to examine this problem at our leisure. But now is not the moment—for even as I exposit, time wanes! Let me simply say here that it is my tentative opinion that the reticence of the Sfondrati-Piccolominis is best explained as the result of their collective shame at the disrepute brought upon their scholarly traditions by the jackanape Houdini Sfondrati-Piccolomini, the which charlatan and rogue did so—"

The mage's discourse was interrupted by a loud clangor. Looking up in surprise, Zulkeh was even more astonished to discover that the large iron gate, the very

item the complexities of whose secret of opening had
been the proximate cause of his study, was even now,
at that very moment, lying flat upon the ledge. The
way to the passage beyond lay open and unhindered.

"I'm sorry, master," said Shelyid. "My hand must
have slipped."

"Several times, it would appear," spoke the mage
stonily. He eyed the many clasps and latches which
were strewn about the ledge, the which had previously
held shut the gate and had, or so the evidence indicated, been detached by the clumsy dwarf.

"Bah!" oathed Zulkeh. He glowered at his apprentice. " 'Tis fortunate for you, my stupid but loyal
apprentice, that Magrit in her cunning has placed here
a common and ordinary gate, cleverly disguised as a
secret entry." He glowered further, then shrugged.

"But what boots it? 'Tis perhaps fitting that the
debauched harridan should be undone by her excessive trickery. Follow me closely, Shelyid!"

This command given, the wizard strode through the
gateway into the passage beyond. A few short steps
were taken by our heroes to the end of this passageway, where, opening to their right, was unmistakable
proof of the sorcerer's prescience. For there, even
before them, was a small and dingy room, empty of
all furnishings. At the far end, but a few steps away,
a narrow and winding staircase wended its way upward.

"Magrit's basement," proclaimed Zulkeh, his voice
filled with satisfaction. "And there lies a staircase, the
which, I have no doubt in my mind, leads to a secret
entrance into the witch's very lair. Leave the sack
behind, dwarf, for you are clumsy enough without it.
And remember—the utmost trickery and maneuver!"

CHAPTER XVIII. *The Witch Encountered.*
Indignities and Introductions. The Dwarf
Behaves Badly. His Conduct Reproved
by a Reputable Agent. The Astonish-
ing Sequel Thereto. Uncouth Merriment
and Wagers. A Salamander Protests!

The creaky stairs climbed up and up. The mage and
his apprentice ascended, moving with utmost stealth
and cunning. At length, they espied a landing above.
Beyond the landing lay a door, standing slightly ajar.

"The utmost stealth and cunning, Shelyid!" spoke the
mage in a low voice. "Even now do we approach the
witch's lair."

"But, master," grumbled the dwarf, "why do we have
to creep around like this in your friend Magrit's house?
I'm tired! Why don't we just go up and knock on the
door?"

"Bah!" oathed Zulkeh. "What absurd proposal is
this? The witch is not my friend—and this, for two
reasons. *Imprimis*, she is not my friend because she
is a crass termagant, a loathsome virago, grotesque
in both habit and mind. *Secundus*, and even were

this not so, she is not my friend because I have long since eschewed friendship. For know, dwarf, that friends are as detrimental to the pursuit of science as enemies. I say this to caution you against your regrettable tendency—so sorrily evident in your recent conduct—to become ensnared by goodfellows, jovial sorts, and the like."

The wizard raised an admonishing hand. "But enough of this nonsense," hissed Zulkeh. "We must hasten—for even as I whisper, time wanes!" And so saying, the mage prepared to step onto the landing.

But he was stilled in his purpose, for at that very moment the door above was flung wide with a great clatter. Startled, our heroes gazed upward and perceived, illuminated from behind, the figure of a woman dressed in an old robe and wearing slippers. She stood there in a most aggressive posture, arms akimbo, fists planted on stout hips, gazing down the steep stairs over a most intimidating bosom, her face—so much was evident even in the dim lighting—disfigured by a sneer of cold disdain. Atop her shoulder, peering down with tiny red eyes, squatted a salamander.

"Thought so!" boomed the woman in a raucous voice. "It's that old fart, Zulkeh. And the little one with him—just as Les Six described. Well, dotard, come on up and stop creeping around—makes me edgy! Come up, I say!" Her figure disappeared from the doorway.

"Well, master," said Shelyid, "we might as w—" But he was silenced by the wizard's glare, like unto the fires of eternal damnation.

"Unspeakable gnome!" oathed the mage. "This disaster is entirely your responsibility! Look you at the result of your cretinous behavior the evening past!"

The dwarf pouted. "It wasn't my idea, hanging out with those drunks. I didn't want to do it. Although, I had a real good time and they were actually real nice to me even though I don't remember a lot of it and today my head really hurts. But," Shelyid concluded, a preposterous tone of accusation in his voice, "it was your idea in the first place, so if anybody's to bl—"

No doubt the dwarf's impertinence would have resulted in a most severe and well-deserved thrashing, judging, at least, from the gathering storm upon the wizard's brow. But, in the event, the wretch was rescued by the intervention of an unforeseen savior. For, at that very moment, the witch's voice was heard to say: "Greyboar! Fetch me these two clowns!"

A moment later, a gigantic form filled the doorway. And a frightful figure it was! Atop a pair of shoulders massive both in size and brutish slope, like unto the forequarters of a great bear, sat a most villainous head—if villainy can be judged from a predatory beak of a nose, beady black eyes, a crop of kinky hair. Not a vestige of a neck separated the head from the shoulders below.

But our heroes were given little time to examine the newcomer, for two hands the size of platters descended upon them, seizing each by the scruff of the neck. In a trice, wizard and apprentice were lofted from their perch on the steps and deposited within the room beyond. This seemed to have been done without effort, which was perhaps not surprising, given that the arms which connected the hands to the shoulders were of colossal proportions, being not only deinotherian in their circumference but possessed of a length which was altogether monstrous.

Looking about, our heroes found themselves in a cavernous room, the which was revealed to be the domicile of the witch Magrit, combining, as it did, the multichambered functions of a sitting room, library, laboratory, museum and curio shop. Within the room, besides our heroes, rested three persons: the witch

Magrit, the giant just recently described, and a third individual. This latter, a red-headed man so small as to border on dwarfdom, sat in a chair to one side, his little legs dangling several inches off the floor. Upon his freckled and pug-nosed face sat an expression which was composed, in strange combination, of equal portions of amusement and dyspepsia.

But our heroes were given little time to examine their surroundings, for the witch spoke again, in an exceedingly discordant tone of voice: "What's the matter, you old fart? My place too messy for you?"

Zulkeh coughed apologetically. "I meant not to offend, madame, nor—I assure you!—is it the plenitude and disarray of objects which disturbs me, nor even the quaint deordination of chamber functions, for I know quite well—being myself, as you doubtless recall, a practicing thaumaturge of vast experience and plenary powers—"

"Who's the windbag, Magrit?" interrupted the salamander, in a voice both sharp and unpleasant. "Is he always like this, or is he just having a bad day?"

"His name's Zulkeh," responded the witch. "He's a wizard. And yeah, he's always been like this. I knew him when he was a little twerp of an apprentice at the University. Even then he was a windbag. I balled him once, just to win a bet, and I swear he was still talking in semi-colons with my legs wrapped around his head."

All eyes fixed on Zulkeh. His apprentice's eyes were the size of saucers. Perhaps the gnome found the image just sketched difficult to reconcile with his master's august person and demeanor.

As for the wizard himself, every fiber of his being, every nuance of his posture, every minute aspect of his expression, not excepting the scarlet color of his cheeks, bespoke with great eloquence his profound indignation.

"These are private matters, madame!" he roared. "I must demand that you respect my dignity!"

He glared at Magrit, then spoke again in a peremptory tone. "Moreover, the event in question occurred long ago, when I was a callow youth subject to occasional japes and escapades. And may I remind you of the unfortunate end of the affair? I should think you—of all persons!—would seek to keep its history hidden."

"Fuck you," said the witch. "Would you believe," she added, spreading her arms and taking in with her gaze the entirety of the room's occupants, "that no sooner did I screw the little cloddy than he runs—the next morning, mind you!—to the Rector of Novitiates and babbles a confession of the sinfulness of his deeds. 'Course, he depicted himself as the innocent party, dragged to the coupling couch by a scarlet woman, pleading for mercy all the while, practically chained to the bed and beaten with whips, to hear him tell it. Never did get around to explaining how he got a hard on. Not," she added unkindly, "that it was much of a hard on to begin with, now that I think about it."

The wizard positively spluttered. But the strumpet was unabashed.

"Yeah, he got me thrown out of the University for—and I quote—'gross and licentious behavior.' Himself, of course, oh, and he was the darling of the deans—'an unfortunate lapse,' they called it, 'but quickly rectified by the honest and timely confession of the fundamentally sound and sterling-charactered apprentice Zulkeh.'" She laughed. "Yeah, but it was just as well. God knows what I'd be like today if I'd stayed in the University!"

She sneered. "And as for you, Zulkeh, you ought to thank me! Probably the last time you got laid, am I right?"

The wizard's answer to this horrendously indelicate

question will forever remain unknown, for at that very moment did the salamander leap from Magrit's shoulder, scurry across the room, and flash beneath Zulkeh's robe. A moment later, the wizard was hopping wildly about, scrabbling in his garment. The salamander had, it appeared, attained to the mage's private parts.

"Out! Out! Out, vile beast!" cried Zulkeh. "Out, I say! Out!"

In a flash, the salamander emerged and scurried back across the room, coming to rest by Magrit's foot.

"Must be true, Magrit," announced the little monster. "He's got wizard's whang. Most advanced case I ever saw."

The witch snorted. "Don't surprise me! As a kid, he had 'prentice's pecker. Most advanced case I ever saw."

Suddenly the tiny horror darted across the room again and disappeared up Shelyid's trousers. And now it was the dwarf who hopped wildly about, scrabbling in his garment. The salamander had, it appeared, attained to the gnome's private parts. A moment later, the foul little beast reappeared and scurried back to Magrit's foot. It peered at Shelyid quizzically, its head cocked.

"Well?" This from Magrit.

"Kid's in the wrong line of business," pronounced the creature.

"Fie upon this monstrous incivility!" oathed Zulkeh. "Madame, you abuse your guests in a most unseemly manner!"

"Guests?" demanded Magrit. "What guests? The only *guests* here are Greyboar and Ignace." She looked to the giant and his tiny companion. "Have you been abused?"

"Not at all," rumbled the giant.

"You've been a most gracious hostess," concurred

the other. "Of course," he added, "we still have to do a job for you, you've made that clear often enough."

The witch glared at the midget. "I know, I know," he said hastily, "'no freebies from Magrit.'"

"Not for you, that's for sure," snorted the witch. She turned back to Zulkeh.

"So much for that! Let me remind you, you old fart, that I didn't invite you here in the first place. You crashed the party. And you didn't even so much as come straight to the front door. Not the great wizard Zulkeh! Didn't the sixth give you perfectly clear directions last night? But no! The magnificent mage has to go crawling through sewers and creeping through cellars."

She glared at the wizard. For his part, Zulkeh coughed in his throat, somewhat nonplussed by this— alas, it must be admitted—not untruthful charge.

"What's the matter," demanded the hellhag, "cat got your tongue?" She fixed Shelyid with her malevolent gaze. "You tell us, shorty! Am I right, or not? Didn't the old fart waste half the day down there? Probably kept telling you"— here the obscene ogress dropped her voice an octave—"'the utmost shrewdery and stealth! the utmost sagacity and cunning! the utmost trickery and maneuver!'"

Shelyid coughed, somewhat nonplussed by this— alas, it must be admitted—not altogether inaccurate description.

"Thought so!" snorted the witch. "And what's your name, anyway?"

"Shelyid, ma'am," replied the dwarf timidly.

"Don't call me 'ma'am'!" barked Magrit. "Silly title! Magrit's the name. People wanting to be respectful call me 'the proper witch.' If I'm in a good mood you can call me 'the old bag,' or 'the salacious crone,' or 'the horrible harridan,' or—oh hell, any one of a thousand things I've been called." She fixed Shelyid with a piercing eye. "But I warn you, at the moment I'm not in a good mood."

"Yes, m—uh, Magrit," stammered the dwarf.

"Well?" demanded Magrit. "Speak up, Shelyid! Am I right or what?"

The apprentice furrowed his brow. "Well, pretty much. I mean, the master didn't actually—"

"Silence, dwarf!" Zulkeh glowered at his apprentice. "What means this craven toadying to the witch's impudent interrogation? Be silent, I command you!"

Discipline restored, the wizard turned back to Magrit.

"I shall graciously overlook the rude manner of your greeting, madame. Not to mention the impertinent behavior of your familiar!" He bestowed a fierce look upon the salamander. "For, I will admit, my method of entry was perhaps not altogether suave in its approach."

With a conciliatory gesture, he forestalled the derisive remark even now foreseeable in Magrit's expression. "Let bygones be bygones, if you will. Soon enough, Magrit, you will learn the cause of my apparently *outré* behavior. But for the moment, may we begin anew? Perhaps with some common civilities! For I have not yet been properly introduced to your other guests."

Then, observing the intemperate remark about to issue from the witch's lips: "Say rather, your proper guests! Or, if you prefer, the other occupants of this room."

With some effort, or so it seemed, the horrid hag restrained her natural inclinations. Taking a deep breath, she shrugged her shoulders.

"What the hell, why not? Zulkeh of Goimr, let me introduce you to Greyboar the strangler and his agent

Ignace, lately of New Sfinctr. They're here at the
moment due to a falling out with the authorities of
that pesthole of a city. Not for the first time!"

The giant bowed politely. "I'm Greyboar. The little
one's Ignace. My card, sir." And so saying, the mage
was presented with an embossed calling card held
between a thumb and forefinger the size of large
sausages. The card read:

GREYBOAR—*Strangleur Extraordinaire*
"Have Thumbs, Will Travel"
Customized Asphyxiations
No Gullet Too Big, No Weasand Too Small
My Motto: Satisfaction Garroteed, or
The Choke's on Me!

"But I have heard of you, sir!" exclaimed the mage.
"Are you not the same Greyboar who throttled the
Marquis de Sangsue?"

The strangler nodded his head. "I have that honor."

"'Twas a masterly stuffocation, by all accounts! And
are you not the author, as well, of the legendary stran-
gulation of the Comte de l'Abattoir and his entire party
of Knights Companion, done at the very feasting table
where they took their pleasure?"

Greyboar shrugged modestly. "It cannot be denied."

"How foolish of me not to have recognized your
name at once! My apologies, sirrah."

The strangler dismissed the matter with a wave of
his hand. Zulkeh turned to his apprentice.

"You are most fortunate, Shelyid, to make the
acquaintance of such a universally admired master of
his profession. In point of fact, not simply *a* master,
but, according to the vast majority of experts, *the* modern exemplar of the chokester's trade. Why, the

Encyclopedia Ozarinica has gone so far as to state that Greyboar is the equal of any of the great asphyxiators of history, at least with regard to fingerwork, if not, perhaps, in force of contraction."

"Sheer tonnage of gullet overpressure is the aspect of the trade which always impresses the amateur," stated Greyboar. "But all practitioners of the craft know the secret lies entirely in the fingerwork."

"I will certainly defer to your professional judgement on the matter," spoke the mage. "As a philosophe, I am in any event more inclined to respect the aesthetic than the muscular aspects of your craft. And all connoisseurs of the art are agreed that the burking of de l'Abattoir and company was a masterpiece, a masterpiece—not alone in the extreme elongation of the several throats, but in the delicacy of detail. As I recall, each of the chokee's necks was tied in a different knot, am I not correct?"

"I was particularly proud of the Blackwall hitch," admitted Greyboar. "Sir Mordicus, that was."

Zulkeh frowned. "I should tell you, sir—I speak now as one professional to another—that your reputation has been somewhat disparaged of late. An article appeared in a recent issue of *The Journal of Contemporary Assassination*, authored by none other than Dashiel Sfondrati-Piccolomini, in which he argues that your abilities, great though he admits them to be, have been cast in the shade by a rising Ozarine phenomenon by the name of Pythoneus."

"That twerp!" cried a shrill voice. Turning, all saw that Ignace had left his chair and was hopping about in great agitation. "That juvenile braggart! That pipsqueak posturer! That no-thumbed puppy!" He glared at Greyboar. "I told you we should have squeezed his fanfaron gullet for him when the swaggering snot came through New Sfinctr!"

Greyboar did not, it seemed, share his agent's concern. He shrugged his shoulders, like an avalanche.

"Why bother? Plenty of room in the trade. Besides, who cares what some pedant says in a scholarly journal? No offense, sirrah"—this to Zulkeh—"but it's precious few of my customers who ever say they've been referred by the latest issue of the *Journal* of this or the *Annals* of that."

"To be sure," agreed the mage. "We scholars tend to settle our disputes in a—physically, at least—less energetic manner."

"Still—" began Ignace, but he was interrupted by Shelyid.

"You mean you kill people for a living? That's awful!"

Reactions to this unexpected comment varied. Magrit chuckled, the salamander smirked, Greyboar looked aggrieved. But the wizard and the agent Ignace were alike in the look of outrage and indignation which sat upon their respective faces.

"Bah!" oathed Zulkeh. "Wherefore am I plagued with such a dolt of an apprentice?"

"Shut your mouth, you nasty little dwarf!" was Ignace's less rhetorical comment.

"Know, Shelyid," spoke the mage sternly, wagging his finger in the gnome's face, "that this upstanding gentleman is a respected practitioner of an honorable profession whose origins date back to the time of antiquity. How could you be such a lackwit as to confuse him for a common murderer?"

"But he kills—"

"Bah!" oathed the wizard. "He does not *kill*—if I may use your crude expression for a moment—anyone. He strangles them. Is this not so, sirrah?"—This latter to Greyboar. "Have you ever once resorted to any method of termination other than the prescribed placement of thumbs and fingers about the weasand and the ensuing application of pressure?"

"Nope," came Greyboar's reply. "Well, on occasion I've used garroting tools—rope, cord, piano wire and such—"

The wizard waved airily. "Those are recognized the world over as legitimate extensions of the art."

"—and, of course, I've often found it necessary to break bones, shred limbs, mangle bodies—but only with respect to secondary persons, bodyguards and the like, who interpose themselves between me and the completion of the job. The job itself is always done with legitimate fingerwork. I'm quite a stickler on this point."

The wizard nodded his approval. "Precisely so! The maiming, mangling and mortification of secondary persons in the course of a strangler's assignment are, of course, hallowed by tradition."

But the impudent dwarf was still not satisfied. "I don't care how he does it! He's still killing people for a living! They *are* dead when you're done with all this fancy choking and stuff, aren't they?" he asked the strangler. And a bizarre sight it was, the little gnome staring up at the person of the chokester, who loomed above him like a buffalo pondering a fieldmouse.

"Aren't they?" demanded Shelyid again. "Dead, I mean?"

The strangler coughed delicately. "Well, yes," he said. "Actually, that's rather the point of the whole thing."

Ignace came between the chokester and Shelyid. "We don't have to take this crap, Greyboar!" he shrilled. He shoved himself up against the dwarf, glaring down at Shelyid—not, let it be said for the record, by such a great height, for the agent barely escaped being a dwarf in his own right.

"Look, shrimp," snarled Ignace, "just shut your nasty little mouth! I warned you already! Who're you, anyway, to question the great Greyboar? A ridiculous dwarf! Ugly as sin, and hairier than a miniature musk ox! You need to learn some manners!"

And so saying, Ignace placed his hand on Shelyid's face and with a shove sent the dwarf sprawling onto the floor. Not satisfied with this indignity, the peppery little agent scurried across the room and stood over Shelyid. He drew a knife and made a great show of testing its edge on his thumb.

"Ignace!" came Greyboar's voice.

"I'll take care of this, big guy!" exclaimed Ignace, waving away the strangler, who was not, as it happens, moving to his assistance.

"See this knife, runt?" demanded Ignace. "Sharp as a razor! Any more crap out of you, and I'll cut off your tongue!"

"I say!" spoke Zulkeh. "I must protest, most vigorously, this uncouth threat to the person of my apprentice! Desist, sirrah! I insist! I admit that Shelyid has behaved badly here, but there is no—"

He spoke no further, for 'twas at this very moment that an extraordinary event came to pass. So extraordinary, in fact, that the entire Alfredae clan rushed as one louse to observe the scene. And so it was that the Alfredae, who were more knowledgeable upon the subject of Shelyid than any intelligences on earth (were we not, after all, blood of his blood?) observed, from divers perches and vantage points upon his brow, his scalp, his ears, and whatnot, what was—all were agreed on this point—the most unexpected and astonishing behavior ever exhibited by the misbegotten gnome.

For the first time in his life, Shelyid lost his temper.

Lost it, moreover, not as one carelessly misplaces

a glove, easily found after a moment's thought. Lost it, not as one forgets a familiar name, and suffers a few minutes of minor embarrassment. Lost it, not as one loses one's way in an unfamiliar city, and spends an unpleasant hour retracing one's steps. Lost it, not as the shepherd loses the stray sheep, and spends an arduous day clambering about the hillside until the lamb is recovered. Lost it—well, I could go on in this pleasant literary vein for some time, but let me just conclude by saying that the gnome Shelyid lost his temper much as Dispater, Archduke of Hell, lost the keys to Paradise and the hope of eternal salvation.

He sprang to his feet before the astonished Ignace, who stepped back a pace. Then, garbling incoherently, the dwarf drew from some fold of his tunic the small poignard given him by Rascogne de Sevigneois. No sooner drawn than utilized! For the apprentice immediately attempted many maniacal gashings of the agent's throat, stomach, chest, indeed, whatever portion of the rapidly receding Ignace's body was closest at hand.

"Shelyid!" cried the wizard. "Desist! Desist, I say! Desist at once!"

But the dwarf evidenced no inclination to obey his master. Such, at least, seemed the only reasonable interpretation of his replies, of which "I'll drink his blood!" was the least profane.

Truth to tell, the agent's predicament soon became extreme. Early in the contretemps, Ignace waved his own blade cunningly, demonstrating both by stance and surefooted poise his expertise in the skill of knifery. But to no avail! For the dwarf, responding at first with a clumsy attempt to exercise the lessons imparted by Rascogne—the which succeeded only in causing him to trip over his own feet—eschewed then and thereafter all subtlety and maneuver. Pitiful and wretched gnome, inept in this as in all things! Instead did he

rely thenceforth entirely on the uncouth force of his
fury, a wild and witless hacking, stabbing, chopping,
hewing and suchlike incompetencies, the which rapidly succeeded in disarming (I should say, disblading,
for Ignace's quick reflexes prevented the actual loss
of his arm at the same moment as his knife went flying) the now-less-than-cocksure agent.

Then, piling error upon error, the crazed dwarf
advanced in utter confusion, while, for his part,
Ignace retreated in a most clever and adept manner,
interposing 'twixt his body and Shelyid's blade all
manner of chairs and footstools, the which adroitness,
however, availed him but little, for the now-howling-
like-a-banshee apprentice did rapidly transform these
shields into so much firewood, mostly suitable only
for kindling.

Backed into a corner, the now-less-belligerent agent
escaped by slithering like an eel between Shelyid's legs.
Abandoning all thought of armor and shields, Ignace
now drew upon that deep reservoir of tactical subtlety
which derives from a lifetime of experience in tavern
set-tos and alehouse disputes, and essayed the time-
honored tactic of fleeing like an antelope.

Alas, it soon became clear that here as well the
agent's well-honed experience was moot, for the now-
baying-like-Baalzebub's-hellhound apprentice tracked
down Ignace and flushed him from every hiding hole
with the same single-minded determination shown by
the wolf in pursuit of the hare, not excepting the
disgraceful exhibition of the gaping jaws and the lolling
tongue.

Yet the tricky little agent retained his capacity to
think and plan, demonstrating yet again the qualita-
tive difference between the experienced combatant and
the emotion-ridden and easily-maddened amateur
brawler, even in those rare instances where the

professional finds himself at a momentary disadvantage. For the now-clearly-irresolute Ignace drew upon that selfsame cool professionalism and put to use his one remaining edge over Shelyid, I speak, of course, of his moderate advantage in height.

The agent leapt into the rafters above. There, he perched beyond reach of the dwarf's blade, the which flashed back and forth below like the futile claws of the lion at the monkey.

Grievous to relate, even this latest demonstration of his haplessness at the hands of a veteran did not dissuade the foolhardy Shelyid from continuing the one-sided struggle. For the witless gnome now flung himself upon the great stanchion which upheld the rafter, hacking and hewing like a miniature lumberjack, apparently intending by this primitive method to bring Ignace within reach of his now-like-the-shark-in-its-feeding-frenzy murderous resolve. Such, at least, seemed the only possible interpretation of the various stuttered declamations and doggerel verses which issued from his foam-flecked lips, of which the phrases "the higher they are, the harder they fall!" and "hey ho! hey ho! it's off to work we go!" were the least incoherent.

But it was even here, when the rapidly mounting pile of woodchips and sawdust seemed fair to result in the early demise of the now-wailing-like-a-lost-soul agent, that the sagacity of the experienced Ignace finally worked its way, much like the chessmaster coolly checkmates the novice who, in his amateurish enthusiasm, mistakes his trove of captured pieces for the harbinger of victory. For, of course, the dwarf's assault upon the foundations of Magrit's house necessarily brought the intervention of powerful external forces.

And where, I can hear the gentle reader asking, has Magrit been all this time? And Greyboar? And Zulkeh?

As for the wizard, he had been nursing his wounds. For the outraged Zulkeh had, on several occasions during the brawl, majestically interposed himself between the dwarf and his prey, commanding the apprentice to cease and desist from his unseemly conduct. Grievous to relate, the maddened gnome had paid no more attention to his lawful master's clear and explicit instructions than a ravenous weasel obeys the admonitions of the farmboy to respect the person of the chicken in the yard. Thrice had the wizard been bowled over like tenpins by the dwarf in pursuit of the agent, until, reflecting upon his bruises, he made his way to comparative safety along the wall. From that vantage point, Zulkeh contributed no further to a resolution of the conflict. Instead, he devoted his prodigious intellect to the development and exposition of a lengthy peroration upon the subject of his apprentice which was, it must be admitted, sullen in the extreme.

But at least it can be said of Zulkeh that he made an attempt to bring the light of reason to shine upon this dark and disgraceful episode. Not so Magrit and the strangler! The conduct of these twain was rather like that of arsonists heaving torches on the conflagration. For the two did roll about the floor throughout the fracas, howling with laughter and cackling like geese!

Worst of all was the contribution of the horrid salamander! The evil little creature summoned forth all the mice from their holes, offering bets on the outcome of the melee. These wagers the rodents declined, even after the despicable amphibian offered ten to one odds on the apprentice.

(Let me say here, by way of a narrator's aside, that from this very episode stemmed that streak of misbehavior on the part of our lousely youth which, in the time to come, was to prove such a burden to the honored elders of the Alfredae. For not only did the disease of gambling henceforth raise its ugly head amongst the youth, but 'twas from this episode that there developed that noxious habit among the more ruffianly adolescents of chanting in unison: "Shelyid's our host! Hoo, hoo, hoo! Shelyid, that's who!" Not to mention the thence-common appearance on the fore-limbs of outright juvenile delinquents of such obscene tattoos as *Born To Raise Hell* and *Shelyid's Slaves*.)

But now, at long last, did Magrit and Greyboar retrieve at least a small fragment of responsible behavior.

"Oh shit," Magrit cackled, "the little barbarian-horde-in-one's gonna bring the whole house down!" And this pathetic jest caused her and the strangler to howl anew, slapping each other's backs with abandon.

"Yeah," sputtered Greyboar, "but at least we finally know what really happened to the Great Wall of Grotum—it pulled a knife on a dwarf!" And this ridiculous quip caused him and the witch to howl yet again, rolling about the floor like lunatics in an asylum.

But at length they recovered, and Magrit, holding her ribs, managed to gasp: "You'd better stop him, Greyboar. I can't afford to rebuild the place, and besides, I don't want to have to mop up what'd be left of Ignace if the dwarf gets to him."

And so it was, still laughing shamelessly, that the strangler staggered to his feet and seized Shelyid by the neck. Suspended in midair, the gnome turned his furious knifework upon Greyboar, but the huge chokester disarmed Shelyid—rather gently, oddly enough—and tucked the apprentice under his left arm. Then, reaching up into the rafters with his right hand, he hauled down the agent and deposited him with a thump on the floor. He then said to Ignace: "Next time, dummy, pick on someone your own size."

And at this latest uncouth bon mot, he and Magrit again fell to hollering and backslapping. It appeared that Ignace did not share the humor, for after a moment the agent jumped to his feet and said to the strangler, in a tone of voice brooking no argument: "Greyboar! Strangle that dwarf!"

Greyboar gazed at his agent, tears of laughter still rolling down his cheeks.

"Why would I do that?" he asked.

"He insulted us, that's why!" came the shrill reply.

"Us?" demanded Greyboar. "What's with this 'us'?" He didn't insult me. Oh, and sure, I supposed you might feel insulted, being chased around like a cat by the Mouse From Hell"—again, he and the witch hooped and hollered disgracefully—"but that's your problem."

"What do you mean he didn't insult you?" shrilled Ignace. "That's how the whole thing started! I was just defending your honor! Didn't he call you a common killer? The outrage! The disrespect to your person! To your professional standing!" Then, with the air of one playing a trump card: "To your philosophy of life!"

The strangler snorted derisively. "What a load of bullshit," he said. "You—of all people—lecturing me on philosophy! Ha!" He glared at his agent. "But I'll get back to that in a moment. First I've got to calm down Midget the Terrible here." Another round of ridiculous gaiety.

Greyboar held up Shelyid before him and shook him like a terrier shaking a rat. More accurately, like a dragon shaking a mouse. This treatment finally snapped the dwarf out of his madness.

"That hurts!" complained Shelyid.

"That's the idea," commented Greyboar placidly.

"Now look, midget—sorry—Shelyid, you've made your point, and made it quite thoroughly, but enough's enough. I'm going to let you down now, but I want no more chasing after Ignace, you hear? He's been my agent for a long time, and he's the best in the business. Besides, I like the little hothead, even if sometimes he is a complete asshole." Greyboar ignored Ignace's squeal of outrage. "Is it a deal? If you still want to fight, well, that's all right, too. But this time you'll have to fight me, and I don't suggest it. In fact, not to put too fine a point on it, I wouldn't even think about it."

The light of reason now having returned, Shelyid carefully examined the figure of the chokester, and nodded his head.

"S'a deal."

"Good." Greyboar set him on the floor, then turned to Ignace.

"Now, let's get back to you," he growled. "Philosophy— ha! From you—ha! First of all, my fair-weather little logician, the kid never insulted me once. Oh, and sure, he indicated reservations concerning the ethics of my trade. So what? Plenty of people have! My own sister Gwendolyn's said more than once—right in front of you, too!—that I wasn't nothing better than a thug and that I ought to mend my evil ways and go back to my honest job in the packinghouse. I didn't see you rise to my defense then, push her in the face and knock her down, stand over her waving a knife and threaten to cut out her tongue. How come? Speak up!"

Ignace coughed. "Well, she's your sister and all. Got to make allowances for family, you know, and besides—"

"What a load of bullshit!" interrupted Greyboar. A great sneer crossed his face. "Naturally, it doesn't have nary to do with the fact that she's almost as strong as

I am and used to gut steers at her job in the slaughter-house—each one with a single stroke of the knife, if you call that great cleaver of hers a 'knife.'"

"Well," muttered Ignace. "Well."

"Well, nothing! Ye olde sorcerer over there"—a massive thumb indicated Zulkeh—"can wax as eloquent as he pleases on the hoary traditions of my 'most honorable and prestigious profession,' but you know as well as I do that the plebes we hang out with don't think choking's anything more than a fancy name for the same stuff what gets them pitched in the hoosegow at the drop of a hat. I get away with it for two reasons." He held up a pair of fingers like cucumbers. "First, I only do it for money. That makes it a respectable profit-making enterprise, rather than a hideous crime of vulgar passion. Second, and more important, I only choke rich people at the request of other rich people, which makes it classy and *haut cuisine*."

"That's not true!" denied Ignace. "You've burked lots of lowlifes!"

"Most of 'em loan sharks or pimps. Or their bullies."

"Well. Well, even so!"

"Loan sharks and pimps don't count. Or their bullies. Makes even the porkers yawn."

"I don't care!" shrilled Ignace. The dyspeptic little agent began hopping up and down in fury. "Forget the philosophy, then! That miserable dwarf pisses me off! Choke him, I say, choke him! Throttle the little runt—as a personal favor to your old friend and faithful agent."

"Not a chance," replied Greybeard. "Three reasons." He held up three fingers like a stack of logs. "First, right now the favor I owe's to the kid, on account of how he just got through providing me with more entertainment than I've had in years." Another sorry round of merriment ensued. "Second, I don't choke people as personal favors to anyone, you included. Professional ethics, you know. And finally, I don't choke shrimps."

"I don't care!" shrilled Ignace. "You—"

"Although," mused Greyboar, stooping over Ignace, "there's always a first time."

Silence fell over the agent. Ignace peered up past Greyboar's great hook of a nose, his beady black eyes visible at a distance. So does the mouse examine the eagle's beak just before lunch.

"You'd be without an agent," he squeaked. "Business'd suffer. You'd go hungry—starve—have to go back to work in the—"

"Nonsense!" cried Greyboar. "Soon as word got out I was throttling obnoxious little loudmouths there'd be a line outside my door. A long, long line. Wouldn't need an agent! Just need to hire a few bouncers to keep the line orderly. Big, beefy lads, phlegmatic types, you know, the kind won't start fights for no reason."

Pondering this line of logic, Ignace soon came to the conclusion that there was some truth in Greyboar's argument. He was perhaps helped along in drawing this conclusion by the learned debate which promptly erupted between Magrit and Zulkeh over the precise length of the line of customers which would form to seek the asphyxiations of offensive twerps. Here the wizard leaned toward the conservative side, opting for a line no more than two miles long, while the witch— exhibiting a more sanguine temperament—firmly placed twelve miles as the lowest conceivable limit.

The argument waxed hot and heavy. Zulkeh, in a rare lapse into empiricism, cited for authority his long experience with the aggravations caused him by his diminutive apprentice. For her part, Magrit ridiculed this selfsame hard-won expertise, advancing the—to your narrator's mind—dubious premise that the dwarf

Shelyid was "rather a fine and sprightly little chap." She went on to depict the sorcerer Zulkeh as a narrow-minded pedant whose cloistered existence had given him no concept of the true essence of the obnoxious little loudmouth, so well-known and despised by the common run of mankind, the which would eagerly scrape together their few coins to see the world rid of this plague.

In the event, the question was settled by the grotesque little salamander. For once again, it rounded up the multitude of mice and put the question to them, asking the rodents what they would offer for the privilege of ringside seats at the apparently-soon-to-be-forthcoming throttling of Ignace at the hands of his client. This question—though obviously framed in a weighted and unscientific manner—soon resolved the dispute, not to mention Ignace's mind. For 'twas but a moment later that the mice, having disappeared into their holes, came pouring forth in a great horde, chittering with glee, dressed in holiday finery, bearing in their tiny paws various crumbs, treasured trinkets, and bits of succulent cheese. One enthusiast went so far as to offer, in a squeaking little voice, "the pelt off my back."

Of course, the rodents were doomed to disappointment, for Ignace promptly announced himself satisfied and went to sit sullenly in his chair, pouting and sulking. A great uproar ensued, with much chittering and squeaking of indignant mice. The salamander was forced to flee onto a nearby table. Magrit, for her part, finally managed to quell the agitated mob of rodents with many pounds of cheese offered by way of a refund.

"Haven't had so much fun in a long time," commented the witch, after the last mouse had disappeared. In a rare good humor, she smiled down at Shelyid and

said: "You can call me the old bag any time you want,
lad."

"Oh, I wouldn't do that, ma—Magrit," protested
Shelyid.

"Just as I said!" proclaimed the witch. "A fine and
sprightly little chap. Well-mannered, too."

Then, with noticeably less pleasure, she gazed upon
Zulkeh.

"All right, you old fart. Now that the fun's over, let's
get to business. You do have business with me, I
assume? It's not likely you're here for the pleasure of
my company. Unless," she added, with a disgusting leer,
"you got horny again."

The wizard chose to ignore this last remark. Instead,
he drew himself up, in a most dignified manner, and
spoke as follows:

"Yes, madame, I have come here on a matter of
business. I find—not with any feeling of pleasure in the
fact, mind you!—that I have need of your assistance.
For it has come to my attention—most unexpectedly!—
that I have enemies. And so—"

But he was interrupted by the salamander, who,
from its perch atop Magrit's shoulder, exclaimed shrilly:

"Oh shit, not another one!"

CHAPTER XIX. *A Wizard's Discourse. Rather, A Horrid Salamander's Précis of Same. A Demand For Payment. An Offer of Payment. An Offer of Payment Rudely Refused. A Wizard's Indignation. A Lunatic Appears!*

"What's your problem, Wittgenstein?"

Such was the question addressed by the witch to the salamander, in response to that latter's vulgar outburst. The creature had a name!

"I *told* you this foety business was a bad move, Magrit," groused the salamander. It looked over to Greyboar and Ignace. "I told her and told her! Would she listen to me? No! She never does!" Its tiny red eyes glared.

"Now look at the situation!" it continued. "That's all we ever get anymore. One sorry-ass so-called wizard after another." Its already-shrill little voice assumed a particularly irritating nasal tone. "'I can't do my spells because some unknown'—what a joke!—'enemies are attacking me in some unknown'—ha!—'manner for some unknown'—ha!—'reason.'" It stopped, glaring at Magrit.

She shrugged. "It's a living."

"It's a *bore*."

"May I continue?" demanded Zulkeh. "I must say, madame, these constant interruptions are an affront to the pursuit of science—the more so, coming as they do from this unnatural beast!"

"Unnatural beast, is it?" shrilled the salamander. "Let's put it to the test! Let's see if this 'unnatural beast' isn't capable of plumbing the so-called depths of your so-called science."

The unnatural beast hopped from Magrit's shoulder onto a nearby table. Then, assumed a most unnatural pose, the which, strange to say, uncannily mimicked the posture and mien of the wizard Zulkeh. It proceeded to speak in a raspy style of voice, the which, strange to say, uncannily imitated the wizard Zulkeh's elocution.

"Madame," it began, "a problem has astonished me in my mind. Yet, still more astonishing than the astonishment itself is the very fact of my astonishment! For, as you well know, I rank among the mightiest of the world's wizards, and hence, by this selfsame nature of my dialectical cunning and metaphysical majuscularity, am incapable of being astonished in my mind. It follows then, as night from day, through the simple application of syllogistic logic, that this paradox can only result from the intervention of—*enemies*."

Here the horrid little salamander began to pace back and forth, its head bowed in the manner of one deep in thought, gesticulating with short but sharply expressive motions of its forelimbs—that is to say, imitated in a most uncanny fashion the mannerisms of the wizard Zulkeh when this latter engaged in profound exposition.

"Alas, due to that selfsame scientific loftiness, I am not an expert on that arcane, uncouth, and obscure branch of the thaumaturgic discipline which goes by the name of foety. Hence—I will speak frankly—have I come to your side, madame."

The miserable little beast ceased its pacing and stood stiffly erect, peering forth intently, exhibiting in every angle of its posture that superlative dignity which was the hallmark of the mage Zulkeh when pronouncing an unpleasant but true truth.

"For you are the witch Magrit, the horrid harridan, the repulsive termagant, the fustigant fury, the lamia rampant, the execrable harpy, the verminous virago, the loathsome she-wolf. Hence are you known the world over as the unquestioned mistress of the lore and practice of foety, this expertise being explained, of course, not simply by its natural attraction to one of your demonic foulness, but, more simply still, by the demands of self-preservation."

The vile little monster ceased and stared at Zulkeh. "Well," it demanded, "has the unnatural beast captured the essence of your thoughts?"

Zulkeh coughed. "As to that," he spoke, "in so far as you explicate the dimensions of my situation, I believe you have succeeded in capturing its focus, if not perhaps all aspects of its permutations." Then he frowned. "But certainly must I take exception to the various descriptions of the witch Magrit which you placed in my mouth! For I can assure you—and all present!—that never once would such intemperate and demeaning characterizations of such a fine and respected sorceress as Magrit cross my lips! I am shocked! I am appalled! I am—"

"Oh no!" interrupted Shelyid. The dwarf took a step toward Magrit, his hands outstretched.

"I can swear to it, ma—Magrit! The master didn't say those things! No, you shouldn't think that!"

The dwarf shook his finger fiercely at the

salamander. "You should be ashamed of yourself, Wittgenstein!" Then, turning back to Magrit, Shelyid continued, in a most earnest tone:

"He never once called you a lamia or a harpy or a fury or a she-wolf, and—"

"You see!" exclaimed Zulkeh. "My stupid but honest apprentice vindicates me! And I can assure you all—"

"—he didn't call you a repulsive termagant or a verminous virago, oh no!—not at all!—instead—"

"—that Shelyid shares with many morons an uncanny accuracy of memory, the which—"

"—he called you a crass termagant and a loathsome virago, and while it's true that—"

"Shelyid!" cried the wizard. "Desist at—"

"—he called you a horrid harridan, I don't think Wittgenstein should make such a big deal about that because he called you all kinds of harridan, not—"

"—at once! Desist I say!"

"—just a horrid harridan but a vile harridan and a noxious harridan and a debauched harridan, too. So you can see—"

"Desist, I say!" This last in a roar, following which Zulkeh smote the apprentice with his staff, knocking the gnome flat. There can be little doubt that this first well-deserved buffet should have been followed by quite the proper thrashing, but his staff was suddenly snatched from his hand.

Turning with indignation, the mage beheld the staff firmly held in Greyboar's giant fist.

"What is the meaning of this outrage!" demanded Zulkeh. "You, sir! Return my staff at once!"

"Do you wish this staff in its most suitable place?" inquired Greyboar, in a very mild tone.

"Certainly! And at once!" The mage extended his hand. "And furthermore—" He paused, considered.

"A moment!" spoke the mage hastily. He pondered again. "It occurs to me, in retrospect, that your inquiry was phrased somewhat oddly. I should—"

"Magrit, I'll need some chicken fat," rumbled the chokester.

"Got lots of the stuff!" said Wittgenstein cheerfully.

"Just give me a minute!" added Magrit, heading toward the pantry.

"One moment! One moment!" spoke Zulkeh. "There is no need—"

He was interrupted by Shelyid, now risen to his feet.

"Why did you hit me, master?" demanded the dwarf, in a most untoward tone of voice. "I didn't do nothing wrong, I was just setting the record straight!"

"Bah!" oathed Zulkeh. "You—"

"Bah yourself!" shrilled Shelyid. The wizard's eyes goggled at this impudence.

"I'm tired of you hitting me all the time," grumbled the dwarf, "especially 'cause most of the time I don't deserve it, and even most of the time when I do, I don't deserve to be hit as hard and as often as you hit me, and even the few times I maybe deserve to be hit as hard and as often as you do, you still shouldn't do it because, well, because it's *mean*." He ceased and stared up at his master, a preposterous look of aggrievement upon his semi-simian face.

The wizard was still speechless, due, one suspects, to his bemusement at the gnome's unwonted impertinence.

"And especially this time it wasn't fair," continued the dwarf, "because I was just telling the truth like it happened. I know I'm real stupid, but you yourself said I have a good memory and I can tell you each time you said what you said about Magrit and where you said and when you said it." He paused, knitted his brow. "Like the time you called her a vile

harridan was when we were still in Goimr, just after
you decided we had to come here. We were in the
study where you had been sitting for days without
moving—and I was real good and I dusted you off and
everything!—and you had just gotten up and called me
and I was sitting on the stool where I always sat when
you were lecturing and—"

"Enough!" spoke Zulkeh. "Desist, I say!"

The dwarf stopped, pouted. Then said quietly: "It's
true. It happened just like I said."

Zulkeh cleared his throat. "Well," he said. "Well,
there is perhaps some modicum of accuracy in your
account—in a vague and general—"

"Oh, shut up, you old fart!" snapped Magrit. "I'm
quite sure that you said everything about me that
Shelyid says you did and I'm sure he could tell me
exactly where and when you said it. Who cares? Do
you think I give a shit what you ever said about me?"
She snorted. "I'd lie awake at night worrying about the
sex life of fungus before I'd lose any sleep over what
you think." She glowered at the mage for a moment,
and then made a small gesture to the strangler.

"Oh, give the fool back his staff, Greyboar! He looks
lost without it." The staff was handed back. Magrit then
said, very softly: "If you ever hit that kid again when
I'm around, you'll find out why they call me the horrid
harridan." And it was odd, this ridiculous threat from
a blowsy, pudgy witch, how it brought such a feeling
into the room, of an ancient, bitter wind, blowing
across a field of ice.

But the moment passed. Magrit turned away and
dropped herself into a chair.

"All right, let's to it. Tell me what your problem is,
Zulkeh, and why you think you have enemies."

Then did the mage launch into a discourse anent
the problem that loomed before him, eschewing not

a full explication of the entire scope and dimension of the task. The clarity and precision of his elaboration of every aspect and nuance of the question were all the more admirable given that he was forced to proceed in the face of frequent interruptions by the salamander, in which the scurvy beast uttered many sour phrases extolling the virtues of brevity and succinct exposition. Yet at length, these uncouth interpositions notwithstanding, the wizard finished with his tale.

"How then," concluded Zulkeh, "may I uncover these enemies?"

Magrit sneered. "Just like that, huh? What do you think I'm running here—a charity?"

"*Most* people offer to pay for her services," groused the salamander.

"I am no beggar!" responded the mage hotly. "I am quite willing to pay for services rendered me!" And so saying, Zulkeh reached into his purse and brought forth a fistful of oddly-shaped gold nuggets, the which he flung onto the table in a manner both imperial and scornful.

In a trice, the salamander scurried over and examined the pile of nuggets. This took but a moment. The miserable little beast cocked an eye at Shelyid.

"You ought to be ashamed of yourself," it said. Shelyid flushed.

"Dwarf shit," sneered Magrit.

It was now Zulkeh's turn to flush. "Well, as to that, madame, gold is gold. 'Tis widely known that the essence of a substance resides in its properties, not—fie on such witless notions!—in its origins, these latter being oft murky and uncertain. Of no substance is this more true than gold! Did not Midas Laebmaunt—"

"Fuck you and your Midas!" exclaimed Magrit. "Save

your breath. I wouldn't fool around with this stuff
under any circumstances. And you'd better watch your
ass! The minute the Consortium finds out about this,
there'll be hell to pay. Pity the poor dwarves of the
world!" At this last remark Shelyid frowned, his ugly
little face filled with puzzlement and apprehension.

"What would you then, Madame?" demanded
Zulkeh. "I am a thaumaturge, not a merchant. Rich
in intellect, logic and lore—yet not, it must be said,
overburdened by material wealth."

"No tickee, no washee," sneered the salamander.
With great disdain, the loathsome little creature flicked
the gold nuggets off the table with its tail.

Suddenly, Magrit grinned. "Never mind," she
laughed, "I just couldn't resist the needle. 'Not overburdened with material wealth'—hah! The fact is,
Zulkeh, I knew you were coming. And I already know
how you're going to pay me for my help. You're going
to do a job for me."

"What?" demanded the mage. "How did you know
I was coming? And what is this—if I may use the
uncouth expression—'job' you are talking about?"

"As to your first question, I found out you were
coming yesterday. An old friend dropped by and told
me. You may know him—Wolfgang Laebmauntsforscynneweëld."

"The fraud!" cried Zulkeh and Ignace in one voice.

"The philosopher!" exclaimed Greyboar.

Magrit sneered. "You're all full of shit. He's no fraud,
and, as for you, Greyboar, I don't suggest you call him
a philosopher to his face. Professional fingerwork be
damned, he's big enough he'd probably tie you in
knots."

"Quite a large individual," agreed Greyboar, not, or
so it seemed, noticeably distraught at the implied
threat. "Eight feet tall, as I remember."

"You've met him?" asked Magrit, surprised.

"We were not properly introduced," explained Greyboar. "But I attended one of his lectures in New Sfinctr some time ago. A most fascinating evening! The philo—uh, how does he respond to 'thinker'—?"

"Prefers to be called a lunatic," said Magrit.

"And quite rightly!" exclaimed Zulkeh.

"—lunatic, then," continued Greyboar, "clarified the powers of madness and amnesia, and their capacity for wreaking good and justice in the world. I enjoyed the exposition immensely! Although, I have to say, I didn't understand most of it, seeing as how it was delivered in a peculiar argot."

"The common, everyday babble of idiots," explained Magrit. "It's his favorite language for public discourse."

"Ah! That explains it, then!" Greyboar scratched his head. "The question and answer period was not especially fruitful, I will admit. Wolfgang answered every question with the statement that he had forgotten the answer."

Now did the wizard, who had been impatiently following this dialogue, interject himself forcefully.

"Madame, you cannot be serious in this project, whatever it is! To bring in the person of Wolfgang Laebmauntsforcynneweëld! Well! Madame! The man is known the world over as a sciolist, a medicaster, a humbug, a hoaxster, a trepan, a—"

"Want me to get the chicken fat, Magrit?" interrupted the slimy amphibian. Zulkeh clamped shut his jaws and glowered at the horrid beast.

"Much as I hate to be on the same side as the pedant," chipped in Ignace, "I've got to tell you I think he's right, Magrit. I was at that same lecture with Greyboar, and let me tell you it was pure and simple gibberish. I mean, that big clown probably couldn't—"

"Shut up!" snarled Magrit. "Both of you! The day I want your opinions, I'll ask for them. Ha! Eternity won't be long enough. Others may laugh at Wolfgang's twin powers of madness and amnesia, but I'm not one of them."

"Besides, she's sweet on him," piped up the salamander. It scampered to the edge of the table, away from Magrit's fierce look. " 'Course, she's sweet on lots of—" It sprang to the floor, evading the witch's backhand. Once on the floor, it looked back at Zulkeh.

"Sorry, old boy," sneered the beast. "I know the truth hurts, but you might as well know your ex-girlfriend's a nymphom—" It darted into a nearby mousehole, one scuttle ahead of a hurled teacup. A moment later, its head popped back out.

"Missed, you slut!" The head disappeared as a volley of teacups landed about the mousehole.

"Madame!" exclaimed Zulkeh. "If you might leave be this interchange with that horrid creature, let us please come back to the subject at hand!"

Magrit turned on him, teacup in hand. Zulkeh flinched. After a moment, she took a deep breath and slammed the teacup back on the table.

"Why'd I have to get a salamander for a familiar?" she demanded to no one in particular. "Sassy little slimeball! Should have settled for a cat like a sensible witch—a cute little furball, sweet, dumb, playful—"

Out popped the salamander's head. "Who'd do your books?" it demanded. "A stupid lazy feline? Ha! Think a cat could cover your accounts payable like an octopus with your accounts receivable like a clam?"

"I know, I know," growled Magrit. "That's why you aren't a wallet."

The squabble apparently over, the creature slithered out of the mousehole and returned to the table.

Zulkeh cleared his throat. "Madame, let us leave

aside for the moment our differing views on the capacities of Wolfgang Laebmauntsforscynneweëld. The question of consulting with him remains moot in any event. For, do I not mistake me, he has been for some time now incarcerated in the world-famed asylum for the insane in Begfat. Under lock and key, so I am told."

"He escaped."

Zulkeh gasped. "Escaped? From the asylum at Begfat? Surely you jest! The institution is noted for its rigorous security, its—"

"Wolfgang escapes whenever he wants to," countered Magrit. "Not hard for him. After all, he owns the place."

"What?"

"You didn't know? Wolfgang founded the asylum. Said he needed a home of his own. He's its main patient." She chuckled. "He's also the head psychiatrist, the chief tester as well as testee of experimental drugs, and the captain of the security guard."

A loud knocking sounded from the floor below.

"That'll be him," said Magrit. She headed toward the stairs, giving the wizard a sneer as she passed. "Some people use the front door."

"Madame!" exclaimed Zulkeh. "This is preposterous! I have no time to fiddle away doing some 'job' for you—certainly not a task which involves such a mountebank as—"

The witch paused at the head of the stairs. "Fuck you," she snarled. "You came here looking for my help. You can't pay anything, except in that dwarf gold I wouldn't touch in a minute. It's like they say: 'no freebies from Magrit.' If you want my help, you've got to do me a service—and the service I need will require Wolfgang. So! There it is—you want my help finding your enemies, stay and wait. You don't need my help, after all? No problem—get lost!"

When Magrit reappeared, climbing the stairs, the wizard was still protesting volubly. His voice was stilled by the sight of the figure who followed, a gigantic man who was only able to negotiate the staircase in a stoop.

"He's even bigger than I remembered," muttered Greyboar.

"Disgusting, the way he drools like that," whispered Ignace.

Once at the top of the landing, the giant straightened up slightly, rolling his eyes toward the ceiling.

"I do wish you'd raise this ceiling a bit, dear," he said. "Last time I was here I couldn't ever stand up straight." A grotesque leer came upon his face. "Not that I spent much time in a vertical position." He reached out a huge hand and patted the witch's ample posterior. Magrit squawked with laughter and slapped the hand away.

Still stooped, the giant turned to the wizard.

"Zulkeh!" he boomed. "Have you led me a merry chase! Been following you ever since you left Goimr!"

"Following me?" demanded the mage. "For what reason? And by what right?"

The giant giggled. "By the right of lunatics to do anything that crosses their silly minds, of course! As for the reason, you're about to hear it."

Wolfgang spread his hands, still giggling. "I now declare this council of war open!" Then, slapping his head. "Oh, but wait! I'm so forgetful! The others!"

He leaned over the railing and emitted a piercing whistle. "Come on up, boys!"

There came the tramp of heavy feet. Then, appearing in a row up the stairs, came six wide grins on six lumpy faces.

PART XV

In Which the Mage Agrees,
Though With Profound Misgivings,
to the Proposal of the Witch and Her
Vile Accomplices, Producing Those Results
Which Reverberate About the World To This
Very Day, Not the Least of These Being the
Earliest Manifestation of The Horror
Henceforth Known, To Friend and
Foe Alike, As The Rebel.

—∞—

CHAPTER XX. A Notorious Council Con-
venes. A Wizard's Objections. A Theft
Proposed. A Wizard's Objections. Motives
Revealed. A Wizard's Objections. Particu-
lars Explained. A Wizard's Objections. A
Plot Set Afoot!

And so was convened the later-notorious First Magrite
Council. The date: October 30, Year of the Jackal.

Presiding over the Council was the witch Magrit herself. Also present were: Zulkeh and his apprentice Shelyid; Greyboar the strangler and his agent Ignace; Wolfgang Laebmauntsforscynneweëld, the lunatic; and six lowlifes, these latter a disreputable crew known to friend and foe alike as Les Six.

The meeting began badly.

"Insufferable!" stormed the wizard Zulkeh. "By what bizarre logic are these—these proletarian jackanapes!—present at this council?"

Six wide grins split six lumpy faces.

"The mage is affronted in his mind!" exclaimed the first.

"Aghast, appalled and taken aback!" added the second.

"And rightly so!" cried the third.

" 'Tis a travesty to have present at such a learned gathering our lowly and loathsome like!" concurred the fourth.

"For are we not uneducated, untutored, unlettered and ignorant?" demanded the fifth.

"Rude, crude, lewd and uncouth, that's us!" boomed the sixth. This was apparently something in the way of a ruffianly toast, for the six scalawags raised their teacups in unison, pinkies politely extended like so many small logs, and slurped noisily.

Zulkeh's expostulation, even now gathering like a storm, was cut short by Magrit.

"Shut up, you old fart! And you! Yeah—you—Les Six! Quit baiting the wizard!" The six scoundrels looked aggrieved.

Magrit glared around the room. "I'm running this meeting, d'you all understand that? None of your clowning around, any of you!"

She settled her ample body back into her chair. Then spoke again:

"All right, here's the deal. There's something that needs to be carried out. It's a task which is almost impossible. But with the people we've got here in this room, I think it can be done. And if it can, each of us stands to gain in some way. What is it? Simple— I want to steal a Rap Sheet."

A collective gasp swept the room.

"A Rap Sheet!" exclaimed Ignace.

"But madame!" protested Zulkeh. "They're all in Ozar—all known ones, that is. Except, perhaps, for the two reputed to be in the possession, respectively, of the Kaysar of All The Kushrau and the King of the Sundjhab."

Magrit allowed the hubbub to quiet down before continuing.

"There are five Rap Sheets whose location is either known or surmised on good evidence, of the original six which Joe is supposed to have made for the cops at the beginning of time. As the wizard says, two of them are suspected to be in the hands of the Kushrau Kaysars and the Sundjhabi Kings. Although recent events cast some doubt on the latter," she mused. "Didn't seem to have done the King of the Sundjhab much good."

Greyboar coughed. "Perhaps my guru left it behind on his recent sojourn to New Sfinctr," he opined.

"His recent, abruptly-ended sojourn to New Sfinctr," stated Magrit, pointedly staring at the strangler. Greyboar coughed again.

"Baloney!" snorted Ignace. "That old fr—uh, wise man—didn't leave nothing behind. Take it from me— I was there! Luxuries like a sybarite's dream, his suite at the hotel—and him squawking about philosophy the whole time!"

Greyboar glared at his agent.

"What's this?" demanded Zulkeh. "Has some

unfortunate accident befallen the King of the Sundjhab? I certainly hope not! A most eminent sage, His Highness—the preeminent expositor in our modern times of ethical entropism. Mind you, I myself do not share the King's belief in the moral supremacy of the second law of thermodynamics, yet still there is no question—"

"The King's dead," interrupted Magrit. "No accident either," she snorted, nodding at Greyboar, "unless you want to reckon him and his thumbs a genetic accident fallen on the unwitting human race."

Greyboar flushed. It took a moment for her meaning to penetrate to the mage's mind. Then did the sorcerer gasp, shock writ plain upon his face.

"What? Do I understand you to say that this—this *assassin* has throttled the King of Sundjhab?"

"And his heir, the Prince," said Magrit.

"That's why we're hiding out here in Prygg," complained Ignace. "It'd been okay if he'd just choked the King—the Prince hired us, and he'd have gotten the porkers off our back. But no!" he shrilled, "Mr. Philosophy Student here"—an accusing finger was leveled at Greyboar—"had to take exception to the Prince's—and I quote—'disrespect for philosophy' and go and squeeze his weasand for him, too! Not that the royal larva didn't deserve it, I'll admit, but still—talk about poor business practices!"

"He hired me to strangle my own guru," growled the strangler. "Imagine! What else was I to do?"

Zulkeh frowned. "Do I understand you to say, sirrah Greyboar, that you yourself are an acolyte of the—former—King of Sundjhab's teachings?"

"I certainly am!" boomed the strangler. "A novice, I admit—I'm still working on my Languor."

"Then why did you strangle him?" demanded the mage.

Greyboar grimaced. "Well, actually I wasn't a follower of my guru when I took on the job. The King—bless him—showed me the Way right at the last moment."

"Greyboar had what you might call a deathbed conversion," chipped in Ignace. "The King's deathbed, that is." He looked innocently away from Greyboar's fierce gaze.

"But still," protested Zulkeh, "the truth once known to you, why did you finish the choke?"

Greyboar looked offended. "I'd already taken the money for the job. Professional ethics, you know."

Zulkeh nodded his head. "Of course, of course. Professional ethics, of course. Yes, quite so!"

"May we get on with our business?" asked Magrit. "Or would you two rather turn this into a leisurely chat on the nature of ethics, morality, and whatnot neither of you knows squat about?"

Wizard and strangler glared at the witch, but fell silent.

"Anyway," continued Magrit, "as I was saying, of the five Rap Sheets known to exist, the other three—this is a certainty—are in the possession of the Imperial Republic of Ozar. Have been for some time, in fact. Helps explain the historic success of the Ozarine—"

"—in its rapacious gobbling up of the world," chimed in Les Six in unison.

"But what's not widely known," said Magrit, ignoring the interruption, "is that one of Ozarae's Rap Sheets has been brought right here to Prygg. Only a few days ago."

"The Ozarine have brought such a precious relic here to Grotum?" inquired the mage. "Whatever for?"

"Is he really that stupid?" demanded the first.

Before the usual round could begin—or the wizard do more than sputter—Magrit took command of the discussion again.

"Keep personalities out of it!" she snapped. "And he's not actually stupid, he just lives in the clouds, on his head, thinking the earth is vapor above." She forestalled Zulkeh's indignation with a sharp gesture.

"In answer to your question, Zulkeh, the Ozarine have brought it to Grotum to aid them in their commercial, industrial, financial and you-can-practically-name-it conquest of our sub-continent. And it will be a big help to them, too, let me tell you. The biggest problem the Ozarines have is suppressing the revolutionary movement of Grotum." She sneered. "That's not from lack of cooperation from the Groutch regimes, of course—in Prygg especially, which over the past two years has become an Ozarean satrapy in all but name. The upper classes in Pryggia today aren't but lackeys for their Ozarine masters."

"Never were much good at their best," stated the second.

"As sorry a lot of drones, churchmen and landlords as ever plagued a land," agreed the third.

"As rapacious as your Sfinctrian aristocrats, as incompetent as your Goimric nobility," concurred the fourth.

"Former worms, current tapeworms," added the fifth.

"Here's to the downfall of parasites!" cried the sixth. This was apparently something in the way of a rabble toast, for the six malcontents raised their teacups in unison, pinkies politely extended like so much firewood, and slurped noisily.

Magrit continued:

"The Rap Sheet rests in the care of the Ozarean sub-secretary to the third consul for agricultural affairs, one Rupert Inkman. He's also the Groutch chief of station for the Ozarean Senate's Commission to Repel Unbridled Disruption."

"A Crud!" exclaimed Greyboar.

"That he is," agreed the first.

"One of your greater Cruds, in fact," commented the second.

"The Butcher of the Rellenos," added the third.

"Reports direct to the Angel Jimmy Jesus himself," elaborated the fourth.

"He's also a subsidiary of the Consortium," embroidered the fifth. "One of their most profitable concerns."

Fortunately, the sixth's contribution—which should no doubt have led to another grotesque toast—was cut short by Zulkeh.

"One moment, madame! I wish to return to the beginning of your exposition. I fear my mind has been so distracted by the news of the sad death of the King of the Sundjhab and the appearance in Grotum of a Rap Sheet that I have let fall aside the chief point. Do I understand you to say that you wish my assistance in the theft of this Rap Sheet from its rightful owner? If so, you may rest assured that I will have no part in such a criminal—"

"Oh, shut up, you old fart! Since when is a Rap Sheet the rightful property of the Senate of Ozar? They stole all theirs from other empires, or took 'em by main force—you know that as well as I do! Cut plenty of throats in the process, too."

Zulkeh stroked his beard thoughtfully. "Well, as to that, I admit there is much to what you say. Still, the Rap Sheets have been in the possession of the Ozarine for some time now, and 'tis a well-known jurisprudential principle—well-buttressed by numerous ontological axioms—that possession is ninety-nine point astronomically large number of nines following the decimal parts of the law."

Now did a new party, hitherto silent, enter the discussion. Since his introduction, the lunatic Wolfgang had sat in a corner, in a special chair designed for his gargantuan frame. He had closely observed all of the participants, reserving, strange to say, the most careful scrutiny for the least significant member of the group—I speak, of course, of the dwarf Shelyid. This latter had squatted on the floor throughout the proceedings, sitting a pace back from the main circle, as was his proper place.

Now Wolfgang spoke, in a tenor voice which contrasted oddly with his size, addressing himself— astonishing to relate—to the apprentice.

"What do you think, lad?" he asked.

Shelyid frowned, stammered, glanced to his master.

"Well, it's not really my place to say. That's for the master to decide."

"Yes, yes, no doubt," spoke the giant cheerfully, "but I didn't ask you what you decided—I asked you what you thought."

Shelyid glanced again at his master. The wizard made a permissive gesture.

"Well," Shelyid said, his brow knotted with thought, "the master always explained that the Rap Sheets were made back in the beginning of time, back when the legends say Joe was froze up by the Old Geister." His face cleared. "I remember now! There was a little poem the master had me memorize—goes like this:

> *Joe made six Pink Slips for the bosses,*
> *to keep the bad in line.*
> *Then Joe made six Rap Sheets for the cops,*
> *to keep track of worse ones.*
> *Then Joe made six Switches for the priests,*
> *to make the worser wail.*
> *And finally Joe made one—"*

Shelyid stopped abruptly, looking guiltily at the mage.

"I'm not supposed to say the last thing Joe made. But it's real awful! He made it for the Old Geister, and—well, I'm not supposed to say." The dwarf fell into a fearful silence.

"Excellent!" boomed Wolfgang. The lunatic gazed benignly at the wizard. "I'm pleased to see that you haven't neglected the boy's education, Zulkeh. Most commendable, teaching him the old gypsy song. Not many sorcerers today even know it themselves." The wizard nodded graciously.

"But what do you think, boy?" continued Wolfgang. "Now that you've recited the song—and, yes, we can skip the last part—not suitable in polite company, that's for sure!—what do you think? Who rightfully owns the Rap Sheets?"

"Oh!" cried Shelyid. "That's easy. They belong to Joe, just like all his other inventions. He's the one gave them to those other people, you know, the ones he invented in the first place—the cops and the bosses and the priests and the Old Geister." The dwarf paused, pondered a moment. "Well, I'm not actually sure the Old Geister's a people, but anyway, Joe just made them so that things would work right. But the cops and the priests and the bosses and the Old Geister—they played him a dirty trick! They froze him right up, like they shouldn't have done! So the way I see it, the Rap Sheets and all really still belong to Joe. Anybody else who has them just has them, well, sort of on loan, I guess you could say." The dwarf pondered a moment more. "Well, sort of more like a mugging kind of loan."

"Marvelous little chap!" exclaimed the first.

"No lawyer long with pedigree could have put it better," agreed the second.

"Ridiculous!" cried the third.

"No lawyer long with pedigree would have put it that way at all," snorted the fourth.

"Your lawyer long with pedigree would have explicated the situation with much the greater circumlocution and the use of fourteen orders of magnitude more the words," stated the fifth.

"And would have concluded, would your lawyer long with pedigree, that the items in dispute properly belonged with their present owners, what just coincidentally happen to be his meal ticket, and that this Joe fellow was no better than a criminal behind bars what's lost his rights," concluded the sixth.

"Bah!" oathed Zulkeh. "Shelyid's opinion—which is, I will admit, deft in its dialectic though crude in its presentation—is beside the point. Joe doesn't exist, if he ever did, so wherein lies his right to property?"

No doubt this latest addition to the brew would have produced yet a further unending round of disputation, save for the intervention of the witch Magrit, who, crude termagant though she was, did possess—it cannot be denied—a talent for focusing the debate.

"Cut the crap!" she exclaimed. "Nobody but you, old fart, gives a screw about the Ozarine's so-called right to the Rap Sheet. The Senate of Ozar grabbed it by force and has used it ever since to suck the world's blood. And right now the leech is attached to Grotum itself. So we're going to take it for ourselves! You want my help in your problem, you pitch in—if you don't, there's the door! Get lost!" She stopped, breathing hoarsely, glaring at the mage.

Zulkeh hemmed and hawed for a few minutes more, but eventually he agreed as to how certain epistemological unclarities regarding the ownership of the Rap Sheet did, in all conscience, allow him to proceed as a participant in the exercise.

"But you have not yet explained, madame," he

concluded, "why you want this Rap Sheet in the first place."

"That's simple!" replied Magrit. "I want it because it'll improve my foety. Wolfgang wants it stolen because he thinks the whole idea's crazy and so naturally he can't resist. Les Six over there need to get it out of the hands of the Cruds, who are getting a wee bit too close to figuring out their hobby—"

"Which is?" queried the mage.

"The abasement of Ozarine imperialism!" cried the first.

"The overthrow of the decrepit Groutch regimes and all their gangrenous cohorts!" added the second.

"The humbling of the haughty Ecclesiarchs!" hallooed the third.

"Justice for the poor and downtrodden!" came the fourth.

"The reunification of all the divided Groutch lands under the rule of a free people!" exclaimed the fifth.

"A nation once again!" boomed the sixth. This was apparently something in the way of a *sansculottes* toast, for the half dozen incendiaries rose to their feet as one man and slurped their tea noisily.

"Churlism!" cried Zulkeh. "Outright murkery! I will have no part in—"

"Oh, shut up, you old fart!" snarled Magrit. "They aren't churls—not proper ones, anyway, though Joe knows they're on good enough terms with murks all over Grotum. Just a band of happy lads pursuing an innocent enough hobby."

She cut short Zulkeh again. "And you didn't let me finish, windbag! I was just going to add that *you* want to get your hands on the Rap Sheet because it'll, like as not, tell you who your enemies are."

Zulkeh frowned. "I fail to follow your logic, madame. How can this Rap Sheet aid me in my quest? Oh, I admit, 'tis a puissant relic, a Rap Sheet, but still and all one of precise and limited powers. On this all tales and legends agree, that whosoever possesses a Rap Sheet will instantly know all evidence pertaining to felonious and subversive activities which is in the possession of any police agency anywhere within the range of the relic's powers, which range is reputed to be great but not universal. But how does this aid me? Surely, were my enemies known to the authorities, they would already have been apprehended and their identity and crimes made known to me by these selfsame authorities!"

"Is he really that stupid?" demanded the second.

"Like I said," growled Magrit, "he lives upside down. Zulkeh, how have you survived so long in this cold and cruel world? Enemies so powerful as yours are presumably great criminals, who have not yet been apprehended because the authorities are involved in some elaborate scheme to ferret out their grand design."

"Yes, yes," mused Zulkeh, "this is sensible."

"Unfortunately," continued Magrit, "you yourself are likely to be squashed in the course of this scheme's unfolding, should you take no steps of your own, for it is well known that your authorities in today's world care less than a fig about the fate of ordinary citizens."

"I am hardly an ordinary citizen!" protested Zulkeh. "But yes, yes, I see your point. Oft have I noted the parlous state of the contemporary temporal powers."

"And finally," concluded the witch, "do you really think that the authorities have the competence to foil this scheme—whatever it is—hatched by your unknown and potent enemies?"

"Certainly not!" exclaimed the mage.

"Well, then?" The witch peered at Zulkeh intently. "Are you in, or not? And can we proceed without these constant philosophical quibbles?"

Zulkeh considered, then nodded his head. "I am with you, madame."

Magrit now looked at Greyboar and Ignace.

"That leaves you two," she said. "We won't be able to steal the Rap Sheet without your help, for reasons that'll become clear in a minute. However, I'll admit there's no real reason for you to do it."

Greyboar scratched his chin. "Well, we do owe you a job."

"Not one like this!" cried Ignace. "Choke one of your rivals, sure. Throttle a customer what owes you money, sure. But this? Steal a Rap Sheet from the Cruds? Take on the whole damn Imperial Republic of Ozarae? Get mixed up in Joe business?"

"It's a bit much," agreed the witch. "And if you don't want to do it, I'll understand. I'm sure I can find some suitable little chore for you instead."

Greyboar cracked his knuckles. The windows rattled. "But you say you won't be able to steal the Rap Sheet without us?"

Magrit shrugged. "No, probably not. Les Six have already agreed to try to fill in for you, if you don't come in. But—well, they're solid lads, but they're not the world's greatest strangler."

Greyboar gazed at Ignace. "My agent makes all the business decisions," he said mildly.

All eyes turned to Ignace. After a second or so, the little agent looked away. His face grew red, his cheeks puffed out. For a full minute, while silence filled the room, Ignace subjected the various objects cluttered about to a fierce and glowering inspection.

Suddenly, he threw up his hands, exhaling mightily.

"All right! All right! We'll do it!"

For a split second, a strange expression crossed Magrit's face. For just that moment, the horrid harridan seemed—soft?

"Are you sure?" she asked. "I'll say it again, this is a lot more than the favor you owe me."

Ignace glared at her.

"It's got nothing to do with that, and you know it! Even if we didn't owe you a favor, we'd go along."

He now transferred his glare to the strangler.

Greyboar shrugged. "You know what chance she'll have, with the Cruds bringing a Rap Sheet to Grotum. There's never been much I could do for her, except that one time we got her out of the police station."

"And much thanks we got for it, too!" shrilled the agent. His face was now beet red.

Greyboar smiled ruefully. "Gwendolyn's always been hard to please." He looked at Magrit, nodding. "We're in."

"Good. Now let me get to the practicalities of the thing. You'll understand why I needed all of you to get the job done."

Then did the witch Magrit present to the assembled party the outlines of her scheme, the which your narrator will briefly summarize:

The Rap Sheet was kept in a small room, deep in the bowels of the Ozarine Embassy. This Embassy was no modest edifice, but an ancient castle, perched high on a crag overlooking the city of Prygg and its harbor. The sole entrance to the castle was a drawbridge and portcullis, guarded by a large company of soldiery.

Within the castle, the room wherein the Rap Sheet was kept was fiercely protected. Entry to the room required passing through, first, a guard room wherein rested at all times the elite of the Embassy's troops; second, yet another chamber in which dwelt some unknown horror; and finally, the Rap Sheet itself, which relic was guarded by bizarre glyphs and wards, the which could only be dispelled by great magic.

"You now see," concluded Magrit, "why we need all of you together. Greyboar can deal with the soldiers in the guardroom. Zulkeh can handle the magic guarding the Rap Sheet. And all of you together, let's hope, can handle whatever horror it is that dwells in the chamber between. Any questions?"

Greyboar spoke. "I see a couple of problems. First, the soldiers. The ones in the guardroom—what are we talking about here? A half dozen or so?"

Magrit nodded.

"That's a piece of cake. But how about the soldiers at the main gate? Must be a couple of hundred at least, if it's like every other Ozarine Embassy." Greyboar grimaced. "That's a wee much. And what about the drawbridge and the portcullis? Mind you, I've got a way with opening doors"—Ignace grinned—"but a whole drawbridge? I don't know." He flexed his enormous hands, gazed down at them. "I don't know."

"Our job, this," stated the first.

"You'll not be needing to worry about the main entrance," added the second.

"You'll be taking a different route," explained the third.

"Coming up from below," elaborated the fourth.

"Through the artist's tunnels," detailed the fifth.

"Paul Gauphin's tunnels," specified the sixth.

"Gauphin?" exclaimed Zulkeh. "He lives yet? I had thought the man dead!"

"No, he's still alive," said Magrit. "He just travels around so much to so many exotic and far-off lands that everybody always thinks he must have died. Actually, he's been back in Prygg for several years now. Keeps himself exclusively to the tunnels he's dug all over the city. Says it's primitive, inspires him."

"Known throughout Pryggia as the Underground Artist," added the first.

"But how can he help us?" asked Ignace.

The second coughed. "Well, it's a bit delicate, this, but you see Paul's—how I shall I put it?—well—"

"He's a lecher," interrupted the third.

"A profligate," added the fourth.

"A satyr," chipped in the fifth.

"A two-legged goat," concluded the sixth.

"The point is," explained the first, "that the Ozarine Ambassador's wife is a most attractive young lady—"

"As is the wife of the Consul," said the second.

"And the wife of the Chargé d'Affaires," added the third.

"And the wife of—"

"Stow it!" bellowed Magrit. "We don't need another of your laundry lists. The fact is, Zulkeh, that almost every Ozarine official anyone's ever met has a gorgeous teenage wife—barely pubescent, most of 'em—'cause they're all a lot of lechers. Would-be lechers, I should say. Big difference between them and Paul Gauphin is that he can keep it up."

"You should know!" piped up the salamander. A teacup went flying. The evil amphibian darted for a mousehole.

"A wallet!" yelled Magrit. Then, turning back to her audience:

"The point is, that the Underground Artist has dug tunnels into every bedchamber in the castle, *including* that of Rupert Inkman himself, the chief of station."

"Wherein lounges his girlfriend," explained the second.

"No Ozarine lass, but a Pryggian minx." This from the third.

"Fair in form and limb," commented the fourth.

"But foul in mind and spirit," countered the fifth.

"A rotten collaborator," stated the sixth, "providing

comfort if not much aid to the Ozarine oppressor of the Groutch masses."

This last bid fair to start another round of canaille toasts, but Magrit intervened.

"Can we keep to the subject?" she demanded. "Anyway, that's how you'll get in—Paul'll lead you through his tunnels right into Inkman's bedroom, which abuts directly to the guardroom."

Greyboar coughed. "Still a bit of a problem here, Magrit. The girl's likely to be there, along with this Inkman fellow. We are doing the job at night, I assume?" Magrit nodded. "Well, then, they'll both be there. And while I certainly don't mind throttling a Crud, the girl—" He fell silent, then spoke again, in a stony voice. "I don't choke girls."

"It's true," confirmed Ignace. "It's a sticking point with him. A lot of business it's cost us, too," he groused.

"Who said anything about choking girls?" asked Magrit. "Or Rupert Inkman, for that matter. They'll both be gone. We're doing the job tomorrow tonight—during the wedding reception for the Princess Snuffy and the Honorable Anthwerp Freckenrizzle III."

"Scion of Ozar's fifth-wealthiest plutocrat!" exclaimed the first.

"Soon to be married to the youngest daughter of the King of Pryggia!" cried the second.

"It's the social event of the season!" proclaimed the third.

"Precisely," said Magrit. "Relax, Greyboar. I've timed this escapade so that just about everybody in the Embassy's going to be stinking drunk in the ballroom, all the way across the castle from where you're doing your business. Satisfied?"

"But will this Gauphin fellow agree to help us?" asked Ignace. "I mean, I don't see why he should. It's a bit risky for him, and I don't see where he gets anything out of it."

"Nonsense!" stated the fourth. "He'll gain the respect and admiration of the toiling poor of Pryggia, who'll certainly pass word of his deed through every hovel and garret of the city."

"Though, 'tis true, this respect and admiration won't translate into purchases of his paintings," commented the fifth.

"Which are priced beyond the reach of the common folk," elaborated the sixth.

"But whose displeasure, should he fail in his patriotic duty, will certainly be felt in the galleries and salons where his paintings are bought by the stinking rich," developed the first.

"The which salons and galleries will, every one of 'em, be picketed by the irate plebeian citizenry," predicted the second.

"Not to mention torched to the ground," foresaw the third.

"Gauphin's effigy burned in the public square," presaged the fourth.

"His name cursed by the masses," divined the fifth.

"Himself hunted like a dog through the—"

"Enough!" bellowed Magrit. "You've made the point. He'll help us. Now—any other questions? If not, let's—"

"A moment, madame," spoke Zulkeh. "I find myself distressed by an aspect of your plan."

"What's that?"

The wizard frowned. "As I understand it, the individuals now present who will actually participate in this enterprise consist solely of myself, my apprentice, Sirrah Greyboar and his agent. Am I correct?"

"Right on the mark," agreed Magrit.

Darker still grew the mage's frown. "Yet meseemeth

that the individuals who stand most to gain from our adventure consist of yourself and these—these half-dozen disreputes here. At least, in a proximate sense."

"Right again," said Magrit.

Black as night was the sorcerer's frown. "'Tis most unseemly, madame!—most unjust! Those who gain the most should not eschew the peril! Nay, fie on such witless notions! Did not the supreme philosophe Aristotle Sfondr—"

"Oh, shut up, you old fart!" roared Magrit. "I didn't say that we wouldn't be playing a role! We just won't be along on your part of the escapade. The four of you will need a diversion. Sure, and there'll be a wedding reception going on, and the booze'll be flowing like a river, but the Ozarine didn't get where it is by having stupid and careless officials. We've got to make sure that the attention of every single Ozarine and Pryggian muckymuck—not to mention their goons!—is riveted to the reception floor."

"We're going to crash the party!" hallooed Les Six in unison.

"I beg your pardon?" queried Zulkeh.

"You heard 'em," said Magrit, grinning widely. "Me and Les Six—and Wittgenstein, he's going to be the star of the show!—are going to attend the reception, representing, so to speak, the little people."

"Who've been most rudely excluded from the event," complained the sixth.

"For fear their gaucheries will disturb the tranquility of high society," explained the first.

"A fear well-founded!" cried the second.

"Indeed so!" agreed the third. "A most boorish lot, your unwashed toilers!"

"Not up on the finer points of etiquette, sad to say," contributed the fourth.

"Certain, in their crude ignorance, to behave improperly," elaborated the fifth.

"Here's to bad manners!" roared the sixth. This was apparently something in the way of a lowborn toast, for the six dregs of the earth raised their teacups in unison, pinkies politely extended like so many small cannons, and slurped noisily.

"I see," mused Zulkeh. His brow cleared. "A cunning stratagem, madame! For if there exist any on the face of the earth most suited to the task of turning a royal wedding reception into a shambles—a public scandal!—it is yourself and this canaille."

Magrit and Les Six nodded in acknowledgement of what was, actually, not a compliment. Then did Zulkeh's brow unclear, resuming its former furrowed darkness.

"And what of Sirrah Wolfgang, here? What is to be his part in the episode?" demanded the mage.

"Well, actually," responded Wolfgang, "I'm not playing any part in the affair—directly, that is to say."

"Then why are you here?" The wizard appeared most aggrieved.

"Well, to begin with, I'm the one who found out about the Rap Sheet. Just got here yesterday with the news. But that's a small thing. What's more important is the key role I play now." Here the giant exuded a vast smugness. "I'm the consultant, you see."

"I beg your pardon?"

"The consultant—the expert adviser." Then, seeing no comprehension on the wizard's face, the lunatic elaborated.

"You need expert advice on something like this, man! I mean, the whole idea's crazy—stealing a Rap Sheet from under the noses of the Cruds under cover of bashing a gala event! Who but a madwoman would come up with such a scheme? Who but madmen would agree to participate? And who then better to serve as your expert consultant," he concluded with pride, "than a demented bedlamite escaped from an insane asylum. At your service!"

Here Wolfgang rose and took a bow, then said: "And let me say—speaking from a lifetime of applying my twin powers of madness and amnesia—that in my capacity as expert consultant I approve wholeheartedly of the plan. It's crackbrained! Nutty as a walnut grove! Deranged beyond belief!"

He resumed his seat. "So it's bound to come off swimmingly."

The wizard did not seem entirely satisfied with this explanation. Indeed, to put it more accurately, Wolfgang's words appeared to reopen in his mind the entire question of participating in the exploit. But the witch Magrit was, as the gentle reader has perhaps already deduced, a fearsome bully, and she soon quelled the mage's incipient revolt. Then did she command the various persons present to retire for rest and refreshment, for the adventure ahead promised great exertions for all concerned.

The assembly dispersed, all going their separate ways. Yet, strangely enough, the lunatic Wolfgang arrested the dwarf as Shelyid was going out the door.

"A moment of your time, little one," said the giant.

Shelyid frowned, glanced at the back of his master, even now receding down the stairs.

"Oh, but, sir," apologized the gnome, "I can't talk now—I have to go get the master's sack from downstairs where we left it and—"

"Bother the sack!" interrupted the lunatic. "You'll have time enough. I just wanted to ask you—have you ever been on an adventure before?"

"Oh no, sir!" exclaimed Shelyid. "I'm just a dwarf, a miserable dwarf. I've never—" Shelyid paused, gulped. "Well, actually I'm real scared, although not

as scared as I would have been a few weeks ago,
maybe, but still—" He paused, gulped again, then said
softly: "I just hope I don't let everybody else down."

"You'll do fine!" boomed Wolfgang. "Why, you've the
makings of a daredevil, you do!"

"You think so?" asked Shelyid, not with any great
conviction. "Uh, sir."

"Don't call me 'sir'—absurd, calling a certified psychotic a 'sir'! And yes, I know you'll take to adven-
turing like a fish to water. Just remember the two
mottoes of all great crazy heroes."

"What're they?"

Wolfgang held up two fingers.

"One: Don't get even, go mad. Two: When the going
gets tough, the tough go nuts."

"I'll try to remember. But I have to go!" And so
saying, the dwarf scurried away.

PART XVI

In Which We
Return Once Again to
the *Autobiography* of the
Scoundrel Sfrondrati-Piccolomini,
this Portion of Whose Story Consists,
Yet Again, of a Crude and Unscrupulous Attempt
to Win the Favor of the Reader, by Means
of Mawkish Romance and Melodrama,
Thereby Confirming—Yet Again!—
His Unscrupulous Character
and Nature.

The Autobiography of Benvenuti Sfondrati-Piccolomini,
Episode 8: Horses, Hurts, Heroes and Halloween

So it was in such a strained silence that Gwendolyn and I began our journey to the General's estate. Two days, the trip would require, or so I had been told. Longer, I suspected, judging from the quality of the nags we were riding.

The expression on Gwendolyn's face was forbidding

and withdrawn. At first, I thought it was hostility directed toward me. Then, I thought it was hostility toward The Roach. Eventually—such is human stupidity—I realized that it was not hostility at all, but a deep grief kept under fierce control.

My own hurt and anger vanished.

"I've been such a petty fool!" I exclaimed. Gwendolyn looked at me, puzzled. I reined in my horse.

"What's this about?" she asked, pulling up her own mount.

"I'm sorry; I've been—preoccupied with my own problems. You don't expect you'll ever see him again, do you?"

She stared at me for a moment, her face pale. "No," she said quietly. "He'll die in Blain. Or Prygg, more likely."

She started her horse moving again. She said nothing for a long time. Just stared straight ahead, a trickle of tears wending down her cheeks.

"You can't be sure of that," I said eventually. "He seems a singularly capable fellow."

She shook her head. "You don't understand, Benvenuti. With a Rap Sheet in their hands, and the Cruds to organize them, every police agency in Grotum—and there's more of them than you can count—will be able to coordinate their efforts perfectly. The Roach's name will be at the top of their list. And he won't be that hard to find, anyway. Where the enemy's blows are hardest, that's always where you'll find The Roach. It's part of the tradition, you know."

My face must have shown my puzzlement.

"What's this?" she demanded. A faint smile came on her face. "Do you mean to tell me that the legend of The Roach isn't told to all Ozarine children, along with all the other legends?"

I shook my head.

"Not surprising. I don't actually believe the legend myself. I don't even know if The Roach does. Whenever I ask, he just smiles and changes the subject."

"What is the legend?"

"Well, it goes like this. Supposedly, way back at the beginning of time, when Joe invented everything, he had one friend—his best friend Sam—who tried to talk him out of it. Tried to tell Joe he was afraid these new inventions wouldn't work out all that well in the end. Joe wouldn't listen to him, saying he didn't see where he had any choice. But after his friend kept pestering him, Joe finally threw up his hands and invented The Boots. He gave them to his friend and said: 'All right, dammit, if my inventions don't work right, you can use these to kick 'em out.' Then, after the inventions went bad, and Joe was frozen up, his friend took it on the lam and he's been kicking ass ever since."

"But that's impossible!" I cried. "The man can't be more than fifty years old."

Gwendolyn grinned. "Well, the legend has it that the original Roach finally realized it was going to take an awful long time to properly stamp out the inventions. So he founded a line—a family line, he said, with a proper pedigree—to give the lowlifes something to match up against the pedigrees of the high and mighty. Every generation since, as far back as you can go in the history of Grotum, there's always been a Roach. It can be anybody, as long as they're a bastard and they can wear The Boots. It was the first Roach who chose the name. He said that since the high and mighty went around naming themselves after predators—eagles, lions, bears, and such—that his line would be named after the most persistent and indestructible animal known to man."

I laughed.

"Isn't it perfect?" said Gwendolyn, chuckling. "When I first heard the name, as a teenager, I was just mortified. The revolution was such a shiny thing to me then, like a crystal vase, and the name seemed so—so undignified. But then I met The Roach himself, and I understood."

She fought back tears. " 'Dignity's not to be found in the word, lass' he said to me. 'Look for it in the deed. Let the enemy have their eagle standards and their roaring lions, and their scepters and their thrones. Eagles and lions are endangered species, anyway. Much rather be a roach. Every time they think they've exterminated us, they come back into the kitchen and—there we are! And boots are a much more useful heirloom than crowns.'

"Anyway, that's the legend. Like I said, I don't actually believe it. I don't believe any of this Joe stuff. But it's a comfort, sometimes, and when I'm around The Roach I almost do believe it. Although—"

I looked over, noticing the sudden pause. To my surprise, Gwendolyn was—blushing, I would have sworn, hard as that was to imagine.

"Although what?"

She shook her head. "Nothing."

My curiosity was aroused. "Tell me!"

She looked at me, smiling oddly. "All right, if you insist. One of the legends is that once The Roach—each new one, that is—puts on The Boots, they never take them off again until they die. Not even in bed." She looked straight ahead. "I happen to know that isn't true."

I started laughing uproariously. "Good God, I should hope it isn't true! Those monstrous hobnailed things? You'd be scarred for life!"

When we both stopped laughing, we were grinning at each other.

"I'm sorry about last night," she said. "I hadn't expected to meet The Roach in the Mutt. Then, when he showed up—well, anyway, I'm sorry."

"There's no need."

"No, I am. That must have caused you pain."

I shrugged. "Yes, it did. But I'm actually not all that fragile. And, in any event, it wasn't—how shall I put this? It wasn't the fact itself, it was that it seemed so—"

"Unfeeling."

"Yes, I suppose." I fumbled for words. "Gwendolyn, I had no right—that is, I had no claim or reason, or—"

"Of course you didn't. But that's all beside the point. This isn't about rights or claims or reasons. People are not property. But they're still people, and pain hurts. And I hurt you, and I don't feel good about it."

I sighed. "Thank you. But now that I understand the situation, I'm—well, I'm not sure what else you could have done."

"That's just what I told that insufferable self-righteous bastard this morning!" she cried. "Would you believe, that pig-headed puritan accused me of using him to put you off?"

I looked uncomfortable. Gwendolyn spotted it right away.

"That's what he was talking to you about in the courtyard, wasn't it?" she demanded.

"Well—"

"That slob! That peacock! It's just like him!"

"It wasn't actually—"

"That puffed up baboon! I can just see it! The gentleman, His Roachness, informing the other gentleman that he'll have no part of the scheming wench's slatternly maneuvers. And you! Probably sat there, nodding sagely—"

"Will you let me get a word in?"

She took a deep breath, let it out slowly, and nodded.

"All right. Tell me what he said."

As we resumed our journey, I conveyed to her the substance of The Roach's conversation. Actually, upon Gwendolyn's insistence, I gave it to her word for word, as best as I remembered.

When I was done, she shook her head.

"He's flat wrong," she said forcefully. "Benvenuti, if I—when I—whatever, the day comes I don't want you around I'll let you know. Directly, mind, not through some scheme."

"And?"

"And what?"

"Confounded woman! Do you want me around?"

"I—yes, I suppose. Yes." She sighed. "When you left the table last night, I felt a great sadness. Well, that's that, I said to myself."

A strange sound. I looked over, saw that Gwendolyn was trying to suppress laughter.

"What's so funny?"

She started laughing aloud. A rich, deep laugh, she had, which warmed my heart even though—I admit—I was a bit irritated.

"Oh, you were such the proper gentleman about it all! The stiff lip, the straight back. God, what an upbringing you must have had!"

Her laughter was so infectious that I could not help joining in. "My uncles have firm opinions on this matter, which they instilled in me at an early age. 'You can't get through life without playing the fool now and then,' they say, 'but that's no reason to audition for the part.'"

We started our horses up again and rode along in a companionable silence.

"You never speak of your father and mother," she said, some time later.

"My father is not known. My mother never disclosed his identity, and she died in childbirth. So I was raised by her brothers. The bar sinister figures frequently and prominently in my family tree—my branch of the clan, that is, the most of the Sfondrati-Piccolominis are quite the proper sorts—so no issue was made of it."

More silence followed, until I screwed up my courage. I reined in my horse again. Gwendolyn stopped.

"I need to say something, Gwendolyn. I—that is, much of what The Roach said was true. We live in different worlds, and—well—"

"You find it hard to see either of us in each other's life?"

I sighed. "Yes. I cannot imagine you in the whirl of the artist's life in the great cities—the salons and the galleries. Though, it would be fun while it lasted! Half the lords and ladies of the land would die of mortification, the ones you didn't kill outright. And while I could see myself in your world, in some ways—as I told you, I am not much given to political thoughts. My sympathies, insofar as I have ever considered the question, lie with you, I suspect. But still—"

I heaved another sigh. "The Roach was right, damn him. I do want to be an artist, just as he said. I do want to sculpt the statues and paint the cathedral ceilings—not because they're cathedrals, but because they're the world's greatest ceilings."

Gwendolyn leaned over and stroked my cheek.

"And you should, Benvenuti," she said quietly. "You will never be happy if you don't at least try it. I know that."

"But—the fact remains. I love you, Gwendolyn."

She looked away. "I love you too, Benvenuti. I've known that for some time. I don't really understand it, actually. Not that you aren't a very attractive man, and all that. But I never would have thought—me! Of all people!"

Her sense of humor rescued us.

"This is so grotesque! It's like a bad novel—one of those Ozarine fantasies I hate! The star-crossed lovers, doomed by fate! It's ridiculous."

Laughing, we resumed our journey. In the few hours of daylight left, I asked Gwendolyn to tell me more about The Roach. Partly, that was done out of my own interest in the man. But more, it was because I knew she needed to grieve. And so she began to talk, and as the time wore on her tales grew lighter and more gay. My initial impression of the man—of a great, quiet dignity—faded somewhat. True enough, in itself, it seemed. But there was also the immense irritability of the man, his famous temper, his rough sense of humor, his pigheadedness.

Of them, she and he, I learned of a long and deep friendship, years in the making.

"The first time I met him, I was much too shy to say anything. The Roach himself! The second time, I was a year older—seventeen, I was—and I threw myself at him." She laughed. "He was always such an righteous lot. 'Lass, I am much older than you', he said, 'and I'll not be taking advantage of youthful infatuation.' And why not? I demanded. The infatuated youth is willing. Well, I was just as stubborn as he. It took me another year, but I finally brought him to my bed. And there he's been ever since, off and on."

She said no more. Shortly after nightfall, we pulled into a roadside inn to spend the night. I saw to the horses, while Gwendolyn made our arrangements. I entered in time to hear her say to the innkeeper, very firmly: "We'll just need the one room."

Once upstairs, in the room, we gazed into each other's eyes, acknowledging the grief in the future. Of the rest, I will say nothing. It belongs to me alone.

The next morning, awakening before Gwendolyn, I spent some time gazing upon her recumbent form. At first, with an artist's eye. *The Lioness Asleep*, I thought I would call it. Oil on canvas. The artist fled, replaced by the man. She awoke, then.

Much later, Gwendolyn gazed up at me, a quizzical look in her eyes.

"You've got a funny expression on your face. Cheerful, like."

"And why shouldn't I be cheerful?" I demanded. "I don't know why I was so stupid about this yesterday."

"About what?"

"All this silly moaning about star-crossed lovers and such—you know, fate takes us down different trails, we shall never meet again, etc."

She frowned. "And what have you figured out that's supposed to change all that? It's still true."

I stopped smiling. "No, Gwendolyn, it's not. I don't know your precise place in the Groutch revolutionary movement. But even someone as ignorant of political matters as I can figure out that you occupy a prominent position in the movement."

"Yes, I suppose. What's your point?"

"I should think it would be obvious. In all our talk yesterday about The Roach's poor prospects for a long life, you made no mention of your own likely fate. But it seems clear to me that the Ozarine and their Groutch accomplices will be coming after you as well. Near the top of their list, you must be."

She frowned. "Yes, that's true." She pursed her lips in thought. "The Roach first, of course. After that— well, Les Six and Les Cinq and Les Sept. The

Mysterious Q, naturally. Then—well, probably me. Among others."

"So that's that!" I said, grinning. "Our personal problems are solved by circumstances."

She sat up straight, her back stiff.

"What the hell are you talking about?"

"My love, surely you don't think I'm going to head off to be an artist in New Sfinctr while you're running for your life?"

"And just what do you propose to do instead? You don't know anything about the work of the revolution! That's not a criticism, it's just a fact." She stared at me a moment. The expression which then came upon her face captured the poet's meaning—*wild surmise*.

"I don't believe this—you idiot! You romantic dunce! You're going to stick with me just so you can go down swinging at the end? Defending the fair and helpless maiden from the ravening forces of reaction?"

"Nonsense! You're neither fair nor helpless nor, for that matter, a maiden." I cleared my throat. "Other than that, well, yes. That is what I propose to do."

"I won't have it! It's a waste! And what's the point of it?"

"The point of it, Gwendolyn, is that it's the way I am. There's no point in arguing about it. I'm not going to change my mind, and you've got better things to do than to worry about how to get rid of me." I grinned. "Look on the bright side. I can make your last days on earth more enjoyable."

She snorted. "That's true enough." Then, grinning herself. "Even though I won't get much sleep."

She lay back on the bed, shaking her head. "What a world, with such mad artists in it. I suppose my worthless brother'll come charging to my rescue next. Make perfect sense—tonight's Halloween."

◆◆   ◆◆   ◆◆

Later that morning, as we rode toward the estates of General Kutumoff, Gwendolyn laughed. "Just like a bad novel—the romantic adventures of an Ozarine hero, gallivanting about the Groutch countryside."

"True," I said. "But I doubt any proper adventurer ever rode on such a sorry nag."

PART XVII

In Which, It Is
Our Sad Duty to Relate,
Our Heroes Commit the Most
Heinous and Horrific Crimes, Thereby
Forfeiting For All Time the Title of "Heroes,"
a Name Which We Shall Therefore
Never Use Again Associated
With Their Now Hopelessly
Blackened Names

—◦◦◦—

CHAPTER XXI. *A Cunning Diversion.
Chaos and Confusion. "Blood, Booze and
Bamboozlement." Divers Family Tragedies
Recounted. A Wedding Cake of Misfortune.
An Escape Foiled. A Capture Foiled!*

And so it was the very next night that our heroes set
forth to purloin the Rap Sheet. Before proceeding with

our narration of the theft itself, however, 'tis necessary
to summarize the events which transpired simultaneously in the Embassy ballroom. As I—the Alfred
of record—was located on the person of the dwarf
Shelyid, himself located in distant portions of the castle,
the tale of the wedding party's disruption was pieced
together from the rudimentary accounts of several of
my apprentices. These latter had I dispatched onto the
persons of Les Six, from which vantage points they
observed the proceedings and took such notes as their
student skills permitted.

The affair began, as Wolfgang had predicted, swimmingly. The motley party gained entrance into the
Embassy by posing as a maid and six servitors. 'Tis
beyond comprehension how this ridiculous subterfuge
succeeded, but no doubt Magrit's large mop and pail
of some substance which she claimed to be soap was
of assistance in lulling the suspicions of the normally
alert guards, ushers and majordomos. As for Les Six,
'twas perhaps the very absurdity of their presence
which gave them their *bonafides*, for who but lowly
servitors could such slovenly proletarians possibly be?

In any event, ere long they made their way onto
the ballroom floor, even as a lively gavotte was in
progress. The seeds of confusion were quickly sown.
Magrit announced loudly that she was here to clean
the floor, and set about that task with great vigor,
upsetting at once four pairs of dancers with great
swipes of her mop. Then, as the substance which she
had proclaimed to be soap spread its oily way across
vast stretches of the ballroom surface, aided in this
progress by the selfsame swipes of this selfsame mop,
not to mention the profligacy with which she used the
substance itself, it soon became clear that the soap was
not soap at all but rather some foul product of the
witch's alchemy, the which was not only malodorous

in the extreme but possessed of the properties of a most efficacious lubricant. Then, as fierce argument erupted between her fishwife self and the irate majordomo come to put a stop to this unseemly swabbing in the midst of revelry, she managed, in the vehemence of her gesticulations, to upend the entire contents of the very large pail. The noxious fluid flooded the dance floor.

Now did a multitude of couples join the initial four, sprawled on the floor, writhing about, howling at the stench, falling again and again as they tried to rise, one stalwart captain of the marines even—sad to relate—stabbing himself in the thigh with his sword, the which he foolishly attempted to use as a crutch; another dashing leftenant of the cavalry—sadder to relate—stabbing his comely partner in her thigh with the sword he had earlier drawn in a demonstration of the saber dance for which the hussars of Pryggia are justly famous; and—saddest of all to relate—yet another gallant officer, this a portly colonel of the artillery, disemboweling himself in his fall upon the sword let fall by his immediate superior, the yet more portly general of the artillery, the which august warrior had held this weapon high, just prior to his unfortunate encounter with the witch Magrit's pseudo-soap, in a glorious gesture of praise for the happy couple in whose honor the festivities were taking place.

The initial bloodletting was but prologue to massacre. For Les Six now heaped chaos onto confusion, charging about with rhinocerine ill grace, attempting to aid divers aristocrats in distress, only, through their oafish clumsiness, to drop half-risen barons onto prone magnates; to elbow still-standing matrons onto prostrate dames in their servile eagerness to aid crawling countesses to their feet, which latter subjects of their assistance invariably suffered mangled fingers, broken toes and bruised jaws in the process of rescue; to slip and fall themselves, time and time again, invariably in such a manner as to flatten what few shaky knots of notables had managed to rise ensemble to their feet, like wheat trampled by oxen.

Then—tragedy piled onto fiasco! A squad of soldiery summoned by officials charged onto the scene, halberds held ready to deal with disruption. Alas, no sooner did this energetic band of warriors charge onto the floor than their feet went flying out from under them. Reacting with natural instinct, the soldiers let go their halberds, which fearsome weapons went sailing into the large knot of eminent strugglers-to-their-feet in the very center of the ballroom floor.

Many were the great inheritances come into that moment. Though even here disorder reigned, as exemplified by the fate of the oldest son of the Ozarean shipping magnate, who, even as he watched his father expire before him, run through by a halberd, had the delighted expression on his face as he contemplated his sudden fortune removed by yet another halberd, the which removed his head altogether, plopping it fortuitously into the hands of his brother, the next oldest son, who in turn soon lost his grin at his own unexpected turn of fortune when, cavorting about his father's corpse and holding the severed head of his brother high, he slipped and fell bellyfirst onto the upended blade of yet a third halberd stuck to the floor, providing another nuance to the old saw: "Easy come, easy go."

The first phase of their plot a smashing success, Magrit and her accomplices immediately set about the implementation of the next. Now posing as a nurse and her assistants, the seven took advantage of the total confusion to guide a full score of dazed and bleeding notables into a portion of the dance floor which had been set aside for the use of the servants, and for that reason segregated from the ballroom proper by a large curtain. There did Magrit, in the tone of voice of the experienced nurse, a tone, as all know, which brooks no dispute, order the sexes separated by yet another curtain, quickly drawn by Les Six, following which she ordered all clothing removed that she might inspect the injuries of the eminent wounded. No sooner said than done, she collecting the clothing of the females, the first through the third of Les Six, that of the males in the adjoining alcove. The clothing now collected, the fourth through the six of Les Six slashed the ropes suspending the divers curtains, thereby exposing the naked bodies of a full score of the most prominent personages of Ozar and Prygg to the ogling stares of their brethren on the main floor of the ballroom.

Great was the consternation which ensued, I speak not simply of the shrieks of outrage, the cries of embarrassment, nor even the peals of glee and laughter which, sad to relate, were heard to issue from the lips of the younger nobility gazing upon the scene. Nay, I speak of positive tragedy! For the Duchess de Trops died on the spot from terminal shame, only to be followed a moment later by her husband, his weak heart overcome by the sight of his naked-but-dead shrew of a wife and his naked-but-alive sister, the Madame Copieux, for whose voluptuous body he had long harbored incestuous passion, only to be followed into death by his sister herself, who promptly committed suicide with a carving knife due to her own distress at being denied the now-at-last-available body of that very same brother for whose stallion-like attentions she had long kept as her secret the identical unnatural lust.

Nor was this the end of the familial catastrophe!

For Madame Copieux's own husband, owner of Ozar's most profitable ironworks, no sooner beheld the corpse of his beautiful wife than he howled his glee at being rid of the adulterous slattern and proceeded to celebrate by guzzling such quantities of potent Pryggian whiskey as to cause him, within the hour, to expire from alcohol poisoning, thus leaving to his son the entire family fortune, the which largess the lad was unable to long enjoy for he himself expired within the next hour, overcome by the same excessive consumption of alcohol due to great joy at great fortune, thus further illustrating the old adage: "Like father, like son."

Nor was this yet the finale of the saga! For the Mademoiselle Copieux, who, in her capacity as daughter and sister was now the sole surviving member of the family, was so overcome by the contradictory emotions of joy at her newfound fortune and grief at the death of all three of her lovers—mother, father and brother, at one stroke!—that she soon went mad and spent the rest of her short unhappy life in such a feverish frenzy of sexual excess as to illustrate anew the old saying: "Keep it in the family."

Stage Two of the plan a roaring triumph, Magrit and Les Six did not rest on their laurels but proceeded at once to Stage Three. Garbed in the stolen clothing of now-naked notables, the witch and her cohorts infiltrated the mob of hysterical ex-revelers and proceeded to spike the huge bowls of refreshment which stood about in profusion with an alcoholic substance whose potency derived, in equal portion, from the theoretical alchemy of the witch and the practical bathtub distilling of Les Six.

The groundwork laid, the scoundrelous septet proceeded to encourage the distraught multitude to drown their sorrows and restore their gaiety with drink, Magrit utilizing for this purpose the soothing tones of the matriarch long experienced in handling misfortune, Les Six the more vigorous methods of vainglorious and successful bigwigs challenging the manhood of similar egoists. And cunning was the ploy! For Les Six, exhibiting a subtlety not looked for in such lowlifes, had divided themselves in the style of their garments, three posing as Pryggian aristocrats, three as Ozarine nabobs. Thus did the first through the third utter coarse comments on the effete incapacity of Ozarine financiers to handle manly drink as compared to the stalwart sons of Pryggian soil. Thus, for their part, did the fourth through the sixth burn into the brains of the selfsame Pryggian noblemen the nasal sneers of Ozarine captains of industry regarding the inability of rustic yokels to handle more than eight stiff drinks without rolling in the mud like the pigs who were not only the sole source of Pryggian wealth— such as it was!—but, judging from appearances, the models from which God in His Heaven had, for reasons of His own, formed the physiognomy of the Pryggian subspecies.

Thus, onto chaos and confusion, was drunkenness laid. And more! For Les Six not only inveigled the assembled gentlemen of Pryggia and Ozar into a turbulent drinking contest, but then, drunkenness rampant, proceeded to embellish their respective insults with such rococo flourishes, such baroque ornamentation, as to produce in but two minutes such a brawl as would shame the lowest alehouses of the scurviest ports in the world. Swords were drawn—and used! Knives, daggers, poignards—not to mention cudgels and clubs of every shape and description!

Chaos supreme! The soldiery overwhelmed—even themselves drawn into the fray—for Les Six had not failed to cast the necessary and necessarily cross-purposed insults on the respective merits of Ozarine Embassy guards versus Pryggian praetorians!

Blood, booze and bamboozlement! For years to come, these were the three words always spoken together, the world over, whenever was told the tale of the Pryggian social event of the season, Year of the Jackal.

But wait! A small knot of sanity remained! The eye of the storm! For there, at the very center of the ballroom, upon the dais, next to the huge wedding cake, stood the Princess Snuffy and her swain, the Honorable Anthwerp Freckenrizzle III. The newlyweds clutched each other, aghast at the shambles, the Ozarine heir's face pale as a ghost, the eyes of the Pryggian princess pouring tears.

"Oh, Anthwy!" the Princess wailed. "Our wedding's ruined!"

Freckenrizzle III comforted his bride. "There now, Snuffy, there now! Let's forget all this—we still have each other, after all. I'll tell you what—let's cut the cake."

And so saying, the scion of Ozar's fifth-richest family drew his ceremonial sword—not too deftly, truth to tell, for the pear-shaped heir's talents and experience lay rather in counting money than the more vigorous of the upper-crust skills—and made to slice the cake.

"You can have the first piece!" he said. The Princess clasped her pudgy hands. "Oh, Anthwy, you're so sweet!"

Alas, 'twas at that very moment that the full dimensions of Magrit's scheme were revealed. Stage Four—voila!

No sooner did the sword touch the cake than the cake collapsed, like a house riddled with termites. The cause? Obvious at a glance! For there, in the very center of the confectionary rubble, his green belly swollen like a pumpkin, squatted the salamander.

"Great cake," it burped. "Try some—I saved you a little."

The Princess shrieked. Freckenrizzle dropped the sword.

Then, eyeing the—actually, quite dumpy—figure of the Princess, the salamander was heard to exclaim: "What a babe!"

This gross remark made, the horrid beast sprang onto the shoulder of the Princess, wrapped itself around her neck, and began uttering foul and lecherous phrases, of which "Dump this chump and let's party!" was only the least obscene.

Now squealing like a pig, Princess Snuffy began capering and leaping about, attempting to dislodge the perverse amphibian, who, for its part, clung the more tightly to her neck, its slimy snout buried in her ear, continuing to speak unspeakable words, of which "Once you've had salamander, you'll never go back" was only the least sordid.

Undignified though the figure of the Princess was, writhing and reeling in a manner which belied her sedentary form, 'twas only this unregal behavior which saved her life. For her spouse, whose wealth was now revealed to be the product of good luck rather than good sense, proceeded to retrieve his sword and hack wildly at the salamander. As the amphibian was still coiled about his bride's neck, 'twas only the clumsiness of the Ozarine heir which made possible the heirs of the future. As it was, he managed to shave his wife's head clean of the long blond hair which was, truth to tell, her only attractive feature. He also inflicted numerous but thankfully minor flesh wounds upon divers portions of her anatomy, most of which, so I am told, left few visible scars to remind her, in later life, of the unpleasantness which attended her wedding.

Alas, the scars on her royal soul did not fade as well. For it was noted, in the years to come, that the Freckenrizzles were not a happy couple. To her dying day, Madame Freckenrizzle, née the Princess Snuffy, persisted on keeping her scalp shaved as bald as an egg, this peculiar habit being, or so it was supposed, a reproach to her husband. For his part, the Honorable Anthwerp Freckenrizzle III became obsessed with the hunting and trapping of all manner of reptiles and amphibians. By middle age, he was eccentric. He wore nothing but snakeskin clothing and lizardskin boots, refused to sit on any item of furniture not upholstered by salamander pelts, ate nothing but turtle soup and frog legs. By old age he was a certifiable paranoid. On one famous occasion, he burned down his mansion, claiming it was infested with toads in the woodwork. He ended his life a suicide, leaping one day into the crocodile pen at the Ozarian Zoo and attacking the prehistoric monsters therein with naught but a sword, in the use of which, all witnesses agreed, he had gained not a whit more skill than he possessed as a newlywed.

For her part, his wife matched his increasing obsession with a similar one of her own. She became the world's foremost amateur herpetologist, the benefactress of countless Reptile Houses and Frog Farms. Following her spouse's arson of their mansion, she moved onto her own estate, from which her estranged husband was barred. There she built a bizarre palace, shaped like a frog. The well-tended gardens were transformed into a fetid swamp, into which she imported amphibians from all corners of the world. She also died a suicide, leaping into the pond at the center of her swamp and attempting to swim about like a tadpole with the aid of a canvas tail encasing her legs, the which soon became water-logged and dragged her to her doom.

But these sad stories belong to the distant future. For the present, their purpose accomplished, the perpetrators of the dastardly deeds recounted above now sought to make their escape. For the salamander, the task proved simple. It soon enough leapt from the neck of the Princess and slithered its way to safety, although, it would later claim, the flight to freedom was made difficult by its bloated, cake-filled belly, the which interfered with the normally sinuous movement of its legs.

'Twas otherwise, however, for Magrit and Les Six. At first their flight from justice seemed assured, for they insinuated themselves, still in their finery, into the horde of notables seeking to flee from the Embassy. And so great was the confusion, that they quickly made their way toward the huge double doors which led from the ballroom into the foyer beyond, and thence to freedom.

But at that very moment, cutting through the din of the maddened crowd, came a voice like unto the demi-divine heroes of yore, piercing, sharp as an ax-blade— at last, the voice of command and authority!

"Guards! Shut the doors!" The guards, ere then confused and witless, sprang to the command. The great double doors slammed shut. The exit was barred to Magrit and her accomplices! Then, the voice spoke again:

"Everyone in the room will be still and silent, on pain of investigation!"

Everyone in the room became still and silent, like dogs brought to heel.

"Damn!" swore Magrit under her breath. "It's Inkman."

Sure enough—'twas Rupert Inkman, Groutch chief of station of the famed and feared Commission to Repel Unbridled Disruption! There he stood, in the center of the ballroom floor, tall, gaunt as a skeleton, garbed all in black. His very posture bespoke one born to command. His icy blue eyes flashed with the look of eagles—keen intelligence combined with deep insight, these qualities in turn but a patina over the loftier aspects of his gaze, I speak, of course, of predation and bloodlust.

"Oh, Mr. Inkman," a majordomo was heard to utter, "thank God you're here to put a stop to this madness!"

"Arrant fool!" came the reply, like a spear to the heart. "There is no madness here! Nay, rather there is dark duplicity—*unbridled disruption*, plotted aforehand and carried through with cunning skill! And in Prygg, there is but one hand—I should say, one mind and six pair of hands—capable of the deed! Yes, yes! They are here! Even now, in this very room! I smell them, like the wolf smells his prey!"

"Who, sir, who?" came the confused cry from several throats.

"The chief enemies of the State in Prygg, you fools! Yes, yes! They are here! At last, I have them!"

"*Who, sir, who?*" came the cry again, this time from many throats, and the tone no longer confused but filled with rising fury.

"SHOW THEM TO US, SIR!" came the roar from a multitude of throats, officers drawing their swords, magnates their bared pens, matrons holding broken lorgnettes like brawlers holding broken bottles.

The situation seemed grim for Magrit and Les Six—then grimmer still! For now Inkman espied them, even through their disguise, like the hawk espies the hares in the brambles.

"There! There!" he cried. He stretched forth his arm, his bony finger about to pinpoint the exact location of the witch and her accomplices. Only a second remained before they would be swarmed by the maddened and murderous *haut monde* mob!

But then! Inkman's finger froze in its track! For at that very moment a gigantic sound was heard—or rather, two sounds, following in close succession. All eyes in the room turned, to behold a terrifying sight.

At the far end of the room, a large door which led to the inner Embassy lay shattered, its splintered pieces lying on the ballroom floor. Such explained the first gigantic sound. And within the door, even now forcing its way through onto the ballroom floor, slouched an immense rock snarl, roaring all the while with demonic fury. Its eyes were fixed upon the person of Rupert Inkman with that flaming, intent, single-minded glare of rage and hatred which immediately reminded everyone present of nothing so much as, well, as the flaming, intent, single-minded glare of rage and hatred which rock snarls typically bestow upon those they intend to devour on the instant.

Chaos and stampede erupted in the room in such proportions as to make the earlier confusion seem like the very balm of Heaven. But in that brief moment before all thought was drowned in mass and mindless fury, two voices were heard to speak, one in a loud cry of distress heard by all in the room, the other in a shocked whisper heard only by a louse.

The loud cry of distress, it needs hardly be said, belonged to Rupert Inkman, whose posture was no longer that of one born to command. 'Twas brief and to the point:

"Oh, shit!"

The shocked whisper belonged to the witch Magrit. For she alone, of the multitude in the room, had immediately spotted the one aspect of the rock snarl which was unusual. All others present had, perhaps understandably, fixated on those features of the monster which were altogether normal for a rock snarl in the grip of murtherous rage—I speak, of course, of the eyes blazing like the ovens of hell, the fangs like cutlasses, the talons like sabers, the lashing tail, the great haunches even now crouching for the death leap, and so on and so forth.

But Magrit had at once seen the oddity, the little hairy face which peeked out through the great neck ruff of the monster.

"I'll be damned," she whispered, "it's Shelyid."

And so it was! Shelyid the dwarf, perched atop the shoulders of the horrible beast like nothing so much as a child riding a hobby horse! How had such an event come to pass?

CHAPTER XXII. *Murals Examined. The Mage's Critique Thereof. A Chamber Devoted to Love. A Dwarf's Inquiries. A Melee. A Pathetic Scene. A Reconciliation. An Historic Event!*

Greyboar was not a happy strangler.

"Couldn't you have made these tunnels wider?" he grumbled.

"For what purpose?" demanded the Underground Artist, Paul Gauphin. "They were not intended for gorillas."

A somewhat injudicious reply, this—so at least is your narrator's opinion. I myself, were I a man rather than a louse, should have hesitated before labeling a man, to his face, a gorilla—especially a man who was, in actual fact, built like a gorilla.

Fortunately for the future of Art, the strangler was of a phlegmatic disposition. He satisfied himself with cracking his knuckles, which act, be it said, caused Gauphin no little terror.

"My God!" cried the artist. "The tunnel's collapsing! We'll be buried alive!"

"It's just the big goon cracking his knuckles," explained Ignace. Gauphin made a sour face, but eschewed comment.

Greyboar's disgruntlement was perhaps inevitable. The strangler had had a most miserable time of it, squeezing his great body through the labyrinth of tunnels below the Ozarine Embassy. The worst of it, he was to say later, was that his discomfort made it impossible for him to fully appreciate the art work which decorated every foot of Gauphin's burrows.

"Of course," he would explain, "I was only interested in the still lifes—marvelous!—the flowers! the bowls of fruit! Pity you had to wade through such a lot of nudes to get to them."

Ignace, on the other hand, due to his miniscule size, was better able to gain the proper perspective on the murals. One would not have thought, based on previously observed behavior, that the little agent was a devotee of the finer arts. But a connoisseur he proved to be, or such, at least, seems the only possible explanation of his reluctance to move at the rapid pace one would have thought more appropriate for daring adventurers on a perilous mission. Indeed, so slow and halting was his progress that his client finally resorted to dragging him forward by bodily force.

Shelyid, whose dwarfish stature gave him an even better opportunity to study the pulchritudinous portraits, took no advantage of the fact. Instead, the gnome kept his eyes firmly on the ground ahead, blushing like a schoolgirl. Of course, he could claim as his excuse that he was bent double by the wizard's sack. His master, on the other hand, scrutinized the murals carefully, and blessed his companions with a running commentary on the Mission of Art, replete with many citations from the ancients, the essential thrust of which was that Paul Gauphin was an arrant

alphabetarian, a nugatory neophyte, a coarse catechu-
men, a posturing parvenu who thought to conceal his
blatant ignorance of the classic methods of proportion,
line, perspective and portraiture by his extravagant
colorism, the which was nothing but a maneuver to
dupe his patrons by passing off crudity as primitivism.

His chief complaint, however, was that the nudes
were not fat.

"'Tis the First Law of Nudistry!" he exclaimed, many
more times than once. "Consider, if you will, the classic
masters of the past—Rubens Laebmauntsforscynneweëld, to name just one! Did that great soul ever paint
the nude portrait of even a single nubile? Nay, fie on
such witless notions! Understood he well that the very
essence of nudistry is the presentation of human flesh,
and thus, it follows as the antithesis from the thesis,
that the more copious the expanse of flesh portrayed,
the greater the Art!"

Gauphin, oddly enough for a temperamental artist,
seemed not at all irritated by this flood of criticism.

"Stuff sells like hotcakes," he remarked, and said
no more.

But at length, Zulkeh's impromptu lecture on Art
came to an end. Gauphin held up a warning hand.
They had reached, or so it seemed, the end of the
tunnel. Ahead of them was nought but a wall.

"Here's my secret entrance to Inkman's bedchamber," whispered the artist. He pointed out a latch
which enabled the wall ahead to be swung aside.

"That's it for my end of the deal," he said. "Give
me ten seconds to get clear."

"Thanks for the help," said Greyboar pleasantly.

Gauphin snorted. "Think I had a choice? I'm not
happy about this, let me tell you—it's probably going
to sour my romance with Inkman's girlfriend." Then,
shrugging: "What the hell, falling out of favor with a

lady beats falling out of favor with Les Six. What's that old saying? 'Hell hath no fury like a woman scorned'? Ha! Try pissing off Les Six some time, if you really want a toasty taste of the underworld! Anyway, I'm gone. If you make it out of there alive, be sure to tell the half-dozen homeboys from hell that I satisfied my end of the bargain."

He disappeared in a flash.

Zulkeh made to unlatch the wall, but Greyboar gently pulled him aside.

"Why don't you let me handle this part? I'm rather good at breaking and entering."

"Of course, of course," agreed the wizard.

Greyboar unlatched the wall and slowly swung it aside. He peered into the room beyond.

"The coast is clear," he whispered. "Nobody's in the room. But keep it quiet—I can hear the guards in the room beyond."

All four members of the party crept into the room. They inspected the furnishings carefully.

"Quite a love nest this guy's got," remarked Ignace, pursing his lips.

Shelyid's face wrinkled in confusion.

"Master," he asked, "why are there all those handcuffs and chains all over the bed? Seems like it'd be uncomfortable, especially those spiked leather collars. I mean, you know, if you rolled over—"

The wizard stilled his apprentice with a gesture. " 'Tis not the time for a lecture, dwarf." He cleared his throat. Cleared his throat again. "An aspect of your education, this, which I have neglected. At some future date, possibly, when you are older. Perhaps a glance at Kraft-Ebbing Laebmauntsforcynneweëld's monographs, or certain of the diaries of De Sade Sfondrati-Piccolomini—expurgated, of course! But not now, my loyal but stupid apprentice."

"Well, if you say so, master," agreed Shelyid uncertainly. "But it all seems kind of peculiar. I mean, all these whips all over the floor, you could trip on them in the dark and hurt yourself. And—"

"Not now, gnome!"

"Yes, master," grumbled the dwarf. Then: "I still think the place is weird—why would you want to sleep on leather sheets? And, boy, this guy Inkman must crap a lot, there's gotta be eight or nine chamber pots lying around. One of them's on his pillow! Pretty vain, too, this guy, there's mirrors everywhere. And what are those funny long wooden things? Look like bananas except bananas don't—"

"Silence!" hissed the wizard. "I command you, wretch!"

Shelyid grimaced, but obeyed. And, in any event, even the dim-witted gnome must have realized that the time for questions and answers was over. For even at that moment Greyboar was standing before a door on the far wall, preparing to sally forth. Voices could be heard in the room beyond, raised in the coarse and uncouth jests of idle soldiery.

"How many, Ignace?" asked the strangler.

His agent listened intently, his ear flat to the door, then stepped back with a smile.

"Seven, maybe eight."

Greyboar grunted, seized the doorframe in both hands.

"Are you ready, Ignace?" The agent shrugged. The great muscles in Greyboar's shoulders began to move, like breaking surf.

"A moment!" hissed Zulkeh. "Perhaps some shrewd stratagem—the disparity in numbers—'twould seem wise—"

He got no further. Greyboar wrenched the door off its hinges and charged into the room. Three startled guards stood immediately before him, uttering cries of surprise. Greyboar swung the door high and brought it down directly upon them. The door splintered into a hundred pieces. So did they.

Five soldiers remained. These had been seated at another table in a corner of the room some steps distant. They were now on their feet, their faces pale with shock, but sharp swords in their hands. Trained and experienced warriors, 'twas plain to see.

Greyboar advanced upon them, flexing his hands.

Meanwhile, Ignace leaned casually against the wall, placidly observing the scene. Shelyid nudged him fiercely.

"We gotta go help Greyboar!" he cried. "He's way outnumbered! And they got swords and he's got nothing!"

Ignace laughed. "Are you nuts, kid? For Greyboar, this kinda thing's a light workout. Knights in armor on horseback, now, he'd of maybe done some warm-up exercises first."

"Yes, Shelyid," concurred Zulkeh sagely, "'tis always wise to let professionals handle matters involving their trade. Best we stay out of the way," he added, matching deed to the word, "lest—"

But Shelyid would have none of it. Exhibiting yet again that cretinous mentality which the gentle reader has, by now, no doubt found excessively tiresome, the pathetic gnome launched himself into the center of the room, clenching his puny fists.

"You guys better watch it!" he cried. "He's not alone, you know!"

"I'll handle this one!" shouted five soldiers in unison, each pointing at Shelyid. "The rest of you take the big guy!"

And so saying, the five stalwarts hurled themselves as one man upon the dwarf.

Two factors alone kept the apprentice from becoming chopped homunculus. The first, ironically enough, was his diminutive stature. For Shelyid, seeing doom advancing in the form of five descending sword blades, immediately threw himself through the legs of the soldier directly before him. This unexpected maneuver caused the soldier to stumble backward and fall upon the dwarf. Shelyid's small arm appeared from below and locked itself around the soldier's neck. His four comrades stood around the interlocked bodies of the duo writhing on the floor, momentarily stymied by the fact that their target was covered by their fellow guard.

This slight hesitation was enough to bring the second factor into play, which was, of course, Greyboar.

As your narrator, let me take the occasion here to state for the record, that whatever slight skepticism I might have heretofore possessed concerning the reputation of the strangler, ended once and for all time within the next four seconds.

Professional fingerwork, indeed.

In the first second, Greyboar removed the spinal column from one soldier, as neatly as an angler filleting a trout. In the next second, he utilized this spinal column as a garrote to decapitate another. Then, in the third second, he deftly snared the falling head and used it upon the skull of a third soldier much in the manner of a gorilla using a stone to shatter a coconut, with much the same result. Finally, in the fourth second, he reverted to more classic form, seizing the last standing soldier by the throat with both hands, stretching his gullet to a truly preposterous length, and neatly finishing the job by tying the now-suitably-elongated weasand into a double bowline.

There remained only to rescue Shelyid from his assailant, who was still lying upon the dwarf. Strangely, the soldier had ceased his thrashing.

"Take it easy, kid," said Greyboar. "I'll handle this."
The strangler reached down and seized the soldier,
preparatory to committing mayhem upon his body.

But he stopped. A look of puzzlement came upon
his face. I might mention, by way of an aside, that
Greyboar's frown has to be seen to be believed.

"Hell," he muttered, "this guy's dead as a doornail."
He lifted the soldier's body upright. The man was
clearly dead, all could now see it. His head lolled at
an impossible angle.

Greyboar peeled Shelyid's arm from around the
soldier's neck, not, judging from the look of strain on
his face, without some effort. He then separated the
dwarf from the corpse, and held Shelyid up before
him, dangling from the great fist wrapped around the
gnome's skinny wrist. With the fingers of his other
hand, Greyboar subjected the dead soldier's neck to
a professional tactile investigation.

"As neat a throttle as I've ever seen," he rumbled.
"Look at this, Ignace! It's a classic choke—windpipe's
like a tapeworm, Adam's apple's so much applesauce,
neck's broke in three—no, four!—places—" The strangler looked back and forth between the chokee and
the choker, the latter of whom was gasping from
exertion, sweat pouring down his face.

"You okay, kid?" he asked Shelyid.

The dwarf gasped, gulped, swallowed, coughed.

"Yes," he squeaked. "I'm okay. I guess." Then,
after some more gasping and gulping: "Put me down,
will you? Please."

Greyboar set him on the floor. Shelyid tottered
about, his face pinched and drawn. The dwarf looked
up at the corpse of the soldier, still in Greyboar's
grasp.

His face grew paler still.

"Is. Is. Is he dead?"

"Like a mackerel on ice." And so saying, Greyboar dropped the corpse on the floor.

Shelyid started to speak, then doubled up and vomited. Greyboar knelt down beside him, wrapping his immense arm around the dwarf's little shoulders.

"Take it easy, Shelyid," he said quietly. "Go ahead, puke it all up." The wizard started to speak, fell silent at Greyboar's stare. Silence was not natural to the mage. But the strangler's stare that moment would have silenced a babbling brook.

A minute or so passed. Then Shelyid spoke softly. "I don't think I've ever killed anything before. Well, maybe a few bugs and such. Even then, it's never on purpose. Never stepped on a bug on purpose. Don't harm nobody, bugs." Then he said only, "Oh, oh, oh, oh, oh," and began to weep like a babe. Greyboar sat on the floor and drew Shelyid onto his lap. The strangler said nothing. His face seemed, if anything, even paler than the dwarf's. Odd, in such a man.

And there the two of them remained, for several minutes. It was a truly ridiculous scene.

The wizard apparently thought so. At length he cleared his throat, and spoke.

"I must say—perhaps—the urgency of the moment— well! That is to say, haste seems—for even as we emote, time wanes!"

"Shuddup," growled Ignace. The agent glared at the wizard, hunched his shoulders, glared around the room, crossed his arms, glared at the universe.

"It's a trade," he snarled, in his high-pitched voice. "Pay's good. Work's steady. What more do you ever get in this world?"

But he went over and tapped the strangler on the shoulder.

"I hate to say it, Greyboar, but the professor's right. We ought to be moving along."

Greyboar nodded. "Let's go, Shelyid," he said, and rose up. He placed the dwarf on his feet.

"Okay?" he asked. Shelyid nodded. He even managed a feeble smile.

Greyboar looked around the room. Except for the two tables and the chairs around them, the room was bare. There were three doors in the room. The first was the one they had burst through earlier, leading to Inkman's bedchamber. There was a second door on the opposite wall, normal in its appearance. The last door, on the other hand, was quite extraordinary. Located against a third wall, it was not only constructed of iron rather than wood, but was held shut by no less than four great metal bars.

"Check that door, will you, Ignace?" said Greyboar, pointing to the normal-looking door. "Pays to be careful. But unless I miss my guess, this great ugly iron door's the one where the business takes us."

A moment later, his investigation completed, Ignace announced that the door led only to a corridor.

"Thought so," grunted Greyboar. "That's how the soldiers get in and out." He grinned. "Can't have common troops parading around while the great Cruddy's engaged in sexual outré-course."

A more solemn expression then came upon him, as he inspected the iron door, very thoughtfully. The strangler pursed his lips and whistled.

"Don't much like the look of this. You'll have noticed, Ignace, that these great bars are all designed to keep whatever's on the other side of that door from getting to the warm little bodies of the people who hang out on this side of the door."

"I am not stupid," came the agent's reply.

"No, no, you're not," agreed Greyboar. "Irascible, yes. Dyspeptic, yes. Unpleasant, frequently. A pain in the ass, as often as not. But stupid, no."

"Me—a pain in the ass?" shrilled Ignace. "You should talk!" The agent glared at the door. "The Old Geister only knows what kind of horror's lurking on the other side of that door."

"Yes, and we're about to find out," responded Greyboar, placidly enough. "Come on, let's get to it." And so saying, the strangler made short work of removing the bars from the door. A moment later, the door itself stood open. A dark passageway loomed beyond, its end not in sight.

"Nothing ventured, nothing gained," announced Greyboar, heading down the passageway. Zulkeh followed, with Shelyid close behind. But before the dwarf could pass through the door, Ignace stopped him with a hand on his shoulder. Shelyid looked up at the agent, suspicion and wariness plain on his face.

"Look, kid," began Ignace, then, after a pause: "Look, Shelyid, I'm sorry about what I did back at Magrit's place. I shouldn't have picked on you the way I did. I just—well, it's like the big guy says, the truth is sometimes I'm an asshole." He stopped, groped for words, found none.

The frown on Shelyid's face cleared, and he said: "It's okay. I don't think probably anybody can get through life without once in a while being an asshole." He stuck out his little hand. Ignace took it and the two midgets shook hands. Acting for all the world like gentlemen!

"We'd better go," said Shelyid. He made to enter the passageway, then turned back. "I'm sorry I chased you around with a knife and tried to chop you into pieces," he said. Suddenly his face contorted, in a most astonishing manner.

And a sight it was, too, to see dozens of the Alfredae rushing to the scene, chittering with excitement. Long hours were spent in the days thereafter, scribe consulting scribe, logs and records examined, notes and diaries subjected to the most detailed scrutiny. Throughout, I kept a dignified silence, as befitted the Alfred. Of course, I *am* the Alfred, and therefore I knew the answer from the beginning, long before the lesser notaries announced, in solemn clan gathering, the official recording of a hitherto unknown event.

Shelyid had grinned.

CHAPTER XXIII. *A Horror Heard. A Wizard's Uninterrupted Exposition. A Horror Seen. And a Horror It Is, Too! The Strangler Prepares. A Dwarf's Folly. The Unforeseen Results Therefrom. The Relic Found. The Mage is Disgruntled!*

The nature of the horror lurking at the end of the corridor was known to our heroes long before it was seen. There was no mistaking the source of the bloodcurdling roars and bellows echoing down the corridor from some place still ahead.

"A snarl," announced Zulkeh. "A rock snarl, if I am not mistaken. The tone and timbre is similar, of course, to that of a mountain snarl. But that slight tremor at the upper registers—no, 'tis a rock snarl, 'tis certain."

"How did the lousy Crud get himself a tame snarl?" demanded Ignace. "I thought the things couldn't be captured and tamed."

"They *cannot* be tamed," responded the wizard firmly. "Indeed, 'tis this very impossibility of domesticating the snarl—in any of its varieties—which most clearly distinguishes the monster from all other manner of wild beasts. On this all scholars agree.

"As for the capture of snarls," he continued, "here there is some confusion in the popular mind. 'Tis not true, as many of the common folk think, that snarls cannot be captured. The beasts are not, after all, supernatural! They can be, and have been, captured on occasion—though very rarely, for the cost in life and limb is invariably immense. And the reward poor! For while snarls can be captured, they cannot be kept in captivity. All too often the creatures escape, for they are not only fearsome in size, strength and swiftness, but cunning beyond all other beasts. And when they do not escape, they invariably perish within a relatively short time, due, it would appear, to heartbreak."

'Twas clear as day, from the deliberate pacing which he now assumed in his progress down the corridor, that the sorcerer was well into his lecture mode. Under most circumstances, his not-academically-inclined companions would no doubt have interrupted him with rude and uncouth remarks. But on this occasion, they listened attentively. So does the prospect of encountering a snarl concentrate even the lowlife mind!

"In all recorded history, there is but one instance of a systematic attempt to entrap snarls. I refer, of course, to the reign of the legendary Panjandrum of the Voracious Regime, whose domain appears to have covered all of Grotum. As recounted by Herodotus Laebmauntsforcynneweëld, this great monarch developed, in the first year of his reign, an obsession with snarl fur. Thus was his army commanded to go forth and hunt down the snarls of the land for their pelts— prairie snarls, meadow snarls, mountain snarls, and the like. By his second year on the throne, the Panjandrum had enough pelts to carpet his throne room. Alas, he had no army. Then was his navy commanded to sail forth and hunt down the snarls of the coastal regions— delta snarls, bayou snarls, mangrove snarls, and the like.

By his third year on the throne, the Panjandrum had sufficient pelts to carpet his bedroom as well. Alas, he had no navy. Then were his officials, the whole of his great bureaucracy, sent forth to hunt down the snarls of the cities and towns—street snarls, alley snarls, house snarls, and the like. Of course, there were no such snarls, for the beasts detested settled regions— as they do to this day. Displeased, the Panjandrum ordered the army to execute the officials. Of course, this mass execution did not take place, as he had no army. Displeased still further, the Panjandrum ordered the navy to execute the army. This mass execution likewise did not take place, as he had no navy. Now greatly displeased, the Panjandrum ordered the bureaucracy to execute the navy. Again he failed in his purpose, due, of course, to the absence of a navy to execute. Now displeased beyond measure, the Panjandrum ordered his lowly subjects to execute the bureaucracy. This they immediately did, with vigor and enthusiasm. Now again pleased, in his fourth year on the throne the Panjandrum ordered his subjects to sally forth and hunt down such snarls as they could find wherever they could find them. By his fifth year on the throne, he had but one additional pelt, enough to cover only his closet. Alas, he had no subjects."

The wizard now stroked his beard, always a sign of deep thought. Then:

"To this point in the tale, all ancient chronicles agree. But here opens up the famed and furious dispute between Herodotus and his arch-rival in ancient historiography, I refer, of course, to Thucydides Sfondrati-Piccolomini. For where Herodotus would have it that the Panjandrum soon died from his inability to feed, clothe and bathe himself—never having needed to learn these simple skills—Thucydides claims, to the contrary, that his palace was invaded by a horde of snarls who tore him limb from limb. 'Tis difficult to choose between these two alternative accounts, for documentation is entirely lacking and the higher truth of Poetic Justice would seem to lie, with equal force, on either side of the dispute. I myself, however, am inclined to place more weight than most scholars on the point advanced by Thucydides' cousin, Xenophon Sfondrati-Piccolomini, in his—"

But there the lecture ended, for at that moment our heroes rounded a bend in the corridor and saw before them the very subject of discussion. A rock snarl 'twas indeed, a most large one to boot. And one which had, at the selfsame moment, espied our heroes.

The adventurous foursome paled as one man, or rather, as three men and a gnome. The huge monster lunged at them, its maw gaping wide. But its charge was brought short suddenly. A great twang was heard, as of a giant bowstring. And now, looking closely, our heroes saw that the creature was held back by a chain which stretched from a collar on its neck to a winch-like contraption to one side.

"Most clever!" spoke the mage. "Note how shrewdly Inkman has designed this chamber wherein the ferocious snarl even now prowls, roaring, lashing its tail, eyeing us with frustrated predatory zeal. The chain is long enough that the beast can seize anyone who ventures into the chamber, but not so long as to devour those who remain in the corridor."

"Then how does Inkman get by it?" asked Greyboar.

"See you the winch?" demanded Zulkeh. "No doubt there is some hidden device, located here in the corridor, which enables Inkman to haul back the monster far enough to allow him access to the room which lies beyond yonder door"—here the wizard pointed to a door at the opposite end of the chamber—"wherein rests, as certain as the sunrise, the very relic we seek."

"Then let's find the device!" exclaimed Ignace, who immediately began a close investigation of the corridor.

"Bah!" oathed Zulkeh. "What would be the point of this entire arrangement could such a device be found by any would-be reivers who came along? Desist, young man! You will not find it, I assure you. Even I, armed with a lifetime's theory and practical skill at the discovery of hidden mechanisms, caches, trapdoors and the like, have no hope of finding it. No, no, I fear we have no choice but to overcome the horror."

"You sure about that?" asked Greyboar.

"I am positive."

"How about using some magic on the critter, then?" queried Ignace. "You know, cast a spell on it or something?"

Zulkeh shook his head. " 'Twill avail but little. The snarl is notoriously resistant to all forms of magic and magery. I will do my best, I assure you, to utilize those few cantrips which have in the past proved to have some slight effect on the monsters. But, I warn you, the cantrips are unreliable and, even at their best, not very effective. At most, I can perhaps slightly dull the beast's normally lightning-quick reactions. I fear me that we have no choice but to rely on physical force. Which," he added quickly, taking a step back into the corridor, "is neither my forte nor my area of expertise."

"Never fails," grumbled Greyboar. "When the chips are down, everybody calls for the lowbrow." He examined the snarl, not, or so it seemed, filled with joyful anticipation of the future.

"A bit dicey, this," he muttered. "I can whip five times my weight in crocodiles, twice my weight in bears. Even wrestled a walrus once in a circus, when I was hungry and down on my luck. Had him pinned, too, till he got cranky and tried to use his tusks. Had to throttle him, then, which irritated his owner no end. Cost me the job." He whistled soundlessly. "Oh, boy. Well, best get to it."

The strangler stripped off his leather jerkin. The musculature now exposed was, depending on one's perspective, an anatomist's dream or an aesthete's nightmare. At once, Greyboar began a regimen of stretching and limbering up exercises which would have crippled your average athletic champion.

Shelyid lowered the sack, his face creased by a puzzled frown. "What are you doing?" Then, as the light of comprehension dawned in his brain: "You're going to hurt the snarl!"

Greyboar looked up, startled. "You're worried about me hurting the *snarl*?" He grimaced. "My concern runs the other way around. Some friend you turn out to be!"

Shelyid looked around wildly, then appealed to his master.

"But, master!" he cried. "We shouldn't do this! I mean, the snarl didn't do us no harm! It's not his fault he's all chained up here—it's that Mr. Inkman who's to blame!"

Zulkeh patted the gnome's head. "Yes, yes, Shelyid, in the broader historical and ethical perspective there is much to what you say. Yet, look you, dwarf, we deal here in a more circumscribed and limited sphere. 'Tis legitimate for us to do so, I might mention. For did he not say himself, the great scholar—"

What the great scholar said—indeed, the identity of the scholar himself—will forever remain a mystery. For at that very moment did the dwarf Shelyid charge into the chamber, directly at the raging snarl, his little hands raised before him!

"Go back, go back!" he called out to the snarl. "Just

go over to the side, out of the way, and you'll be okay. Greyboar doesn't really want to hurt you, we just want to get into that door over there and what do you care anyway, I mean, it's that Mr. Inkman what put you in th—"

He got no further. With one monstrous swipe of its talon-tipped paw, the snarl smashed Shelyid's body to the floor, like a giant swatting a fly.

"Oh horror!" cried Zulkeh. Greyboar and Ignace looked away, grimacing.

"Oh horror!" cried Zulkeh. "The diminutive cretin's at it again!" Greyboar and Ignace looked back, astonishment upon their faces.

And indeed, the now-certifiably-moronic dwarf had risen to his feet, somewhat shakily, and advanced again upon the snarl. This time, however, his hands were not raised high in appeal, but clenched in pigmy petulance.

"That hurt!" shrilled Shelyid. The monster's head plunged down, jaws gaping wide.

Shelyid punched its snout.

The snarl pulled back its head abruptly. Its jaws snapped shut. For a moment—insane moment!—monster and dwarf gazed at each other, their eyeballs not more than two feet apart. Shelyid was glaring, if such a fierce description can be applied to the gnome's ridiculous little face. The snarl's expression was impossible to describe at all. Uncertainty, puzzlement, surprise, confusion—perhaps a bit of all of these. But perhaps not—'tis difficult to ascertain the mental state of a beast which is, after all, mindless.

The impasse was broken by Greyboar.

"Don't move, Shelyid!" he shouted, advancing rapidly toward the pair, his great hands outstretched in a wrestler's pose. "I'll take care of it!"

The snarl's head turned. Seeing Greyboar approach, the monster's hackles rose, a great snarl issued from its maw—and they don't call the beasts "snarls" for nothing, let me assure you!

"Stay away!" shrilled Shelyid. But Greyboar's attention was wholly fixed on the snarl, which was even that moment matching wrestler's stance with predator's stalk.

"Stay away!" cried Shelyid again. Rushing at the strangler, the dwarf stretched out his hands and thrust them into Greyboar's belly—if such a word as "belly" can be used to describe a stomach like the plastron of a giant weight-lifting tortoise.

Greyboar landed on his rump. "Utter shock" best describes the expression on his face.

"You knocked me down!" he bellowed.

Shelyid grimaced. He started to speak, then spotted the head of the snarl, which was even then pushing past him, jaws wide, flaming eyes fixed on the form of the strangler.

"And you stop it too!" shrilled the dwarf. He smacked the snarl's snout. Then smacked it again. The enormous beast backed up a pace, stared at Shelyid. Whined. Sat back on its haunches—for all the world like a dog brought to heel!

"You knocked me down!" bellowed Greyboar.

Shelyid turned back to the strangler. Grimaced again. Shrugged apologetically.

"You knocked me down!" bellowed Greyboar.

Shelyid wrung his hands—and well he should! He began to apologize: "Well, gee, Mr. Greyboar, I didn't mean to but—"

Greyboar, still seated, looked over at Ignace. "Did you see that, Ignace?" He pointed an accusing finger at the dwarf. "He knocked me down!"

Ignace nodded, his face pale. "Yeah, I saw it." The agent whistled tunelessly. "Word of this gets out, our fee'll be cut in half. If we're lucky."

Zulkeh tugged urgently at the agent's sleeve. "Mr.

Ignace," he spoke, "I must urge you to exercise whatever ability you possess to restrain your client! I apologize for my apprentice's unseemly behavior, but I am quite certain the miscreant gnome" (here he gazed fiercely at Shelyid, shook his finger, and admonished his apprentice: "Apologize at once to Mr. Greyboar, unworthy wretch!" "I'm trying to," complained Shelyid, "if people'll just let me fin—") "did not intend any actual bodily harm or discomfort to the esteemed chokester—nay, fie on such witless notions! And I can assure you and your client that I shall certainly chastise the insolent youth in a most—"

"Shuddup!" cried Ignace. "Just shuddup! You don't get it, dummy! I ain't worried about 'bodily harm'— ha! Look at the great bruiser! Does he look 'bodily harmed' to you?" And, indeed, it did not appear that any actual physical harm had befallen the strangler.

"It's his reputation, that's the problem," shrilled Ignace. "He's never been knocked down before, it's part of the mystique. Customers pay through the nose for that, don't you know."

"Not actually true," said Greyboar, now rising to his feet. "The Chevalier d'Escroc knocked me down."

"Not in the record book!" shrilled Ignace. "He only put you down on one knee and you right off used the position to tear off his leg and you snatched him falling off the other side of the horse and had him throttled before he even hit the ground—and with his helmet still on! The Records Committee ruled the kneedrop was a maneuver!"

Greyboar grunted. "Yeah, I know, you talked a good line to 'em—but I was there, I know it was a knockdown." He flexed his shoulder at the memory. "Good man with a morning star, the Chevalier."

"Who cares?" demanded Ignace hotly. "D'Escroc's the only one who could argue the point, and he's pushing up daisies. Record says you've never been knocked down!"

"Not any more," commented Greyboar, quite calmly. "Not even you can argue this one. Or what kind of 'maneuver' you want to call me landing plunk on my ass?"

Ignace shook his head in despair. Then, a thought come to him, he turned to Zulkeh.

"Listen, professor, maybe there's no real reason you gotta go public with this. I mean, who knows? Maybe Greyboar and Shelyid were just clowning around, you know, just friendly-like, and maybe Greyboar just pretended to fall down, you know, maybe just—"

"Calm yourself!" spoke Zulkeh. "I have no intention of broadcasting the recent event to the world at large— quite the contrary! I simply wish to retain the services of my stupid but loyal apprentice, who will be of little assistance to me if Greyboar takes umbrage at his recent offense and throttles the wretched little—" He turned to Shelyid, shaking his finger. "I denounce you again, miserable—"

But his admonition was cut short. The wizard was speechless, jaw agape.

The cause of this unwonted silence was plain to see. For even at that moment did the snarl, which had whiled away the preceding minute sniffing at Shelyid's person, seize the dwarf in both paws and begin a vigorous licking of the apprentice's face. Shelyid giggled in protest, trying to fend off the great purple tongue.

"I'll be damned," whispered Greyboar.

" 'Tis true, then," mused the mage, stroking his beard, "the dwarf is, in actual fact and not his fancy, a snarl-friend."

"What's that mean?" queried Ignace.

"It is difficult to answer the question," spoke the wizard. "The essence of 'snarl-friendness' remains a complete mystery to all scholars and sages. Though, 'tis true that in his memoirs the world-famed snarl-friend Tarzan Laebmauntsforscynneweëld claims—well, perhaps not at the moment! And, in any event, his thesis is vigorously disputed by no less an authority than Mowgli Sfondrati-Piccolomini, who for his part advances the argument—well, perhaps at a later time! Suffice it to say, sirrah Ignace, that snarls are known to take a strange liking for certain individuals—not many! no more than a handful in each historical epoch—for reasons which are quite unknown. Based on what records exist, only two factors seem to demonstrate a frequency beyond the limits of statistical accident: hirsuteness, especially among males, and great size."

The wizard paused, stroking his beard vigorously. "Of these factors, Shelyid certainly exhibits the first—perhaps to such an extreme as to outweigh his utter lack of the other. For, as all can plainly see, the dwarf does not possess great size. To the contrary! The dwarf is actually—well, actually, he's a dwarf."

More vigorous beard-stroking. "Yet there seems no question that he is a snarl-friend."

Indeed, 'twould be hard to question, for even as the wizard spoke were the dwarf and the snarl engaged in that childish pleasure in play which so typifies the savage beast and the dimwit. The twain romped about, the apprentice shrieking with glee as he slapped the snarl's snout, the latter, for its part, gaily seizing the dwarf in its great maw and swinging the gnome about like a cat shaking a mouse.

"That looks kind of risky," said Greyboar, frowning.

"Nonsense!" spoke the mage. "I admit my apprentice appears scrofulous, but I can assure you that I have always insisted on a regime of hygiene and cleanliness. The snarl is in no danger of contracting—"

"That isn't what I meant!" bellowed the strangler. "I mean it looks risky for Shelyid. Look at the size of that—" He gasped in horror, for the snarl had just swallowed the dwarf whole. Shelyid's peals of laughter could be heard faintly from within the monstrous jaws. But the strangler's disquiet proved unbased. The snarl opened its jaws and Shelyid popped out, none the worse for wear. Actually, he was howling in positive ecstasy at the experience.

Eventually, dwarf and snarl ended their foolish rompery. Shelyid, now inspecting the beast closely as he worked to unfasten its collar, turned to the wizard and said shrilly: "Look, master, the snarl's all scarred up and everything! He's got"—a moment's pause for examination, then:—"she's got all these fresh cuts and sores all over her!"

The wizard nodded his head. "Yes, Shelyid, and I am not surprised. For look you!" Here the mage pointedly dramatically at a great cat-o'-nine-tails hanging on the wall behind. "Clearly 'twas part of Inkman's trap! Not only to keep a snarl chained here in the chamber, but to keep the beast maddened by frequent scourgings. No doubt he also kept the monster on starvation rations! A shrewd man, Inkman, there can be no doubt of it. Anyone who attempts to pass through this chamber to the treasure room beyond must deal not with a snarl, which is bad enough, nor even a starving snarl, which is worse, but a starving snarl driven to the height of rage by torture and torment. Most ingenious! Most sagacious! Most—"

"He's mean!" interrupted Shelyid. He flung the collar to the floor.

"Well, as to that," spoke the mage, "ingenuity and sagacity have, in themselves, no moral character. Nay, fie upon such witless notions! Do we not have before

us the splendid historic example of Borgia Sfrondrati-
Piccolomini? Not to mention, of course, the—"

"Speaking of treasure rooms," boomed Greyboar,
"shouldn't we be getting on with it?"

"Quite so, quite so," admitted the mage. "Some
other occasion, Shelyid, will be more suitable for this
lecture. But be sure to remind me! 'Tis essential, for
your education, to discern with sure precision 'twixt
the higher faculties of Reason and the maudlin morass
of Emotion."

From the sour expression on his face, it appeared
that Shelyid was not filled with anticipation at this
promised lesson of the future.

Our heroes crossed the room and opened the door
to the chamber beyond. The foursome entered—
fivesome, I should say, for the snarl squeezed itself
through the door after them. Greyboar looked back,
paused, shrugged.

"Why not?" he asked no one in particular.

"Treasure room," the wizard had called it, but in
truth, the chamber was utterly bare save for a table
in the center. Upon the table rested a small book,
bound in green leather. Such were the only objects
in the room.

Ignace advanced to the table, reaching out his hand.
"That's got to be it!" he exclaimed.

"Stop!" cried the mage. "Stop, you fool!"

Ignace looked back, frowning.

"What's your problem, professor?"

"Dolt!" spoke Zulkeh. "Yon object is a great relic—
ancient, potent beyond belief. Think you it is not
guarded by fell wards and gruesome glyphs, guardian
daemons and the like?"

"Well, maybe, but I don't see anyth—" Ignace
choked, then fell silent.

'Twas not, one suspects, so much the size of the

great wraith-like serpent which even now appeared, coiled above the book, which convinced Ignace that the wizard had reason on his side. 'Twas probably not the coal-red eyes, nor the dagger-like fangs, nor even the drops of misty poison which fell from said fangs. No, one suspects it was the spirit-snake's voice—throaty, sibilant, seductive—hissing the words: "Oh you stud! Kiss me! Kiss me, you stud!"

"More your line of work, this!" muttered Ignace to Zulkeh, as he beat a hasty retreat.

"Indeed so," concurred the mage, examining the guardian spirit with an expert eye.

"Bah!" he oathed. "A naga!" Clear enough, Zulkeh was displeased.

"And not even a purple," he added darkly, "but a green." He glowered with ill-humor. Then spoke again:

"I am deeply offended at this disrespect!"

CHAPTER XXIV. *A Thaumaturge Insulted. A Daemon Destroyed. A Sorcerer Demeaned. A Glyph Dispelled, A Wizard Offended. A Ward Dissolved. A Mollified Mage. The Seal Is Broken!*

"Disrespect, master?" queried the apprentice.

"Of course, disrespect!" spoke Zulkeh. "A slur, a sneer, a gesture of base contempt!" He pointed accusingly at the naga, which was still coiling and writhing about, its glowing eyes now fixed on the wizard.

Shelyid's brow wrinkled. "Well, I don't know, master, sure and the thing's a fright, and it's kind of obscene the way it keeps telling you to kiss it and all, but I'm not sure it's really being disrespectful. Actually, I think it's trying to trick—"

"Bah!" oathed Zulkeh. "Dolt of an apprentice! What boots it, the naga's words? 'Tis the very presence of the thing which offends me!"

Shelyid eyed the snake-spirit again. "Well, yes master, I can see where the thing's ugly, and I know you have real refined—"

"Bah!" oathed Zulkeh. "Cretin of a gnome! What

boots it, the naga's appearance? I say again, 'tis the very presence of the thing which affronts!"

"Well," said Shelyid uncertainly, then, in a small voice: "I guess I don't understand, master."

"Bah!" oathed Zulkeh. "Of course you don't! You are a lowly apprentice—naturally you do not grasp the insult which is here delivered unto me."

Seeing no understanding on Shelyid's face, the wizard threw up his hands with exasperation. Then, with the look of resignation of one forced, for the thousandth time, to explain the obvious yet again:

"What am I, my loyal but stupid apprentice?"

"O master, you are the wisest and most powerful sorcerer in the world!" came the instant response.

"At last! A glimmer of intellect! And what am I doing here?"

Shelyid frowned. "Well, you're here to take that relic thing that's sitting right there under the naga."

"Good, good. Two correct statements in a row. And what is the purpose of the naga's presence?"

Shelyid frowned, hesitated, then said: "Well, I guess it's here to keep the thing from being taken."

"Very good! Three correct statements in a row." The mage smiled, patted Shelyid's head, then glowered deeply at the naga.

"And therein lies the insult!" he spoke. "For to put a naga—and a green, at that!—to prevent the mightiest mage of the world from seizing yon relic—O infamy! O insult!"

"That's a lot of fancy talk," commented Ignace, pressed against the far wall, face pale, eyes fixed fearfully on the naga, "but how's about some action?" His sentiment seemed shared by Greyboar, who was pressed equally flat against the same far wall. Even the snarl kept its distance, sidling with agitation, growling at the naga.

"Action, you say? Observe, then, the dispatch of a naga!" And so saying, the wizard advanced upon the spirit-snake, who, for its part, hissed: "Oh you stallion! Kiss me! Kiss me, you stallion!"

"Which scroll do you want, master? I'll get it for you!" The dwarf began scrabbling in the sack.

"Bah!" oathed Zulkeh. "Think you a thaumaturge of my puissance needs to consult a library to dispatch a mere naga—and a green, at that?" He was now almost upon the thing.

"Oh my gander! Kiss me! Kiss me, my gander!" Now great was the naga's excitement.

"Bah!" oathed the wizard. "Think you I would not know from memory the hexes of the great scholar and serpentbane, I speak, of course, of Rikki-Tikki-Tavi Sfondrati-Piccolomini?"

At the name, the naga recoiled in terror. Too late! For even now did Zulkeh purse his lips, like a lover, and speak the words of snakedoom:

"Oh mon goose! Kiss me! Kiss me, mon goose!"

A great wail filled the room, as of a lost soul—the naga was gone, vanished like smoke!

"I'll be damned," said Greyboar. He and Ignace stared at the wizard, a new respect in their eyes. But Zulkeh took no notice, for he was even now inspecting the relic at close hand—though 'twas noticed by all that he kept his hands away.

"There will now appear a glyph," he predicted. Sure enough, but a second later did a great rune appear on the book's cover, elaborate in its calligraphy, glowing a baleful crimson.

"O outrage!" cried Zulkeh. "O dishonor!"

"What's the matter, master?" queried Shelyid.

The mage's eyes seemed almost as red as the rune. "The matter? *The matter?* Look at the glyph, diminutive dolt!"

The apprentice approached and examined the glyph. "Looks like a rune, master," he said. "A nasty-looking one, too."

"Bah!" oathed Zulkeh. "Of course it's nasty-looking! Not just nasty-looking, I might add, 'tis nasty in actual fact. Touch the thing without first draining its power, and your body will be blasted by lightning."

"No kidding?" This from Ignace, still plastered to the wall.

The wizard bestowed his hot-eyed look upon the agent. "Do you doubt me?" he demanded. "Touch the thing, then!"

"No, no," replied Ignace hastily, "wouldn't doubt you for a minute!"

"Never question a professional at his work, myself," added Greyboar. Even the snarl looked away from Zulkeh's glare.

Zulkeh turned back to the table. "A rune!" he snorted. "A miserable, wretched, ridiculous rune. Not even an ideogram, much less a hieroglyph!

"Barbarous things, runes," he grumbled. "To be expected, of course! Barbarous folk, northmen. Crude, uncivilized, not much better than savages."

Seeing Shelyid inching toward the sack, the wizard made a peremptory gesture. "Cease and desist, lilliputian librarian! Think you I require assistance to remember the phrase which drains all power from a rune-glyph? Fie on such witless notions! Exists not a journeyman warlock in creation who could not, in his sleep, recite the infallible weird of those masters of barbarian lore, I speak, of course, of the Runettes Laebmauntsforscynneweëld!"

And so saying, the wizard began dancing and shuffling about, snapping his fingers, crooning the following tune:

"Who put the rune on the book, the book?
"Who was that man?
"He thinks himself quite grand!
"But he's so very plain to see!
"Bebop! Shebop!"

The glyph faded away in less than a second.

Ignoring the exclamations of praise coming from the duo still plastered to the far wall, Zulkeh—not yet touching the book—announced, in a tone of supreme confidence:

"And now for the ward."

All eyes were fixed on the Rap Sheet, at first in anticipation, then in puzzlement.

"The ward always takes a bit of time, Shelyid," explained Zulkeh. " 'Tis always the third of the four relic guards, and its appearance is always delayed— this in the hope of lulling the ignorant would-be reiver to lay his hands upon the relic. To do so before unlocking the ward, of course, would be disastrous."

"Would you be, like, fried alive or something?" queried the gnome.

"Bah!" oathed Zulkeh. "The cruder of the dooms we have already surmounted. Nay, Shelyid, the unwary seizer of still-warded relics finds himself drawn into the relic itself, there to spend eternity in the utter boredom of relichood. A horrible fate—even for a scholar!"

Zulkeh stretched his limbs, looked about. "Perhaps we could take some refreshment, Shelyid. 'Twill be some time yet before the ward, its hope of an easy snatch frustrated, becomes manifest. The more potent the ward, it goes without saying, the greater its patience. The legendary wards of old were known to lurk as much as two full days before making their appearance. In these modern times, however, I doubt

me we shall need to wait more than four hours, perhaps not more than—*what*? *Already*?"

Great was the sorcerer's indignation.

"O scurrilous discompliment! O scabrous disesteem!
O insult piled onto insult!" He stalked about the chamber, fists clenched above his head. Smoke and lightning issued from his ears. Shelyid quailed, for he
naturally recognized in Zulkeh's circular pacing the
famed and dreaded *peripatis thaumaturgae*—counter-
clockwise, eleven steps to the circuit, with, of course,
the semi-hop following each third completion of the
circuit to throw off what demons might be tailing
behind in the netherworld.

"Look at the thing!" he spoke. More accurately,
bellowed with rage.

"It's like a cage of glowing red bars, master," said
Shelyid. "Like the door to a vault, maybe, if a vault
door was made of molten steel."

"Precisely!" snarled Zulkeh. "It's a vault ward! The
most primitive, simple-minded, rudimentary, oafish,
hebetate and thick-witted of all wards! I was tossing
the things off like a short-order cook my first year at
the University!"

He stopped his pacing. Glowered for a moment
more, then began to speak. But before even a single
word was finished, he hesitated.

"Bah!" oathed the wizard. " 'Tis so long ago I have
forgotten the exact phrasing. Infuriating! To have such
simple problems posed that one has to grope to
remember the answer!"

He sighed. "Still, best to get it right. Even a vault
ward can be dangerous if improperly unlocked. Shelyid,
get me the *Memoirs* of Sutton Sfondrati-Piccolomini."

The dwarf disappeared into the sack, reemerged not
more than a minute later with a volume in his hand.
The mage quickly flipped through the pages.

"Now, where is it?" he muttered. "Ah! Here is the relevant passage." At once he recited the following:

" 'Willie, why do you rob banks?' 'Because that's where the money is.' "

The glowing bars had already begun to fade before he was well into the passage. By its end, they were gone.

The wizard handed the volume back to his apprentice. "And what insult comes next?" he demanded. "There is still the last guard, the seal. In what manner will my dignity be affronted now?"

He glared at the Rap Sheet, then seized it with both hands and shook it fiercely.

"O master!" cried Shelyid. "Be careful!"

"Bah!" oathed Zulkeh. "The seal is not dangerous! It is the final guard because it is the last resort. The relic reiver having avoided the grasp of the daemon, the blast of the glyph, and the snare of the ward, there is naught can stop him now but the prevention, by sheer sealing away, of his ability to use the relic. Such is the purpose of the seal. I can now safely take the relic in hand—indeed, I could travel the world with it, use it as a footstool, a pillow!—but can I use it without opening it, without breaking the seal? Of course not! Even now, look you as I attempt to open the book!"

And so saying, the wizard made what was clearly an effort to turn the pages. As well turn the pages of a solid block of marble!

"And so what demeaning seal will appear?" demanded Zulkeh. "Solomon's Seal, I expect, which can be broken by any half-literate herbalist in her hovel in the woods!"

He began to utter more phrases of contempt and contumely, but stopped. For now had a seal appeared, like unto a great blob of wax plastered across the open edge of the book.

"But what's this?" he demanded. He frowned, gazing at the seal which was rapidly taking form. Odd ridges and whorls solidified, spotted gold and black.

"Fascinating! Extraordinary!" he cried, as soon as the seal had taken its final shape and structure.

"What is it, master?" queried Shelyid.

"Why, why, 'tis a Leopard Seal! Astonishing!"

"What's a Leopard Seal, master?"

Zulkeh stared down at his apprentice, thoughtfully.

"Truly, 'tis early in your apprenticeship for an introduction to the higher seals, yet—recall, dwarf, that I predicted this journey would expose you to new knowledge and lore!"

"Oh yes, master!" cried Shelyid.

"Know, Shelyid, that all of the higher seals take their inspiration from the souls of animals. For who could keep their counsel better than dumb beasts? I might mention, in this regard, that we see here the absurdity of the popular belief that Solomon's Seals are the greatest of seals. Preposterous! How could a seal inspired by the soul of Solomon—that vainglorious babbler, that opinionated chatterbox, that obsessive-compulsive spouter of judgments and pronunciamentos, that—well! Suffice it to say that the expression 'pillow talk' finds its origin in Solomon's liaison with the Queen of Sheba."

Here the wizard wagged his finger in Shelyid's nose.

"Nay, fie upon such witless notions! To inspirit a seal with real power of mutery, 'tis necessary to draw upon the souls of dumb beasts. True, such beasts utter sounds, but sounds without meaning. Likewise, should I shatter the seal on this binder by force rather than science, I should reduce the contents within to pure babble. Such is the reason that all the higher seals are inspirited of animals."

"Oh, I understand, master!" cried Shelyid. "So this seal is, well, inspired by a leopard soul." The dwarf frowned in puzzlement. "I would have thought maybe a tiger or a lion would—"

"Nay, nay!" spoke Zulkeh. Shelyid fell silent. The wizard stroked his beard.

"I am perhaps responsible for your confusion," he admitted. "There are, it is true, excellent seals derived from the felines. And, 'tis true enough, the tiger and lion seals are the best of the lot. The seals inspirited by leopards—which are properly called 'panther seals,' by the way—are noticeably weaker. But this is not such a seal, Shelyid. Nay, nay, this seal is of the greatest of the seal families, I speak, of course, of the pinnipeds. For what animal soul could better inspirit a seal than a seal?"

The wizard paced back and forth, gesturing with the book in his hand.

"Within the seal seals, there are of course gradations. Weakest are the Harbor Seals. The Harp Seals are famed for—well, time presses! Suffice it to say, Shelyid, that of all the seal seals, the most potent—on this all scholars agree—are the Leopard Seals."

He held up the relic in both hands, his face positively glowing. "So!" he cried. "At last I am shown proper respect!" A frown. "But why would such a great seal be combined with such a wretched set of daemons, glyphs and wards?" The wizard pondered for a moment, before his expression cleared.

"Of course!" he exclaimed. "I had forgot me that the relic is a Rap Sheet, long in the possession of the Cruds. No doubt it was the Angel Jimmy Jesus himself who set the daemon, glyph, ward and seal. This explains all! The grandeur of the seal, its well-nigh perfection of mutery, derives from the most outstanding characteristic—personality trait, you might say—of the

Angel Jimmy Jesus, which is known even to babes in swaddling clothes."

"He's a total paranoid," said Greyboar.

"Claims friends are enemies," elaborated Ignace, "and the better the friends the more certain their enmity. Why else would they be your best friends, except to get close enough to stab you in the back?"

"Precisely!" agreed the wizard. "A classic paranoid. He actually believes that the whole world is out to get him, when all studies have shown that not more than three-fourths the global population actively seeks his death, although, in all fairness, one should add that a good three-fourths of the one-fourth remaining would certainly cheer from the sidelines as the multi-millioned mob tore him limb from skeletal limb."

"Then why was the other stuff so rotten?" asked Shelyid. "You know—the daemon and glyph and stuff?"

" 'Tis obvious, youth!" spoke the mage. Zulkeh turned to Greyboar and Ignace.

"Enlighten my apprentice, good sirs. What is the second most prominent characteristic of the Angel Jimmy Jesus, known to schoolboys at their desks?"

"He's a total incompetent," stated Greyboar.

"Worst thing ever happened to the Cruds, him being put in charge," added Ignace. "I remember once when some Senators tried to get rid of him, there was mass demonstrations and riots in the streets of Ozar, every revolutionist and insurrectionary gathered the world over demanding he keep his job."

"Exactly! A complete nincompoop—in all but one thing, which is keeping his mouth shut. And certainly we cannot sneer at this seal," he mused, gazing down at the book in his hand.

"So! Let me to work! 'Twill take hours, no doubt, for this is a challenge worthy of my science!" Happily muttering to himself, the wizard headed over to his sack and began rummaging. Soon enough he realized that rummaging in the great sack was difficult with the Rap Sheet still in his hand.

"Shelyid!" spoke the mage, extending the relic toward his apprentice, "hold this for me a moment." Then, seeing the look of apprehension on Shelyid's face, Zulkeh snorted. "Come, come, dwarf! I have already explained the thing is harmless!"

Gingerly, Shelyid extended his hand and took the book.

At once the great seal shattered into a thousand pieces, which fell to the floor and melted away into nothing. The Rap Sheet was open!

CHAPTER XXV. *A Paradox, Followed By a Quandary. The Wizard's Wrath. The Wizard's New Experience, and His Later Reflections Thereon. "Shelyid's Wild Ride." A Lousely Schism. The Crud's Doom. A Parting!*

"Unspeakable gnome!" oathed Zulkeh. "What have you done?"

"I didn't do anything, master," whined Shelyid. "I just took the thing like you gave it to me."

"The seal is broken! Look you, 'tis broken!"

"It's not my fault," pouted the dwarf. "I didn't break it. I didn't do nothing!"

"Anything," corrected the mage. Then, still glaring, he stroked his beard. "'Tis true," he mused, "there is no way such a novice as yourself could have broken the seal. Still, 'tis odd. 'Tis most odd!"

"Who cares how it got broken?" interjected Ignace. "It *is* broken, right—the seal, I mean?"

"Certainly!" snorted the mage. "Can you not—"

"Then it don't matter how it got broken!" cried Ignace. "And don't bother with my grammar," he added, forestalling the mage, "I'm to old to change habits. The important thing is to get out of here quick. We got what we came for, so let's go!"

"But the paradox—" protested Zulkeh. 'Twas of no use. Ignace snatched the relic from Shelyid's hand and headed out the door, Greyboar close behind. After a moment, the wizard threw up his hands in frustration.

"Bah!" he oathed. "I fear Ignace is right. Come, Shelyid, we must depart." And so saying, the mage followed the strangler and his agent. "Still," he was heard to mutter, "'tis most mysterious, most enigmatic!"

Shelyid came after, followed in turn by the snarl, like a giant puppy following a child. Rapidly, the bizarre-looking party made their way through the snarl's former prison chamber and into Inkman's bedchamber. No sooner had the snarl squeezed its way into the room than it began a fierce sniffing of the bed. 'Twas apparent the beast had smelled his ex-captor's scent, for the monster suddenly roared—causing all others present to jump with alarm!—and then proceeded, in but three seconds, to transform the bed into so much wood and leather wreckage.

"Inkman did not win the heart of his pet, I'd say," commented Greyboar drily. The strangler stooped and entered the tunnel in the far wall.

"Here we go again," he complained. "I'll be a hunchback before the night's over."

Greyboar was followed by Ignace, then Zulkeh, then Shelyid, then—

—a problem presented itself.

Hearing a whimper, Shelyid turned and beheld the snarl's head at the entrance to the tunnel, its hitherto-fierce eyes filled with a look of sorrow. It whimpered again.

"Oh, wait!" cried Shelyid. "She can't fit into the tunnel! We'll have to find a different way out!"

There followed a most absurd dispute. For the dwarf, exhibiting that petulant stubbornness which was perhaps his most unattractive characteristic, refused to listen to reason, even as his master advanced the most cogent arguments and clever dialectic, the thrust of which was that there was no other possible escape route than Gauphin's tunnels.

"He's right, Shelyid," said Greyboar, as the mage paused to catch his breath. "The only other way out is through the main corridor into the Embassy. Place'll be crawling with soldiers. If I thought we'd have a chance, I'd be willing to try it. But there's limits, I'm afraid, even for a strangler."

"Let's just open the door into the corridor and let the snarl out," suggested Ignace. "Maybe she can escape on her own—what the hell, the soldiers probably won't try to stop her." The agent looked up at the great horror. "I sure as hell wouldn't."

"Bah!" oathed Zulkeh. " 'Tis a ridiculous scheme! No doubt she could deal with the soldiers, but how is the great creature supposed to open the various doors along the way? The snarl could break through some of them, certainly, but an Ozarine embassy is sure to have any number of bronze portals, iron gratings and the like, cunningly locked and barred, which no amount of brute force can overcome. 'Twould require deft fingers to pass through such, and—well." He shrugged. "Examine the beast's paws, if you will!"

All looked. And 'twas clear at a glance, even to the dwarf, that the snarl's extremities were not well suited for lock-picking. Other tasks, yes—gutting, rending, disemboweling, mangling—but opening cunningly barred and locked metal doors, no.

"So, you see," concluded Zulkeh, "we have no option." In a rare gesture, he laid a kind hand on his apprentice's shoulder. "I am unhappy myself at the fact, Shelyid, for

I abhor the thought of leaving the poor creature to Inkman's mercy—the more so as our recent theft of his relic will no doubt greatly enhance his already, judging from all evidence, exceedingly sadistic bent. But here as in all things, must Reason be our—"

"I can open the doors for her," said Shelyid.

Before his master could fully grasp the meaning of these words, Shelyid darted out of the tunnel and seized a tuft of the snarl's throat fur.

"Come on!" cried the gnome, tugging the monster toward the far door, "you and me'll go the other way! I'll meet you back at Magrit's house, master!" he shouted over his shoulder.

"Shelyid!" exclaimed Zulkeh. "Halt! Cease and desist in this madness!" His voice rang with sure command.

The dwarf stopped abruptly. His little shoulders hunched. He turned around and looked at the wizard.

"No," he said. Very softly, very firmly.

Zulkeh's face assumed the aspect of apoplexy. "Impudent dwarf!" raged the sorcerer. "Disobedient wretch! Not only stupid but-now-revealed-to-be-disloyal apprentice!"

"I'm not disloyal," stated Shelyid. "I'm not at all, that's not fair, and besides you'll be all right because you'll have Greyboar and Ignace to look after you." He stopped, groped for words, then said: "It's just, well, I have to be loyal to her too."

But 'twas clear as day the wizard was in no mood for argument.

"Bah!" he oathed. "My safety is beside the point! The issue here is your impertinence! Your rebellion 'gainst my authority! Your—"

The silence which now fell upon the mage was total, sudden, complete.

In later time, Zulkeh would reminisce more than once on the new experience he was now undergoing. On such occasions he would allow, with quite atypical modesty, that the vast theoretic knowledge which he had acquired beforehand, even when added to his own empirical observations, had never prepared him for the actual reality of Greyboar's choke.

"'The Hand of Fate,' 'tis called in southwest Grotum and the Grenadine," he would comment to his rapt audience. "In the Crapaude, *Mortemain;* in east Grotum, 'Doomclasp'; throughout the Ozarine, of course, 'the Great Crunch' is common, though many prefer 'the Devil's Grip'; in Alsask, 'tis invariably called simply 'the Squeeze,' which is further embellished among the Kushrau to 'the Big Squeeze.' But"—here he would wag his finger solemnly—"I have personally experienced the phenomenon, and I can assure you that none of these names—though they each capture some aspect of its essence—approaches in exactitude the phrase which is universal in Greyboar's own home-land of Sfinctria, I speak, of course, of 'the Thumbs of Eternity.'"

"You know," growled Greyboar, "sometimes you piss me off."

"Take it easy, big guy, take it easy!" exclaimed Ignace, prying himself between Greyboar and the mage.

"You don't want to piss him off," he said to Zulkeh. "Trust me on this one."

'Twas apparent, by his gestures, that the mage was attempting to indicate his full agreement with Ignace's last point. Words, of course, failed him.

"Greyboar," came Shelyid's shrill voice, "let go of him!" And, astonishingly: *"Now!"*

A moment's hesitation, then the strangler released Zulkeh. The wizard gasped for breath. Greyboar turned to Shelyid.

"I was just—" He stopped, stared.

Truly an incredible sight! For there was the dwarf, perched on top of the snarl's shoulders, for all the world like a tiny mahout riding a carnivorous elephant!

"I know," said Shelyid, "but you still shouldn't choke the master. He just gets excited sometimes, especially when I irritate him, which happens pretty often." Then, to Zulkeh: "Are you all right, master?"

The wizard wheezed and whistled. "Of course . . . not . . . all right . . . imbecile! Just been . . . throttled . . . world's . . . premier strangleur . . . what a . . . question! Rattlepated runt . . . half-witted homunculus . . ."

"He's okay," announced Ignace.

"He's right, master!" cried Shelyid. "You'll be back to normal—"

"—moronic midget . . . pinheaded pygmy . . ."

"—in no time!" The dwarf tugged on the snarl's left ear, turning the beast around—for all the world like a champion equestrian! "We gotta go! I'll see you at Magrit's house later!" And so saying, dwarf and snarl-mount headed toward the door leading to the main corridor. But Shelyid stopped almost at once and turned to look back, consternation on his face.

"Oh! I almost forgot! The master's sack!"

He looked appealingly at Greyboar. "I really can't take it with me," he said, "I was wondering if, well, maybe you could—"

"Don't worry about it," rumbled the strangler, "I'll make sure the wizard doesn't lose his precious bag."

"Oh, thank you!" cried Shelyid. A moment later, he and the snarl disappeared.

"Good luck, Shelyid!" shouted Ignace. Turning back, he said: "Well, let's hope he makes it. Come on, Greyboar, pick up the sack and let's get out of here!" The agent grabbed Zulkeh and shoved the still-wheezily-denouncing mage ahead of him into the corridor.

Greyboar bent over, reached down a hand, seized the sack, and flung it over his shoulder.

And collapsed to the floor.

"What's in this thing," he complained, "lead bricks?" The strangler rose again and lifted the sack anew, this time firmly braced and using both hands. His knees bent, his great thews rippled with effort. The sack now on his shoulders, he stooped and entered the tunnel, grumbling: "How does that tiny little guy manage to carry this thing, anyway?"

The events which now followed caused such excitement and consternation among the Alfredae as to completely overshadow the fierce debate which had erupted among us not more than a few minutes earlier. The debate, of course, centered on the proper significance to be given Shelyid's defiance of his master. Was this, as some argued, the first act of rebellion in his life? Or rather, so countered others, but a continuation of the insolence which had first manifested itself in Shelyid's behavior at the tavern and been shortly followed by his refusal to heed Zulkeh's commands to cease and desist his murderous attempts on the person of Ignace?

As the Alfred, it was naturally left to me to decide the issue. At the appropriate time I did so, coming down firmly on the side of those who advanced what came to be known as the Thesis of First Revolt. For 'twas clear, I explained in my authoritative judgement, that Shelyid's earlier acts of insubordination occurred while the gnome was incapacitated due to strong drink and frenzy. Whereas in this instance, we had to deal with conscious and sober insurrection, committed by the dwarf in full possession of his faculties (such as they were).

All this, however, came later. For no sooner had the

debate begun to wax hot, than the events which piled upon us swept all other considerations aside.

In the official annals of the Alfredae, it is known as The Snarlrun, but noble and common louse alike invariably refer to it in the vernacular: "Shelyid's Wild Ride."

The madness began at once. For no sooner had Shelyid and snarl entered the main corridor than they ran right into a squad of soldiery—a platoon, I should say. These wights were hastening forward, led by a leftenant with drawn sword, who was even at that moment shouting:

"Faster! You all heard the alarm! Someone's—"

The leftenant's speech ended, as invariably happens when a speaker's head is bitten off by a snarl. A snarl in full fury, as the soon-decorating-the-walls-of-the-corridor entrails of half a platoon attested. The other half retained their innards by utilizing the classic methods of rout and stampede, though 'twas clear from the smell that these innards were no longer continent.

Even then, there is little doubt the snarl would have hunted them down with ease save that Shelyid restrained the great beast, not without difficulty.

"Stop! Stop!" he cried, tugging at the monster's ears. This availing little, the dwarf leaned over the snarl's forehead and slapped the horror's snout.

"Cut it out, dummy!" The snarl stopped in its tracks, whether out of obedience or out of astonishment that a bite-sized idiot would slap a snarl on the snout even while the snarl is rending flesh, it is difficult to say.

Shelyid hopped off the snarl and raced back to the corpse of the leftenant. A moment of groping, and the dwarf was racing back, holding up a large key ring.

"See? See?" demanded the gnome. "I had to get the keys—we'll need them later!" He leapt back aboard his huge mount. "Okay, let's go!"

The scenes of carnage which followed appalled even the hardened scribes of the Alfredae. Limbs strewn about like confetti! Torsos severed! Skulls shattered like melons! Blood pouring down corridors like a river! Intestines flowing down staircases like a mudslide! Grue and gore—gore and grue!

And the hideous scenes of individual tragedy, which burn deeper into the memory than the general slaughter! The elderly Seneschal of the Keep, cornered, crying: "Down, boy, down!" 'Twas perhaps the snarl's annoyance at this confusion of her sex which caused her to linger over the dotard's demise. The young Captain of Cuirassiers, stripped from his half-armor like an oyster from its shell, yet still possessing that *savoir faire* which is the hallmark of the aristocracy to which his handsome-though-ashen features clearly marked his membership, down on one knee in a clever stratagem, snapping his fingers, saying: "Here kitty, kitty, kitty!" Alas, to no avail! The distinguished Chamberlain—but enough! I grow nauseous at the memory!

Worse than the snarl's bestiality was the dastardly role played by the gnome Shelyid. 'Twas only the apprentice's aiding and abetting which permitted the slaughter to continue. Time and again, clots of fleeing officials and soldiers would yet retain the presence of mind to close and lock behind them the great iron doors which separated the various sections of the castle. On such occasions—each and every one!—would the pitiless dwarf leap from the snarl's shoulders and open the locks. The locks once turned, of course, no weight of officialdom leaning on the other side could for an instant prevent the snarl from forcing its way through. Then! Ambassador Salad—tossed! Flank of Diplomat— shredded! Plenipotentiary Steak—chopped! Loin of Legate! Envoy Bouillabaisse! Not to mention, of course, the steady diet of Ground Round Dragoon.

Worse yet than the butchery of bodies was the spiritual anguish of unshriven souls. For oft were cries of rue and chagrin heard issuing from the lips of the doomed! And, as is known by man and louse alike, 'tis bad enough to die, but 'tis worse to die in the grip of hopeless regret.

"I told him not to use the whips!" were the last words of a consul, even as he disappeared into the great maw.

"Damn all Cruds and their schemes!" came from a stalwart Colonel of Lance, expiring on the chandelier whence a single blow of the snarl's paw had sent him and his several and separate portions.

The most common expression of regret, of course, was the ubiquitous phrase: "He could have at least fed the thing!"

In this entire holocaust, I can hear the reader's shaken query in my mind's ear: was there a single instance where the dwarf Shelyid used his influence to stay the monster? Even for a moment? Even if in vain?

Not one.

To the contrary! The gnome urged the ravenous beast on! Yes! Yes! I say it again! Time and again, Shelyid was heard to say, in the childlike tones of a boy excusing his pet's misconduct: "That mean Mr. Inkman! Starving you like that!"

From this day, came a sea change over the attitude of the Alfredae—of its scribal class, I should say— toward the dwarf. Of Shelyid's pathetically addled mind, of course, our view remained unchanged. But where, in times gone by, superior and subordinate notaries alike—even Alfreds themselves!—were oft heard to say: "Still and all, a sweet-tempered little fellow"—never again! Nay, never again! In the stead of such benevolent comments came the frequent habit, on the part of superior and subordinate notaries alike, of referring to the evil-souled apprentice by those cognomens which were to become, all too soon, the common property of the civilized world entire:

Shelyid the Terrible.

Shelyid the Merciless.

Shelyid the Cruel.

The Runt Rampant.

The Thuggee Dwarf.

Kali's Gnome.

The Midget *Sans Merci*.

Pygmy the Impaler.

And, of course: The Rebel.

But worst of all was the sea change which now also began among the lesser lice—the pen-fumblers, the ink-spillers, the mis-spellers, the lack-grammars, the declension-bunglers, the—well!—in sum, that entire motley rabble which is known as the class of louselouts.

For these dregs reacted otherwise than the cultured strata. Oh, otherwise indeed! Throughout The Snarlrun, while their betters stood silent, aghast, able to keep quill to paper solely by dint of long training and stern regimen, did the canaille gather upon Shelyid's shoulders and cavort shamelessly. Disgusting slogans did they chant:

"Two, four, six, eight! What do we appreciate? Masticate! Masticate!"

Most popular of all: "De Flense! De Flense!"

In defiance of all custom, 'twould be from this time forward that the lower lice would develop their own terms and definitions. The insolence began with the rabble's own nicknames for the apprentice, which cognomens became, all too soon, the common property of the globe's *sansculottes*:

Shelyid the Plucky.

Shelyid the Bold.

Shelyid the Brave.

The Runt Rambunctious.
The Disabused Dwarf.
The Gnome Unleashed.
The Midget *Sans Peur et Sans Reproche*.
Pygmy the Mahdi.
And, of course: The Rebel.

Soon enough, sentiment would lead to deed. Began then that period in Alfredae history known as The Troubles. Mad philosophies appeared, swept the mob, only to be discarded in favor of outlandish ideologies, which, in turn, were casually cast aside for doctrines still more extreme. Bands of savage young louselouts arose, who scuffled shamelessly with the respectable apprentices and sub-scribes. It became dangerous for an educated louse to scurry at night through entire sections of Shelyid. Why, the hooligans even declared the dwarf's left leg a "No Go Area"— and woe to the penlouse who ventured thereon!

But I race ahead of our tale. The Troubles lay still ahead—though not far distant! But 'tis well said that "narrative must follow its own course," and so do we return to the moment:

Shelyid and snarl were now in a great corridor on the ground floor of the Embassy. Ahead of them, at the end of the corridor, a door was open. Beyond, the lights of the city could be seen.

"That's the way out!" cried the dwarf. "Come on, let's go!"

The snarl made its way quickly down the corridor, approaching a door to their right, through which could be heard a great hubbub. Then, just as the beast was passing the door, the hubbub was stilled by a piercing voice.

The words could not be made out, but the snarl froze, twisted its head, swung forward its ears. The voice was heard again. Again. And yet again.

Now did the beast's features assume that expression which gives the snarl its name. Without warning, the monster hurled itself at the door!

The door splintered under the blow. The snarl forced its way through, uttering such a roar as to waken the dead. They were in a great ballroom, filled with people, all of whom were at that very moment transfixed with terror at the sight of the snarl.

But, in truth, the huge crowd was—in its overwhelming majority—quite beyond danger. For the snarl's attentions were fixed entirely upon the person of a single figure within the room—a thin man, practically skeletal, tall, dressed all in black. The man stared back at the snarl with equally rapt fixation, his blue eyes flashing with the look of eagles.

Such eagles, at least, as have aroused the mortal fury of the legendary roc.

"*Oh shit!*" he cried. But the Savior of the Rellenos was made of stern stuff. Even as the great monster bounded toward him, maw gaping wide, Inkman stood his ground.

"Soldiers, arrest that beast!" he ordered.

Then, seeing the soldiers fleeing the scene, Inkman's voice rang with paramount authority: "Notables of Ozar! Nobles of Pryggia—arrest the soldiers!"

Then, seeing the nobility and the plutocracy trampling the soldiery underfoot in their mad rush for the doors, Inkman's voice grew stentorious with imperial command.

"Traitors! Arrest yourselves!"

Then, even as the doom was upon him, Inkman faced his end with that *sangfroid* which is the hallmark of all great champions of law and order. His last sentence, crackling with a tone which can only be described as Olympian:

"Stop, beast—*on pain of investigation!*"

Alas, crackling tone was now replaced by crunching bone.

So passed Rupert Inkman, Crud among Cruds, Groutch chief of station, brilliant investigator, dazzling interrogator, the Scourge of Sedition, the Hammer of the Right, and many other prestigious titles, positions and cognomens—but hereafter known among the Groutch masses, I am grieved to relate, as The Just Dessert.

Eventually Shelyid was able to coax the snarl to leave aside its frenzied Crud-crunching, though not before Inkman's last finger bone disappeared into the horrid maw.

"C'mon, baby," he whispered urgently into the beast's ear, "we gotta go!" The snarl, apparently sated both in body and soul, obediently ambled through the double doors leading to the entry beyond.

A moment later, dwarf and beast were padding through the deserted streets of Prygg. It seemed that word of the slaughter had spread throughout the city. Even many blocks from the embassy, all doors were shut, all shutters barred. No one walked abroad that Halloween night!

Or, almost no one.

"Psst! Shelyid!" came a low and hoarse cry from an alley to their left. The snarl's hackles began to rise, but fell soon enough as it became clear that Shelyid was ecstatic.

"Oh, it's Magrit!" cried the dwarf. "And Les Six!"

Sure enough, 'twas the disreputable septet in the flesh. They ventured out from the alley and came up to the dwarf—keeping a certain distance, to be sure.

Amazingly, Les Six were speechless. Magrit was not, quite.

"I've seen everything now," she muttered. Then, to

Shelyid: "You want to come with us? My house is just around the corner."

The apprentice hesitated. "Well." He stroked the snarl's shoulder. "Well, yes, I guess I'd better." He started to climb down from the monster, then hesitated.

"Maybe I should stay with her just a while longer," he said. "Just to make sure she gets out of the city all right."

Good fortune is always brief. Les Six found their voice.

" 'Tis true!" cried the first.

"The snarl needs a shepherd to guide it through the streets!" pleaded the second.

"The perilous streets of the Pryggian night!" gasped the third. "Filled with ruffians and footpads!"

"I can see the horrid scene now!" wailed the fourth. "The snarl ambushed!"

"The bloodthirsty cutpurse advancing, knife in hand!" moaned the fifth.

"The snarl at bay! Cornered! Back to the wall! Whimpering for mercy!" This from the sixth, and back around to the first.

"But 'tis a pitiless rogue, yon blackguard of—"

"All right! All right! You've made the point!" shrilled the dwarf. He climbed down from the snarl. For a moment, dwarf and monster stared at each other, their eyes not two feet apart. The beast licked Shelyid's face with a great purple tongue. The dwarf giggled, then clutched the terror's neck. His puny little arms didn't reach halfway around.

"Take care of yourself," he mumbled into the mass of fur, then stepped back. Another moment of this absurd mutual admiration. Suddenly the snarl was gone, flitting down the alleys like a ghost, heading toward the great rocky crags to the west, which shone in the moonlight above the rooftops.

Now afoot, like a proper gnome, Shelyid followed Magrit and Les Six in the opposite direction. Once only he looked back.

CHAPTER XXVI. *A Wizard's Wrath. A Dwarf's Biography Retold. Unfortunate Misunderstandings Thereof. The Wizard Abashed. A Dwarf's Decision. A Contract Is Negotiated!*

And so it was that the first sight which greeted the wizard Zulkeh upon entering Magrit's chamber was that of his apprentice, perched on a couch, a shawl wrapped about his little shoulders, a steaming mug of hot chocolate in his hands. Magrit sat next to him on the couch. Les Six were scattered about on various seats. Wolfgang sat in his special chair in the corner, his features hard to discern in the dim lighting.

The gnome was chattering away as if he had not a care in the world. He was immediately disabused of the notion.

"Miscreant!" oathed Zulkeh from the doorway. "Disobedient rascal! Insubordinate delinquent! Mutinous—"

His peroration was cut short by Greyboar, who pushed him into the chamber from behind.

"Do you mind letting the rest of us by?" growled

the strangler. He staggered into the room and let fall the sack off his shoulders, heaving a great sigh of relief.

"Am I glad to be rid of this thing!" he puffed. He eyed Shelyid with respect. "How long have you been lugging around this—this burden of eternal damnation, anyway?"

"Ever since we left Goimr!" piped up the dwarf. "Thanks a lot for taking care of the sack. I know it's real heavy. It was hard at first, but I've gotten used to it, and besides, it's like the master said! This trip's improved my muscular tone and strengthened my stamina, just like he said it would!"

"Bah!" oathed Zulkeh. "Think you this feeble praise will deflect the force of my chastisement? Which even now sweeps toward your diminutive person as the cyclone of the tropics falls upon the monkey chattering in his palm tree!"

The mage shook his staff and advanced to the center of the room, glowering down at his apprentice. "Gnome, you have displeased me beyond measure! Aroused my temper! Wrothed my wrath! Incited my—"

"SHUDDUP!" came the united cry from every throat in the room save Shelyid's. And as, among the throats numbered in the room, were those of the witch Magrit and Les Six—I leave aside the now-revealed-to-be-stentorian voice of the normally-soft-spoken-though-possessed-of-windpipes-like-unto-the-moose-of-the-north Greyboar—the wizard was stunned into silence.

"You are an asshole," stated Magrit.

"A gaping asshole," clarified the salamander.

At this point, Les Six would no doubt have contributed a round or two, but Ignace—of all people!—rose to the mage's defense.

"Still and all, he's a good wizard," said the agent.

"I wouldn't have thought so before this little escapade—but there's quite the hexman underneath all that verbiage!"

Magrit looked at Ignace, then back to Zulkeh.

"Yeah, I know," she said sourly. "That's why I knew it would work." She adjusted the shawl around Shelyid's shoulders, saying: "He's a windbag, he's got an ego would paralyze Narcissus, he's self-righteous like the Old Geister in his cloud-shrouded citadel wishes He could have wet dreams about, he could dry up a middle-sized lake with hot air, he could bore an oak tree into falling over in the hope of escape, he—" She paused, took a deep breath. "He has the screwiest ideas about the real world—gravity's caused by graveness, can you believe it?" Another deep breath. "But when it comes to real magic, he's a hell of a wizard. I hate to admit it, but he's probably the best actual sorcerer in the world."

She rose suddenly and advanced upon Zulkeh, who was standing as rigid as a post. Seizing the mage's shoulders with her thick hands, she shoved him into a chair. Then, returning to her seat, she spoke again:

"While we've been waiting for you, Shelyid's been telling us all about his life."

"Cheerful little fellow," commented the first.

"Nary a complaint uttered," added the second.

"Not a peep!" emphasized the third.

"Naught but a recital of events," summarized the fourth.

The round now took an ugly turn.

"Difficult to fathom such innocence," mused the fifth.

"In light of selfsame events," agreed the sixth.

"'Tis not the beatings, of course," protested the first.

"Certainly not!" concurred the second.

"Good for sprouts to be switched now and then!" snorted the third.

"Though perhaps not with oaken staffs," qualified the fourth.

"Nor with the frequency of pellets in a hailstorm," added the fifth.

"Should at least let the wounds heal," developed the sixth.

"The blood dry." The first again.

"The scars fade." This from the second.

"Nay, 'tis the other little matter," stated the third.

"The selling into slavery," specified the fourth.

"The attempted selling into slavery," quibbled the fifth.

"The distinction is of little moment," countered the sixth.

"From the moral standpoint," explained the first.

The round now took a very ugly turn.

"As has oft been expressed by the toilers in their various congresses and assemblies," began the second.

"Speaking with one voice, and in no uncertain terms," added the third.

"The downtrodden masses," continued the fourth, "have declared the traffic in human flesh an abomination."

"An historical anachronism," chipped in the fifth.

"A monstrous crime 'gainst humanity," concluded the sixth.

"To be dealt with by any representatives of the suffering classes—" The first.

"Elected in formal congress—" The second.

"Or self-appointed—" The third.

"Due to the press of circumstances." The fourth.

The round now took an extremely ugly turn. Such, at least, seemed the best interpretation of the fact that Les Six had put down their teacups, risen to their feet, circled the mage, clenched their meaty fists.

"You wouldn't happen to have the odd bucket of tar lying about, Magrit dear?" asked the fifth.

"Forgotten in a corner, perhaps?" queried the sixth.

"Hot tar," clarified the first.

"The unused pillow here and there?" inquired the second.

"We'll be needing feathers," explained the third.

Fortunately for the dignity of the mage, a new party interjected himself into the scene.

"Just hold on a moment there, lads," rumbled the strangler. Les Six turned as one man and glared at the strangler. Greyboar raised a huge hand, in a calming gesture.

"I'm a man likes peace and tranquility," commented the strangler mildly. "And what's all this about, anyway?"

The minutes which followed did not, one suspects, take their place among the mage's fondest memories. For Les Six and Magrit proceeded to provide Greyboar and Ignace with the biography of the dwarf Shelyid, as the youth had recounted it to them over the hours gone by. Particular emphasis was placed on the apprentice's relationship to his master. More precisely, on the wizard's notions of discipline, and his concept of the rights of masters over their wards.

As the story unfolded, Shelyid attempted, on several occasions, to lighten somewhat a tale which, it is difficult to deny, would seem dark to the uninformed listener.

"Oh no!" he cried in one instance, "You're exaggerating like you shouldn't! The master only beat me seven times that day, not ten! And it's true, I was really slow to learn the lesson." He blushed. "I'm never good at theology, especially the part about how God's love of man is expressed in crippling diseases and such." Then, in a small voice: "It's 'cause I'm so stupid, and you have to be real smart to understand theology. Really, really smart—like a genius. Like the master."

"And there's another point we'll be needing to discuss, good my mage," stated the first.

"The constant emphasis on the youth's lack of brains," explained the second.

"As contrasted with the brilliance of the scholar," elaborated the third.

"With which we ourselves will soon be blessed!" cried the fourth.

"As the illuminatus corrects our dull-witted mistakes—" The fifth.

"Our crude technique—" The sixth.

"Our disrespect for the classics—" The first.

"Our gross ignorance of the fine points—" The second.

"As laid down in the writings of Jack Ketch Laebmauntsforscynneweëld—" The third.

"Vigilante Sfondrati-Piccolomini—" The fourth.

Fortunately for the mage, this particular round was again quelled by Greyboar. Even more than the strangler's warning growl, however, it was perhaps the sight of the little apprentice moving over to stand by Zulkeh's side which caused Les Six to settle back in their chairs.

The strangler himself made no comments throughout the entire tale. Early on, Greyboar rose and went to the fireplace. He returned to his seat holding the great iron poker which stood by the mantel. In the minutes which followed, the strangler proceeded to idle away the time twisting the poker into a succession of knots. During the recital of Zulkeh's various attempts at the Caravanserai to sell Shelyid to slavers and circus owners, Greyboar tired of knot-tying. He now stretched the poker into a long iron wire, with which he idled away further minutes making a cat's cradle.

For his part, Ignace spoke just once, saying: "Boy, I thought my pop was bad, before he died. And he had the excuse of being a drunk."

At length the biographical project came to an end. There followed a minute's silence, which was broken by Greyboar.

"There's one thing in all this puzzles me." He looked at Zulkeh and said: "I've had the dubious privilege of carrying that weight of the world's sins you call a sack. I doubt you could even pick it up, much less move with it. So who was supposed to carry your sack? After you'd sold the kid into slavery, I mean?"

Zulkeh frowned, stroked his beard.

"Actually," he began. Stopped. Then: "Well, that is to say, actually." Stopped. Then: "I confess I had not considered the point. No doubt I should have engaged a porter."

"You'd have needed to hire a crew of teamsters, more like," grunted Greyboar. The strangler shook his head. "What a genius. He tries to sell his apprentice into slavery so he can get enough money to go on saving the world, but in order to save the world he needs his sack, so he'd have to use the money to hire people to carry the sack the apprentice was already carrying all by himself for—what was it?—a shilling a year and, in good times, maybe the odd meal once a day." A snort. "You always hear about absent-minded professors—but!"

Then he rose, stretched his muscles. This awesome action was perhaps not done unconsciously, for the strangler proceeded to say to Les Six:

"Boys, you'll have to be forgetting about lynchings and such. There's better ways to handle the situation, and besides, in case you hadn't noticed, Shelyid's making it pretty plain he'll stand by the mage. What're you going to do? Restrain the kid while you string up

Zulkeh? Shelyid might be harder to restrain that you think—he's a lot stronger than he looks, and I'm telling you, the lad's got the making of a chokester. Besides, the snarl might be hanging around, lurking in the shadows like."

A moment followed, in which the united glare of Les Six was met by the strangler's calm stare. Les Six looked away. Greyboar then turned to the wizard.

"Now, as to you: I hope you've got plenty of money, because you'll need to be hiring some idiots to carry your sack. The kid'll be staying here."

At this last statement, Zulkeh raised his head, began to protest. But the sight of Greyboar's face stopped him. And it was odd, how the strangler's gaze could have this effect upon people. For there was not a hint of anger, not a trace of a clenched jaw, not a blink of an eye, not even the slightest flush on the cheeks. Just—impossible to describe!

Of course, in the time to come, the wizard would describe it often.

"'Destiny's Glime,' 'tis called in Begfat," he would explain to a rapt audience. "In the Crapaude, *le Visage Impitoyable*, or simply *l'Implacable*; in the bustling streets of Ozar proper, 'tis 'the Mirror of Mortality,' but in the slower-paced Ozarine as a whole, 'the Mirror of Imminent Mortality'; in the mystic land of Sundhjab it has many names: most common among warriors is the terse 'Kismet,' but the higher castes prefer 'the Contemplation of the Endless Round of the Wheel,' which is shortened by the fellah classes to 'the Window on Infinite Pain'; in Grotum itself, these elaborate terms are discarded in favor of the simple 'Basilisk.' But"—here he would wag his finger solemnly—"I have personally experienced the phenomenon, and I can assure you that none of these names—though they each capture some aspect of its essence—approaches in exactitude the phrase which is universal in Greyboar's own homeland of Sfinctria, I speak, of course, of 'the Time to Reconsider.'"

But we leap ahead of our tale. Greyboar continued to speak as follows:

"Magrit, you can put the kid up, at least for a while. Your place is plenty big enough, and I'm sure Shelyid'll be helpful around the house."

"Hell, I'll take him on as *my* apprentice. Won't be able to teach him all that high-falutin' stuff, but he'll get a lot more practical education. And if it turns out the kid decides he doesn't really want to be a warlock"—here she looked pointedly at Les Six—"I'm sure the lads here can set him up in a suitable trade."

"'Tis a certainty!" boomed the first.

"Any one of a hundred!" cried the second.

"The possibilities are endless," added the third, "shoemaker, baker, turner, drayer, forgeman, welder, blacksmith, ironmonger—"

"'Course these'll be but the means to pay the rent," interrupted the fourth.

"While the lad learns his true and proper profession," explained the fifth.

"The art of insurrection," concluded the sixth.

"Here's to the new comrade!" bellowed Les Six in unison, rising to their feet, clenched fists held high like hams in a smokehouse.

Then Ignace spoke.

"Before you all start planning out the kid's life," he snarled, "why don't you ask Shelyid what he wants?" Surprised, all stared at the agent. The little redhead's face was flushed and angry. "You all remind me of my aunts and uncles!" he shrilled. "'Do this, Ignace! Do that, Ignace! You'll make a right proper little whatever, Ignace!'" He glared furiously. "Poor guy'll wind up like I did—take to the streets just to get away from it all."

"He's got a point," rumbled Greyboar. He looked over to Shelyid, who was still standing next to the mage. Zulkeh remained in his chair, his head bent.

"Well, Shelyid?" asked the strangler.

The dwarf's face was a study in uncertainty. Uncertainty but, it soon became clear, not confusion. He placed a hesitant hand on the shoulder of the wizard.

"Well, actually," said the dwarf, "I'd really rather stay with the master. If he's willing, of course."

The faces around him filled with surprise.

"We've been together a long time," explained Shelyid, "ever since I was—well, found in a basket. I don't know where I was born, or who my parents are, so the master's really been my only family. Until I went on this trip, I didn't even have any friends—well, I had one, but—well, never mind."

Seeing that his words were not having much effect, the dwarf hurried on: "And besides, it's not been as bad as you all make it out to be. Sure and the master thrashed me a lot, and he's impatient with me, and maybe I think I'm not really as stupid as he always says, but the truth is I actually learn a lot and this trip's been really exciting even though I didn't want to go and I only went because he made me but it really has turned out just like he said it would, I really have gotten better—really, I can tell! I'm stronger and smarter, and I made a bunch of new friends and before in my whole life I only had one and it—well." He fell silent for a moment, then said: "I miss—well. But it'll be so nice when I get back! I'll be able to tell—" Again, a moment's silence. Then, quietly: "It's my secret."

When the dwarf spoke again his voice was filled with a quite unusual firmness. "I want to stay with the master. The reasons may not make any sense to anyone else, but they're good reasons to me. It's not always fun, being the master's apprentice. Truth to tell, it's not any fun at all. But it's best for me. I don't want to be just a wretched little dwarf. I'm tired of it. But even though the master treats me bad, well, I don't know any better way to learn what I have to learn."

He looked around the room. All visible faces were blank in expression. The wizard's head was still bent. Wolfgang's face remained invisible in the darkness of his corner.

"You all think I'm crazy," muttered Shelyid, "but I know what's the right thing to do."

"Of course you do, boy!" boomed Wolfgang's voice. Everyone jumped.

"What a fright you gave me!" exclaimed Magrit. "I'd forgotten you were even here!" She gazed at the lunatic quizzically. "You've been silent as a clam. Not like you, at all."

Wolfgang pulled his chair into the light.

"As the mage would say—'bah!' You sane types have an altogether irrational faith in the power of speech. Babble, now, there's a useful skill!"

He gazed about the room, beaming like an idiot.

"I think the boy's quite right! Not stupid at all! Of course he should go with the wizard! Where else would he learn the things he's learned? Why, think about it! A mere sprout, and he's already sown confusion and havoc! Fed a high and mighty Crud to a snarl! Which of you had accomplished such mad deeds at such an early age? Not to mention stealing a great relic!"

"Oh!" gasped Shelyid. "The Rap Sheet! We haven't even looked at it! We've wasted all this time talking about me!" He grasped the sleeve of the mage's robe and tugged vigorously. "We should look at the Rap Sheet, master—it'll tell you who your enemies are!"

Zulkeh's head lifted a bit. His face, it could now be seen, was pale and drawn.

"Later, Shelyid," said the mage. "It will keep. At the moment, there are more important things to deal with." He gazed down at the dwarf's hand, still resting upon his sleeve.

"You are firm in your resolve?" he asked. "To remain as my apprentice?"

"Oh yes, master!" cried Shelyid.

"Be not so quick, Shelyid. The road I must travel, though its exact route remains uncertain, will undoubtedly take me to distant and perilous lands. 'Twill be long, perhaps very long, before we shall return to Goimr."

"Oh, I'm not afraid!"

The wizard shook his head. "That is not my meaning." He snorted. " 'Tis certain that the timid gnome who left Goimr is no longer timid! Rash, yes. Foolhardy, yes. But certainly not lacking in courage."

He paused, took a deep breath. "I raise the question of our return to Goimr because, listening to your earlier words, I was struck by your references—three of them, if I am not mistaken—to the friend left behind, the one you so look forward to seeing again and telling of your adventures. Your 'secret,' you called it."

Zulkeh raised his eyes to Shelyid's face. "You are referring to the spider in the lower catacombs."

The dwarf's mouth fell open. "You know?"

"Certainly. Only a fool could have missed your expeditions to the lower levels. After a few such, I became curious. I followed and observed you with the spider."

He raised his hand. "I did not eavesdrop! I departed the scene after no more than a minute, and never followed you again. 'Twas clear enough—well. I am not unaware of my inadequacy as a source of emotional comfort. To anyone, much less an orphan. Some happiness the spider's company seemed to give you, and I saw no harm in it. 'Twould have been sheer cruelty to intervene."

The wizard paused, took another breath. "I am not cruel, Shelyid. Cold, yes. At times, I admit, even harsh. Perhaps other terms could be used—"

"We shall assist!" cried the first.

"The word 'callous' immediately springs to mind," mused the second.

A single gesture from Greyboar brought silence.

The pained look on Zulkeh's face faded, to be replaced by a frown.

"Doubt me not on this, Shelyid," spoke the mage. "These—gentlemen—may mock, but if you travel with me you shall soon enough learn the meaning of true cruelty. Inkman gave you but a taste of it."

"I never said you were cruel, master. I never even thought it." A guilty look crossed Shelyid's face. "I did say you were mean a few times." A look of greater guilt. "And I thought it a lot more times."

"I will allow 'mean,' dwarf." The wizard sighed. " 'Tis perhaps not far from the mark. But look you, Shelyid, we have drifted from the point. If you truly wish to see your friend again, you cannot accompany me. You must return to Goimr now. For she has not much longer to live. Certainly she will be dead before spring comes—and we are already well into autumn."

"The spider's sick!" gasped Shelyid.

"Nonsense!" snorted the mage. "A most hale and healthy arachnid! She has already lived to a ripe old age. Spiders do not live long, Shelyid. Your spider has done exceedingly well in that regard, actually."

The dwarf fought tears. "I never knew. And I promised—it's a she? A female spider? I never actually knew which sex my friend was."

"Bah!" oathed the mage. "Who cannot distinguish between the male and female arachnid is a—" His jaws clamped shut.

"Amazing!" cried the fifth.

"Who says you can't teach an old dog new tricks?" demanded the sixth.

Another gesture from Greyboar stilled the round.

After a moment, Shelyid spoke.

"Well, it makes me feel better, knowing that she had a full life. And it's nice to know what sex she was, after all this time. Maybe you could teach me more about spiders, master."

"Certainly!" spoke the mage. "A most fascinating breed, the arachnids! 'Pound for pound,' as your lowlifes would say, the fiercest predators in the animal kingdom. Moreover—" He stopped. "But let us save this for a later occasion. For the moment, we must resolve the issue before us. Do you still wish to remain with me, knowing what you now know?"

Shelyid pondered the question for perhaps a minute, then nodded his head.

"Yes, master. It's true I promised her, but there wouldn't be much point going back just to see her die. And I don't think she'd like it, anyway. Actually, I always knew she was pretty fierce, and I think she wouldn't like me, well, you know, fussing over her deathbed, and such. I'll sure miss her, though." A tear formed, but he wiped it away. "So I'll stay with you."

Then the dwarf squared his shoulders, stepped back a pace, and stared the wizard straight in the eye.

"But there's going to be some changes made!" he said shrilly.

The scene which followed is painful to relate. For the dwarf Shelyid not only behaved in a most reprehensible manner, insisting upon the most

preposterous rights and privileges, but was shamelessly aided and abetted in this impudence by Les
Six.

Their brazen role began at once.

"The lad needs a new contract!" cried the first.

"A complete overhaul of his terms of employment!"
exclaimed the second.

"But he's a youth," moaned the third, "inexperienced
at the negotiating table."

"A pawn in the hands of the boss," wailed the
fourth, "sure to be shackled in the exploiter's cunning
twist of phrase and subtlety of clause."

"Desperately in need of experienced counsel, lest
he sign himself over to helotry," opined the fifth.

"Stewards, to the fore!" bellowed the sixth. And with
these words, Les Six pulled up their chairs, forming
a semicircle around the mage.

Zulkeh stared at the half-dozen great and grinning
faces, much as a cornered fox examines the muzzles
of the hounds.

"Perhaps," said the mage, coughing, "we should first
examine the great relic which we have—just this very
night!—obtained in order to determine the nature of
our enemies. Our enemies, gentlemen! Who are—
perhaps this very moment!—closing in, their black
hearts filled with—"

"Do not concern yourself with the enemies of the
future," counseled the first.

"When you are surrounded by the enemies of the
present," advised the second.

Here Magrit intervened. "The Rap Sheet'll wait till
tomorrow, Zulkeh. And whatever enemies we've got
are so fuddled tonight they'll have a hard enough time
finding their peckers to take a piss. No, you just concentrate on this business—it'll take you hours as it is.
The rest of us can go to bed."

And so saying, she strode out of the room, stopping along the way to take Wolfgang by the hand.

"C'mon, tall and handsome, let's get laid."

Greyboar rose, stretched. "I think Ignace and I will turn in, also. Been a long day."

The wizard looked at him with appeal. "Sirrah Greyboar! Perhaps—you have been a most calming influence—the heat of negotiations—"

"Me?" cried Greyboar. "You want *me* to stick my nose into the affairs of a different trade?" He shook his head, clucking. "'Tisn't done, just isn't. Not at all proper! Besides, I wouldn't be any help, anyway. I don't really know a thing about negotiating complicated labor contracts. The fine points just don't come up in my profession. The basic provisions of my contracts are simple and straightforward, so I hardly ever run into difficulties with my employers. They pay me what they owe me when the job's done, or"—he cracked his knuckles; the house shook—"I collect from the estate."

He turned to his agent: "C'mon Ignace. Let's hit the sack." The two departed.

"Down to business," said the third, rubbing his hands.

"Point one," stated the fourth. "This 'master' business has got to go."

"'Tis demeaning to the laborer," explained the fifth.

"And most inaccurate," happily added the sixth, "as you'll soon see for yourself when examining the provisions which are about to be included in your new contract with the dwarf Shelyid."

The first: "Who is hereafter referred to as the short-statured-but-fully-qualified-apprentice Shelyid."

And this was but the beginning!

CHAPTER XXVII. *Enemies Revealed— But a Deeper Mystery Bared. A Lunatic's Exposition. A Mage's Great Disquiet. A Resolved Apprentice. Traveling Companions Found. Forward the Mage!*

"Magrit!" spoke the mage. "I require your expert assistance here. Can you not leave this—this obscene chortling and plotting to a later time?"

The witch looked up from mixing potions. "Huh?" she asked. "Oh. Yes, I suppose so." She rose, muttering fiercely, and stamped over to the table where Zulkeh was examining the Rap Sheet.

"I still can't believe," she snarled, "that two-faced rat! That smiling little slimeball! All this time, pretending to be my friend—and he even had me fooled, I got to admit."

It had been some time earlier, in mid-morning, when the various parties involved in the theft of the Rap Sheet had reconvened in Magrit's chamber. Greyboar and Ignace were alone absent, off on some business of their own. The witch had demanded to be the first to examine the relic. Zulkeh began to protest, then

531

wearily nodded his assent. And truly the mage seemed exhausted by the events of the night past—not from the adventure itself, but from the rigors of the bargaining table.

"From that day forward," he was known to say in later life, "the chambers of the Inquisition held no fears for me. The rack—I laugh! The wheel—I sneer! The whipping post—beneath my contempt!"

And so had Magrit delved deeply into the Rap Sheet, cackling with glee as the name of one unsuspected enemy after another appeared, faithfully recorded in the relic as informers of the various police agencies which had taken a keen interest in the doings of the witch. So great was her enthusiasm, in fact, that she soon broke off further examination of the Rap Sheet and began happily plotting her revenge against the half-dozen now-doomed individuals whose identity she had already ascertained.

'Twas at that point that the wizard was finally able to scrutinize the relic for his own purposes. After a few minutes, a great frown took form on his features. It was then that the mage called for Magrit's aid.

"What is it, Zulkeh?" asked the witch.

"I am totally baffled," admitted the wizard. "Look you on what is revealed herein! Of my enemies—at least, those who have been thwarting me in my attempt to decipher the meaning of the King's dream—there is not a trace! Not a whisper! Not a hint! But—well! See for yourself!" He thrust the relic before her.

The witch examined the Rap Sheet, which was now attuned to the wizard Zulkeh. Listed on its magical pages was all information concerning the mage known to all authorized, semi-authorized, quasi-authorized, pseudo-authorized and unauthorized official agencies charged with police, regulatory or espionage powers anywhere in Grotum. Many sheets did Magrit scan, her eyebrows rising steadily.

She whistled. "Oh, boy! Have you pissed off a lot of people!"

"Practically every authority in Grotum and Ozar has me listed as an arch-criminal!" cried the mage. "Me! Who has always been the most loyal of citizens! A model of propriety!" He was livid with indignation.

Magrit summoned the crowd. "You got to see this!" she boomed. A moment later, all were examining the relic.

The first to react, to Zulkeh's everlasting chagrin, were Les Six.

"Comrade!" they bellowed in one voice, surrounding the mage and pounding his back vigorously. The wizard's protestation of innocence was to no avail.

"You can't be innocent," declared the first.

"You've been accused," explained the second.

"But there have been no charges filed!" protested the mage. "No warrants issued! No subpoenas! No inquest! No trial!"

"What nonsense is this?" demanded the third.

"Would you waste the taxpayer's hard-earned money?" inquired the fourth.

"Fie on such witless notions!" exclaimed the fifth.

The round was cut short by Wolfgang.

"You're all missing the important thing!" he cried. "The cryptic cypher! It's on every page!" The lunatic grinned like an idiot. "Look here, for instance!" He pointed his finger at a notation on the page.

Zulkeh peered closely. "Yes, yes, I had noticed that—and, as you say, it appears frequently, at least once on each page. Magrit, you are more conversant in these matters than I. What is the import of this notation?"

Magrit examined the cypher, then shook her head.

"Got no idea. Surprising, too—there's not much in the way of foety gets by me."

"Of course you don't know what it means!" boomed Wolfgang. The madman cackled like, well, like a madman.

Magrit glared up at him. "Do you know something I don't, you fucking loony? Yes! I can tell by that drooling grin! Spit it out, Wolfgang! What does AVEXBU mean?"

"It's an acronym," replied the giant. "It stands for Avatar Extermination Bureau."

Magrit and Zulkeh looked puzzled. "Never heard of it," said the witch. "Nor I," chimed in the wizard.

"Of course you haven't!" agreed Wolfgang cheerfully. "It's the most secret secret society in the world. Not more than a few thousand people anywhere have ever heard of it—and most of them work for the Bureau."

"Is it an Ozarine cabal?" demanded the first.

Wolfgang shook his head. "Not exactly—although it has close ties to many Ozarine spy agencies. Very tight with the Cruds, for instance. No, it's sort of a unique outfit. Ancient, it is—traces its origins back to the Knights Rampant. The Ecclesiarchs have always encouraged it on the highest levels—by which I mean the Twelve Popes. I doubt if even most Cardinals know of it. The Popes have provided much of AVEXBU's funding for centuries. But even they don't control it. It's truly marvelous! An independent spiral of organized insanity, institutionalized madness, passed on down through the generations like syphilis!"

"Then how do you know about it, you nutcase?" demanded Magrit.

Wolfgang blushed like a schoolgirl. "Well, actually, I myself have been the subject of their inquiries. In fact, it's one of the reasons I decided to go mad. Always a good alibi, lunacy."

"You? Why would they go after you?" Magrit's face expressed disbelief.

"I'm not positive, love," responded Wolfgang, "because as soon as I found out they were sniffing around I had my first breakdown. And a doozy it was, too!" He beamed around the room. Then: "But I've always thought it was probably my size."

"You are almost certainly correct," came the quiet voice of Zulkeh. Magrit turned, gasped. The wizard had collapsed into a chair, his face pale as a ghost, a trembling hand stroking his brow.

"Are you all right?" asked Magrit.

"Yes, yes," came the impatient reply. "A moment's weakness, no more. It all makes sense to me, now. I should have known from the beginning! What other subject would so arouse the deepest enmity of the fiercest powers of the Universe? 'Tis no wonder I have not been able to interpret the King's dream!"

"What are you babbling on about?" demanded Magrit. "The both of you!"

Zulkeh coughed. "Madame, please do not take offense at what I am about to say, but—as I recall—history was never your best subject at the University."

Magrit snorted. "Hated the stuff. Dry bones, chewed over by mangy dogs."

An intemperate remark began to emerge from Zulkeh's lips, was choked back. A moment later, the mage spoke:

"I will not dispute the question now. Wolfgang, it was the acronym which confused me. 'AVEXBU' is new to me. I assume it is of recent origin. What I mean to say—we are talking about the Godferrets, are we not?"

"Right as rain! Always thought that was a crazy expression, actually. Why should rain be right? Why not wrong rain? Or left rain, maybe?"

"Wolfgang!" roared Magrit.

"What? Oh. Sorry, dear, my mind wandered. Can't be helped—I'm nuts. Yes, yes! Business first! Zulkeh, you are absolutely correct! We are indeed talking about the Godferrets—also known, at various times and places, as the Weasels of Righteousness, the Almighty's Knout, the Fangs of Piety, the Guardians of—well! I could go on—and on and on. And those, of course, are the names given by admirers! Others—heretics, infidels, suchlike monsters—have preferred other cognomens: the Darkworms, the Slime of Creation, the— well! There's a lot of names. Lot and lots of names! Not surprising, they've been around for a long time."

"Yes, they have," agreed Zulkeh. "But whence this AVEXBU?"

"Oh, that's the new name! Modern times, you know! Separation of Church and State, rights of the individual, freedom of conscience, all that folderol. Slavering sanctimony needs a secular face, nowadays! And besides—acronyms are all the rage among the upper crust, don't you know?"

"Wittgenstein!" bellowed Magrit. "Start the pot boiling—the big one! If I don't get some sensible answers out of these two we're going to have psychopath stew tonight—garnished with chopped sorcerer."

"Right away!" squeaked the salamander, scurrying toward the kitchen. Its voice came back: "Oh boy oh boy oh boy oh boy oh boy I love psychopath stew! Especially the brains! Melt in your mouth like butter!"

"Madame, this is uncouth!" protested Zulkeh. Then, seeing the inevitable riposte, he held up a hand.

"'Tis simple, witch! This—AVEXBU—is but a modern incarnation of the oldest, and easily the most vicious, of the Church's inquisitory agencies. Though, as Wolfgang says, the Ecclesiarchs long ago lost their grip on the leash. The Godferrets! They claim to answer to no one but the Old Geister himself. The most secret of secret societies—and easily the most powerful! Their influence reaches into the chambers and corridors of all the world's mightiest institutions—temporal and spiritual alike. All this, devoted to one general purpose—the ruthless extermination of Joesy. And to one specific purpose—the sniffing out and destruction of Joe's avatars."

"Joe's avatars?" demanded Magrit. "You mean—Joebacks?"

"That is, I believe, the popular name, yes."

"But that's just a fable!" protested the witch.

"Is it?" demanded the wizard fiercely. "You have, then, suddenly become an expert on Joetrics?"

Magrit snarled. "You know damn good and well I got thrown out of the University before I could qualify for the Arcanum! You should know, you rotten—"

"Please, please!" interjected Wolfgang. "Some calm! Tranquility! My nerves are shot—liable to break down any minute!"

Magrit and Zulkeh fell silent, glaring at each other. Wolfgang picked up the conversation.

"Magrit, dear," he said mildly, "what the wizard's trying to say—with his usual charm!—is that all questions surrounding Joe are mysterious and convoluted. Not to mention dangerous! Nobody can really claim to be an expert on the subject. Well, except my dear aunt Hildegard, I suppose."

"There is one recognized authority," said Zulkeh, his calm returned.

Wolfgang pursed his lips. "Well, yes, there's Uncle Manya. But he's crazier'n a loon, you know. Would have been locked up years ago except his family's so rich they can keep him on the estate—has a whole mansion to himself, I hear!"

A thought apparently came to the lunatic. "Wait a

minute," he mused. "What if he's not really crazy? The
Godferrets were never happy with him. Tried to kill
him a few times, in fact! Nutty idea, of course—
trying to kill a Kutumoff on Kutumoff soil. The
Godferrets ought to have themselves institutionalized,
the idiots! But maybe the General got tired of running assassins—told Uncle Manya to pretend he was
a fruitcake, so his dogs could get a rest."

"Sort of like you, you mean," piped up Shelyid from
his chair.

Wolfgang bellowed in outrage.

"Like me? What an insult! I'm a certified psychotic!
The head psychiatrist at the world-famous asylum at
Begfat has said so himself! Many times! And in any
number of articles published in the most prestigious
psychological journals!"

"You're the head psychiatrist at the asylum at
Begfat," protested Shelyid.

"Yes, that's true. What of it? The man's still a giant
in his field! One of the most respected figures in
psychoanalytic circles the world over! Wolfgang the
great psychiatrist says Wolfgang the big nut is a
madman—who are you to question his word?"

Shelyid frowned, scratched his head. "There's something about this that doesn't make sense."

Wolfgang now appealed to the wizard. "You know,
Zulkeh, you really have to concentrate more on the
psychological subjects in the boy's education. Look at
the poor tyke! Totally confused by the most basic
concepts!"

Zulkeh waved the protest away. "Yes, no doubt. But
for the moment, I must discuss a more pressing matter
with my apprentice. Shelyid, have you followed this
conversation?"

"Oh yes, mast—*professor*."

The wizard glared fiercely at his apprentice, but

the dwarf held his ground. "It's in the contract!" he shrilled. Shelyid dug into his tunic, took out a booklet. "It's right here—right in Article I. 'The apprentice is henceforth to address the wizard as *professor*. Under no circumstances is the term *master* to be used, except under the following provisions: clause a: at such times as—'"

"Cease! Cease!" roared the mage. "Remind me not of that nefarious contract! That—that product of coercion!"

"And when was a labor contract ever squeezed from a greedy exploiter other than by coercion?" demanded the second.

Wolfgang interjected himself again. "Please, please! My nerves! My fragile grasp on reality! Even now I can feel it cracking!"

All fell silent. Then Zulkeh glowered and spoke again.

"What I was about to say, wretched dw—"

"No slurs based on stature!" piped the dwarf. "Article II, clause a."

Zulkeh ground his teeth. "Misbegott—"

"No slurs based on genetic origins!" piped the dwarf. "Article II, clause b."

Zulkeh face's was now beet red. He leapt to his feet, gesticulating wildly. "Anthropophage of Reason! Creature of darkness! Minion of the lowest sort! Base cur of low degree!" He continued in this vein for a minute or so.

When he was done, Shelyid brows were knitted in thought. "I think those're all okay," he said uncertainly. He appealed to Les Six: "Aren't they?"

"Within the letter of the contract," stated the third.

"Though 'base cur of low degree' rather bends the spirit," opined the fourth.

Where this would have led will remain unknown,

for 'twas at that very moment that Greyboar and Ignace came into the room. Ignace's face was flushed with pleasure.

"Good news!" he cried. "The heat's off in New Sfinctr! We can go back—in fact, we're headed off today!"

Zulkeh's attention was distracted. "But the King of Sundjhab and his heir are barely cold in their graves!" he protested.

"Actually," rumbled Greyboar, "I think the Sundjhabi practice is cremation. Be that as it may, it seems there's been some little changing of the guard in the Sundjhab. Whole new dynasty, in fact. And of course they'd just as soon everybody forgot all about the old monarch. Whose official name in the Sundjhab is now 'the Devil's Spawn.'" The strangler frowned. "Don't much care for that kind of disrespect for my guru. May just go down there some day and speed a few souls along the wheel of time."

"Later for that!" exclaimed Ignace. "There's been too much of this philosophy business as it is. Right now we're off to New Sfinctr!"

"If you don't mind my asking," asked Magrit, "why in the world are you so eager to get back to New Sfinctr? The city's a cesspool!"

"Pesthole of the planet," agreed Ignace cheerfully. "Armpit of the world. It's great for business!"

"When are you leaving, did you say?" asked Zulkeh.

"Within the hour," said Greyboar.

"A moment, then, if you please," said the mage. "I have a favor to ask. But first—" Here he turned back to his apprentice. A frown began to appear, then faded. Zulkeh sighed.

"Shelyid, if you will kindly leave aside for the moment the fine points of our new contract, I am attempting to commit a kindness. How much of the preceding discussion did you actually understand?"

"All that stuff about the AVEXBU and the God-ferrets and stuff?" asked Shelyid. Zulkeh nodded.

"Well," admitted the gnome, "not actually a whole lot. I was paying real close attention, too, 'cause I could tell it has something to do with Joe, and I've always liked the Joe stuff you teach me. But I really didn't understand what it was all about, except that everybody seems real nervous."

Zulkeh snorted. "Nervous indeed! The key point you must understand now, Shelyid, is that there is no subject in all the world which is more perilous to meddle with than what you call 'Joe stuff.' And it is now clear that in some manner—I remain completely mystified as to how it all happened, by the way—I have become thoroughly enmeshed in 'Joe stuff.' 'Twas not by my choice, I can assure you! I am not pusillanimous, mind you—no practicing sorcerer can be—but I am not foolhardy."

He frowned, stroked his beard. "But there is no point in bemoaning the reality which faces one. Entwined in 'Joe stuff' I have become, and I must seize the tiger by the tail. Thus will my road forward be even more fraught with danger than I had foreseen. I say this, Shelyid, by way of a preface. For once again, my loyal but stup—not brilliant apprentice, I offer your release from my guard'anship."

"You mean you don't want me to come?" asked the dwarf, his voice little with hurt.

"I did not say that, gno—short one," snapped the mage. "For myself alone, I would prefer that you did come." Zulkeh was silent for a moment, then: "In truth, it would be a great comfort to me. But I would not needlessly expose you to the perils ahead."

"Oh, that's okay!" cried Shelyid. "I told you before,

mas—professor—I'm not afraid. And besides, I really like Joe stuff. I'm real good at it, too! I've always been good at the Joe stuff you teach me! I never forget any of it." The dwarf blushed, then said hesitantly: "You know, I think it's my best subject."

An expression of surprise crossed the wizard's face. He looked to Magrit and Wolfgang.

"You know, Shelyid's right. He always did soak up what little Joetrics I taught him." The wizard stroked his beard. "Odd, really, very odd. 'Tis normally the most difficult subject for apprentices. Apprentices! Wizards themselves fumble at Joetrics, in their great majority. Of course, I didn't expose the boy to but the simplest aspects, you'll understand! But still—" He fell silent, musing.

"Of course the boy's good at it!" boomed Wolfgang. "I've said it before, I'll say it again—the little tyke's got a knack for madness! And nothing's crazier than— what'd the lad call it?—'Joe stuff', yes, 'Joe stuff'!"

The lunatic waved his arms around wildly, like, well, like a lunatic.

"It's mad! It's insane! Heresies galore! Schisms enough to turn a schizophrenic green with envy! And talk about paranoia! Whisper the words 'Joe's back' in an alley somewhere—Church and State both will scream for your blood! Ask any priest to tell you about Joe and he'll shame a deaf-mute! And—"

"Enough!" roared Magrit.

The wizard now addressed himself to the strangler.

"Sirrah Greyboar, as I mentioned before, I have a favor to ask."

"What is it?"

"As I understand it, you and your agent are departing for New Sfinctr within the hour?" Greyboar nodded. "My apprentice and I, for our part, must wend our way to the Mutt. For 'tis clear that I must, before all else, attempt to consult with Uncle Manya. Sane or insane, he remains the world's authority on Joetrics. If there is anyone who can shed light on the mysteries which surround me, 'twill be he."

Zulkeh paused, coughed apologetically. "I am, per-haps—what is the popular expression?—yes, 'beating about the bush.' The point is this. For some consid-erable distance, we shall be traveling the same route. Of course, our paths will diverge at Blain. But for the first many days, well—"

"You want to come with us?" asked Greyboar.

Zulkeh coughed again. "It seemed to me, you under-stand, the occasional footpad or highwayman—"

"No problem, professor," said Ignace, grinning widely. "Sure and you can come along. Greyboar'll no doubt enjoy the philosophical conversation. And, it's true," he added, his grin now evil, "we're not likely to be bothered by cutthroats."

"Haven't actually been mugged since I was eight," rumbled Greyboar. "The thing went badly for the footpad, and word got around. He survived, of course, I was too short to reach his throat, but—well—"

"Best thing that ever happened to the guy!" chipped in Ignace. "He made lots more as a beggar than he ever did as a cutpurse. People always chipped into his hat, feeling as sorry for him as they did, all twitchy and mangled up like that."

"Yeah, sure, it'd be a pleasure," said Greyboar. "On the way, I think I'll teach Shelyid a little fingerwork. Kid's got a great natural choke." He forestalled Zulkeh's protest with an upraised hand.

"Nothing fancy, nothing fancy. But the boy can't study sorcery every minute of the day. And you never know when a little professional fingerwork will come in handy, even in your trade."

"Well, yes," allowed Zulkeh. "There is the occasional

rowdy demon. Oft cranky, your demons, especially if you summon them during copulation."

"If you want to come, we're leaving now," announced Ignace.

"We are ready. Are we not, Shelyid?"

"Oh yes, professor. The sack's right here."

"Let us be off, then. For even as I speak, time wanes!"

"Wait! Wait!" cried Shelyid. "We forgot something!"

The wizard frowned. "And what is that?"

"Well, it's the first of the month, right?"

"Yes, 'tis November 1, Year of the Jackal," replied the mage. "What of it?"

A huge grin split the gnome's face. Shelyid extended his arm, palm facing up.

"Payday!"

A black frown began to take form on Zulkeh's brow. But it faded, to be replaced by a rare smile.

"Why, so it is," spoke the mage. "As the contract says—Article III, clause a, if I am not mistaken—'the short-statured-but-fully-qualified-apprentice shall earn the wage of one shilling a month, to be paid on the first day of the month.'" The wizard fumbled in his purse, drew out a coin, and placed it in Shelyid's hand.

"Of course," spoke the mage, "from a logical standpoint this entire business is somewhat absurd. You are yourself, after all"—he coughed—"well, let us simply say that the funds actually originate from you in the first place."

"Is it not ever so?" demanded the first.

"Is not all value created from the toil of the suffering masses?" asked the second.

"Only then seized in its entirety by the grasping hand of the exploiter!" added the third.

"To be added to his already-obscene accumulation of plenty!" This from the fourth.

"From which bloated mass of wealth but a pittance is returned to the laborer!" The fifth.

"Upon which starvation wages the downtrodden working classes eke out their miserable existence," concluded the sixth.

No doubt a long-winded economic debate would have ensued, save for the intervention of Wolfgang.

"Crazy thing, money!" he boomed. "And they say we lunatics are insane! Nonsense—just another example of the superiority of lunacy over lucidity! Only sober-minded rational people with their feet planted firmly on the ground would ever come up with such a goofy idea as money! Won't find us demented types worrying over money! We've got real things to fret over! How do unicorns propagate when they've got this fetish about virginity? Why does a troll's tongue drool when it's naked as an egg and has sweat glands? Why are krakens extinct? Are they extinct? Did they ever exist? Why do—"

"Come, Shelyid, let us be off!" cried the mage, hustling his apprentice out the door. "For even as the lunatic raves, time wanes!"

PART XVIII

In Which We Conclude This
Volume of Our Chronicle By Resuming,
With Firm Resolve Though Great Distaste,
Our Skeptical Scrutiny of the *Autobiography* of
That Sfondrati-Piccolomini Fellow, in This
Portion of Whose Tale Are Related Impudent
Revelries Over Recent Reverses Suffered
By The Lawful Order of Grotum As Well
As Divers and Dramatic Encounters
and Leave-Takings.

The Autobiography of Benvenuti Sfondrati-Piccolomini,
Episode 9: Dogs, Divas, Dements and Departures

So it was on such a wretched horse that I rode onto
the estates of General Kutumoff.

As I thought, the trip had taken a day longer than predicted. It was not until the morning of November 1
that we arrived at our destination. The estates were
vast, or so they seemed to me. But when I made
comment to that effect, Gwendolyn told me that they
were actually quite small, by Groutch standards. I

realized again the impossibility of gauging Grotum by
Ozarine scales. Though rich and mighty, the Ozarine—
not to speak of Ozarae proper—is small in geographic
size. Whereas Grotum! A world in itself, it sometimes
seemed to me.

Truth to tell, I had no idea we had entered onto
the estates until Gwendolyn told me. To all outward
appearances, the estates seemed much like the rest of
the countryside of the Mutt. Prosperous, well-tended
fields; farmers busy about their business; modest but
well-kept farmhouses.

"Not quite what I had expected," I remarked.

"How so?"

"Well, from all you've told me of what you call the
Groutch land question, I'd rather been expecting to
see miserable, half-starved serfs, stooped in their
labor, overseers cracking whips, that sort of thing."

Gwendolyn was shocked. "On the estates of *General Kutumoff?*"

I saw the storm gathering on her brow. This experience, if you've never undergone it, is somewhat akin
to watching a mounting tidal wave. From the vantage
point of a very small, very flat island.

"Obviously I misunderstood!" I hastened to add.

"I should think so!"

I was relieved to see the storm pass. After a
moment, Gwendolyn even laughed.

"I keep forgetting how little you know of Grotum.
The Mutt is—not like the rest of Grotum."

"I can believe that! Not that I've seen much else
beside the forest and Goimria."

At that moment our conversation was interrupted
by a great baying sound. I looked ahead. My blood
ran cold. Toward us, racing like the wind, was an
enormous pack of—dogs? Wolves? Snarls? I couldn't
really tell. Whatever they were, they were utterly

horrifying. It wasn't simply their size, but the gaping jaws, the slavering tongues—most of all, the frenzy with which they were bounding toward us. Futile though it was, I reached behind me for my sword.

"Oh, will you relax? It's just the General's puppies. They're always excited when people come to visit."

"Those are *puppies*?"

But it could not be gainsaid. Once the—creatures—reached us, they began acting just like eager and undisciplined pups. Gwendolyn leapt off her horse and the beasts swarmed all over her. A minute or two of rough play followed.

I myself remained on my horse. A vast horde of the things gathered about me, peering up with puzzlement, whining and whimpering with confusion at my unseemly behavior. I remained, I say, on the horse.

"Oh, Benvenuti, you're such a spoilsport. You'll hurt their feelings."

"Let them die of heartbreak. I am not romping about with puppies the size of timber wolves."

Laughing, Gwendolyn shook off a half dozen of the brutes and remounted. She gave me a mischievous sidelong glance.

"And here I thought you wanted an adventurous life."

"And so I do, Gwendolyn. A life full of drama and romance and high adventure. Reasonable adventures. Rescuing fair maidens from ogres. Slaying dragons in their lairs. Storming the gates of hell. Not—I repeat, *not*—suicidal acts involving puppies the size of timber wolves." A horrible thought came to me. "Do the adult dogs roam loose?"

"All over the place. The General doesn't believe in kennels." She was giggling now. "The look on your face—it's priceless! But you can relax. The grown-up dogs are very dignified. Very aloof with people, until they get to know you. Especially Fangwulf."

"Who—or should I say, what—is Fangwulf?"

"He's the General's head dog. The leader of the pack." Again, that mischievous sidelong glance. A grim foreboding filled my heart. Immediately confirmed.

"I'll have to make sure the General introduces you to Fangwulf," she said.

Some time later, a great mansion loomed on the horizon. A lane led to it from the main road, shaded by trees on either side. I had expected to turn down that way, but Gwendolyn continued straight ahead. In response to my quizzical eyebrow, she explained: "The General won't be there. He's always at his shack, except for a few evenings when Madame Kutumoff forces him to attend one of her soirees."

A mile or so further on, we turned down a trail leading off from the left of the road. Then, through a small wood, and into a clearing. At the far edge of the clearing, nestled under the overhanging boughs of a huge sycamore, rested a hut. It was easily the most ramshackle structure I had yet seen in the Mutt.

I pointed to it, chuckling. "Now that's more what I thought housing for the downtrodden serfs should look like."

"Ostentatious, isn't it? It's the General's shack. I think he overdoes the thing, myself. But he's quite proud of the tradition."

I forbore comment. Odd place, the Mutt, I believe I've mentioned before. As we drew near, I noticed some mounds scattered about in the clearing near the hut, looking for all the world like little haystacks. As we came nearer, they began to move. The truth dawned upon me.

"They're the size of buffalos," I whispered shakily.

"Nonsense! Any decent buffalo will weigh in at around a ton. The dogs don't average but three, maybe four hundred pounds."

"Dogs are not supposed to be that big," I hissed.

"Why are you whispering?" boomed Gwendolyn. The sound of her powerful voice brought the monsters to their feet. But I was relieved to see that they made no move in our direction. They simply stood there, watching us impassively.

As Gwendolyn drew up before the hut, a man emerged. Rather short, perhaps a bit on the heavy side. Altogether, completely unremarkable in his appearance. A battered campaign hat was perched on his head. He leaned on a cane held in his left hand. In its right he held a short, very pungent cigar.

"Hello, General," said Gwendolyn.

"Gwendolyn," responded the General, nodding his head. Gwendolyn began to introduce me, but before she got two words out of her mouth a pack of raggedy children came boiling out of the hut.

"Gwendolyn! Gwendolyn! Gwendolyn! Gwendolyn!" they shrieked, capering about. A moment later Gwendolyn was off her horse and repeating—more gently—her earlier antics with the puppies. I was forced to the painful conclusion that the love of my life had no sense of aristocratic reserve whatsoever.

Eventually, she extracted herself from the squealing pack.

"General Kutumoff, meet Benvenuti Sfondrati-Piccolomini."

A look of interest came into his face. "So this is the young man I've been expecting."

I was taken completely by surprise. So, judging from her expression, was Gwendolyn.

"How did—I didn't say anything about Benvenuti in my note."

The General looked at her. "Oh, I wasn't expecting him to come with you, Gwendolyn. But I received a letter from his uncles a month ago saying he was coming to Grotum. Ludovigo and Rodrigo said the boy was bound to get into some kind of trouble, which means he'd wind up here sooner or later. And since he's here with you, I'd say he's in serious trouble."

A plain-looking fellow, but I learned then that he was perhaps the most observant man I ever met. What he saw in Gwendolyn and me at that moment—some subtlety of expression, or posture—brought a gleam into his eyes.

"Young Benvenuti," he said, puffing on his cigar, "I believe you have committed the gravest of sins. I speak as a soldier."

"And what is that?"

"In classic Sfondrati-Piccolomini manner, you have engaged yourself simultaneously on two fronts. I predict you will have an adventurous life."

I flushed, as did Gwendolyn. The General chuckled.

"I don't disapprove, mind you. Love is not war, appearances and popular opinion to the contrary. Gwendolyn, it's nice to see a softness, for once, on that blade of a soul. As for you, young Benvenuti, it's always a pleasure to see a bloodline run true. You are, I trust, illegitimate?"

I gaped like a fish. Nodded.

"Excellent, excellent. I approve of Sfondrati-Piccolomini bastards. Got no use for the rest of that lot." He turned back into his hut. "Come in, come in."

Entering, I found that the hut was much bigger on the inside than it had seemed from without.

"You've added on," said Gwendolyn.

The General looked uncomfortable. "Yes, yes, I have. It's still the smallest residence on the estate, mind you.

But I admit I'm stretching the limit of tradition. Still, I had no choice. The children needed more room to play, and Fangwulf was getting grumpy, not being able to stretch out properly."

I could see it coming, tried to head it off, but Gwendolyn was too quick.

"Benvenuti's just dying to meet Fangwulf!" she cried. The words out, she gave me an immense grin. Completely unfazed, she was, by my answering scowl.

Amusement gleamed in the General's eyes. "Well, *of course* he wants to meet the top dog." He stuck two fingers in his mouth and emitted a piercing whistle. A moment later, a batch of children's heads were in the door.

"Go fetch Fangwulf," said the General. The faces disappeared in a flash.

"And mind you follow protocol this time!" he roared after them.

"He's a good dog, Fangwulf," explained the General. "But as he gets on in years, he's getting prickly about the formalities."

A minute or so later, a girl—perhaps six years old—skidded into the hut. She drew herself up into a rigidly military posture. Then, in a shrill voice, intoned the following:

> *"All hail Fangwulf! Fangwulf of Wide Fame!*
> *"All hail the Fleshripper! The Hideous Hound!*
> *"Fangwulf of the Loping Stride!*
> *"The Ravening Gullet Himself!*
> *"Sired by Consumption out of Omnigorge!*
> *"The Slouching Rough Beast!*
> *"Its Hour Come Round At Last!"*

How shall I describe the dog who came into the hut? From a dispassionate, scientific, objective standpoint, the task is not too difficult. The beast was something of a triple-lifesize cross between a mastiff and a wolfhound, combining the most fearsome features of both—the great jaws of a mastiff with the long legs and teeth of the wolfhound. The fur was relatively short and bristly, colored black and brown except for a white spot above one eye.

But all this was trivial. For I am an artist, with an artist's eye, and I could not help but think of a portrait of the great horror. The difficulty was in choosing a suitable title.

Death Incarnate would be too abstract. The phrase doesn't capture the saliva dripping from the great canine fangs.

Slavering Beast of Hell, on the other hand, connotes a certain mindless rage. And while I could not miss the oceanic fury in those glowing red eyes, neither could I escape the great, cold, pitiless intelligence which gleamed there also.

Other titles flashed through my mind as well, in that last moment of my life: *Satan's Nightmare. The Big Crunch. Doom Itself.*

I thought Gwendolyn's description was utterly inappropriate.

"Isn't he just the most beautiful dog!" she cried. And so saying, Gwendolyn flung herself onto the monster. When my horrified paralysis passed, I discovered that the thing was licking her face. While she, for her part, rumpled his fur and nuzzled his jowls. Fortunately, the more energetic antics she had conducted with the puppies earlier were forgone.

I saw the General's eyes upon me, weighing and judging.

"I—that is, he's certainly quite impressive," I said, very weakly.

"Nonsense. He's a hideous creature from the darkest

pit of hell. Not even a snarl could stand against him, except perhaps an ancient forest snarl. Snarls are just great natural killers, while he's been bred for it, generation after generation."

He gazed at the affectionate embrace, took a puff on his cigar. Then, with a gesture, he drew me out of the hut. Once in the clearing, he drew another puff on the cigar, and shook his head.

"You don't understand Grotum yet. You may never. It's a handicap, being Ozarine."

I started to speak. He held up his hand.

"Please, please. I was not criticizing. Your uncles were fine officers. Two of the best that ever served with me. Bitter men, of course. Couldn't really accept Grotum. And born at least a century too late to be Ozarine. Not the least of Ozar's many crimes, that it drives its best to become mercenaries."

He took a last puff on his cigar and threw the butt away. "Enough of that. You've a lifetime to learn these things, and you seem to be off to a decent start. Very good start. Precious few men in this world have a heart big enough to give to Gwendolyn. Fewer still have a heart big enough to win hers. I congratulate you, sir."

I didn't know what to say.

"Don't know what to say? Excellent, excellent. It's a fine and proper thing for bold young men to be tongue-tied by the sagacity of their elders. A fine and proper thing."

He turned back to the hut. "And now, I need to speak to Gwendolyn. I have news."

At that very moment, Gwendolyn herself came out. "I need to talk to you, General. I just found out a few weeks ago that the Ozarine are sending a Rap Sheet to—"

"I know, Gwendolyn, I know."

Gwendolyn was stunned. "How did you—"

The General smiled. "I found out about it the same way I found out that the problem's already been taken care of. From Hildegard."

Gwendolyn was speechless. The General's smile widened.

"Don't know what to say? Excellent, excellent. It's a fine and proper thing for bold young women to be tongue-tied by the sagacity of their elders. A fine and proper thing."

He took Gwendolyn by the elbow and moved her toward the horses. "Why don't you go up to the house? Hildegard's there. She can tell you about the whole thing."

Gwendolyn leapt on her horse and took off toward the mansion at a gallop. I followed at a somewhat less precipitous pace. By the time I reached the front door, Gwendolyn had disappeared inside. I was in such a hurry to hear the news myself that I didn't take the time to examine the building. Only an impression of great size registered.

I entered through a pair of double doors and found myself in a large foyer. There was no one present. Down a hallway to my left I heard voices— Gwendolyn's, and others. I followed the sounds, and found myself in a large room with high ceilings. My artist's eye was at once drawn to the marvelous paintings on the ceilings, which depicted scenes from various great operas.

The room was sparsely furnished. A grand piano stood toward the far wall, a few chairs and music stands scattered about it. At the near end of the room were several large and comfortable looking sofas and easy chairs clumped around a couple of low tables. Most of the space in between was empty, exposing a beautiful parquet floor. The room was very brightly lit from an entire wall of windows. The other walls, covered in a pale apricot watered silk, were decorated with an extensive collection of antique musical instruments.

Gwendolyn was standing by the piano, her back to me. A middle-aged woman, rather pretty, was sitting in a chair nearby. Another woman, elderly but very vigorous looking, was standing behind the piano. She was almost as tall as Gwendolyn. Her hair was white as snow, drawn back in a tight bun. A serene smile graced her face.

"But, Gwendolyn, I insist!" she said. "You must hear this aria first."

Without waiting for Gwendolyn's reply, the white-haired woman leaned over and began playing the piano. It was only then that I realized she wasn't standing behind the piano—she was sitting. She must have been well-nigh eight feet tall!

A beautiful melody filled the room. Gwendolyn clenched her fist and raised it over the piano. Her whole body exuded anger and frustration. But the melody was too much. After a moment, her fist opened, her hand fell to her side. Slowly, the tension eased out of her shoulders. By the end, she was even humming along to the tune.

The giant woman finished the melody with a flourish.

"There! Isn't it just grand? It's from the Big Banjo's new opera. He's here, you know? He came two weeks ago, in order to put the finishing touches on the opera. It's called *I Ladro*. Such a dramatic libretto! It's about a highwayman who wins the love of the beautiful wife of an old miser while he's robbing them. Then, after the old man and his young wife get thrown in prison, the highwayman rescues them and then—"

"*Hildegard!*"

The old woman sighed with exasperation. "Gwendolyn, you are such a monomaniac. Very well, then. I suppose we'll have to discuss this Rap Sheet business first, or I won't get any peace. But when we're done, you must promise me to read the libretto. So dramatic! Everyone's dead at the end, of course. After the old miser slays the highwayman with his cane in a duel, his wife commits suicide and he—"

"*Hildegard!*"

"—dies of heartbreak after repenting his lifelong obsession—"

"*Hildegard!*"

"—with money. There, I got it out! All right, dear, I'll tell you all about the Rap Sheet. But first, who is this very handsome young man standing behind you?"

I hadn't realized she'd noticed me. The old woman—Hildegard, apparently—had never looked in my direction once. Gwendolyn turned. Her face was set in its hawk look. But for just that one moment, when she first looked at me, a trace of softness came into her face.

"Oh," said Hildegard. "I see."

Gwendolyn turned back. "See what?" she demanded.

Hildegard's only reply was a smile and a quick flurry of notes on the piano. Not a tune, really, just a sudden air of joy and happiness. Gwendolyn's face reddened a bit.

The third woman in the room suddenly stood up and came over to me, her hands outstretched.

"Welcome! Welcome! I am Madame Kutumoff."

I took her hands in mine and bowed.

"Enchanted, Madame. I am Benvenuti Sfondrati-Piccolomini."

"Which branch?" asked Madame Kutumoff.

I began to explain where my immediate family line

fit on the complex hereditary tree of the Sfondrati-Piccolomini clan, but before I got very far into it she began nodding her head.

"Yes, yes, I know it. Two of your uncles—Ludovigo and Rodrigo, if memory serves me correctly—served with my husband some years ago." Still holding my hands, she looked at Gwendolyn and then back at me.

"I predict you will have an adventurous life," said Madame Kutumoff.

Hildegard laughed. Never, in all my life, had I heard more melodious laughter.

Gwendolyn spoke. "If you two gossips are through chortling over my love life, can we get on with the business at hand?" But she was smiling.

"Very well, dear." Hildegard placed her hands on top of the piano, fingers interlaced. "Last night—right at the stroke of midnight on Halloween—I had a vision, you see."

"Where was this?"

Hildegard frowned with puzzlement. "My vision? It was in my head, of course."

"No, no. Where were you—when you had this vision?"

Hildegard was still frowning. "Why, let me see. I believe I was sitting in that chair over there—the one against the wall. We were all here, discussing the Big Banjo's latest—"

Gwendolyn threw up her hands with frustration. "Hildegard! What were you doing *here*? The last time I saw you was at the Abbey, when you told me you were being watched too closely to leave and you needed me to take your message to Zulkeh in Goimr. So what are you doing on the loose?"

"But that was then. This is now. The past and the present are different, Gwendolyn. That's the one truth you can always be sure of. I keep trying to explain that to the Old Geister, but He's just so set in His ways. I'm afraid all that omnipotent nonsense has quite gone to His head. Why, do you know that in His latest tablet He claims—"

"Hildegard, please! Never mind. You came here. Then you had a vision. Let's please stick to the Rap Sheet, if you don't mind. I've been charging all over central Grotum, warning everybody about it."

"Well, I should hope so! Such horrible things, those Rap Sheets. But we won't have to worry about this one they sent to Grotum."

"Why not?"

"Because it's been taken away from them, dear— from the horrid Ozarines." Hildegard looked at me, an apologetic expression in her face. "Please don't take that personally, Benvenuti."

I waved it away.

"How?" demanded Gwendolyn. "And how do you know that?"

Hildegard looked confused. "Well, I don't actually know how it was done. But I imagine we'll find out from my nephew when he gets here. I expect him any day now."

"Who? Wolfgang? He's in Prygg—at least, that's where he said he was going."

"Oh, yes. He's just leaving there today."

Gwendolyn sighed. "Hildegard, Prygg is hundreds of miles away—as the crow flies. It'll take Wolfgang weeks to get here."

"Oh no, dear. Not Wolfgang."

Gwendolyn sighed again. "Never mind. But if you don't know how it was taken, how do you know that it was taken at all?"

"I told you—I had a vision. Last night, at midnight, I suddenly saw a monster. Two monsters, actually.

There was a little monster inside a big monster, although the little monster was actually bigger than the big monster. And then there was another little monster and he was suddenly inside the big monster too, except that he wasn't bigger than the big monster the way the other little monster was. Oh no, not at all! Instead, the second little monster got smaller and smaller until he disappeared. And then I heard a great wailing in the sky, and a great singing in the earth, and I knew."

"Knew what?"

Again, Hildegard looked confused. "Why—so many things. I knew the Rap Sheet was taken away from people who shouldn't have it, and I knew the time was here. Sooner than I'd expected. I had so hoped I could convince the Old Geister to set things right beforehand. But one has to look facts in the face. He refused to listen to me, and now things will be unpleasant. Very unpleasant, I'm afraid."

Gwendolyn shook her head. She spoke between gritted teeth.

"Hildegard, you are making no sense at all! What is this 'time is here' you're talking about?"

Hildegard looked away. For a long moment, she stared out the window. When she turned back, the expression on her face was a strange mix of serenity and fatalism.

"Joe's time, dear. He's coming back."

Gwendolyn frowned. She started to say something, but Hildegard suddenly reached out and placed her fingertips on Gwendolyn's lips. If the gesture hadn't been done so gracefully, it would have been grotesque, so incredibly long was her arm.

"Hush, Gwendolyn. I know you don't like to hear about Joe, but just this once, listen to me. Don't say anything, just listen. Because he is coming back, and whether you like it or not, you'll have to deal with it. We all will."

She took her hand away. "Actually, it's not that simple. Joe—the old Joe, I mean—is gone forever. So he can't actually just come back. But he's—well, returning. Let's put it that way. It's perhaps a fine distinction, but it's important to me."

Suddenly she laughed, that amazing musical laugh.

"Of course, it's not an important distinction for some people! God's Own Tooth, for instance—not to mention that whole pack of Popes."

Gwendolyn walked away a few steps. She radiated frustration and impatience. Hildegard stood up and went over to her. I could now see that she was almost as tall as Wolfgang. She stroked Gwendolyn's great mane of black hair.

Gwendolyn smiled.

"I don't know what is it about you, Hildegard. But I can never stay angry with you."

"Well, I should hope not! I am, after all, the Abbess of the Sisters of Tranquility."

A moment later they were both laughing. When they stopped, Gwendolyn looked up at Hildegard with a rueful expression.

"Just tell me this, Abbess. I can't make sense of the rest of it—but are you sure the Rap Sheet's been taken from the Ozarines?"

Hildegard looked shocked. Madame Kutumoff was scandalized.

"Gwendolyn!" she cried. "How could you say such a thing? Hildegard's visions are infallible!"

In desperation, Gwendolyn looked at me.

"Does any of this make any sense, Benvenuti?"

I pondered the question, reviewing my uncles' advice. Nothing seemed relevant to the question of the infallibility of the visions of a gigantic Abbess. So I applied common sense.

"Gwendolyn, precious few things have made sense to me since I landed in Grotum. So why should this be any different? But the solution is obvious—we wait a few days for Wolfgang to show up and clarify everything with his twin powers of madness and amnesia." When the laughter settled down, I continued: "If he doesn't show up, we reexamine our situation. And in the meantime—" I turned to Madame Kutumoff. "Did you say that the Big Banjo was still here?"

"Why, yes, he is."

"I would take it as a great privilege if you would introduce me."

"I shall be delighted, young man."

I turned back to Gwendolyn. Suddenly, I was bathed in her smile.

"Good!" cried Hildegard. "That's settled. And you, young lady, are going to sing. We haven't heard your voice in ages. The Big Banjo was complaining about it, just the other day."

Madame Kutumoff was clapping her hands. "Oh, yes! That will be such a joy." She stuck two fingers in her mouth and emitted a piercing whistle. A moment later, a very proper looking butler appeared in the doorway. Tall, spare, polished, groomed within an inch of his life. Aplomb personified.

"Madame whistled?"

"Yes, Andrew. Gwendolyn and her friend, Benvenuti, will be staying with us. Can you see to their rooms, please?"

Gwendolyn took my hand. "We'll just need one room."

Madame Kutumoff eyed us thoughtfully. "Such vigorous young people. Best make it the room at the far end of the second floor, Andrew."

"My very thought, Madame," said the butler, nodding his head.

Madame Kutumoff smiled at us. "You'll find the bed in that room is very comfortable. And those of us who are insomniacs will find it very comfortable, too. It doesn't squeak."

The next morning, following breakfast, I was introduced to the Big Banjo. It was a great moment in my life, although, truth to tell, the man didn't pay much attention to me. He was far too busy trying to convince Gwendolyn to be the prima donna for his next opera.

No, I am not joking. It came as a surprise to me, I can assure you. I had come to adore Gwendolyn's unique voice, but the thought had never crossed my mind that she could sing—at least, by operatic standards. Yet here was the world's greatest opera composer—such, at least, was my opinion—intently waging a campaign to convince Gwendolyn to take the stage.

"Not a chance," she said, over and again. But the Big Banjo was stubborn. He sat in his chair, his back ramrod straight, glaring at her down his long nose.

"But it's such nonsense, Gwendolyn! The Rap Sheet's a thing of the past. There's no reason you can't forego agitation for a few months. And the part's perfect for you! No, not even that—the part *requires* you. I don't know another singer could fill the role."

An innocent smile came onto Gwendolyn's face. "Oh, that can't be true! Why, I hear these new singers for the Gesamtkunstwerkgenie put everyone else to shame."

The Big Banjo's eyes blazed. "That's not singing! Bellowing, grunting—call it what you like, but don't call it singing!"

Gwendolyn's smile became angelic. "How can you say that? Why, the whole world's waiting with bated breath for the grand opening of his new opera house next year. He's a genius—no, that's not quite right. He's *the* genius of all time! Everyone says so." Her smile now radiated holy beatitude. "They even say you're learning a few tricks from him."

The Big Banjo shot to his feet like a rocket. For a moment, he stood glaring down at Gwendolyn. Then, suddenly, he began to laugh.

"Yes, yes, it's quite true. I've tried to keep it a secret, but it's no use. I am a child at the feet of the master. But I fear I shall die of old age before he finishes the first act."

In the end, he was able to prevail upon Gwendolyn to sing an aria he had written for her part in the projected opera. No sooner had she agreed than Madame Kutumoff was bustling about rounding up a pack of musicians from various nooks and crannies of the huge mansion. It wasn't but ten minutes later that the first bars of the music started, and Gwendolyn began to sing.

I was stunned. All the deep strength of her voice, put to that marvelous music, was like the soaring of a great heart. A heart with the power of the universe, unleashed, triumphant, filled with hope and glory. The Big Banjo had not been wrong. I could think of no other voice which could possibly have conveyed that music.

When she finished, there was no applause. Applause would have been—trivial. After a moment's silence, Gwendolyn said: "It is wonderful. Where does this aria come? In the first act?"

"No, Gwendolyn. It's the finale."

"The finale? But—this is a song of—of joy, and victory. It's not at all tragic."

The Big Banjo shrugged. "I am becoming weary of tragedy. Our people have had enough of it. I thought I would compose something different. And besides, I wrote it for you, and you're just not the tragic type."

Gwendolyn grinned. "How can you say that? Haven't you been telling me for years that I'm doomed to an early grave?"

The Big Banjo dismissed her words with a gesture. "Not the same thing, at all. Tragedy's when the young heroine dies on stage from a dainty stiletto, moaning, at the last, of her broken heart. Stage left, in good view. Whereas you will die in an alley from a hundred great saber wounds. Howling defiance, like a wolf. And nobody will be able to see your body, because it will be buried under a dozen corpses of your foes."

These grim words brought silence to the salon. Gwendolyn and the Big Banjo stared at each other. A contest of wills, I thought at first, until I recognized the respect. And the regret.

The moment passed. The Big Banjo smiled ruefully, and said, "At least promise me this much. After the revolution, sing in the opera. I will have it ready by then."

"I will." She laughed. "Who knows? I may sing before then—if the occasion is right."

Actually, she sang quite a bit the rest of that day. Mostly compositions by Hildegard, who, I discovered, was a great composer in her own right. As I might have expected, the Abbess' music was not at all dramatic. But it conveyed an immense serenity, a calm acceptance of life which evoked not so much resignation as understanding.

In the course of the afternoon, the Big Banjo told me some parts of Gwendolyn's life which I had not known.

"I first met Gwendolyn at Hildegard's Abbey," he

explained. "Just a girl she was then, hiding out from the police. Hildegard had started her singing, as a way to relax the child. But when the Abbess discovered that voice! She wrote to me, and I came right away. I was astonished. No, more!—I was consumed by the desire to set Gwendolyn's voice to music."

He chuckled. "Still am consumed by the desire. But Gwendolyn wouldn't agree. 'After the revolution,' she said—hard as iron, even then. And she's never budged since."

Late that afternoon, after tea, Madame Kutumoff took me on a tour of the mansion. Quite an extraordinary place. As you can imagine, having grown up in Ozar apprenticed to my uncles, I had been inside many of the palatial homes of the idle rich. Grand salons, innumerable rooms, lavish gilding, elaborate bronze and marblework, paintings, sculpture—I had seen it all, and had found most of it tasteless and ostentatious, jumbled displays of sumptuous opulence intended more to impress and stupefy than to delight and uplift the soul. The Kutumoff mansion, however, was altogether different.

When I made comment to that effect, Madame Kutumoff said: "Well, yes, I should think it would be different. It's because of the traditions of the Mutt, and the Kutumoffs. Do you know about that?"

"Somewhat," I replied. "I know the General is the latest of a long line of Kutumoffs who have achieved world renown as military leaders, and have repelled all attempts by others to dominate the Mutt. As for the Mutt, all I know is that people here take a great aversion to money and all its wicked ways."

"Quite so! Well, every time one of the Kutumoff generals leads the people of the Mutt to a victory, the various tradesmen of the Mutt come here and do some more work on the house. It's the tradition, you see. And since there have been so many victories over the centuries, well, the house has grown. Two hundred and seventeen rooms, I believe we're up to now."

I felt I was on delicate ground, so I tread lightly. "Ah, I notice, ah, however, ah, that the General himself doesn't seem to spend much time in the house."

"Oh, certainly not! That would be most improper! A modest man of the people, he is, just like all the generals have been. So he mostly lives in the shack. That's also part of the tradition, you see?"

The expression on my face caused Madame Kutumoff to laugh.

"Oh, Benvenuti! The people of the Mutt are passionately attached to their traditions. The world's greatest general has to be a plain and simple fellow, scorning luxury and ostentatious display. But in order to do that, he has to have a luxurious and ostentatious mansion he can scorn. Don't you see? It all makes perfect sense!"

We toured for over an hour and yet I did not see all of it. Indeed, during the days I spent at the Kutumoff residence, I got lost any number of times in the multitude of stairways, turrets, galleries, hallways, passages, loggias, rooms and rotundas.

The lower floor consisted of the most commonly used rooms: the music salon, the breakfast room, the morning room, the dining room, the great dining room, the feasting hall, the drawing room, the office—each with its attendant cloakrooms, antechambers, closets and alcoves. Belowstairs was a virtual warren of storerooms, pantries, a buttery, a bakery, the small kitchen, the morning kitchen, the big kitchen, the really big kitchen—not to mention a beer and wine cellar of truly legendary proportions.

The upper floors were divided into the family wing with divers bedrooms, nurseries and suites, and the guest wing, again with many spacious rooms. There was even a padded cell, built especially for Wolfgang on those occasions when he escaped from the asylum. In addition, there were two ballrooms, a conservatory, a library, a smoking room, and a whole shoal of rooms and salons devoted to the special passions and interests of Kutumoffs past and present. There was also a trophy room, which, I was surprised to notice, was empty. Madame Kutumoff explained that the Kutumoff generals were really only interested in bagging whole armies, and that the ancient practice of mounting the heads of defeated field marshals had been discontinued several generations earlier.

"Modern times, you know. Nowadays it's considered uncouth."

There was even a large and well-equipped art studio, which I eyed hungrily.

Several of the rooms came equipped with their own stories and traditions. One of the rooms, of course, was haunted. And several closets were full of skeletons. Another room was locked and barred—the "locked room," Madame Kutumoff explained, where all were forbidden to enter lest the secret therein be revealed.

"What's the secret?" I asked.

"Who knows?" replied Madame Kutumoff. "You'd have to ask the workmen who built the room. They felt a proper mansion should have a locked and barred room holding a dark secret. But they're all dead now, I imagine—that was four generations of Kutumoffs ago."

At last, Madame Kutumoff and I returned to the music salon, where nobody seemed to have noticed our absence. Later that evening at dinner, however, everyone asked me about my tour, and it soon became clear that each one had his or her own favorite room or part of the house. I discovered that there was hardly a single inhabitant of the Mutt who didn't know every nook and cranny of the mansion, and didn't have a favorite room where they had spent many happy hours. I caught a glimpse, then, of the reason the Mutt had broken every army sent against it over the centuries.

The next several days passed quickly. Peaceful days, at first. But by the third day, I could feel Gwendolyn's increasing agitation. Soon she was spending most of her time with the General, discussing the prospects for future struggle. I came along, the first time, but their conversation really meant very little to me.

It was then that I remembered the figurine I had obtained in the Doghouse, and I resolved to create my own version of the piece. Madame Kutumoff readily granted me permission to use the studio, and so I went happily to work. After an initial period of indecision, I finally decided to make a carving— inspired by finding an exquisite baulk of walnut. By the end of the week, I felt satisfied with my work.

Yet, as enjoyable as the time was, there was always a little cloud of unhappiness lurking in a corner of my heart. It could not last, I knew. But I thrust the thought from my mind.

We were awakened, the morning of the seventh day, by a great, booming, familiar voice. Before I was even out of the bed, Gwendolyn was clothed and rushing through the door.

A minute or so later, I arrived downstairs in the music salon which seemed to double as the mansion's all-purpose gathering place. Sure enough. It was Wolfgang. When he heard my footsteps, he broke off his conversation with Gwendolyn and Hildegard.

"Benvenuti!" he cried. "I hear you've had the most heroic adventure! Such a hair-raising exploit!"

I shrugged modestly. "It was nothing—not much more than a hike through the woods."

"Not that, you silly boy! I'm talking about seducing Gwendolyn—such a daredevil! Such a credit to his family!"

Gwendolyn slapped him playfully. Anyone but the gigantic lunatic would have been flattened.

"Stop that, Gwendolyn, stop that! You mustn't strike a psychopath—it's very bad therapeutic technique. Not at all modern!"

Gwendolyn laughed. "It was a sad day for the world when they did away with snake pits."

Wolfgang rolled his eyes. "Oh, but they didn't! They just turned the whole world into a snake pit, so nobody could tell the difference."

"And I'll have you know he didn't seduce me, anyway. Ha! I had to drag the screaming virgin to the bed. Then I had to teach him everything."

My upper lip grew stiff.

"I'll admit, he's been a good student. Doesn't fumble near as much, although his stiff upper lip still gets in the way when he tries to—"

"Gwendolyn!" cried Hildegard.

Gwendolyn chuckled. "Bait me, will you? Make fun of the dour fanatic, will you? Ha! All right, Wolfgang, enough of that. What happened to the Rap Sheet? And how did you get here so fast, anyway?"

Wolfgang sighed. "Oh, Gwendolyn, always so serious. Business, business, business. It's not good for your mental stability, you know? The head psychiatrist at—"

"Wolfgang!"

The giant rolled his eyes. "Where should I start? How did I get here so fast? Well, I was so eager to tell you the wonderful news that I just started off. I'm so impulsive, you know, I forgot how far it was. So it didn't take me any time at all, naturally." He waved his arms about. "Space—time—people are much too concerned about all that. Slows them down terribly."

Gwendolyn rubbed her face. "Never mind. I should have known better than to ask. But what happened to the Rap Sheet? Can you at least give me a straight answer to that question."

Wolfgang scratched his head. "Oh, that's so difficult! I'm really not very good at straight answers. Not good at anything straight, actually. And it gets me in so much trouble. Like this man I met once who told me he liked straight shooters, but he wasn't telling the truth at all. Because when I went and got a bow and started shooting arrows at him I could tell right off that he wasn't angry at me because I was missing him but because I was shooting at him in the first place. He couldn't fool me! I'm not stupid, you know—just crazy. But then—"

"*Wolfgang!*"

"Oh, dear. I've made you angry again. Very well, then, I'll do my best. It was really so grand! Such heroes they were! The wizard and his apprentice— such a splendid little fellow! He's a dwarf, you know?"

"Who's a dwarf?"

"The wizard's apprentice, of course. Anyway, where was I? Oh, yes—and your brother was there! And his friend, that little Ignace fellow."

Gwendolyn's jaw fell. "My brother? What was he doing there?"

Wolfgang looked puzzled. "Well, of course he was there. Where else would he be? We couldn't have stolen the Rap Sheet without him. Oh, no—it would have been utterly out of the question! You need serious muscle for this kind of thing, Gwendolyn. Don't you read any novels?"

Suddenly the lunatic was howling like a lunatic. "But the funniest thing was—was—" He was unable to speak for a few seconds, hooping and whooping and drooling. "The funniest thing was that in the end most of the muscle came from the dwarf! Ho! Ho! Sort of, I mean—actually, what I mean is that most of the muscle came from the snarl who carried the dwarf, so it was really the snarl who did most of the shredding and gobbling and rending and all that. But he couldn't have done it without the dwarf!"

He wiped tears of laughter from his eyes. "Even so, we couldn't have done it without Greyboar. Because Greyboar had to carry the sack, you see? Except for the dwarf, he's the only one strong enough."

He beamed down at Gwendolyn. "So that's how it happened."

Gwendolyn shook her head. "That's all gibberish, Wolfgang."

Wolfgang cackled. "Of course it's gibberish! What else do you expect from a lunatic?"

Hildegard interrupted. "Nephew, let us leave aside for a moment the ins and outs of the thing. Where is the Rap Sheet itself?"

"Oh! I forgot! I have it—it's right here." The giant dug a hand into his tunic. He brought it out, clutching a green book.

"That's it?" demanded Gwendolyn. "It doesn't look like much."

"Of course it doesn't, dear," said Hildegard. "Joe was a plain and simple fellow. None of his relics look like much. But don't be fooled by appearances. That—that horrid thing—is worth the lives of thousands."

"Oh, at least!" exclaimed Wolfgang. "It's such a

clever gadget! Let me show you!" He opened the book and began thumbing through the pages.

"Look, Gwendolyn—here you are!" He handed her the book. "The life and times of Gwendolyn Greyboar!"

Gwendolyn scanned the page the book was open to. Then she began turning more pages. More pages. More pages. After a minute or so, she closed the book. Her face was pale.

"This—relic—knows more about me than I do. I'd forgotten half the things in it."

Shaking her head, she started to hand the book to Wolfgang. Suddenly she drew it back, and reopened it again. She scanned a few pages, closed it. The expression on her face was strange—relief, tinged with sadness.

"What's wrong, dear?" asked Hildegard.

"Nothing's wrong, Hildegard. I just—needed to know something."

She gave the book to Wolfgang and walked over to a window. She stood there silently for a time, staring, thinking. Then she squared her shoulders, took a deep breath, and turned away from the window. She looked at me.

"You're not mentioned anywhere in the Rap Sheet, Benvenuti. Not once. That means none of the authorities have any idea of what you've been up to since you came to Grotum."

The news should have pleased me, but it didn't. I had a sudden premonition, which Gwendolyn immediately confirmed.

"So you should go. Now, while you still can."

I opened my mouth to speak, found no words. I tried again, and found no words.

At that moment, General Kutumoff came into the room, followed by his wife. I was relieved to see them, although I knew the respite was only momentary.

"General! And Madame!" cried Wolfgang. "So good to see you! How are the children? And the dogs?"

"Everyone is fine, Wolfgang," replied Madame Kutumoff.

"I must apologize for this interruption," said the General, "but there is pressing business which we need to discuss."

Wolfgang rolled his eyes. "Business, always business."

The General smiled. "I'm afraid so, Wolfgang. What are you going to do with the Rap Sheet?"

"I'm supposed to give it to The Mysterious Q. Magrit decided it wasn't safe to keep it herself. Ozarae is bound to retaliate, you know, and it'll strike at Prygg first. The poor witch! It just broke her heart—all those enemies she'll have to pass up. Of course, the list she did compile will keep her busy for several years. But you know Magrit! Once a horrid harridan, always a horrid harridan!"

The General pursed his lips. "Yes, that's probably best. If the Rap Sheet will be safe anywhere, it'll be safe there. And The Mysterious Q can make the best use of it."

"Use it?" exclaimed Hildegard. "That horrid thing?"

The General's face grew bleak. "Yes, Hildegard, use it. We'll be able to keep track of the activities of the police and the Ozarine spies. The enemy has suffered a double blow here, don't you see? It's not just that they won't be able to use the Rap Sheet, but that we'll be able to use it against them. And why not? It seems fitting to me."

Hildegard shook her head. "Oh, it's not the justice of the matter that bothers me, General. It's—well, perhaps you're right. I'm certain that Joe wouldn't mind. After all, he made the thing to keep track of the baddies. Not the baddies he originally had in mind, of course, but then things have turned out differently than he thought they would."

She shook her head. "Still, I don't much care for the idea. And I don't think it will really stop the Ozarines."

"Of course it won't stop them," replied the General gruffly. "To the contrary—now that their favored methods of conquest are neutralized, they'll fall back on simpler methods. Direct military intervention—starting at Prygg, I imagine."

Hildegard looked distressed. "I had so hoped to avoid this unpleasantness," she said softly.

A look of sympathy came to the General's face, but when he spoke his voice was like iron. "It was never possible to avoid it, Abbess. Never. And it won't just be a military intervention, either. The Ecclesiarchs will drop their facade of holy dispassion. Soon enough they'll bring out the Switches—and who knows what other relics they've been hoarding for centuries?"

"Don't forget the Godferrets!" cried Wolfgang.

"I have not forgotten them," replied the General. "They'll be right in the thick of things. In many ways, they'll pose the greatest danger because of their magical powers. God's Own Tooth is probably the world's most powerful sorcerer."

Wolfgang cackled. "Oh, I don't think so, General! Oh no, not at all! In fact, the world's greatest sorcerer is on his way here this very minute."

The General frowned. "Who is this? And why is he coming to see me?"

"Well, actually, he's not coming to see *you*. He's coming to see Uncle Manya. His name's Zulkeh—Zulkeh of Goimr, physician."

"Oh, dear," said Hildegard.

The General looked at her sharply. "What's all this about, Hildegard? Do you know this Zulkeh?"

"Oh, yes, General. I've known him for years."

The Abbess bestowed a look on Wolfgang which

fairly reeked of disapproval. "You had to go and do it, didn't you, nephew?"

Wolfgang rolled his eyes. His body began twitching. "Oh! Oh!" he cried. "I think I'm having one of my attacks! Oh! Oh!"

"Stop it, Wolfgang!" exclaimed Hildegard. "Stop that this instant! I want a straight answer and none of your foolishness!"

The lunatic ceased twitching. He beamed at the Abbess.

"Hildegard—such a disciplinarian! So medieval! That's not at all the proper approach to a demented seizure, you know? The head psychiatrist at the asylum says—"

"A straight answer, I said! Now!"

"Oh, all right," pouted Wolfgang. "Well, yes, I did think your approach was altogether too placid. We argued about this years ago, if you remember. And I don't see what you're so upset about—or are you still hoping you can change the Old Geister's mind?" Wolfgang broke into a fit of howling laughter. "It was always such an idiotic idea, my dear aunt! How can you change God's mind? He's omniscient, you know?"

"He most certainly is not!" snapped the Abbess.

Wolfgang shook his head. "Such heresy! Such *outré* theology!" He looked at the rest of us. "It's why they excommunicated her, you know? Can't say I blame them! What kind of a proper abbess goes around saying God's got an ego problem?"

"Yes, Wolfgang, we know that's why they excommunicated her," said the General patiently. "But I'm afraid I'm not making much sense out of all this—and spare me the line about expecting sense from a lunatic!"

Wolfgang pouted. "But it's one of my best lines!"

The General smiled. A very wintry smile.

"Perhaps Fangwulf needs a good run. He's been getting a little fat lately."

Wolfgang smirked. "Fangwulf won't chase me, General. He's partial to lunatics. Uncle Manya's influence, that is."

The General glared. I might mention that the glare of the world's greatest general is a fearsome sight to behold. Fortunately, Wolfgang came to his senses. So to speak.

"The reason Zulkeh is coming here to see Uncle Manya, General, is because he's gotten thoroughly mixed up in Joe business."

"To put it mildly," interjected Hildegard.

"And as for who he is," continued Wolfgang, "the fact is that he's the world's greatest sorcerer. Oh, yes! God's Own Tooth couldn't hold a candle to Zulkeh!"

"Then why haven't I heard of him?" demanded the General.

"Well, that's because it's often been noted that he's the least notable wizard of Grotum." Then, forestalling the General's looming outburst: "It's because he's such a goofy pedant, General. You know the old saying of the wise man? 'Wherefore profit it a man to be learned, if he remains stupid in his mind'?"

"Everybody knows that saying."

Wolfgang grinned. "What everybody doesn't know is that the wise man said it after he met Zulkeh."

The General threw up his hands with frustration. "Then what good is he? And whose side is he on?"

"What good is he?" exclaimed Wolfgang. "General, he's the world's greatest sorcerer! Such a magician! Such a thaumaturge! Why, we couldn't have stolen the Rap Sheet without him!"

The lunatic looked confused for a moment. "As for whose side he's on, well, that's a bit difficult. He's a reactionary, of course—all your great sorcerers are, you know. But the thing about Zulkeh is, that he's such a really great sorcerer that his reaction sort of gets very strange. Leads him to do the wildest things!"

The General shook his head. "Never mind, Wolfgang. Since this Zulkeh is coming here, I'll get to meet him anyway. In the meantime, we have lots of other things to do."

He turned to Gwendolyn. "The warnings you've been spreading about the Rap Sheet will have the movement on its toes by now."

"I'll feel a little foolish when these latest developments come out," said Gwendolyn ruefully.

"Don't be stupid. We want the movement on the *qui vive*. All hell's about to break loose—bigger hell than the Rap Sheet would've produced, actually. But we're better able to handle this kind of action. And with the Rap Sheet in the hands of The Mysterious Q, we'll have the best intelligence we could ask for."

The General paused for a moment, groped for a cigar in his vest.

"Not in the house, dear," said Madame Kutumoff. The General got that unmistakable look on his face. Some day I should capture it on canvas: *Guilt and Frustration—The Thwarted Smoker*.

"Sorry. Anyway, Gwendolyn, I think the first thing you should do is try to find The Roach. He'll be at Blain by now, I imagine. Then, you've got to step up the Railroad's work immediately. There'll be a wave of pogroms coming, as sure as the sunrise, and there's no one better than you—"

He stopped then, seeing Gwendolyn's expression. Her face was pale. The General cast a quick, shrewd glance at me.

"But we can deal with all this tomorrow," he said gently. "You'll want today for other things, I imagine."

Gwendolyn nodded faintly. She reached out and took my hand.

"Let's go outside, Benvenuti. We need to talk."

As we headed out the door, I heard the General speaking. "Now—lunatic! I want some straight answers."

"Shall I take him to the kitchen, dear?" asked Madame Kutumoff. Wolfgang began howling with fear.

"No, love," said the General. "I think it best to remain within the guidelines of the rules of war. Very loosely interpreted, of course."

The rest of the day was unlike any other of my life. Islands of joy, in a sea of pain. Time and again, I tried to find a way out of the dilemma. But Gwendolyn had a will of steel.

"We always knew this time would come, Benvenuti. It won't help to draw it out. There'll just be more pain. And I have to leave soon anyway. It's true, what the General said. The Ozarines will set Grotum on fire. My kind of fire, what I was made for."

"But—"

"But what?" Her face was like a stone mask.

That night was spent in a frenzy of passion. In the morning, exhausted in body and soul, I packed my belongings. Gwendolyn and I descended from our room to the foyer. Madame Kutumoff was there, holding a satchel, which she extended to me.

"Take this, Benvenuti. Rations for your trip." She made a wry face. "I know the stuff tastes terrible, but it'll keep you going."

When we stepped through the door, we found Wolfgang waiting outside. I was surprised to see him.

"But why are you surprised, dear boy?" He waved his arms about. "You are going to New Sfinctr, aren't you?"

I hesitated, but Gwendolyn was implacable.

"Yes, he's going. He's not happy about it—neither am I—but it's for the best."

"Of course he should go!" cried Wolfgang. "You're absolutely right, Gwendolyn! There's nothing for him here. Except you, of course. But you're going to be very, very busy now, aren't you? Things are going to be getting hot in Grotum soon, oh yes! The Ozarines are going to be making such a fuss."

He looked at me, grinning from ear to ear.

"So it's the perfect time for you to make a splash, my boy! New Sfinctr will be a whirl! High society dancing on the edge of the volcano! Oh, it'll be splendid! You'll be famous in no time! Oh, yes! Trust me!"

I opened my mouth to speak, found no words.

"And besides," added the lunatic, "I'm heading that way myself. So I can show you how to get there."

"Why are you going to New Sfinctr?" asked Gwendolyn.

"Oh, I'm not. I'm going the opposite direction, so it'll be easy for me to show Benvenuti where to go. The other way from me. I'd love to go to New Sfinctr, mind you. Such a crazy place! But I've got to get back to the asylum before they discover that I escaped."

"You escaped months ago," I said. "They're bound to have discovered by now."

"Oh, yes, certainly. But the captain of the security guard has such a bad memory! He's probably forgotten all about it."

Madame Kutumoff laughed. Gwendolyn snorted.

"But I've still got to get back. You never know—he might remember any time now! And if he does—" Wolfgang shuddered. "He's a monster! A brute! He'll beat me to a pulp! The man has fists like hams!"

"You're the captain of the security guard, you idiot!" roared Gwendolyn.

"Yes, I know! That's what's so terrifying! I know the man well and—believe me!—he's a sadist! A psychopath! Ought to be locked up himself!"

He reached out a gigantic arm and took me by the shoulder. "So let's be off!"

I pulled back. "Wait! I'm not—" I turned to Gwendolyn. She was in my arms in a rush. Her embrace was like a python's. She gave me a quick fierce kiss, and then pushed me away.

"Go, love," she said, fighting tears. "Go now. Please."

I was unable to speak. I looked around. Madame Kutumoff seemed distressed. Wolfgang was watching me with a look on his face I couldn't decipher. Amusement, almost, but there was not a hint of malice in it.

I tried to kiss Gwendolyn again, but she fended me off. Gently, but with that incredible strength.

"No," she said. "Just go."

Wolfgang took me by the arm and gently pulled me away. But after I had taken a few steps, I stopped and turned back.

"Wait. I have something for you, Gwendolyn. I've been working on it for the last two days. It's a copy I made of a piece I found in the Mutt. I thought you would like it."

I dug in my pack and brought out the carving. When I handed it to her, Gwendolyn gazed down at it and gave a little gasp.

She looked up at me, frowning. "I thought you said you'd never met him."

"Met who?"

She held up the carving. "Him. My brother. That's who this is."

"I had no idea. It's just a carving I made from a piece I found in a shop. Here, I'll show you." I pulled forth the original.

"But—what would this be doing in a shop?"

"Oh, those!" exclaimed Madame Kutumoff. "Why, those figurines are all over, Gwendolyn. The peasants in the Baronies started making them a year or so ago. It was after Greyboar—well, after he disposed of the Comte de l'Abattoir and his Knights Companion. He's become something of a folk hero among the serfs, actually."

Gwendolyn's face grew hard. "He didn't do it for them!"

"Well, of course he didn't!" boomed Wolfgang. "He did it because some other baron paid him to do it—stupid peasants! Just like the ignorant sods to make a hero out of the man who throttled the most vicious lord in creation for the wrong reason." He clucked his tongue. "That's the whole problem with the Groutch peasantry—no understanding of psychology!"

He reached out his hand. "May I see the carving?"

Gwendolyn handed it to him. Wolfgang gazed down at it for a moment, and then handed it back. He began shaking his head vigorously.

"Oh no! Oh no! It just won't do! It's a beautiful carving, of course. Excellent work, Benvenuti—but I'm afraid it's ruined by that typical Sfondrati-Piccolomini touch. Just like that painting of your uncles! The marvelous suggestion of a great nobility of soul within that brutish exterior—preposterous! Greyboar's not like that at all! Oh no! The man's a monster, a fiend! A heartless killer! Why, my soul shudders when I think—"

"Wolfgang, shut up!" roared Gwendolyn.

The giant pouted. "But, my dear, your brother is a renegade from the human race. A two-legged beast, with the philosophy of a weasel. You've said so yourself—many times, in fact. I was just elaborating on your words."

Gwendolyn glared at him. "I never—" She fell silent. "Well, maybe I did." She looked down at the carving in her hand. After a moment, her face softened and she looked up at me.

"Thank you, Benvenuti."

Before I could say anything, Wolfgang was hustling me down the lane.

"We're off! We're off!" he cried. When we reached the road, I turned back. But Gwendolyn was gone.

Four days I spent, walking north from the Mutt with Wolfgang. All things considered, he may have been the best companion I could have had then. In his bizarre way, he made it impossible for me to wallow for long in my misery.

He talked constantly, an unending stream of idiotic babble, with those odd insights popping up like bubbles. Of what he said, I remember nothing, except his last words. Those came at a crossroads at the start of Joe's Hills.

"Just keep going north, Benvenuti. It's safe enough, walking through Joe's Hills, as long as you stick to the road. And when you get to Munching, you can take the barge down the river to New Sfinctr. They're wretched barges, I warn you. But they'll get you there."

Suddenly I was enfolded in his huge arms. When he released me, he was grinning in his inimitable style. Quite a fetching grin, actually, if you ignored the foam.

"Don't look so woebegone, boy!" He cackled. "The heart's just a muscle, you know. It doesn't really break, it just gets bruised. Bruises go away. Especially if the muscle's healthy. So that's it! Just exercise your heart!"

His grin was replaced by a rare look of seriousness. "I have come to cherish you, Benvenuti."

The look vanished.

"I know what I'll do! I'll tell you the secret of the

universe!" He leaned down and whispered two words in my ear. A moment later, he was shambling down the road in that unique stride, waving his arms.

"I must be off!" I heard him cry. "It's my longest escape ever! Oh! They'll be furious! They'll beat me! Whip me! Oh! Oh! I can't wait!"

Three seconds later, he was out of sight around a bend. His voice lingered a few seconds longer.

I made my camp that evening atop the highest hill I could find. From there, I was able to look south over the Mutt. The setting sun bathed the land in purple and ochre beauty. I found some comfort, then, knowing Gwendolyn was somewhere in that splendor.

Two days I spent there, paralyzed. A hundred times, I started back south, only to return to the camp. A hundred times, I started north, only to return to the camp.

In the end, staring out over the Mutt on the evening of the second day, I found my answer. A cold answer. But I took some pride in the fact that it had nothing to do with my ambitions.

I would only be a burden to her.

Sometime around noon of the next day, as I walked north, I remembered Wolfgang's last words to me. And it was strange, that it was those words which brought the first smile to my lips in days.

Two words. "The secret of the universe," according to a lunatic.

Things change.

American freedom and justice versus the tyrannies of the seventeenth century

1632 *by Eric Flint*

Paperback • 31972-8   **$7.99** ___

"This gripping and expertly detailed account of an episode of time travel that changes history is a treat for lovers of action-SF or alternate history... it distinguishes Flint as an SF author of particular note, one who can entertain and edify in equal, and major, measure."

—*Publishers Weekly*, **starred review**

1633 *by David Weber & Eric Flint*

Hardcover • 7434-3542-7   **$26.00** ___

The greatest naval war in European history is about to erupt. Like it or not, Gustavus Adolphus will have to rely on Mike Stearns and the technical wizardry of his obstreperous Americans to save the King of Sweden from ruin, but caught in the conflagration are two American diplomatic missions abroad. . . .

MERCEDES LACKEY
Hot! Hot! Hot!

Whether it's elves at the racetrack, bards battling evil mages or brainships fighting planet pirates, Mercedes Lackey is always compelling, always fun, always a great read. Complete your collection today!

DAVID WEBER

<u>The Honor Harrington series:</u> *(cont.)*

Field of Dishonor

Honor goes home to Manticore—and fights for her life on a battlefield she never trained for, in a private war that offers just two choices: death—or a "victory" that can end only in dishonor and the loss of all she loves. . . .

Flag in Exile

Hounded into retirement and disgrace by political enemies, Honor Harrington has retreated to planet Grayson, where powerful men plot to reverse the changes she has brought to their world. And for their plans to succeed, Honor Harrington must die!

Honor Among Enemies

Offered a chance to end her exile and again command a ship, Honor Harrington must use a crew drawn from the dregs of the service to stop pirates who are plundering commerce. Her enemies have chosen the mission carefully, thinking that either she will stop the raiders or they will kill her . . . and either way, her enemies will win. . . .

In Enemy Hands

After being ambushed, Honor finds herself aboard an enemy cruiser, bound for her scheduled execution. But one lesson Honor has never learned is how to give up!

Echoes of Honor

"Brilliant! Brilliant! Brilliant!"—*Anne McCaffrey*

continued

DAVID WEBER

The Honor Harrington series: *(cont.)*

Ashes of Victory

Honor has escaped from the prison planet called Hell and returned to the Manticoran Alliance, to the heart of a furnace of new weapons, new strategies, new tactics, spies, diplomacy, and assassination.

War of Honor

No one wanted another war. Neither the Republic of Haven, nor Manticore—and certainly not Honor Harrington. Unfortunately, what they wanted didn't matter.

AND DON'T MISS—

—the Honor Harrington <u>anthologies</u>, with stories from David Weber, John Ringo, Eric Flint, Jane Lindskold, and more!

HONOR HARRINGTON BOOKS by DAVID WEBER

On Basilisk Station	(HC) 57793-X /$18.00	☐
	(PB) 72163-1 / $7.99	☐
The Honor of the Queen	72172-0 / $7.99	☐
The Short Victorious War	87596-5 / $6.99	☐
	7434-3551-6 /$14.00	☐
Field of Dishonor	87624-4 / $6.99	☐

continued ☞

PRAISE FOR
LOIS McMASTER BUJOLD

What the critics say:

The Warrior's Apprentice: "Now here's a fun romp through the spaceways—not so much a space opera as space ballet.... it has all the 'right stuff.' A lot of thought and thoughtfulness stand behind the all-too-human characters. Enjoy this one, and look forward to the next."   —Dean Lambe, *SF Reviews*

"The pace is breathless, the characterization thoughtful and emotionally powerful, and the author's narrative technique and command of language compelling. Highly recommended."
—*Booklist*

Brothers in Arms: "...she gives it a genuine depth of character, while reveling in the wild turnings of her tale.... Bujold is as audacious as her favorite hero, and as brilliantly (if sneakily) successful."   —*Locus*

"Miles Vorkosigan is such a great character that I'll read anything Lois wants to write about him.... a book to re-read on cold rainy days." —Robert Coulson, *Comic Buyer's Guide*

Borders of Infinity: "Bujold's series hero Miles Vorkosigan may be a lord by birth and an admiral by rank, but a bone disease that has left him hobbled and in frequent pain has sensitized him to the suffering of outcasts in his very hierarchical era.... Playing off Miles's reserve and cleverness, Bujold draws outrageous and outlandish foils to color her high-minded adventures."   —*Publishers Weekly*

Falling Free: "In *Falling Free* Lois McMaster Bujold has written her fourth straight superb novel.... How to break down a talent like Bujold's into analyzable components? Best not to try. Best to say: 'Read, or you will be missing something extraordinary.' "   —Roland Green, *Chicago Sun-Times*

The Vor Game: "The chronicles of Miles Vorkosigan are far too witty to be literary junk food, but they rouse the kind of craving that makes popcorn magically vanish during a double feature."   —Faren Miller, *Locus*

MORE PRAISE FOR
LOIS McMASTER BUJOLD

What the readers say:

"My copy of *Shards of Honor* is falling apart I've reread it so often. . . . I'll read whatever you write. You've certainly proved yourself a grand storyteller."

—Lisa Kolbe, Colorado Springs, CO

"I experience the stories of Miles Vorkosigan as almost viscerally uplifting. . . . But certainly, even the weightiest theme would have less impact than a cinder on snow were it not for a rousing good story, and good story-telling with it. This is the second thing I want to thank you for. . . . I suppose if you boiled down all I've said to its simplest expression, it would be that I immensely enjoy and admire your work. I submit that, as literature, your work raises the overall level of the science fiction genre, and spiritually, your work cannot avoid positively influencing all who read it."

—Glen Stonebraker, Gaithersburg, MD

" 'The Mountains of Mourning' [in *Borders of Infinity*] was one of the best-crafted, and simply best, works I'd ever read. When I finished it, I immediately turned back to the beginning and read it again, and I can't remember the last time I did that."

—Betsy Bizot, Lisle, IL

"I can only hope that you will continue to write, so that I can continue to read (and of course buy) your books, for they make me laugh and cry and think . . . rare indeed."

—Steven Knott, Major, USAF

Got questions? We've got answers at
BAEN'S BAR!

Here's what some of our members have to say:

"Ever wanted to get involved in a newsgroup but were frightened off by rude know-it-alls? Stop by Baen's Bar. Our know-it-alls are the friendly, helpful type—and some write the hottest SF around."
> **—Melody L** *melodyl@ccnmail.com*

"Baen's Bar . . . where you just might find people who understand what you are talking about!"
> **—Tom Perry** *perry@airswitch.net*

"Lots of gentle teasing and numerous puns, mixed with various recipes for food and fun."
> **—Ginger Tansey** *makautz@prodigy.net*

"Join the fun at Baen's Bar, where you can discuss the latest in books, Treecat Sign Language, ramifications of cloning, how military uniforms have changed, help an author do research, fuss about differences between American and European measurements—and top it off with being able to talk to the people who write and publish what you love."
> **—Sun Shadow** *sun2shadow@hotmail.com*

"Thanks for a lovely first year at the Bar, where the only thing that's been intoxicating is conversation."
> **—Al Jorgensen** *awjorgen@wolf.co.net*

 Join BAEN'S BAR at
WWW.BAEN.COM
"Bring your brain!"